Praise for

THE PERFECT EQUATION

"Smart is the new sexy, and Elizabeth Everett does both better than anyone else!"

—Ali Hazelwood, *New York Times* bestselling author of *The Love Hypothesis*

"Sparkling, smart, moving, original—just delightful from start to finish."
                                            —*USA Today* bestselling author Julie Ann Long

"Splendidly entertaining . . . detonates with an ingeniously orchestrated display of wit and whimsy that dazzlingly celebrates the importance of both STEM research and love in a lady's life."

                                            —*Booklist* (starred review)

"Poignantly feminist and perfectly feisty! Letty and Grey's romance is a delicious journey from sharp-tongued disdain to smoldering desire."
                                    —Chloe Liese, author of the Bergman Brothers series

"Elizabeth Everett's writing absolutely dazzles. Fiercely feminist, deliciously sexy, and bursting with intoxicating enemies-to-lovers goodness, *A Perfect Equation* is an instant historical romance classic and Everett an auto-buy author."

                                    —Mazey Eddings, author of *Lizzie Blake's Best Mistake*

"Enchanting . . . the characters' intense chemistry keeps the pages flying. This is a winner."
                                                        —*Publishers Weekly*

"When a spirited mathematician and the straight-laced nobleman she loathes are thrust together to protect Athena's ~~~ liners, corsets, and sparks fly. A brilliant balance o ~~~

romance, and smashing the patriarchy, the second installment of the Secret Scientists of London is a triumph!"

—Libby Hubscher, author of *If You Ask Me*

"The second book in Everett's Secret Scientists of London series stands out among recent feminist historical romances thanks to a fierce enemies-to-lovers plotline and a sexual tension that is built slowly and expertly."

—*Kirkus Reviews*

Praise for

A LADY'S FORMULA FOR LOVE

"Fizzy, engrossing romance . . . a whole-hearted celebration of women who choose to live gleefully outside the bounds of patriarchy's limitations."

—*Entertainment Weekly*

"Explosive chemistry, a heroine who loves her science, and lines that made me laugh out loud—this witty debut delivered, and I'd like the next installment now, please."

—*USA Today* bestselling author Evie Dunmore

"A witty, dazzling debut with a science-minded heroine and her broody bodyguard. Fiercely feminist and intensely romantic, *A Lady's Formula for Love* is a fresh take on historical romance that's guaranteed to delight readers."

—Joanna Shupe, author of *The Devil of Downtown*

"A brilliant scientist and her brooding bodyguard discover that love can find you when you least expect it. *A Lady's Formula for Love* is full of wit, charm, and intrigue. You don't want to miss this exciting debut from Elizabeth Everett."

—Harper St. George, author of *The Lady Tempts an Heir*

"With its beguiling blend of danger, desire, and deliciously dry wit, the brilliantly conceived and smartly executed *A Lady's Formula for Love* is an exciting debut and a first-rate launch for Everett's The Secret Scientists of London series. Fans of Evie Dunmore's A League of Extraordinary Women books or Olivia Waite's historical romances will savor this fiercely feminist, achingly romantic, and intensely sensual love story."

—*Booklist* (starred review)

"A sweet, swoon-worthy tale."

—*Woman's World*

"Smart, sassy, sexy, and sweet . . . it's *The Bodyguard* meets *Pride and Prejudice*. Mr. Darcy, with his brooding sexiness, doesn't have a damned thing on Arthur Kneland. This book is an all-around winner."

—Minerva Spencer, author of The Academy of Love series

"A secret society of rule-breaking women . . . irresistible! You're going to love Elizabeth Everett's adventurous debut."

—Theresa Romain, author of The Holiday Pleasures series

"A sparking debut full of humor, heart, and sizzling romance."

—Jeanine Englert, award-winning author of *Lovely Digits*

"A fabulous debut filled with danger, imperfect but fierce found family, and the love story of two stubborn protectors, *A Lady's Formula for Love* is everything a romance reader who likes to ponder as well as cheer could want."

—Felicia Grossman, author of The Truitts series

ALSO BY ELIZABETH EVERETT

THE SECRET SCIENTISTS OF LONDON

A Lady's Formula for Love
The Perfect Equation

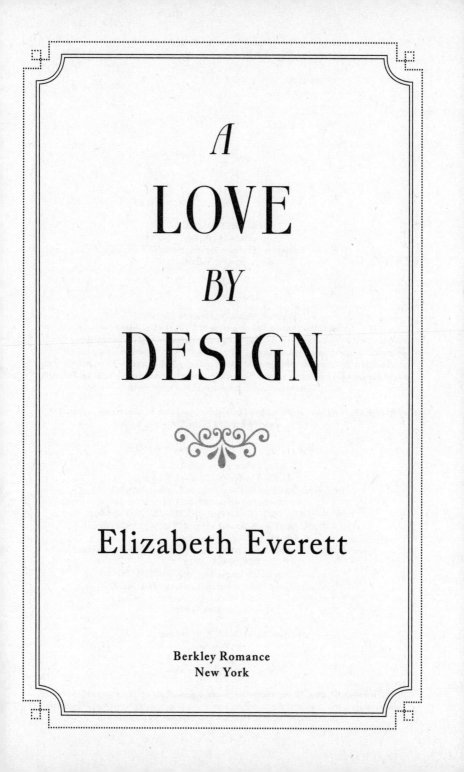

A
LOVE
BY
DESIGN

Elizabeth Everett

Berkley Romance
New York

BERKLEY ROMANCE
Published by Berkley
An imprint of Penguin Random House LLC
penguinrandomhouse.com

Library of Congress Cataloging-in-Publication Data

Names: Everett, Elizabeth, author.
Title: A love by design / Elizabeth Everett.
Description: First Edition. | New York : Berkley Romance, 2023. |
Series: The Secret Scientists of London ; 3
Identifiers: LCCN 2022017732 (print) | LCCN 2022017733 (ebook) |
ISBN 9780593200667 (trade paperback) | ISBN 9780593200674 (ebook)
Subjects: LCGFT: Love stories. | Novels.
Classification: LCC PS3605.V435 L68 2023 (print) | LCC PS3605.V435 (ebook) |
DDC 813/.6—dc23
LC record available at https://lccn.loc.gov/2022017732
LC ebook record available at https://lccn.loc.gov/2022017733

First Edition: January 2023

Printed in the United States of America
1st Printing

Book design by Alison Cnockaert

*This book is dedicated to my husband,
a real-life romantic hero.*

*I'd also like to dedicate this book to all the
health care workers who went to work every day while we
remained safe at home, who held the hands of dying
patients while their own loved ones were dying as well,
who went without protective clothing or re-used masks
and slept away from home so as not to infect their
families, who were a great, shining light in the dark days
at the beginning of the pandemic. I am so incredibly
grateful for your tenacity and bravery, and I will never
forget all you sacrificed to keep us safe.*

A LOVE
BY DESIGN

Prologue

Lincolnshire, 1820

GRASS THINNED BENEATH the willows, giving way to patches of cool, hard earth. The scent of wet stone itched the inside of Georgie's nose as he made his way to the streambank. Black water rushed toward a distant outlet and giggled against the silent rocks. A rare contentment settled in his chest.

Pushing aside the curtain of willow branches, Georgie paused. Below the chimes of the stream's rapids came a low, snuffling noise.

He knew that sound.

Disappointment washed through him. Someone had breached his refuge and the excitement of the morning was lost now. For a moment, he considered finding another place downstream where he could be alone.

When the sound came again, Georgie rolled his eyes up to heaven and shook himself all over, like a dog shaking off the wet, ridding himself of his frustration.

Small for his eight years and good with neither letters nor numbers, yet already George Willis knew when a woman was crying, a man was generally the cause of it.

Huddled in the nest of interlaced roots at the bottom of the tree, a scrawny lass in a sky blue frock lifted her head and peered at him. Her fiery red hair had been plaited and hung limply over one shoulder, crimson splotches around her eyes, nose, and mouth contrasting with the milky whiteness of her skin.

"Hullo. Broken heart, izzit?" he asked, letting the branches fall behind him as he walked under the dome of the great willow.

"A broken heart? Don't be stupid," the lass said with the ladle-like dip of a well-heeled accent.

"Are you lost?" he asked.

The girl couldn't be from the village with that accent.

Pulling a lace-trimmed handkerchief from a pocket in her pretty half apron, she blew her nose, honking like an angry goose.

"No. I'm a guest at Grange Abbey." Folding her handkerchief, she finally stared at him straight on, scrutinizing him with a mixture of interest and distaste.

Ah. That made sense. The stream lay on the border of the Viscount Grange's vast estates. The viscount had four daughters—could have been five. They were loud and constantly moving so Georgie had a difficult time telling them apart except the oldest, Violet, who was his same age and obviously up to no good. He liked her.

If this girl were a guest, why wasn't she at the Abbey with the rest of the family? He'd glimpsed them playing pall-mall in the garden, the youngest girls lisping their displeasure at having to hit the balls with their mallets and not one another.

Perhaps she was a poor relation like Mam had been before his father put a baby in her belly and had to marry her. Maybe she was like the girls in the stories Mam told him, the ones down on their luck until a handsome prince showed up to rescue them. That was ripper, then. He'd save her, wouldn't he, then on to some fishing.

"Hungry?" he asked. "I've some tommy I can share with you."

She turned her cherry red nose up at his overture, but Georgie didn't take any offense. Instead, he clambered over to the pile of rocks where she sat and squatted, unwrapping the bundle the Abbey's cook had given him. A gorgeous aroma of yeast and wheat had him near fainting with pleasure.

He'd been at the estate asking for work. His father had been gone for months now and what coin his mam brought in with her lace could not keep them fed and clothed for much longer.

Although his father disavowed them most times, Georgie's mam swore they had been married before he was born. Most of the villagers didn't believe her but they were kind to her just the same. Georgie tolerated her trying to raise him like a gentleman's son, but his empty belly and threadbare clothes had finally convinced her to leave off with lessons and let him earn some coin on his own.

With great reluctance, Georgie kept himself from yothering the rest of the bread. He would save it for supper and let Mam have the last of the stew. The gardener had given him a job starting tomorrow including a penny as footing. Georgie would be the man of the house from now on and his mam would never have to suffer his father's wrath again.

To distract himself from the gnawing in his belly, George inspected the lass more closely. Her frock was clean, and she wore real kidskin boots, but her collar needed mending, the boots were dirty, and a faded and frayed ribbon pulled back her hair.

"Was Miss Grange cruel to you?" he guessed.

"No." The girl rested her chin on her knees. "Not Miss Grange. She's not cruel, a' tall."

"Witch locked you in a tower and you've gone an' escaped?" he guessed.

The lass snorted in derision.

Hmmm.

"Suffering a curse?"

"Don't be daft. I'm not cursed!" she exclaimed. "I'm not . . ." She swallowed, then fixed her gaze on the water. "I'm not anything special."

Georgie's good humor deserted him as she curled into a secret. This was his private space she'd invaded for no good reason as far as he could see. He'd come here to celebrate his good fortune, to throw stones at things and avoid going home to his mam's worried sighs and the slate board that mocked him with its unanswerable questions.

No broken heart, money enough for sturdy shoes, and a belly so used to food, she could refuse a slice of delicious bread without a second thought. This lass didn't need rescuing. He leapt to his feet, fists on hips, and scowled down at her.

"If no one was cruel and you're not lost, why don't you go home and cry to your mam?"

With a guttural roar, she rose to her feet. George had to tilt his head to see the top of her. Lawk, the lass was tall.

"Why don't *you* shut up?"

Later, much later, he claimed the element of surprise sent him falling back onto the hard-packed earth when she punched him in his empty belly. The truth was this girl had the power to bring him to his knees with or without a blow.

When he looked at her, she appeared almost ethereal, backlit by the prisms of sun that shone through the diamond-shaped spaces between the willow leaves.

Georgie considered for a moment that she might be an escapee from an asylum like he heard tales of from Mrs. Morgan, the postmistress, who read aloud the stories from the broadsheets of London.

"You din't have to kill me," he complained.

"You're not dead," she retorted.

Being a gentleman, born if not raised, he wasn't allowed to punch her in return. He stood, brushed off his clothes, and slapped his threadbare cap against his knee, watching her all the time, ready for the next assault. Scowling at him, she crossed her arms and tapped her foot as if her show of ill temper would drive him away.

This was his secret spot. He wouldn't give up his refuge to an interloper, no matter how terrifying.

She huffed, staring at the water as though the crisp patter of the stream was a confidence she'd been longing to hear.

"I apologize," she muttered. "I have a most unladylike temper."

As well as a most unladylike left hook. He left that part unsaid. Apologies could be more difficult to part with than coin. A linnet serenaded them from the other side of the stream and Georgie lifted his face to the early May sunshine.

"Is your mam dead?" he asked.

With a sharp intake of breath, she pulled her hands into fists and he braced for another attack.

"No, but I wish she were," the lass said boldly as if daring Georgie to condemn her.

For wasn't that the worst thing you could say?

He came to stand next to her, pretending to stare at the water as well. The skirts of the willow behind them billowed protectively around their bodies as they stood in silent communion.

"I wish my father were dead as well." For the first time, he said aloud the words in his heart.

The stream took their secrets on its way and the side of her arm brushed his shoulder. A skitter of odd sparks followed the touch.

Open and closed, her fingers curled around invisible balls until she stooped and grabbed a handful of rocks.

"Can you hit that tree over there?" she asked. Not looking at him, she held the rocks out in her open palm. An offering of solidarity.

Surreptitiously rubbing the ache where she'd punched him, he took a rock. The linnet's song and the plunk of stones falling into the water filled the silence between them that day as Georgie Willis fell irrevocably in love with Maggie Strong.

1

London, 1844

Y OU WILL TAKE that *monstrosity* back to where you purchased it, or I remove your spine with my bare hands."

"If you put your tiny hands anywhere near my perfectly fashioned body, I will crush you. What do you have against sweet little bunnies? Everyone loves bunnies."

George Willis, Earl Grantham, stood in the foyer of a large town house off Kingsbury Road and held a toy rabbit aloft, safe from the threatened predations of his onetime romantic rival, Arthur Kneland.

Two years ago, Grantham had proposed to his best friend, the Lady Violet Greycliff. Violet, a genius chemist, and the founder of a secret society of women scientists, had chosen instead to marry Kneland, her former bodyguard. Grantham had opined—aloud and on multiple occasions—that her choice was a consequence of inhaling a few too many gases in her quest to prove Avogadro's law. Kneland had responded by dosing Grantham's tea with emetics.

The affection between the two men bordered on unseemly.

"Listen, Kneland," Grantham said with the patience of a saint, "I allowed Violet to marry you—"

Kneland—whose sense of humor matched his height—rudely interrupted.

"Violet chose to marry me. You had nothing—"

"—despite your obvious *short*comings," Grantham continued. "If she saw fit to spend the rest of her days leg-shackled to a dour little Scot, who was I to stop her? However, I will not begrudge my goddaughter the attention and belongings she so richly deserves."

Ever since the arrival of Violet and Arthur's daughter, Mirren Georgiana, Grantham had brought a baby gift when he came to visit. Kneland, being an aforementioned dour little Scot, had objected to the increasing size and elaborateness of the gifts.

In fact, Kneland had called the steady stream of presents—culminating in this four-foot-tall stuffed rabbit made with costly angora wool and clad in a custom-designed silk dress with sapphires for eyes—"outrageous, exorbitant, and unreasonable."

Admittedly, tweaking the former counterassassin with increasingly preposterous trinkets did provide the *tiniest* bit of amusement. Who would begrudge Grantham a sliver of light in an otherwise gloomy and miserable autumn?

"I will take that rabbit and shove it so far up your . . ."

Kneland, that's who.

A tiny flush high on the man's cheekbones stood out against his weathered white skin, eliciting the sole clue he enjoyed himself as much as Grantham.

"If you keep holding that monstrosity above your head, it leaves your underbelly exposed to any sharp blade that happens to be in someone's hands," said Kneland through gritted teeth.

"Tiny hands that can't fit around a knife handle," Grantham observed. Tired of holding the damn thing in the air, he set his other hand on his hip. "Well, where is Vi? Let's ask her if Baby Georgie would like a bunny."

"My child's name is Mirren, and my wife is not at home. She is fetching a guest from the train station," Kneland informed him. His brows met and he craned his neck to peer around Grantham into the street. "I believe that's her carriage now."

Grantham looked at Arthur.

Arthur looked at Grantham.

Grantham looked at the rabbit.

A grin ghosted across Arthur's face . . .

And they were off.

"What on earth?" the housekeeper, Mrs. Sweet, said, entering the foyer as the men tore past her.

"Good day, Mrs. Sweet. Don't you look radiant?" Grantham called as they ran by.

While Grantham had the superior muscular physique, Arthur was slippery like a weasel and the men were well matched as they raced through the hallways of Beacon House. Turning the corner into the kitchen, they both headed toward a thick oak door which led to what was once a series of outbuildings but had been transformed some seven years ago into Athena's Retreat, the first social club for ladies in London.

Grantham took the opportunity to jab Arthur in the ribs with his elbow.

Hard.

While Arthur slowed, using precious breath to utter an *impressive* curse, Grantham flung open the door and slammed it shut behind him.

Breathing heavily, he approached a fork in the hallway. Each corridor ended in a door. The door to the left led to the public rooms of Athena's Retreat. There a group of members attended lectures on the natural sciences, drank tea, and held discussion on topics such as the use of botanicals in household cleansers.

The door on the right led to the true Athena's Retreat. Behind the facade of the public rooms were workrooms and laboratories given over to women scientists from all over England. Women who were forced to keep their work secret from society due to myriad prejudices found a haven in this warren of strange sounds, nasty smells, and the low vibrations of brilliance.

The carriage house serving both Athena's Retreat and Beacon House was at the back of the public-facing rooms. However, a stairway stood outside the second floor of the hidden rooms and might get him there quicker if he—

Too late. The evil little Scot caught up to him and used his cursed assassin tricks to swipe Grantham's legs out from under him.

"Damn, but I love the sound of your giant arse hitting the floorboards," Kneland twittered as he flew through the door on the left.

Feck.

Grantham heaved himself up and resumed his journey at twice his original pace while plotting another baby gift.

Perhaps a live circus including pygmy monkeys?

Shouldn't Baby Georgie have her own boat?

Contemplating how he might haul a yacht down Knightsbridge Road, Grantham slammed open the door to the outside staircase and decided to leap from the second-floor landing onto a patch of brush in the kitchen garden rather than waste time taking the stairs.

In the seconds before his brain reminded him any decision prompted by his manly bits never turned out well, he caught sight of Violet Kneland and her companion.

Maggie.

Instead of neatly dropping feet first into the shrubbery—for which cook might scold him, but he'd soon charm her into forgetting—Grantham lost his footing and fell headfirst in an ungainly heap atop an untrimmed hedge of dog roses.

Maggie had returned.

Of course, she was now known as Madame Margaret Gault.

Try as he might, Grantham could never twist his tongue around the name.

Almost his whole life, he'd called her Maggie.

His Maggie.

From upside down, he watched as she turned the corner of the carriage house, the wind unfurling the hem of her simple bronze pelisse. A brown capelet hung about her shoulders, and a matching muff hid her hands. Catching sight of him, she paused, tilting her head so he caught a glimpse of lush auburn curls peeking out from beneath her tea-colored bonnet trimmed with bright red berries. Margaret's fair skin showed no hint of the freckles that had once plagued her every summer, and thick brown lashes shielded her hazel eyes.

She was unusually tall for a woman; nevertheless, she moved with effortless grace, and not even the blazing clash of colors adorning Violet next to her could detract from her beauty.

For she was a beauty, Margaret Gault. Once wild and graceless, she'd bloomed into a woman of elegant refinement.

A woman who was more than met the eye.

A woman who would rather feast on glass than give him the time of day.

For eleven years, the first day of summer meant Margaret would be waiting for him beneath the willow where they first met. She and Violet attended the Yorkshire Academy for the Education of Exceptional Young Women together. While Violet came home to her large, affectionate—and very loud—family, Margaret had no one waiting for her at home. Her father had died of a stroke when she was ten and her mother had little interest in Margaret's whereabouts or well-being.

Violet and Grantham had been Margaret's family. The three of them had been the best of friends until one hot afternoon when

Margaret had smiled a certain way and the ground went out beneath his feet. A year later he was soldiering in Canada and Margaret lived in Paris and their summers together were nothing but a memory he pulled around himself like a blanket on cold lonely nights.

"Good afternoon, Grantham," Violet greeted him, seemingly unaffected by his headfirst dive into her rosebushes. She wore a shocking yellow day dress beneath a burgundy velvet paletot and atop her head sat a garish blue bonnet topped with a life-sized stuffed parrot.

Swallowing a barrelful of curses, Grantham tried wriggling out of the bushes, every single thorn piercing his flesh a hundredfold as Margaret stared without saying a word.

"Ahem." He cleared his throat as he managed to get to his feet despite being trapped in the center of one of the bushes. As he pulled a branch from his hair, a shower of wrinkled brown rose petals drifted down his shoulders. "You are especially . . . vibrant today, Violet. I brought this for Baby Georgie."

He thrust the torn, dirtied rabbit at Violet, who received it with a bemused air. One of the buttons had come off and the silk was stained green and brown.

"Madame Gault," he said, bowing to Margaret. "So lovely to see you again."

No matter how strongly Grantham willed it, Margaret did not speak to him in return. Instead, she bent her knee a scant inch in a desultory curtsey, her lush mouth twisted like the clasp of a coin purse, no doubt to hold inside the names she was calling him in her head. He had a good idea what some of them were, considering he most likely had taught them to her.

Grantham hadn't seen Margaret for thirteen years until their reunion—if one could call it that—a year and a half ago in the small parlor of Athena's Retreat. He hadn't exactly met the moment then, either—although to be fair, there'd been a hedgehog involved. The handful of times he encountered her since, she'd avoided meeting his eyes with her own, as though he were an inconsequential shadow cast by their past.

Someone to be dismissed.

Someone who had broken her heart and whom she would never forgive.

"See who is come to live in England for good." Violet linked her arm with Margaret's and beamed at her friend.

This was news.

When Margaret had come to stay at Athena's Retreat a year and half ago to complete an engineering project for her father-in-law's firm, Grantham had hoped she'd stay but she returned to Paris after three months. He'd asked Violet if Margaret might ever return, but Violet had doubted it.

"She's one of the only women engineers in Europe with an excellent reputation. Why give up a dream hard fought to come back to England and fight all over again?" Violet had asked.

Something had changed, however, and now Margaret was home.

His heart leapt in his chest and the bitter orange flavor of hope flooded his mouth.

"Clean yourself up and come inside for tea," Violet said to him now.

Margaret did not echo the invitation. Instead, she tightened her hold on a stylish carpet bag and accompanied Violet and Arthur into the building.

There are moments in life when the world shifts as though a door has opened somewhere out of sight. Whether a person runs toward that opened door or not depends on how fast they're stuck in place. Grantham considered for a moment how painful it would be to get himself unstuck.

Although the tangle of branches in front of him twisted menacingly, he pulled a deep breath of resolution into his lungs alongside the scents of roseships and crushed greenery. Gritting his teeth, he made his way through the thorns toward the open door.

"HOW WONDERFUL YOU are back to stay, Margaret. Grantham visits nearly every day when he is in London. It will be like our summers at the Abbey—the three of us together again."

Margaret Gault avoided comment by sipping her tea. Violet sat at her side on a low settee, serving her guests small plates of rock-hard biscuits.

Arthur, Violet's taciturn husband, stood across the room, giving off the impression of a coil poised to spring. His nearly black eyes somehow remained on Violet at the same time they roved over the room.

Violet favored this small blue parlor. The velvet curtains had faded over the years from violet to periwinkle and a cheerful fire lent its warmth to the wan October sunlight, revealing delicate etchings on the glass-shaded sinumbra lamps. Training her gaze on a charming print of a tiny cottage amid the gorse-covered hills of the Scottish Highlands, Margaret let Violet's words wash over her in a comforting stream.

"... the members of Athena's Retreat are over the moon at the news you've returned for good," Violet said. "You will miss seeing Letty and Greycliff. They have decided to remain in Herefordshire until the baby is born."

Last spring, Violet and Arthur went north to Yorkshire for half a year. Violet had suffered a miscarriage and needed time to heal, and as luck would have it, Margaret needed to be in London to work on a project for her father-in-law's engineering firm. She'd stayed in rooms at Athena's Retreat and served as the club's temporary secretary.

Her time at the Retreat served as an awakening. Meeting women scientists from various disciplines and learning about their work had inspired new ideas of her own. Margaret had made friends with like-minded—and sometimes not so like-minded—women who had both relied upon her and challenged her.

She'd become especially fond of Letty Fenley, an extraordinarily talented mathematician who had fallen in love with Violet's first husband's son, Lord William Greycliff. Watching her fierce and prickly friend bring the reserved viscount to his knees had been delightful if somewhat bittersweet.

Upon returning to Paris afterward, Margaret's perfectly ordered life lost its previous appeal. For the first time since her husband's death seven years earlier, she was lonely. While she and Violet had carried on a lively correspondence for years, the letters were not enough.

Loneliness alone wouldn't have precipitated moving to England but for her father-in-law's sudden announcement. In the absence of a son to carry on the work of the family engineering firm, he would be closing Henri Gault and Son.

Once more, because of one man's unilateral decision, Margaret's life was upended. For a few days she'd railed against the perfidy of men who, in their shortsightedness, could not imagine a woman taking the reins of such a prestigious firm, despite her status as daughter-in-law. No argument could sway Henri, however. He'd valued her work but would not leave his legacy in the hands of a woman.

Unlike the last time she'd been abandoned by a man, Margaret was not a lovesick seventeen-year-old with no other prospects in sight.

This time, she was a grown woman with a *Plan*.

Never again would a man have power over how she lived her life. Nothing would stop her from achieving her dreams. There would be an engineering firm bearing the Gault name after all. Her name. Margaret Gault, Engineer.

Within hours of her decision, Margaret wrote to Violet, asking to again stay at Athena's Retreat. Tonight, she would unpack her belongings and settle in. In two days, Margaret had a meeting with a prospective client. In the meantime, she and Violet had planned an evening of catching up and cuddling the baby. Tomorrow, Margaret would reunite with her friends, Althea and Mala, for an afternoon of tarts and port-soaked wisdom, and she would find a set of rooms for her new offices.

She had anticipated everything.

"I didn't say pony," said a low voice. "I said ponies. Plural. A herd of them. Don't you think Baby Georgie—"

"Her name is Mirren," Arthur growled.

"—would like a herd of ponies?"

Everything except for *him*.

Seated diagonally across from Margaret, somehow taking up most of the space in the room, was the Earl Grantham.

George Willis.

Georgie.

Oh, Margaret had known she would see him eventually. Violet had kept her apprised of his whereabouts and sudden change in fortunes. She'd hoped to be prepared, but how do you ready yourself to meet a piece of your heart that had been torn away?

The painfully thin boy who'd been a collection of elbows and feet that had never stopped tapping and twitching had grown into this giant of a man, golden maned and powerfully built. He slouched with leonine insolence in an enormous chair, which appeared delicate beneath his large frame. When he gestured, the reach of his muscular arms strained the costly wool of his topcoat at its seams.

Grantham's face was a study in contrasts; full lips so perfectly shaped, they appeared feminine were set in a squared jaw, the elegant line of his nose ending abruptly at a small white scar and continuing thereafter at an angle. With his fair skin, sky blue eyes, and flaxen curls, he could be a picture of angelic perfection if there weren't a hint of wickedness in the set of his dark brows.

Distracted by his beauty and his perpetual good cheer, one almost missed the pale lines at the corners of his eyes and mouth, deeper than one might expect in a man of two and thirty even though he'd spent a half-dozen years in the wilds of North America.

In the handful of times Margaret had been in Grantham's presence since their reunion, she'd seen only the tiniest glimpses of the man who'd forged those lines. A flash of something hard and desperate beneath his usual cheer had her wondering in the dark of night how his life had been since they parted so many years ago.

What had hurt him.

Whom he'd hurt in return.

The last time Margaret was here, she developed a preternatural sense for when Grantham was nearby. Immersed in her work, she'd only had to endure his company a handful of times before she'd returned to Paris. She'd watch him from the corner of her eye, stepping around the edge of his voice, and turning sideways in the wake of his presence like a child walking along a cliff encounters a wind strong enough to push her off her feet and send her falling.

Margaret had thought herself inured to him. Safe from any falls.

She'd been wrong.

The summer they'd turned sixteen, the world changed forever. There had been no thunderclap from the heavens, no trembling of the earth beneath her feet. One second, he'd been her playmate, then he became her world. Thirteen years, a marriage, a career, and home had come between them, yet Margaret *still* knew where he stood in any room she entered and could taste the salt of his warm skin on the tip of her tongue. Her body didn't understand what Grantham had done; her traitorous heart raced in her chest fueled by memories and the scent of him that somehow reached her from across the room.

He addressed Violet now.

"The last time I visited Grange Abbey, two of your sisters tried to trap me into marriage and your mother made certain to seat me directly in front of where she used to set the Christmas pudding. D'you remember the year we decided to improve on the size of the pudding's flames?"

Even Arthur's face cracked when Grantham told the story of how the three of them managed to burn a hole through the massive dining table that had previously withstood the depredations of nearly two hundred years of Grange offspring until Violet came along.

"My theory was sound," Violet insisted. "The problem was in the execution."

"The problem," Grantham said, "was the two of you scientific geniuses relying on a henchman who thought a cup full of brandy was a piddling amount of fuel if we were to make the Christmas pudding a true spectacle."

"It wasn't brandy," Violet explained to Arthur. "I'd been researching accelerants and conceived a formula to create the highest flames with the smallest measure of liquid."

Arthur let his piercing gaze rest on Margaret. "Did you perhaps inject a note of sanity into their madness, Madame Gault?" he asked.

"I am afraid not, Mr. Kneland," she confessed. "After estimating the height and intensity of the flames according to Violet's formula, I designed the optimal platform atop which we set the pudding. I should have used less flammable construction materials, for once the pudding was lit—"

"And my father's eyebrows were singed—" said Violet.

"And your sister Poppy wet herself from screaming." Grantham chuckled.

"And my other sister Lily bruised her forehead from ducking under the table—"

"And your other sister Iris wet herself from laughing—" Margaret reminded her.

"The flames from the pudding consumed the platform, most of the tablecloth, and a good deal of the table beneath it," Violet finished.

"It was a terrific fire for all that it demolished the pudding," Margaret said wistfully. Violet and Grantham sighed in agreement and Arthur frowned.

"No disrespect, Madame Gault," he said, a note of fear in his voice. "But for how long, exactly, will you be staying at Athena's Retreat?"

Margaret laughed in appreciation as Violet scolded him.

"Margaret is the most sensible woman I know. She'd never let Grantham and I talk her into anything so dangerous now."

For this first time since she'd arrived, Margaret let her gaze meet Grantham's.

"You have nothing to fear, Mr. Kneland," she said. "I learned the hard way to never again trust Lord Grantham's proposals."

2

TWO DAYS LATER, while her maid paid the driver, Margaret stepped down from a hired hack, and breathed in the stench of the city—a combination of coal smoke, the muck of the nearby Thames, and the accumulation of horse droppings and hay littering the street.

Compared to the interior of the hackney cab they'd exited, it smelled like a garden.

"I think someone might have died in there, madame," the maid, Maisey, confided after the hack had departed.

Being a widow, Margaret had fewer restrictions on her ability to travel alone than an unmarried woman. However, she took a maid with her whenever she visited a prospective client. Her late husband, Marcel, had drummed into her from the beginning of their partnership that an independent woman must never appear so.

"Imagine if a man walked about with his purse open and gold coins clanking for all the world to see," he would say. "Everyone would blame the man if he were robbed, no matter the coins belonged to him. Men are the same way with power, my dear. If you show it off, they will take it away and blame you for their actions."

She'd met Marcel Gault two days after arriving in Paris thirteen years ago. Violet's father, Viscount Grange, had sent ahead a letter of introduction to Henri Gault, founder of the city's most prestigious engineering firm. Henri hesitated to take on a woman engineer as an apprentice, no matter how much he admired Lord Grange. His son, Marcel, had no similar qualms.

"Engineering is the perfect science for women," Marcel had told his father, winking at her. "They have the common sense that is characteristic of their sex but none of the ego which causes men to overestimate and underfund."

Tall and thin with a Gallic eye for fashion and a head for accounting, Marcel Gault was a steady presence with a dry wit. While she never gave him her heart, they had a happy marriage full of laughter and friendship. Margaret had mourned his early death from consumption as deeply as his father. Their shared sorrow had made Henri more accepting of Margaret as a senior engineer—but not accepting enough to leave her his firm.

As her late husband's words rattled in her head, Margaret took a moment to study the tall, narrow building before her. A series of unadorned columns stood sentry on either side of its greenish copper doors. A plain grey lintel carved with a single medallion topped each window and skylights studded the metal roof. Stuck between two crumbling old stucco houses built in the last century, it resembled a long, thin face, pinched in disapproval of the neighbor's bow windows and blackened timbers.

"I don't know how long my appointment will go, Maisey," Margaret said once they'd entered the building and climbed the main staircase with care as the polished granite was slippery beneath the smooth soles of their boots. "You are welcome to read while you wait, and do not let anyone say otherwise."

"Yes, madame," said Maisey, huffing as they reached the second floor.

A shiny brass plaque announced their destination and a personable young clerk greeted them in a bright antechamber. He made certain of Maisey's comfort before tapping at a gleaming oak door. Taking a deep breath, Margaret tried to shove the events of the past two days out of her mind.

Having Grantham land at her feet only hours after arriving in England had unsettled her equanimity. That he'd done it arse up and covered in rose thorns had made her want to greet him with a jest and she'd resented the impulse. She hadn't come home to forgive or forget.

She's come home with a Plan, and Grantham was not part of it.

The Plan was her destiny and hers alone.

"Why, I've never looked a woman in the eye. I suppose it's going to take some getting used to."

It took every ounce of willpower in Margaret's body not to react to Sir Royce Geflitt's bemused surprise as he opened the door to his office and ushered her inside.

"If that is your only complaint about doing business with me, I shall take it as a compliment," she told him, injecting a note of cheery dismissal into her voice as if it didn't matter that her size was the first topic of conversation.

Taller than most men, Margaret had hoped to become inured to the jokes about the weather where she stood or the veiled innuendos from men happy to be eye level with her bosom. This hadn't happened yet, but she'd learned to accept one more irritant in a long line of them that came from working with the opposite sex.

Without waiting for Geflitt to offer her a seat, Margaret took her place in the chair opposite his desk and forced her lips to smile around clenched teeth.

One of Sir Edwin Landseer's paintings hung on the far wall. The horses' melancholy gazes were partly obscured by the pale lemon sunlight of an October afternoon falling through the window. Beneath the painting, a credenza filled with a few shiny leatherbound books sported a small collection of horse figurines, a stack of *Gentlemen's Monthly* magazines, and numerous volumes of shipping ledgers, periodicals, and atlases. Oak wainscoting wrapped around the room, broken only by the green marble mantelpiece framing a grate full of smoking ash.

Geflitt's offices sat in the middle ground between well-worn grandeur and the actual trappings of work—much like the man. His baronetcy stretched back at least three generations, but nevertheless he engaged in business. The air of a gentleman somewhat bemused by finding himself in these circumstances wafted about him as he took his seat. His clothing was a conservative mix of fawn-colored trousers and a dark blue frock coat accented by a salmon pink cravat and a plain brown waistcoat. He was clean-shaven and she could smell a hint of sandalwood in the air.

Geflitt lifted one eyebrow in good-natured acknowledgment of her tone once he'd settled himself opposite her. The grey hair at his temples caught in the sunlight and his expression was confident as he steepled his hands.

"These are singular circumstances, my entertaining your bid for this project," he said. "I'd never heard of a woman owning her own engineering firm, but I have assurances from the Henderson Brothers, the Ainsley Consortium, and even the Lords Crespley and Grimshaw that you are the preeminent railway bridge engineer to be found in the British Isles now you've returned."

Both Henderson Brothers and the Ainsley Consortium had employed Margaret through her father-in-law's firm to design and consult on their railway bridge projects last year. While neither project had been completed yet, both were ahead of schedule, under budget, and already drawing praise for their innovations.

"I am flattered by their kind words," Margaret said, pretending humility as displaying too much confidence was dangerous. "I would not say I was the *preeminent* engineer for there are so many brilliant Englishmen in this field. What I would say . . ."

Margaret leaned forward as if to share a confidence, happy to see Geflitt mirror her position.

"What I would say is there are few engineers who are also experienced in running a business, whether they are male or female. If you hire me for this project, I can assure you I will never underestimate the timeline of the work nor saddle you with superfluous expenses."

She dropped her eyes to her hands clasped demurely on her lap. "My late husband, Marcel, taught me everything he knew about planning and thrift. Although I will miss working with my father-in-law, I cannot live away from England any longer."

Geflitt nodded, pushing his lower lip out to signal the weight of his pronouncement. "There is no place in the world that compares to England. It must have been a trial for you to be living amongst the French for so long."

Yes, such a trial to see beautiful clothes in every shop, eat delicious food, and drink gorgeous wines with her meals.

Margaret brought the conversation back to where she needed it to go.

"If you hire me as your engineer, I will bring the secrets that made my father-in-law's firm, Henri Gault and Son, the largest and most prestigious in all of Europe. However, since my own firm is an unknown quantity, I will bill you only half the amount I would have commanded had I still worked for Henri."

A light went on behind Geflitt's eyes.

"Already you are beginning your bridge construction at a profit," she added.

"Ahhh." Geflitt held up a hand. "You have a reputation as a railway bridge engineer but so do Elmsworth and Hitchens."

Margaret's heartbeat sped up. Elmsworth was a mediocre engineer and Hitchens benefitted from the work his father had done to build their reputation. She, on the other hand, had sacrificed the dreams of her father by choosing engineering over theoretical physics and the love of her mother for choosing to become a scientist in the first place. For every single commission, she'd put in twice the hours and one hundred times the effort as anyone else in her father-in-law's firm.

More than anything, Margaret wanted to stand and announce her achievements and trumpet her ambitions.

That would be a mistake.

Instead, she nodded agreeably. "Both of them are fine engineers."

"You, however, have a reputation for . . . shall we say, original ideas?"

Geflitt's mouth twitched as though a smile sat behind his lips and wanted out. The slightest tingle of foreboding touched the base of Margaret's spine when he rubbed his hands together in anticipation.

"I have something to show you."

Gesturing to a table behind them covered in rolls of parchment, Geflitt rose and, with the air of a street performer, unrolled the largest one, setting an inkpot on either side to keep it flat.

"What is . . ." Margaret joined him at the table but could not comprehend at first. "What is this?" she asked.

Even before she uttered the last words, she understood. These weren't preliminary plans for a bridge. This was a plan for . . .

"A tunnel?"

Geflitt chuckled with genuine glee. "Yes. I want you to design and build an underwater railway tunnel."

Only one underwater tunnel existed in the world. The sheer brilliance—and remarkable perseverance—of Marc Brunel had made the Thames Tunnel possible. Its construction had been, in a word, *disastrous.*

"The Thames Tunnel took twenty years to build, killed six men, and cost half a million pounds. It may be an engineering marvel, but it doesn't even achieve its original purpose." The survey maps clearly showed the site of the original Thames Tunnel and a proposed site only a few miles away. "Why on earth would you repeat such a debacle?" Margaret asked.

Geflitt's eyes sparkled as he traced the diagram with a gloved forefinger.

"You are correct. Right now, Brunel's Thames Tunnel is little more than a sightseeing attraction—an underground collection of trinket and pasty sellers." He scrutinized her as if measuring her backbone. "Railways will remake the economy of not just this country, but all of Europe. I'm part of a consortium of men who will start a private line of our own."

Margaret recognized the banked excitement in his voice as ambition. Not something the British upper classes were supposed to possess.

"I've had surveys done. The conditions at the riverbank here and here make a bridge expensive and unwieldy. A tunnel, however, would allow us to bypass the costs of a bridge plus allow us to outshine the rival railways. Ask yourself. Why travel over ordinary bridges when you can take a subaqueous journey? Traveling at breakneck speed right beneath the most storied river in England, now that would be worth the cost of investing in such a venture."

Margaret shook her head, ready to take her leave even as a low hum started in her head. The diagrams on the parchment turned from dotted lines to lengths of cast iron and barrows full of dirt. Sounds of water rushing overhead drowned out Geflitt's voice and the smell of brick and mortar filled her nose.

While the rest of the students in physics class at the Yorkshire Academy for the Education of Exceptional Young Women had seen abstract formulas on their slate boards, Margaret alone had heard the grate of stone on stone, felt the weight of a hammer, and tasted sawdust on the back of her tongue.

Science asked questions but for Margaret that wasn't enough. She needed to find the answers to them—she needed to make those equations *real*. Theories were important only because they guided her toward creating actual change in her environment.

Beneath the parchment were four more sheets of paper. Margaret rummaged through, catching sight of measurements of the soil height and rock layers at the tunnel site, weather reports, iron prices, all the information necessary to build a tunnel.

A tunnel.

Margaret pushed the papers away and set her hands on her hips.

"No. No matter how well I plan, I have only myself and perhaps an assistant. It would be a thankless job taking years of my life and is bound to end poorly."

Geflitt cocked his head as if disappointed, but a half smile remained on his face. "Are you certain, Madame Gault? I came to you out of all the other engineers in the country thinking this might be the first true challenge anyone here has set for you."

Oh, he was wily was Sir Royce Geflitt. The other jobs had been simple, far below her capabilities. A tunnel beneath the Thames was something else altogether. Already Margaret's head filled with plans to improve upon the Brunel's designs.

"The logistics . . . ," she argued half-heartedly.

"I suspected you might be hesitant, Madame Gault," Geflitt said swiftly. "I can assure you with my next words your worries will be forgotten."

Hardly. She couldn't imagine what might convince her to put her name to such a project.

Until he named a sum.

A staggering sum.

A sum too good to be true based on her preliminary investigations of Geflitt's consortium and financial backers.

"I will be blunt. Your consortium members' finances are public knowledge," Margaret said. "I don't see—"

Geflitt interjected. "My *known* consortium members. I have acquired a silent partner since publishing our last written notice of incorporation."

Temptation had her round the ankles and was pulling her in, but Margaret had to remain untouched. So much depended on her making the right decision. "Be that as it may, I cannot agree to this project without knowing the identity of this partner so I can assure myself of their financial stability."

"He is the publisher of a monthly men's magazine and leads a social reform group called the Guardians of Domesticity." Geflitt gestured toward the credenza at a stack of magazines. "Have you ever heard of Victor Armitage?"

GRANTHAM STARED AT a scarlet bed canopy, reflecting on the life of a belted earl in the year of our Lord Eighteen Forty-Four. Surrounded by privilege and exempt from the hardships plaguing the populace crammed into this capital, you might think he lived a life of contentment and ease.

Instead, Grantham's backside ached from a two-story fall, his stomach was unsettled with the residual humiliation of having made that fall in front of a beautiful woman, and he'd slept poorly. He'd been plagued by dreams of an . . . amorous nature, featuring a scantily clad and beguilingly furious Margaret Gault.

Grantham yawned and stretched, wincing at the sudden pain in his back. Was this a portent of aging? He'd only passed his thirty-second birthday. Would forty see him limping with a cane and losing his teeth?

He got up and covered himself with a banyan while his valet, Jameson, left a steaming mug of tea and a pile of broadsheets on the small table where he sat to break his fast in the mornings. At the top of the pile lay *Gentlemen's Monthly*, the magazine owned by Victor Armitage.

Armitage was the leader of the Guardians of Domesticity, a group of men who blamed everyone but the people *in charge* of the government for the most grievous acts *by* the government, who lauded the aristocracy for simply existing, and who demonized women for supporting their families. The magazine was mainly a pile of tripe, but Grantham found it helpful to know what those fools might be planning.

Taking a sip of tea, he opened the paper, then uttered a curse that made Jameson, a connoisseur of fine curses, nod in approval.

"Why, that's me!" Grantham exclaimed, mopping up the tea he'd spit over the table with the sleeve of his banyan.

A caricature on the first page of the magazine portrayed him as an over-muscled, half-naked Pied Piper wearing a pair of devil's horns leering at a young girl as he led a group of children down to hell.

For what Purposes does The Untamed Earl want to take your Children away? read the caption. **And why is he so determined to include your daughters?**

This summer, Grantham had helped shepherd through Parliament the Factory Act, which capped the number of hours a child could work, although no one was under any false impressions the factory owners would comply.

Now, Grantham and others had turned their attention to education reform which proved even more controversial. They had drafted an Education Reform Bill to make education compulsory, unify the voluntary schools alongside the lesser "ragged" schools and fix fees so places didn't go to only the middle class.

"Look at this! It's on the front page alongside an article about how the Education Bill will ruin the economy and tear down the Church," Grantham shouted as Jameson bent to clean a black polish that had fallen on the bedroom carpet. "Says my insistence on mandatory education for girls alongside boys smacks of perversion. How else are we to ensure girls get the same education and aren't doing needlework and cooking the whole day long instead of learning to read and do sums?"

Grantham pushed back his chair and paced the room.

"Ruin the British way of life? Tear down the Church? Perversion?" he roared. "Does the British way of life celebrate ignorance? Is the Church in danger if kitchen boys learn to read? Is it depraved to offer girls an equal chance for education?"

Grantham stormed into his dressing room and pulled his clothing out of drawers, ignoring Jameson's protests about matching waistcoats to cravats or some such nonsense.

"That poxy fool Victor Armitage must be siding with the Anglicans against the bill," Grantham complained. "I'm simply trying to extend the chance for education to more children than those in workhouses and factories, but the entire issue has become a fight between the Church and the Dissenters. They care more about which bishops will make appointments and less than nothing about whether we can help children out of poverty."

He tore through a drawer of cravats. "Reprinted that old tripe that I am a rake and carouser."

Jameson laughed and shook his head. "If they could only see you asleep before ten with a book open on your chest."

Rake and carouser. Hardly. Simply because Grantham paid attention to lonely women, listened to what they had to say, and treated them with respect, he'd been labeled as a lothario. These sorts of rumors were part of what caused the rift between himself and Prince Albert.

"Grey said he would take care of that weasel, Armitage." Grantham ran his fingers through his hair in frustration. "Instead, he lost his mind over Miss Fenley and scarpered off to Herefordshire with her. Now it is up to me to finish off Armitage once and for all."

Jameson took the crumpled magazine, smoothed it out, and laid it on the pile of broadsheets. Grantham opened his mouth to order the magazine tossed in the fireplace when the front page of the broadsheet beneath the magazine caught his eye. He pulled out the broadsheet and stared at it while the germ of an idea formed.

"*The Capital's Chronicle.* Now that sounds familiar. And why is that?" Grantham asked.

"Because you own it," Jameson answered.

"Because I *own* it," Grantham crowed. "Here's a tidy solution to this mess." He strode toward the wardrobe. "Jameson, where is my cravat?"

"You're wearing . . ."

"Never mind, I'm already wearing one."

Within two minutes Grantham had finished dressing and was out the door. With St. Clemens Dane church at his back, his carriage made its way past the office of the Anti-Corn Law League to the corner of Whitefriars and Fleet streets. It pulled up in front of the three-story building proclaiming itself the home of *Gentlemen's Monthly Magazine.* The ubiquitous coal smut covering everything in London had darkened the bow window, but the brass knob was polished, and the front steps swept.

This portion of Fleet Street housed the offices of many of London's newspapers, known as broadsheets. In the mornings, rivers of hawkers streamed out of the backs of these buildings, barrows full of the latest news, gossip, and outright libel.

Libel was the very subject Grantham wished to discuss as he threw open the door and stormed into to the magazine's office.

Within minutes he stormed back out into the street.

Victor Armitage was not in the offices, and no one there knew when he would appear. The artist who penned the caricature did so anonymously, unlike his famous and more talented contemporaries like Cruickshank, and no one knew where to find him. Finally, as to Grantham's bellowed threats of litigation, the slope-shouldered clerk had stared at him dispassionately and recited to him Lord Campbell's Libel Act, as though Grantham hadn't sat through endless discussions of the act last year before it became law.

The Untamed Earl.

Oh, the name stung, no matter he tried to deny it.

Going from Georgie Willis to the Earl Grantham had been a difficult transition.

The old earl had ignored his existence for years owing to his father's scandalous ways and the doubt cast on his mother's claim of marriage. After the earl died, the family's lawyers had found the marriage lines and proclaimed Grantham as the heir.

From that day forward, his life ceased to be his own. The needs of his estate and the tenants were overwhelming to a young man whose only dream had been to buy a farm of his own. He'd found himself at sea when he returned to London and was thrust into the machinations of the *bon ton*—London's aristocratic social world.

In the early days of Prince Albert's marriage to the Queen, he, too, was an outsider. Albert found Grantham's uncomplicated demeanor refreshing, and Grantham had agreed to help the prince on a few small matters since Albert wasn't certain whom he could trust at court.

However, Albert had quickly found his bearings. He and the

Queen's careful crafting of an image of domestic harmony left no room for an "Untamed Earl" with an undeserved reputation as a flirt and a reformative political bent.

The ton ridiculed Grantham behind his back and he'd shown his indifference by playing up his uncouth ways on occasion. It disarmed his political opponents when the man they'd labeled a hopped-up peasant could hold his own in the House of Lords.

Might he have carried it too far?

Guilt soured the contents of his stomach. Like most men, Grantham preferred to pretend he was never in the wrong, but he'd been cursed with a conscience. If his own foolish actions threatened the bill, he had a responsibility to make things right.

Grantham straightened his topper, sighing at the burden of his own nobility. Ten feet along the road he gazed at the worn stucco and worm-riddled beams of an ancient building, a cracked wooden sign hanging over the scuffed door.

The Capital's Chronicle was one of the late earl's last investments. What with the disrepair of the estate and his half-hearted courtship of Violet, Grantham had assured its editors he had no interest in its day-to-day running.

Armitage had his magazine through which he could spew nonsense about the reform act and his noxious views about society in general. In theory, Grantham could do the same with his newspaper.

His neck itched as he inspected the latest edition displayed in the dirty windows—a sure sign his ballocks had motivated an idea rather than his brain box. There was no question which was the bigger portion of his anatomy.

And, after all, what did he have to lose?

3

ROLLING UP THE rough designs, Geflitt collected keys from his clerk and showed Margaret to a set of rooms on the third floor. Three times as large as the offices of her father-in-law's firm, Geflitt offered them at a paltry rent if she agreed to the project.

Margaret walked through the rooms as though inspecting them for flaws while tamping the excitement building in her chest. If she said yes, she would climb to a summit she'd never imagined when, heartbroken and afraid, she'd left England to apprentice with Monsieur Gault.

And yet . . .

What would the women of Athena's Retreat say if they knew how she'd managed to finance her firm?

Victor Armitage's group, the Guardians of Domesticity, had risen in prominence over the past three years, born out of a reaction against the excesses of the late King George IV, the unsettled post-war economy, and the ushering in of a woman to the throne.

The Guardians had targeted Athena's Retreat the year before, protesting the existence of a social club for ladies. They'd argued it was against the natural order for women to leave their homes to learn more about the world! Thank goodness the Guardians had no clue about the true nature of the Retreat. Margaret shuddered to think what might happen if they did.

"What will Mr. Armitage do when he discovers the engineer for your tunnel is a woman?" Margaret had asked.

Without pause Geflitt had waved aside her concerns. "Whatever slogans Victor bandies about in his appearances have nothing to do with how he runs his businesses. Outrage is profitable—until it isn't."

Ah. So Armitage was as false as his slogans. Margaret grew even more disgusted with the man, but it did mean he wouldn't interfere with her work.

"Hiring a woman as an engineer is a revolutionary act," she reminded him. If she were going to take the job, it behooved Geflitt to understand the truth. "You are titled and—"

Geflitt cut her off with a chuckle. "I am hiring you as an engineer, not having you to dinner."

Despite the sting of his words he meant no offense. This was the truth of Margaret's decision so many years ago to turn her back on her family and take up a profession. Margaret was no longer acceptable company to the higher circles of society. Her friendship with Violet was an outlier. For the rest of the aristocracy, Margaret was an invisible cog in a great machine that worked to do their bidding.

After having given Geflitt a date by which she would decide, Margaret donned her cloak and collected Maisey. They made their way down the gleaming stairs, holding tight to the wrought iron balustrade. Wan sunlight wafted over them from the skylights in the ceiling and Margaret glanced upward, admiring the symmetry of the leaded panes.

The wind tugged at their skirts upon leaving the building and Margaret turned her body away from the street to avoid the dirt and smut that rose when a strong gust whipped around the corner and threatened to dislodge her hat. Coal smoke and dust got in her eyes, and she staggered to the side, only to collide with a soft dun-colored wall.

"I beg your pardon," said a voice.

Margaret jumped when she realized the wall was an actual human being.

"Oh!" Margaret rubbed her eyes. "I'm so sorry."

"It's no hardship, madame. Women are always throwing themselves in my path."

Grantham.

"What are you doing here?" she asked, glancing at the building behind her as if Geflitt might come charging out at this moment and say something about Victor Armitage.

". . . put an end to Victor Armitage and his Guardians of Puerility."

"What?" she cried.

"I said"—Grantham exaggerated his words through a maddeningly charming lopsided grin—"I am here to put an end to Victor Armitage and his Guardians of Puerility."

When Margaret blinked, both to clear her eyes of soot and to take in the incongruity of Grantham appearing in front of her and uttering that name, he repeated himself.

"Puerility. It's a play on the name of his group. The Guardians of Domesticity."

When she remained silent, his enthusiasm wavered. "Never mind. Not as funny the third time. What are you doing here? Come to give Armitage a scolding?"

"How . . . ?" Margaret surveyed their surroundings. Next to her, Maisey coughed into her handkerchief, but she was the only other person on the sloping wooden walkway. A long wagon filled with barrels pulled to a stop in front of a tavern and a single rider on a piebald horse passed them. Other than the large tan and gold carriage which must belong to Grantham, the street was empty.

"I don't see anyone. Is he nearby?" she asked.

"Why, that's the offices of his magazine right there."

Sure enough, in painted black lettering across the bow window of the building next door was the name **GENTLEMEN'S MONTHLY MAGAZINE** in large print and beneath the words **NEWS FOR THE GOOD AND THE GODLY AMONG US.**

What rubbish. Nothing good nor godly came from bullying women who were trying to provide for their families.

"I had no idea," she said. The ties between Geflitt and Armitage were strong indeed.

Damn.

"Then what are you doing traipsing 'round Fleet Street?" Grantham asked.

Maisey interrupted, calling to her. "There won't be many hacks to be had this time of the day, Madame. Should we walk toward the Strand?"

"Hack?" Grantham frowned. "Walk? You will ride home in my carriage."

"I will not," Margaret shot back before he'd finished his sentence.

Geflitt's offer, the idea of a tunnel, the revelation that Armitage would fund the project, and the empty office with all it symbolized had left her dizzy. Despite Geflitt's assurance that Margaret was not worthy of a peer's attention, here was an earl accosting her on the street.

The last thing she needed was Grantham intruding into her life while she had to sort through the choices presented to her and integrate them into her Plan.

No part of that Plan included a man telling her what to do, no matter how distinguished he looked now there were no green stains on his trousers or rose leaves in his hair.

Margaret wished for the stains and the leaves. She wished he was still the boy who had no care for his consequence—only for when the fish were rising and whether the Grange's cook had set up her black-berry jam.

She missed that boy.

Georgie would know what to do. He might not understand more than basic arithmetic and constantly assume he would win a fight with gravity, but he'd an inbred sense of fairness no amount of abuse or derision could alter.

This man who stood before her was not the boy she once knew. He was a former soldier, now an earl who spoke in the House of Lords and was on friendly terms with Prince Albert.

He'd grown up but the ever-present joy which had buoyed him through a difficult childhood still seeped from his pores as though he'd swallowed sunlight. His skin glowed and his eyes shone with humor. His beauty was almost preternatural set amid the dirt and gloom of the city's streets.

A long time ago she would have pressed herself against his skin, hungry for the way only he could pull her from her head back into her body. He would put his nose to the crook of her neck while she set her lips to his cheek and they would lie like that, simply breathing in the scent of late afternoon sun and unfulfilled longing. There had only been a handful of embraces that summer and she remembered each one. His arms had been thinner, but long enough that they wrapped her in a cocoon so tight he'd imprinted himself upon her like an invisible daguerreotype, felt rather than seen.

Lust didn't weaken Margaret's knees so much as remembrance of touch; an awakened craving for contact while he whispered the right words to soothe her worries and heat her blood.

But that was then.

This was now and any comfort he might offer came far too late.

Margaret cleared her head of the past and straightened her shoulders.

"We came here in a hackney, and we will be perfectly fine traveling home in one," she insisted despite Maisey's hopeful mien.

"What about the rain?" he asked.

"Rain?"

As she spoke a large wet drop plonked on the brim of her cunning new poke bonnet replete with a pretty spray of blue watered-silk roses.

"Damn London," she muttered under her breath. The rain here was filthy and would ruin the white ermine trim of her pelisse.

Again, Maisey gazed at her with hope in her eyes and Margaret clicked her tongue in resignation. "Yes, Maisey. We shall take the earl up on his offer."

Grantham beamed and Margaret's eyes rolled heavenward. A footman hopped down and pulled out the stairs for them. Ever the gallant, Grantham helped Maisey into the carriage first, hoping aloud the conveyance would be smooth enough for her.

When he turned and held out his hand to Margaret, however, the smile wavered.

"Madame?" he asked softly.

Where had he gone, her Georgie? Did he live deep within this giant who burst through the world recklessly as though he'd never broken anything of consequence? Would he hold her, if she asked, taking care of the thinnest, most fragile parts of her?

Ugh. When had she become so maudlin?

Margaret kept her hand at her side and ascended the stairs on her own, avoiding his touch and ignoring the dimming of his glow. A pebble of guilt sat neatly between her chest and her stomach like an invisible busk.

Grantham heaved himself in after, taking up far too much space on the seat across from Maisey and herself. His long legs brushed against Margaret's skirts and his feet nudged hers as they rounded the corner. He addressed not a word to her, however, instead engaging the maid in conversation about Violet's baby.

"Cries all night, does she? Excellent. Strapping pair of lungs in her. Want her to favor the Yellowbelly side of the family. Folks from Lincolnshire are nothing if not opinionated. If she were quiet, you'd have to worry," he said. "That would be the Scottish side coming out."

Margaret twisted her lips around a rebuke and swallowed it, unwilling to be baited. Maisey, however, patiently explained to him a parent's birthplace did not cause colic.

The scent of horehound filled the carriage, taking her back to damp summer days spent hiding from Violet's sisters in a treehouse high in the willow. Sucking on the ubiquitous candied drops, Georgie would pace the warped wooden floorboards, eager to be fishing by the stream. He was a wild thing then, never happier than running like mad, arms flung out to embrace the world.

He and Violet both possessed an inborn confidence they would land safely no matter how high the perch from which they jumped. Margaret, on the other hand, had been the one to measure the distance and flag the dangers. Her body, unnaturally tall without a corresponding center of gravity, made her wary of sudden flights, figurative or otherwise. Each of her footsteps echoed with her mother's admonitions—how Margaret's shoulders were too broad, her neck too long, and her height set her too far apart from the other girls. Why couldn't she be softer, rounder, smaller?

Why was she forever calculating, scribbling . . . taking up space?

That voice of doubt never left her. No matter how many accolades Margaret won for a project there always came a moment when she was certain someone would step forth and expose her. One day everyone would figure out Margaret was not bold and assured nor extraordinarily gifted or special. She was a woman trying her best to survive by pretending to be all those things.

The carriage jerked as the wooden wheels caught on the pock-marked road leading toward Beacon House and Margaret grabbed hold of the strap attached to the side of the conveyance. Grantham laughed as he slid on the padded cushions, teasing Maisey about her book.

He glanced over at Margaret seeking her approval, but she withheld it. If she gave in, even the tiniest bit, he would run roughshod over her attempts to keep her distance. No matter how beautiful his eyes or how tempting it might be to revisit the comfort of those long ago embraces, the fact remained that Grantham had hurt her badly. Margaret no longer had an unshakable belief in the wisdom of her heart.

She did, however, still have the determination that led her to leaving England alone at the age of seventeen and cutting ties with her mother to continue her engineering studies. Sentimentality had no place in her life.

All her attention must be given to her work. Margaret's accomplishments were the product of resolve and a fiery temper she'd learned how to channel into a single-minded perseverance. That same perseverance meant she would have to overcome her ambivalence about taking Armitage's money.

When women were offered positions of real power, they always came with a price.

Either they had to sacrifice their dreams of motherhood, or they had to sublimate their attractiveness, or some other measure of blood was extracted.

The price for establishing Britain's first woman-owned engineering firm might be the end of her friendships with the women of Athena's Retreat if they found out about the money. Certainly, Violet would be upset. Would Margaret lose her as well?

Margaret had never told Violet what happened between her and Grantham that summer. Up until now, he had been the only secret she'd ever kept from her friend. That secret paled in comparison to this one.

Armitage was yet another man poised to ruin her life, but this time Margaret would not let him, or anyone else, separate her from her destiny.

GRANTHAM OPENED THE sliding hatch between the cab of the carriage and the driver and called out the name of his club then leaned forward, hoping to catch one last glance of Margaret—and possibly her ankles—as she marched up the front steps of Athena's Retreat with serious little Maisey behind her, hurrying to keep pace.

He could have told Maisey not to bother. When Margaret had her sights set on some goal, she never looked back, only always forward.

What exactly had Margaret been doing earlier? She'd deftly avoided his questioning why she'd been on Fleet Street. There weren't any engineering firms in that part of London, as far as he knew.

The thought that she might have been visiting a man flitted through his head and he swatted it away, jaw clenching. What Margaret did was none of his concern. Determined, as always, but a hundred times more self-possessed than she'd been as a girl, she gave off an enigmatic aura that made him itch to untie her bonnet ribbons or pull at the cuffs of her gloves.

Like a damned pup trying to catch a girl's attention.

Pathetic.

His sneer of derision made the club's doorman flinch as Grantham bounded up the stairs. Inside he wavered, peeking into the billiards room. A few young lordlings lounged therein, the familiar fug of expensive cheroots and mediocre brandy drifting toward him.

He contemplated wasting time among their shallow company talking nonsense and hitting balls with sticks—indulging in the simple joys of being a man.

But no.

Grantham did not want to return for the next session of Parliament. He needed time alone, time to learn the land of his estate and settle matters with his mother and sister. To that end, he must do what he could to find support for the Education Reform Bill while it had a chance of passage before Parliament adjourned at the end of next month.

"Well, if it isn't the Untamed Earl himself. Where's your flute, my lord? Unless that's the bulge in your trousers?"

Putting his back to the lure of the clacking billiards balls, Grantham spun about to face Lord Alfred Barnesdown, known to his circle of friends as Barney.

"You are a wit, Barney." Grantham faked a chuckle and clapped the other man on the shoulder.

Barney was *not* a wit, but he was powerful; a combination of his father's doing and an innate ability to know which way the political winds blew and how to get in front of them. Grantham had been working hard for Barney's support of his bill, but the other man hesitated.

With no clear momentum either way, Barney would sit on the fence unless Grantham could figure out a way to pull him off onto the right side. As the days went by, it became more difficult to keep his tone light and spirits up. The urge to take these men around him by the collar and shake some sense into them became powerful indeed.

Girls needed to go to school to learn more than domestic skills. The truth of this statement was so stark and obvious to Grantham yet so intangible to an astonishing number of aristocratic men who saw women as either bedmates or broodmares.

"Armitage is growing more powerful by the day with his magazine and group of agitators. You should take yourself out of his sights," said Barney.

As if Grantham hadn't considered that.

"I'm not worried," he lied. "I've got an idea or two of how to put him in his place. "

Barnes lifted one eyebrow into a perfect triangle of disbelief. "Leave off the ideas and get on with the actions, then. If you don't want folks thinking you're haring around after little girls like his cartoons suggest, settle down and get married."

Married?

"Married?" Grantham said. "How will that make a difference?"

Barney examined him for a moment. Leaning forward, he spoke in a conspiratorial tone. "If I can be honest."

At Barney's dramatic pause, Grantham nodded, irritated with the man's demeanor but curious as to what he might be about to say.

"You've made a valiant effort with the Reform Bill, but your influence is diminished now Prince Albert has distanced himself. Get yourself a wife, preferably from an established family, spend more time at parties and dinners than at Lords . . ."

A sour taste at the back of Grantham's mouth caused his lips to twist in discomfort as he listened to the man's words.

Barney hesitated for a moment but, unable to refrain, finished his lecture with one final thought. "You are friends with Greycliff, but you should limit how often you are seen with his former stepmother. Between her ill-advised marriage and her ladies club, that association does your cause no good."

Whatever expression Grantham wore, it shut Barney up and had him beating a hasty retreat to the smoking room. Grantham on the other hand remained in the hallway, half listening to the clacking of billiards balls and the overloud laughter of foolish men.

"Fancy a game, my lord?"

One of the young cubs from the billiard room gestured to him, but Grantham waved him away.

My lord.

The Earl Grantham.

It took him years to answer to that name—Grantham. That was the name his father would mutter on his infrequent visits home when he was in his cups; the great-uncle who left George and his mam to a life of abuse and penury until his father died and his mother was able to remarry a gentleman farmer.

His father had gotten his mother, a poor relation to the earl's wife, pregnant. Although his mother had written the earl to tell him of her child's birth and ask for assistance, she'd never received any acknowledgement in return. His father had blamed the marriage for his subsequent bad luck, but drink and gambling were the sole reasons for his father's decline.

The title hung about Grantham's neck like an anvil and the only way he'd found to lessen the burden was to use it for something clean, honest, and decent. Girls needed to be educated so they would not be at the mercy of men as had happened with his mam.

The idea of balancing out his father's sins with his own actions carried Grantham forward when his worries brought him too low to see the horizon. Those days were more and more frequent, and Grantham did not like to think about what might happen should his attempt at atonement fail.

Before he became the earl, he'd been a soldier with the 24th Foot. Life had been simple. If you had an enemy, you shot them. Terrible, but direct. As Grantham grew older, his enemies had become more amorphous.

While he couldn't shoot his adversaries in Parliament, he could indulge in a more direct sort of warfare than giving speeches and attending dinners. The thought of taking on a weasel like Victor Armitage lifted his spirits. Grantham left the club with a spring in his step as he headed to the one place his project would be met with words of praise and approval.

4

"Go away, Grantham."

"I'm trying to help. You need to use a gentle touch," Grantham said. "It's a delicate thing."

"I mean it." Margaret's jaw ached from grinding her teeth. "Shut up."

"Worked perfectly at the auction house. I don't know what's—why don't you push that button there over to the left."

Margaret was tempted to push *Grantham* right out of a window if he opened his mouth one more time. Calculating his approximate weight and the distance to the window, she decided to strangle him instead. Her hands could be around his throat in seconds.

They knelt side by side in Mirren's nursery. Margaret and Violet had been having a lovely time that afternoon sorting through children's primers on physics and chemistry in anticipation of setting up Mirren's schoolroom when Grantham and a footman had interrupted them, lugging a huge package into the room.

"The auctioneer swore this was made by the same craftsmen who worked on the Jaquet-Droz automata," he'd exclaimed while tugging at the twine wrapped around a three-foot box. "Maggie, you must see the insides."

Before she could remind him yet again to stop calling her Maggie, he'd unwrapped the gift and opened the crate. Within sat a wooden doll dressed in a beautiful pink silk gown perched before a rosewood organ, lifeless fingers hovering above miniature ivory keys. An automaton, one of the clever toys that moved when wound like a clock, the doll was supposed to play music, her slipper-shod feet pushing at miniscule pedals, head bobbing in time with the lullaby.

"Can you see what might be wrong?" Grantham's breath, when he spoke, stirred a ribbon hanging from Margaret's day cap. The sensation sent a tingle up her spine. His broad shoulders were only a hairsbreadth from hers, and if she swayed in the slightest, her hip would brush against his. Licking her dry lips, she tried to focus on the gears in front of her.

Beautifully folded in the front, the doll's dress gaped widely in the back, exposing a wooden panel Grantham had removed to wind it up. Nothing happened, so Grantham had stuck one of his enormous fingers in the cams, causing Margaret's head to ache.

"Don't touch it—"

She'd stopped short of calling him a giant oaf.

Grantham had a core of sweetness to him he'd hidden with jokes and hurried movements. More than once since her return, he'd made fun of his great size and she wondered if he was self-conscious about his body.

He'd no reason to be. From what she could tell, beneath his beautifully tailored clothes, his hips were trim and his stomach flat. Long muscles in his legs stretched the fine wool of his trousers when he crouched by her, and she averted her gaze from his backside.

Imagine if he caught her ogling him, what he might say. The fear he would ridicule her or, even worse, guess she harbored some vestige of attraction to him, led her to jab at the parts more fiercely than was prudent.

"The Jaquet-Droz family are brilliant watchmakers." Margaret spoke loudly to Violet as she worked, hoping to distract herself. "They make intricate gears that provide incredibly precise ratios."

When Violet said nothing, Margaret paused and peered around, but Grantham motioned to the automaton.

"She left to put the baby to bed. If you hurry, we can fix this before the lass wakes after dinner."

That they were alone in the room did not help Margaret's powers of concentration, such as they were. She kept talking, not caring if Grantham could understand her.

"As I'm sure you know, gear ratios determine the speed of an escape wheel. You can have multiple gears allowing for different movements at different times. This is how you have one hand that tells minutes while another tells the hour in a normal clock."

How beautifully exact and orderly the mechanism before her was made. A glorious mix of predictability and imagination. Appreciation for the design lent warmth to her cheeks and set her heart to beating faster.

Yes, admiration for the scientific principles and not the large, handsome man forcing himself into her awareness, distracting her so that her words slurred as though she'd had too much champagne.

"In some ways, automata are similar in design to watches. You have a master driving wheel"—Margaret pointed to the wheel at the base of the doll—"controlling the speed at which the cams—this column of discs here attached by the small linkages—move up and down or side to side. These control the different parts of the doll and it is why the fingers can move at a different speed than her foot when it presses on the pedal."

Beside her, Grantham leaned forward, his face so close to hers, the sound of his breath echoed in her ears.

"Cams and linkages," he murmured.

Oh, those brilliant blue eyes of his. They stroked the bridge of her nose and the curve of her lips like a line of flames. In response, her skin heated, and she shifted away from him.

For all she spent her days working with men, her nights were spent alone.

Seven years without a caress or embrace.

Margaret must not have the same constitution as other women who were happy to live alone once widowed. The way her body leaned in toward Grantham's, the yearning for the feel of skin beneath her lips, the craving to be encircled by another living body . . . Certainly, the result of a weak character and nothing to do with Grantham himself.

"I cannot tell why it won't work," she said. "Perhaps something was bent during transit, although most of the pieces seem sturdy."

"That might be," he agreed.

The scent of him, linen and licorice and sandalwood soap, made her dizzy and her legs squeezed together in response to a tiny pulse throbbing at the center of her. She leaned slightly forward and squinted at the brass fixtures. Nothing was wrong with the doll, so why couldn't she force herself to stand and move away from him?

"Margaret, look here."

His mouth was almost touching that place beneath her ear that made her wild. Close enough so if she turned her head, they would kiss.

Grantham reached out and set the tip of his finger to the three gears sitting in the center of the driving wheel, his other hand resting between Margaret's shoulder blades as if to balance himself. His touch burned through the paisley shawl that covered her day dress right down to her skin. If she leaned back into his touch, it would start a conflagration the same way a key would start the mechanism of the automaton. Also like the automaton, Margaret would have no control over how hot the fire might burn or when it would end.

By God, she was a fool.

She shot to her feet, unbalanced by a sensation of standing on the other side of a wall of glass.

"You've made a bad bargain, my lord," Margaret said, stumbling for the door. "Somehow you took something precious and broke it. However, my time is too valuable to spend it fixing your mistakes."

Hurrying down the corridor and into the kitchens, she trailed her fingers along the wainscoting in the hallway connecting Beacon House with the public rooms of Athena's Retreat. Not many members lingered before dinner hour, so she didn't have to worry about carrying on a conversation when what she wanted to do was punch something.

Someone.

"Margaret."

Him.

She'd hoped he would think better of pursuing her this far. Of course, Grantham did not *think*, did he? He simply acted on impulse, assuming his smile and cheerful manner would get him past any obstacle as it had so many times in the past.

Well, Margaret was not going to be swayed by Grantham's transparent allure. He could whisper sugared words and flash his most attractive grin, but it didn't change their past.

IT TOOK GRANTHAM years to figure out how to live in his body. For the beginning of his life, he was small—made of skin and bones, his mam had said. Most of this great height and breadth came in the space of the first two years as a soldier, much to the amusement of his fellows and the despair of the Army's lackeys, who had to procure him new trousers every three months.

As a result, he sometimes forgot how intimidating his physical presence could be to smaller folks. Margaret, on the other hand, had reached her height early on in her girlhood. Nothing in her posture indicated his size impressed her when he caught up to her and blocked her path.

When her shoulders went back as if in preparation for a battle, her shawl fell around one elbow and exposed the clean line of her neck and the supple curve where he had once laid a thousand tiny kisses in a necklace of adolescent desire. Grantham remembered the taste of her skin in the same way he could summon the yeasted tang of fresh bread and the bitter sweetness of gooseberry jam.

As they knelt side by side in the nursery, every inch of his skin had buzzed with awareness. Her unique scent of oranges and sawdust had filled his nose until he'd become clumsy, overwhelmed by sensation almost too painful to bear. He'd had to reach over and touch the cool slide of the metal wheel to steady himself, but when his palm landed on her back, the world had tilted and left him breathless.

The time had come to speak of their past.

It sat like a menhir in the room every time they'd seen one another, and although Margaret seemed willing to ignore it, Grantham could no longer live with the pain he'd caused her standing between them.

"Go away, my lord."

Margaret's voice dripped with a reserved disdain that would do even the Queen proud. Eliciting a hint of her childhood temper would be quite the feat. A tingle of excitement pricked Grantham's spine like the claws of a kitten, and he cleared his throat.

"You know my name, Maggie," he said. "None of this 'my lord' business."

Margaret huffed an exasperated breath and pushed at his shoulder. "Will you get out of my way, you great gawk."

That was a fine old Lincolnshire insult. Outrage suited her; eyes of hazel widened beneath her thick lashes, her cheeks flushed, and lips slightly parted.

"I've missed your temper," he told her. Common sense fled in the wake of her familiar scent of citrus and heat. "I've missed *you*. Maggie, we need to talk about what happened."

With the force of a blow, she finally met his gaze, and he lost his wits. There she was—the girl he'd fallen in love with at the tender age of eight. Always three inches taller and miles ahead of him in wit and intelligence. Grantham hadn't cared if Maggie was smarter, fiercer, and funnier than him. All that mattered was *she* cared for *him*.

A wave of lust awoke as well, and with a roar, it coursed through his body. Inconvenient.

Inevitable.

Without consideration that anyone might pass by, he backed her up against the wall, reveling in the closeness. Only the last vestiges of will-power kept him from pressing his hips against hers. Noble thoughts of repairing a childhood friendship turned to smoke in the flames of de-sire. He almost resented the strength of the attraction because it fogged his brain and he needed to convince her to listen to him.

Stroking her skin with his gaze, he kept his hands at his sides. No matter how great his urges, he wouldn't touch her unless she touched him first. Softening his voice from brass to honey, he drizzled his words over her.

"Perhaps we could dine together tonight? It has been so long, and we've had no occasion to speak with one another. We can reminisce about our childhood. Remember the house we built in the old willow?"

Margaret stubbornly averted her gaze again, so he admired the prim curve of her eyebrow. He wanted to trace the upside-down V with his tongue.

"Speak with one another," she repeated. "Reminisce," she echoed.

The last piece of that word broke off, and Grantham understood he'd pushed her too far. Intending to charm her into lowering her guard, instead he'd reminded her of what lay between them.

The hurt he had caused her. The wounds still festering.

"As a matter of fact, I'm reminiscing right now," she said. "Shall I tell you what I remember?"

Damn.

Why had he done such a clumsy job of this? That flush unfurling high on her cheeks might have been a church bell sounding the warning of a storm approaching.

"Uh." Grantham stepped away from her. "I don't—"

Faster than he could credit, Margaret's arms shot out and pulled him close. Despite common sense, he relished the feel of her breasts against his chest. Bliss.

"I'm *reminiscing* about how I felt when you broke your vow to me, George Willis," she said. "I'm remembering it felt like this."

A split second of what might have been desire flashed across her face before she brought her knee up between his legs.

Holy Christ on the cross.

Pain flooded his entire body as he slumped to the floor, then keeled sideways into a boneless heap of agony. Falling headfirst into a rose-bush was a tap on the shoulder compared to this.

Margaret peered at him with the same dispassion one might display when selecting a fresh-caught fish for dinner.

"I only wanted . . . ," he wheezed, the words emerging as a smear of syllables meaning nothing. "I simply wanted to say . . ."

An avalanche of words waited on the tip of his tongue; a vow to correct the mistakes of their past, a plea to give him a chance for redemption, an appeal for grace.

Too late. The last he saw of Margaret was the hem of her skirts as she calmly stepped over his body and continued on her way.

5

MARGARET STOOD IN the center of her near empty office, alone except for her misgivings. Her fingers drummed against the top of a cast-off table she'd had hauled here alongside a drafting desk she'd borrowed from the Retreat. The rolls and rolls of plans, surveyor's maps, and copies of Brumel's designs for the original Thames Tunnel were in heaps on the floor next to a pile of lumber.

Around her front, she'd wrapped one of the Retreat's canvas aprons, and a bag of ha'penny nails shone in the bright daylight streaming into the offices from the newly washed windows on the roof. She'd devised a set of shelves to hold her rolled parchments, but Geflitt had interrupted her before she could begin construction.

In her hand was a cheque, the first installment of her payment, advanced to her so she could outfit her office and hire an assistant.

An assistant. What would the Guardians of Domesticity do if they discovered their founder paid a woman's salary? Did this balance out the derision they heaped on the scientists of Athena's Retreat? Margaret hadn't told her friends about the project, yet. There hadn't been time.

This was a lie.

She was putting it off.

When he'd arrived earlier to present the cheque, Geflitt had beamed as though he were a proud parent. It made her uncomfortable. Even more discomforting was the list he'd set on the table in front of her.

"These are the suppliers who have connections with the consortium," Geflitt had explained as she pored over the names. "As you can see, our network runs widely and among those are—"

"I do not see Morgan's Foundry on the list," Margaret interrupted. A prickling beneath her skin made her fingers clench. "None of these names are familiar from my last trip to England."

Pretending not to care she'd spoken over him, Geflitt tapped the top button of his waistcoat, assuring himself of his own presence.

"You will find that Adams and Sons Foundry will fulfill your requirements nicely."

Margaret scrutinized the list again, while Geflitt appeared bemused as though trying to understand why she might question him.

She cleared her throat. "While I am grateful for your list, there are other foundries with which I have connections. I'm certain you won't mind me speaking to them as well."

Now Geflitt's posture stiffened, head shaking as though to clear his ears of the nonsense she'd spouted.

Margaret had followed the steps of this dance dozens of times.

Step one. A man told her what to do.

Step two. She asked why.

Step three. He told her what to do again. Because she must not have understood him the first time. She certainly couldn't be *questioning* him. Impossible for her to not *defer* to him.

He was a man.

She was a woman.

It so followed that he was correct.

One, two, three, and four. Back and forth and to the side. Over and over again until it sank into his brain that she *was* questioning him. That she did *not* defer to him.

Astonishing.

Lucky for Margaret although Geflitt was a proud man, he was not stupid, and it took less time than she'd imagined for the confrontation to occur.

All pretenses of bonhomie disappeared. It had taken years of practice, but Margaret did not look down or away and kept her gaze locked on him.

The other night Margaret had begrudged Grantham his self-assurance. Who would gainsay him with the power of his sex and his title? Nobility alone didn't fuel his confidence. George Willis was born knowing which fights to pick.

The stubborn boy who refused to sour beneath the blows of his father's drunken fist had been the one to convince Margaret she was important even when she did not believe it herself. If that boy were here, he would whisper in her ear to stand her ground, not back down, and for the love of all that was holy, keep her temper in check.

"It is common enough practice to favor certain firms," Geflitt said. "This is how business is done, madame. You would do well to insinuate yourself with the consortium members and their friends. They will be useful to you in the coming years."

Why were men so determined to get in her way? When would they simply step aside and let her get on with the work?

"This project will carry my name," Margaret said, the skin of her face rigid while she enunciated her words in an effort to keep her voice from rising. She gestured to her office, to the Plan she'd begun to construct with both her hands and her heart. "Gault Engineering will not be known for anything other than excellence. If Adams and Sons meets my standards, I am happy to give them my business. If not . . ."

Hands clasped against the tension in her belly, she dulled the sharpest of the edge from her words. "Well, I suppose we will delay that conversation until the time comes."

While he did not outright oppose her, Geflitt did leave her with a discouraging thought.

"I admire your courage in staking out your claim in a man's world, Madame Gault. You have an undeniable talent and good business sense."

He'd glanced out the window at the racing clouds and patted his top hat firmly on his head. "Your stature and safety will nevertheless always depend on the goodwill of the men around you. You have no title or family to protect you. No husband to stand between you and men who assume they can take advantage of a woman. No reputation other than the one you build from here on out."

Margaret glanced at the list of names then at him.

"No one will think less of you for accepting our help."

His words attached themselves like burrs to her skin, no matter how hard she scrubbed in the bath later that evening. They pulled at the hem of her ballgown and dangled from her shawl that night as Margaret squeezed Violet's hand upon approaching the bright lights of Hemming's Assembly Rooms.

"Are you ready to descend into a veritable swamp of stultifying, aggravating, and condescending folks with narrow minds and even narrower waists?" Violet asked.

Grateful for the distraction, Margaret leaned in toward her friend, admiring how Violet's indigo gown contrasted with her creamy skin and ebony curls.

"My goodness, when you put it that way, what are we waiting for?" Margaret asked.

They were waiting, however, for Violet's steps slowed as they approached the entrance.

"I have forgotten how to dance," she whispered.

"I promise it will come back to you at the first note of a waltz," Margaret assured her.

Violet huffed in disbelief while perusing the crowd. This was her first reentry into society since she'd had the baby. Arthur had received an urgent summons from their former doorman, Henry Winthram, and had begged off the event so Margaret agreed to escort Violet in his stead to a public ball. Unlike private assemblies, public balls were ticketed events, often for charities. Tonight, the aim was to raise funds for the widows and children of fallen soldiers.

For all the confidence Violet had gained since the death of her first husband, crowds like this intimidated her. Margaret's heart hurt to see her friend so apprehensive.

"I am too fat to wear a gown like this," muttered Violet.

"You are luminous tonight with a décolletage that will have every man here drooling with desire."

Violet turned to Margaret and snickered. "Drooling with desire over my décolletage? Is your French influence taking over? Why not just say they'll be ogling my bubbies?"

"How insufferably English, my dear," Margaret chastised her as they entered the foyer. "Much more elegant to use alliteration to point out the gentlemen will be considering your *coker-nuts*."

Violet's laughter faded when a pair of older women passed by. She made to approach them, but one woman turned her head quickly in the other direction and pulled her friend along with her.

A fire leapt to life in Margaret's breast at the cut direct.

"How dare they—" Margaret began.

Violet shushed her, squeezing Margaret's arm to divert her attention. "This is neither the time nor the place to contemplate ramming anything down anyone's orifices."

Biting her lip to keep from snickering, Margaret patted Violet's hand where it rested now in the crook of her elbow.

"You know me too well. Except I was not contemplating ramming anything down. More like shoving something up."

Somewhat cheered, they fell into a line to greet the charity's patronesses.

"Is it your marriage to Mr. Kneland that caused their reaction?" Margaret asked.

"Hmmm, it could be." Studying her dress, Violet smoothed a wrinkle in the bodice. "It could also be my association with Athena's Retreat."

Violet's husband, Arthur, was a commoner with a twenty-year-old scandal attached to his name. Even though he'd recently received a public display of approval from the Queen and had the support of Violet's former stepson, Lord Greycliff, the marriage had raised more than a few eyebrows. Added to this, Athena's Retreat was a popular subject in some of the tawdrier broadsheets and gossip columns. The idea of a women's club struck many as unseemly.

A terrible thought occurred to Margaret. Pulling Violet to a halt, she let the group of women behind them go ahead.

"Violet, I have returned to start my own engineering firm."

Violet's eyes rounded in question. "Yes, I know, dear. I am proud of you for it."

"Won't it diminish your standing even more to be seen in friendship with a woman who works for a living in a man's occupation? Perhaps I should leave and have Althea—"

In their girlhood, Margaret had always been the one with a temper and Violet forever smoothing ruffled feathers. Time had a way of flipping things on their head, for Margaret's urge to slink away and protect Violet was met with a fierce glare and clenched fists.

"Don't you even think of leaving my side, Maggie Strong." Violet linked her arm with Margaret's and pulled her forward. "I wasted too many years diminishing the best part of myself to meet a ridiculous standard. I almost missed out on the happiest moments of my life because I feared what others might think or say. You cannot believe I would end our friendship over concerns for what others may say about your accomplishments. Why, I am as proud of you as I would be if any of my sisters were to strike out on their own."

A wave of gratitude swept through Margaret as they greeted the patronesses.

"You are an angel, Violet Kneland," Margaret whispered to her friend.

"Yes, an angel with enormous breasts."

They pinched each other hard—an old habit they'd learned to keep from bursting into laughter in public.

Margaret understood she'd lost any claim to gentility by choosing a profession where she must work alongside men on a construction site, haggle with tradesmen, and engage in bidding for contracts without the shield of a husband or father. Rumors would inevitably circulate about how she won jobs or secured fair prices.

Despite her friend's declarations, Margaret would eventually have to separate herself from Violet.

She cleared her head of worries for that night and smiled when Althea Dertlinger and her mother approached them. Althea was one of the first scientists Margaret met when she stayed at the club a year and a half ago. Thin and tall, although not as tall as Margaret, she had large brown eyes that squinted when she went without her gold-rimmed spectacles and her chestnut hair had been braided and wrapped into a somewhat lopsided chignon at the back of her head. She wore a simple, yet elegant gown of buttercup yellow that hung loose on her straight figure.

When Althea pushed her spectacles up her nose, Margaret could see tiny purple crescents beneath her eyes contrasting sharply with her fair skin, which appeared almost translucent in the dusk.

"How lovely to see you, Mrs. Kneland. Hallo, Margaret." Althea beamed with undisguised relief at their presence.

Althea was engaged in the study of minuscule animals known as *bacteria*. Named for their sticklike shape, they could be discerned only through the lens of a micro-scope and her research required long hours hunched over her specimens in a small laboratory at the Retreat. Having become increasingly worried about her daughter's chances on the marriage mart, Althea's mother had forbidden her from remaining at the club past supper.

The poor girl now rose with the costermongers and coffee sellers to work at her science after being hauled about to balls and parties only hours before.

Thanks to her height, Margaret could see above the heads of the chattering ladies in front of them and into the assembly rooms. From a distance, it appeared as though flocks of directionless pastel butterflies were quivering about. In their wake lumbered the larger males of the species vibrating at a different frequency. Towering floral arrangements lent a cloying scent to the humid fug of too many bodies cramped together and Margaret twitched her shawl from her shoulders in anticipation of the heat.

"I see my particular friend, Mrs. Elizabeth Donatelli, over by the ratafia," said Mrs. Dertlinger. "I will trust you to lead Althea in, Mrs. Kneland. Althea, if you . . ." She sighed as Althea pulled at the bodice of her gown and scowled at a knot of young men laughing loudly.

"We shall keep Althea company and ensure she has appropriate dance partners," Violet promised. "You must enjoy the ball."

Mrs. Dertlinger sniffed. "I would *enjoy* a good book and my feet up before the fire." The annoyance in the glare she sent her daughter was tempered with a hint of bemusement. "However, my poor aching feet are doomed to be stuffed into dancing slippers until Althea makes an effort to speak to at least one man without looking as though she were sucking on a dead fish the entire time."

Margaret laughed despite Althea's huff of annoyance.

"Can you not spare me a modicum of sympathy?" Althea asked as they made their way past clumps of chittering debutantes and laconic young gentlemen who preened beneath the flickering candles.

"I do, Althea. You would much prefer to be in your workrooms," Violet said. "Even so, a ball is not a torture session. One can always find like-minded gentlemen who can carry a conversation without stepping on toes."

"I haven't met many of those," Althea complained.

Margaret had nothing to add. If her mother had had her way years ago, she would have been in the same position. Instead, she'd left England at seventeen and missed out on the traditions Althea had to suffer as a female member of the British upper class. The balls, the teas, and the musicales—events designed to show off young women and prove their eligibility for a society marriage.

Much of this reminded Margaret of the paces show horses were led through in the ring at Haymarket. If there were a way to pry open a woman's mouth and inspect her teeth in a genteel manner, there would no doubt be some societal event created to celebrate it.

When Violet paused to greet an acquaintance, Margaret continued toward the dance floor with Althea.

"I wish you would tell my mama a woman can make her own way in the world without having to rely on matrimony," Althea complained.

Men and women met in the center of the room, bowing and curtsying, judging each other from the corner of their eye and totting up subtle clues to decide if it were worth engaging in conversation.

"You forget," said Margaret, "I relied on matrimony to attain my position in my father-in-law's firm. I never would have been able to contemplate starting on my own without the protection of my husband's name. Marriage is a means by which ladies secure their future in one form or another."

Althea's shoulders bowed as she, too, watched the dancers. On the far side of the room, chairs were arranged so matrons could supervise their charges and judge their friends' children. Gossip was traded behind fans, sparkling heads bowed one to another passing rumors like water carriers passing buckets at a house fire.

Fortunes were made or lost at such events. A large part of the British economy was decided not in the houses on the Exchange, but by the women in those chairs.

Margaret squeezed Althea's arm in sympathy. "I wish it were otherwise and I could save you from this."

Before Margaret had returned to Paris last year, Althea had broken down in tears one night after a similar ball.

"Why does she insist on my attendance when she knows I will never marry one of them?" Althea had asked, thin fingers wrapped around a teacup full of port. "Over and over, I am forced to endure the company of an endless line of men who want nothing to do with my mind and care only for the width of my hips or the amount of my dowry."

Her distress had been so acute, Margaret grew afraid for her.

"Is your reluctance to marry because you desire women over men?" Margaret had asked her. "Althea, if this is the case, I will help you find a way to tell your mama, so she does not force you to marry."

Most proper ladies would have been shocked at Margaret's question, but there were more than a few scientists at Athena's Retreat who loved those of their own gender. One couple, Mildred Thornton and Wilhelmina Smythe, had lived together happily for over thirty years.

"I do not desire one over the other," Althea had said, blowing her nose. "This may seem unnatural, but I find them equally appealing. The problem is I do not want to be told what to do. Either I marry and my husband will have control of me, or I remain unmarried, and my parents will hector me until I grow old and bent."

Margaret had nothing but sympathy for Althea's plight.

Now, as they made their way to the refreshments, a young man hovered nearby, long fingers picking at the knot in his cravat. Althea refused to return his gaze, keeping her focus on Margaret.

"Marriage may mean security, but at what expense?" Althea asked. "Even Mrs. Kneland is now constrained in her work with the arrival of her child. No matter how kind the man you find, when you enter a marriage, you sacrifice some of yourself."

Margaret had no rebuttal for this.

Henri Gault had been daring enough to take her on as an apprentice, but he would never have given her the position she occupied at his firm had she not married his son, Marcel.

If Margaret remarried, it would be as Althea said. She would lose everything all over again.

"You are still young and there is hope society will change," Margaret told her friend not without sympathy. "For tonight, perhaps if you dance with a few fellows, your mother will let me chaperone in the future. Shall I arrange an introduction to that young man over there? He is interested and has all his teeth."

"*Et tu, Brute?*" Althea asked. She waved her hand in dismissal when Margaret cringed. "It's fine. Hallo, Gerald." Althea waved to the young man, and he lurched toward them, delight written on his face.

She turned to Margaret. "If Mama asks, I'm dancing with Gerald Hurlebut."

"I will be waiting for you by the terrace, I promise," Margaret said, stepping out of Gerald's path and clasping her hands in a plea for for-giveness.

The young gentleman led Althea out for a polka. He'd taken the current style for facial hair to heart. It looked as though a beaver had been sewn to either cheek.

"Good God, the boy better not emigrate to Canada, they'll shoot him for his pelt."

Grantham.

Margaret tried not to smile as he loomed over her.

"I find his attention to fashion appealing," she lied. "You might better use your time squiring an eligible lady out on the dance floor instead of mocking a gentleman who does his duty. Poor Violet has been trapped in conversation for ten minutes by that ridiculous Sir Limpenpot. Go rescue her."

Grantham rocked on his heels in mock surprise. "Is that my duty? Smashing the toes of half the ton after paying a king's ransom to be here in the first place? Listening to that fool Limpenpot natter on about dragons?"

When Margaret turned her attention from the dance floor to give him another scold, the words curled in her mouth.

He was staring at her shoulders.

Most of Margaret's gowns were almost two years old, although no one would be able to tell, considering how far London was behind the fashions of Parisienne dressmakers. Tonight, she wore a gown of rus-set silk she'd had made for a night at the Paris Opera and the draping bodice flattered her full figure.

Grantham blushed when he realized she had caught him out.

"Don't know why I took lessons for the quadrille when they play those maniacal polkas." He spoke rapidly to distract from his reaction. "Can't master the steps."

Margaret enjoyed the new dance imported from Bohemia although it had not taken hold in London the same way it did in Paris. Lively enough to occupy the dancers, the polka allowed for less posturing and more genuine enjoyment. Clusters of smiling couples bustled about beneath the candlelight like petals caught and tossed by a spring's breeze.

Grantham said nothing, merely tapping his toes until the dance ended and the orchestra played the slow opening to a waltz.

"Now . . ." He leaned over, and his lips grazed the rim of her ear when he spoke. Margaret squelched a shudder at the sensation this awoke in her. "The waltz is made for a man such as I who has trouble counting past three but likes nothing more than holding a beautiful woman in his arms."

She meant to object, but she was somehow already settling her hand in his as his arm came around to the small of her back. Her skin beneath his palm tingled and the inches between them hummed with awareness. Beneath the layers of silk and muslin, her breasts swelled. A blush of her own warmed her cheeks.

"You are a terrible dancer," she said without rancor as they entered a series of turns, nearly knocking another couple off their feet. She and Grantham were the tallest people in the ballroom and the other dancers wisely kept their distance. Her great height wasn't the cause of folks staring. They were entranced at the sight of this ridiculously beautiful man, his enjoyment clear to see, his sparkling blue eyes near blinding in their brilliance.

"Not fair. I'm a decent dancer when my ballocks aren't swollen to twice their size," he said matter-of-factly.

Margaret could not help herself. She tipped her head and let go a laugh. The sound caused Grantham's lazy charm to flee, and his jaw hardened, leaving him with a dangerous air. A tiny pulse between her legs throbbed at the sudden charge between them and she swallowed a gasp when his hand slipped dangerously low on her back.

Within seconds, Grantham steered them both toward the three sets of double doors at the back of the room leading out onto a flagstone terrace. There were a few couples out enjoying a respite from the overheated room and a small cluster of matrons stood in the doorways, watching with an eye toward gossip.

Margaret was too old and low placed to draw their interest, but Grantham was a known figure in society, and she did not want talk to circulate and possibly harm Violet. She kept her face turned away from them as he walked her to the edge of the terrace where four shallow stairs led to a dying garden. The lights of the ballroom illuminated heaps of browning chrysanthemums the gardeners had yet to cut.

Grantham had been a softer, hungrier-looking boy than the man he'd grown to be. When they were children, she'd find him some mornings sleeping in the treehouse, hiding from his father and pretending not to need the day-old scones she'd hidden in her handkerchief to bring him.

Now he was well-fed and rich, and no one could hurt him.

The shadows from the party behind them served to soften the lines bracketing his mouth, a visible reminder of how many times he must have frowned as well as smiled.

"Walk with me," he said. Not a question and yet he paused, waiting for her consent. She pulled her gossamer-thin wrap over her shoulders and took hold of his arm. The simmering attraction that warmed her in the ballroom cooled as memories of similar nights alone warred with the sting of betrayal that dogged Grantham's presence.

It occurred to Margaret they'd been apart for longer than they had been friends.

They were almost strangers.

"I know nothing of how you spent your years with the 24th Foot. You were in Canada, were you not?" Margaret asked as the dried leaves crunched beneath their feet.

"And I know nothing of your years married to . . . what was the fellow's name?"

Margaret paused. So, there was to be no idle chatter tonight.

"His name was Marcel," she said softly.

"Marcel," he repeated, a curl of chagrin in his voice at the warmth with which she said his name. He paused. "Do you miss him?"

"I do."

He frowned slightly, hearing the truth in her voice.

Margaret did miss Marcel. Not desperately, but as one misses a dear friend. He had been a good man and she'd owed him a great deal.

As they walked, Grantham's boots pressed the loose gravel beneath him into the ground with his great weight. Margaret marveled again at how he'd grown.

"I'm sorry," he said.

She said nothing in return, considering instead the night sky. The air was so cold, the few stars one could see glittered like a set of dowager's diamonds.

What to say to the man who once broke her heart about the man who helped to heal it?

"He was kind," she told Grantham. "I don't think he would have married had I not come to work for his father."

Grantham had no interest in the skies and had kept his gaze fixed on her. "Did you work on projects together?"

"Not quite. Marcel never had much interest in engineering. He was an accountant and loved nothing more than to perform audits on his father's books. Everything had to be perfectly aligned and make sense."

What Margaret didn't tell Grantham was how Marcel carried his love of order into their home. The furniture in their apartment was set at right angles, her gowns hung according to color. He laughed at himself easily and was so softhearted, she had to keep an eye on him lest he be taken advantage of by the beggars who lived under the bridge by the river. How he took his toast dark in the mornings and made her tea when she was sick. Although they never fell in love with one another, they did enjoy each other's company.

"He married me so I could take the Gault name. It was the only way for me to get a commission. They thought I was him."

Unwilling to speak any longer of marriage to Grantham, of all people, Margaret turned away from the sky.

"Did you like it?" she asked. "Being a soldier? You were so eager to leave, I remember—" She cut herself off. Hadn't she resolved not to speak of such things?

As a boy, Grantham's hands had always been grubby, covered with small cuts, grime forever trapped beneath his short nails. Now, they were hidden from her beneath a pair of dove grey gloves. A trace of golden hair darkened as it disappeared beneath his cuff and she wanted to touch him there.

"I liked parts of it some of the time," he said noncommittally. Grantham rubbed his neck as though her gaze had weight, his eyelids fluttering.

He was lying.

"Parts of it some of the time?" she repeated.

Grantham shook his head then stopped moving. Margaret waited at his side while he stared at the wilted plants and scattering of leaves on the slate that made up the border of the garden.

"I was never meant to be a soldier," he confessed. "Mam told me a hundred times. You and Vi did as well, and so did the Viscount Grange, but I was sure I'd make something of myself. My stepfather kept telling me I was wasting my life, but my seventeen-year-old self knew better than him—knew better than anyone."

He shook his head. "I should never have tried to be like you."

"Be like me?" Margaret fumbled for his meaning.

"Everyone told you no and you never listened," Grantham explained. "Your mother told you to marry a rich man and you never once considered it. Your father told you to study physics, but you chose engineering. The whole of polite society would tell you to get married instead of taking up a profession and yet you've never looked back. You've never needed anyone. I thought if you could go your own way, so could I. I was in awe of you, Maggie."

"In awe of me?" The words cracked in her throat. "Is that why you left me, Georgie? Was it too much for you to contemplate, marriage to a woman who filled you with awe?"

Grantham rubbed his face and glanced at the folks on the terrace, but Margaret's rage had snapped loose the tethers binding her to propriety. She did not care who heard her.

"Were you in awe of how desperate I was to believe you? How I trusted you when you said you loved me? *Awe* made you propose to me, only to go back on your word and leave me behind?"

The strains of a waltz drifting from the ballroom into the chill air sounded off-key.

Violet had invited Grantham to the ball, but he would have skipped it if not for Barney's warning the other day that he ought to find a wife. Once he'd spotted Margaret, his intentions of sussing out a prospective countess had flown out the door.

Tonight was the first time he'd ever danced with her. When they were younger, their only touches had been few and furtive; adolescent fumbling squeezed between long hours of stupid lustful longing.

It hurt him to the core to think of the men who'd had the pleasure of resting their arms at the small of Margaret's back. Of her secret

damp and hidden places pressed against strangers. Of the years spent
in bed with a husband she missed.

"I told you I didn't want a season. You said we would elope, and
you would take me with you to Canada." Margaret's words hung in a
cloud of ice between them. "I sacrificed everything to run away with
you that night and instead you turned me away and told me you didn't
want me."

A public ball was not the ideal place for this conversation, but it
could no longer wait. Grantham rubbed the space between his brows
and gathered his thoughts, terrified he would say the wrong words in
the wrong order. Pushing aside his envy of the places—and people—
that had stood between them over the years, he conjured the picture
of her the last time they saw one another in the tree house.

He had been waiting for her.

Maggie had hauled herself through the trapdoor onto the warped
floor of the willow tree house they'd built when they were children,
and she sprawled there for a moment, sweating and disheveled.

"I could only carry one trunk with me, so I wore the clothes I didn't
want to leave behind," she'd explained when she caught sight of him.
"Is there time to write one last note? I'm wondering if we should have
told Violet after all. If only she weren't the worst secret keeper in all of
England. Where did you hide the cart?"

He'd said nothing when she repeated her question. A nearly full
moon had cast petals of silver over the floor, and he could pick out
only a few of her features in their light.

After years of steadfast friendship, something had altered between
them that summer. It began with a casual brush of his arm against her
shoulder that sent his senses rioting. Light-headed and stupid at the
merest hint of a smile from her—every expression held a deeper meaning, every glance an invitation.

Heat and hope burned brighter and brighter until neither one had the fortitude to deny it. They'd plummeted headlong into a passion they never saw coming, yet once they had a name for it, neither was surprised.

What might have happened had her mother not appeared that summer? It had been Mrs. Strong's first visit with her daughter in four years and she'd informed Maggie her time at the Academy studying engineering was at an end.

"She says I am to prepare for a season. Even Lord and Lady Grantham cannot talk her out of it. She is my mother and has control over my finances." Maggie had come running across his stepfather's fields to find Grantham and deliver the news. He'd held her close in a copse of alders while she fought for breath, drowning in a sea of fear and anger.

Grantham couldn't stand the thought of her torn away from the work she loved and thrust among a group of strangers—a group of strange men—to be assessed and valued for her appearance instead of who she was and what she could do.

"We'll marry, Maggie," he'd whispered into her ear, picturing himself as standing between her and the world. "We'll go to Scotland. They can't stop us. You'll come with me to Canada while I soldier, and we'll make a life together."

They had been the most selfish words he'd ever uttered.

Now, what felt like hundreds of years later, they stood inches apart amid the frozen wastes of a formal garden.

"Do you remember the first bridge you ever designed?" he asked her.

Margaret narrowed her eyes in annoyance, as if his question were an evasion of her earlier accusation.

"Yes, of course," she said.

She had been fifteen and Violet's father had given her permission to use the marble blocks from an old Roman ruin on the far side of the property. Grantham had spent every free moment not working on his stepfather's farm carting those blocks to the stream bank and placing them exactly where she'd told him to. It had been a marvel to be part of such a construction.

"You told me the perfect bridge—the strongest and most aesthetically pleasing of them—is not just a way to span a distance. It is a physical expression of the balance between tension and compression."

Margaret rubbed her arms to warm herself. "You remember that?" she asked, a hint of disbelief in her voice.

He did, though. Grantham remembered everything she'd ever told him, even if he understood only the half of it.

"That night on my way to fetch you, I crossed over your bridge. You called it a negotiation with gravity. What goes up will always be struggling not to fall back down."

Was he saying this right?

Tiny clouds floated from her mouth, and Grantham moved closer to lend her his heat. She stepped around the curve of the path, and they were hidden from view of the ballroom. He couldn't stand to see her shiver and gave in to the urge to pull off his jacket. She said nothing when he settled it over her shoulders.

"I thought of those words as I stood atop that bridge," he said. When she remained silent, he pulled the jacket tighter around her.

"Damn it, Maggie. Marrying you would have been one long fall to earth. I wouldn't have rescued you. I would have crushed you with the weight of being without your studies, your friends, your teachers, or anyone who would give you a chance to practice your discipline. Do you know what life is like for women who follow the drum?"

Grantham could not regret his choice. A lowly soldier's wife, she would have lived in a tiny set of rooms, surrounded by men who fought and died for a living. Her soft white hands would have turned red and cracked from doing the cleaning and cooking. There would have been scant coin for books, let alone the graphite and parchment she'd used in her work.

She would have been isolated and frustrated, and it would have been his fault for not being something more.

Grantham had made the right decision, but he would regret forever that the decision hurt Maggie's heart.

"Look at what you did without the weight of me." The words were heavy and thick with the determination and regret he'd carried inside him since that night years ago. "You created a life all your own in Paris. You built a career. More than I ever did. More than most."

How to make her understand?

"A piece of your genius will now survive you, will survive generations of women like you. I couldn't take that away," he said, his voice cracking with emotion.

"If I'd married you, there would have been no bridges."

This was what he'd needed to tell her since first setting eyes on her again.

Margaret's teeth chattered from the cold. Moving closer, he set his hands on her shoulders. She remained motionless aside from her shivering, and he rubbed her arms brusquely. Soon, he'd usher her into the ballroom and liberate brandy from someone to put color in her cheeks.

"If I'd been a little older or less of a lummox, I might have found the words to explain," he said.

"You told me you'd made a mistake." Margaret's voice sounded thin and metallic in the frigid air, and it sliced through him like a knife. "You said I wouldn't suit the life of a soldier's wife and to ask Lord Grange to help find a way out from Mama's thumb."

Grantham didn't remember the actual words he'd used, but Margaret's rendition sounded right.

He'd been so damned in love with her, but his tongue had been clumsy with grief and fear.

"If I'd said you were meant for something better, I would have had to admit that meant better than me," he confessed. "To my everlasting regret, I had too much pride."

She had thought he was a hero. She had loved him—a gift he treasured then and treasured still.

"I am sorry, Margaret."

Margaret nodded once in acceptance, remaining silent for a terribly long time. A thick lock of her hair fell from an amber-studded comb and he drew her toward him into a tentative embrace.

"You're so cold," he whispered.

When she rested her head on his shoulder, he tensed, his knees coming together in a flash of fear.

"I'm not going to hurt you, Georgie. Not this time," she told him.

Inside, the orchestra struck up another song. Past time for them to return to the world they'd made without each other. Grantham took the opportunity to bury his nose in Margaret's hair and fill his senses with her rich, spicy scent. No insipid rose or lilies for this woman. She smelled like oyster shells, like freshly cut lemons and graphite. He'd no name for her scent but wished he could keep a bottle of it near him always.

"I'm sorry, Maggie," he said once more.

Taking a step back, Margaret tilted her head the tiniest bit, for now he was the taller of the two of them, and she placed her hand on his cheek. Her gloved fingers were like ice, but he didn't flinch as he sank deep into her solemn gaze.

"Be at ease, Georgie," she said. "When you left me, it hurt, but I never believed you didn't love me."

Everything he'd lost over the years tugged at his ankles and pushed at his knees. Like a blessing, like a curse, Margaret closed the distance between them.

Her lips were cold but so unbearably soft. Perhaps she'd meant the kiss as a token. If he were a better man, he would have taken it as such, wrapped it in a piece of linen, and kept it in his breast pocket to think upon on special occasions.

Because he was not truly an earl but the hungry son of a broken father, Grantham pulled her close and deepened the kiss. He stole from her the sighs of summers past, pushed open her mouth, and tasted her secrets. He kissed her and kissed her until his lips were numb and hers must be swollen, unable to stop, so hungry for her tongue and her teeth on his skin and the night was burning.

Even after she'd pulled her mouth from his and handed back his jacket, lifted her skirts so they didn't drag on the loose gravel, and made her way into the ballroom, Grantham remained. Protected from the cold night air by the fire in his veins and the burning sensation of certain heartbreak.

6

. . . WOULD HAVE BEEN home much later if Margaret had not been kissing Lord Grantham."

Margaret jerked, spilling port over her sleeve, mouth agape at Althea's indiscretion.

"I . . . that is to say . . . what?" she stammered.

Althea clicked her tongue and handed Margaret a handkerchief to mop up the port. "I said I would have been home much later if you and Mrs. Kneland hadn't intervened with Mother to give me a reprieve last night after Mr. Simon Ponsonby stepped on my toes."

Plopping into a heap of cushions that once had been a chair, Althea commenced to filling three remaining teacups with the last of the port.

"Not so full," Mala said without sounding very convincing. "It's only ten o'clock. I cannot return home in an altered state. James's mother already has reason enough to complain about me—we don't need to add buffy to the list of my flaws."

Violet shook her head and put a hand over her teacup, sighing. "If

I have a cup of port, I will fall asleep right here and not wake for a week." Her words slurred as she fought a yawn.

"Is the baby still waking all hours? And Mr. Kneland insists on getting up to rock her to sleep?" Althea asked.

When Margaret last lived at Athena's Retreat, she'd been in the habit of meeting Althea and their friends Mala Hill and Letty Fenley—before Letty became the Viscountess Greycliff—once a week for an afternoon repast. They'd indulged in jam tarts flavored with the spice of being naughty in the middle of the day while they washed them down with port and spoke on subjects ranging widely from details of correspondence with the former Court Astronomer, Caroline Herschel, to the most titillating of scandals setting London all aflutter.

They met in Letty's old workroom, clustered around a tiny fireplace, bottoms sinking into the sagging cushions of an ancient settee and broken-back chairs. Slate boards took up the length of one wall and the smell of chalk dust lingered despite it having been ages since anyone worked a problem on them. Letty had remained at Greycliff's estate during her confinement so the workroom was bare of her books and papers but her cabinets were well stocked with purloined bottles of port and biscuit tins.

"Mirren is getting so big and so pretty. Will you add a nursery to your workroom?" Mala asked Violet.

While her friends spoke enthusiastically about Mirren, Margaret stifled a yawn. When she and Violet had been much younger, they would lie together in bed like spoons in a cupboard and talk about their futures. Both had envisioned marriage to a handsome man who could overlook trifling flaws like Violet's propensity to set things on fire and Margaret's desire to take things apart to see how they worked. They would have lovely homes and dozens of children, who would grow up together and be playmates the same as their mothers.

Violet's life had been less than idyllic, but finally she had what she'd dreamed of—a beautiful baby and a husband who said nothing about the occasional explosions that rocked his floorboards.

Margaret had no similar desire to have a child, no matter how sweet Baby Mirren was or how content Violet appeared to be. Was it unnatural, not to want to trade her profession for time spent in the nursery?

As for a husband . . .

Last night's kisses with Grantham had left her muddled and a tiny bit sad. His mouth had been hot and hungry, and he'd stoked a desire that had been softly simmering since they'd locked eyes that first day back in Violet's sitting room—but those kisses had come after his confession and Margaret struggled to separate the two.

All this time, she'd thought Grantham had called off their elopement because he'd come to his senses and realized she wasn't womanly enough to marry, or he hadn't loved her enough. To hear his misgivings about his suitability as a husband had changed the narrative Margaret had listened to in her head for years.

What would become of them now?

"Ever since the fire last year, we've been under siege." Althea's panicked voice interrupted Margaret's thoughts. Her friends had switched topics and begun speaking of the Guardians of Domesticity. Margaret's stomach lurched as she set down her port.

"Three more club members have resigned and Mrs. Dibleton's husband has forced her to stop her experiments. The men he works with are Guardians and he fears for his position were they to find out about her membership." Pulling her spectacles from her nose, Althea set about polishing them with vigor. "Everyone is frightened and uncertain as to how we might stop them. I am grateful to Mr. Kneland for organizing security for our lecture series, but this must end. We need a strategy to either turn their attention away from us or bring them down altogether."

She turned to Mala. "Weren't you going to ask James to write something in our defense for the *Morning Times*?"

Mala frowned. A delicately boned woman with dark brown eyes, tawny skin, and thick black hair, she left off studying the trim of Violet's gloves and clasped her hands in her lap.

"Yes, I asked James and he wrote an excellent article comparing the Guardians to a gang of ruffians. They menace women who are simply trying to better themselves and their families. He talked about how they harassed one bookbinder in St. Pancras who apprenticed young women. It became so unbearable that not only did he let the women go, but he closed shop altogether and moved to Scotland."

Mala's husband, James Hill, was a gentleman from a distinguished family. They'd caused a minor scandal when they married since Anglo-Indian marriages had fallen out of favor since the early days of the East India Company. James's mother, a formidable force in the ton, spent a great deal of her capital ensuring polite society received the couple.

"The *Morning Times* absolutely refused to have anything to do with the piece," Mala continued. "He tried *The Quarterly* as well, but even John Lockhart wouldn't print it and his daughter, Charlotte, has attended lectures at the club. It didn't matter. James said no one wants to draw the Guardians' attention, even if they think Victor Armitage is a blustering fool."

Violet turned and put a hand on Margaret's arm. "What do you think we should do about Armitage?" she asked.

"Me?"

Margaret's three friends sat staring at her guilelessly as she fought a blush.

Time to tell them everything, she supposed. Margaret set her teacup on the low table in front of her. They would be disappointed—angry even—but they were her friends. They would understand why she had to take Armitage's coin.

Wouldn't they?

What about Violet? Armitage's Guardians had threatened all she held dear. If Violet didn't understand, Margaret would lose her dearest friend.

She swallowed and readied herself to defend her Plan, even if it meant she'd never see the inside of the club again.

It wouldn't be the first time Margaret had to construct a new life on her own.

She began her confession with the good news first.

"If they don't approve of lady bookbinders," Margaret told them, "they most certainly will not be pleased when they hear about what I have planned."

"This is about the meeting you had Thursday?" Mala asked. "You said you'd a chance of a commission?"

Violet clapped her hands with pleasure. "Is it good news?"

Partly.

"I met with Sir Royce Geflitt. He is a baronet of good repute who has created a railway consortium."

"Oh, Margaret," Althea interjected. "Is it your suspension bridge idea?"

"Not exactly." Margaret clasped her hands in her lap. "He has hired me to design a railway tunnel beneath the Thames."

The three women sat silent for a moment as they digested the news.

"A *tunnel*?" Mala asked. "But . . . they already have a Thames Tunnel."

Making a shushing noise at Mala, Althea raised the bottle of port in Margaret's direction. "One can never have too many tunnels. I'm certain yours will be magnificent, Margaret."

"You are a genius," Violet enthused. "I'm sure your tunnel will be the most innovative in all of Europe."

While her friends heaped praise on her, Margaret concentrated on appearing unmoved. The more accolades she received for her work, the larger her fear they would discover her secret. That she was an imposter, a woman who spent her life hanging on by a thin thread while the rest of the world assumed she was in complete command.

A sensation of standing far away made Margaret dizzy and she gripped the arm of her chair to stay in place.

"But we should have a party to celebrate," Violet said.

"Oh, no," Margaret objected. "I don't think—"

Mala huzzahed in approval and Althea held up a teacup as a toast.

"A party is an excellent—"

A loud crash interrupted them.

"Careful with those boxes, men. Can't have any broken pieces."

Grantham.

A fizzing sensation ran through Margaret's veins at the sound of his voice.

"This gift has made it from Denmark without a scratch. All we have to do is sneak it through the kitchens," he called.

Yesterday, Arthur had declared the staff at Beacon House were not to accept any parcels from the Earl Grantham. Violet had stopped him from banning Grantham from the house altogether, claiming if Arthur stopped complaining about the gifts, Grantham would stop sending them.

Obviously, Grantham had found a way around the ban by entering through Athena's Retreat rather than the house.

"Go right down this hallway," Grantham ordered the workmen, who tramped past the open doorway with arms full of large wooden crates. "Don't mind the smells, or the smoke. Or the screams."

Violet hurried to the doorway at the commotion, glancing at Margaret in apology. "What are you doing?"

He popped his head in the entrance and grinned. Gone was the reflective man from last night's ball. In his place stood the public facade of the earl, chest out and merriment fair blazing in his eyes. No hint of any ambivalence or depth of feelings; he was once again his normal charming self.

Why must he be so damned compelling?

Margaret's body came awake as he entered the room as though her skin were made of tiny magnets that felt a pull only from him.

"Bit of a miscommunication twixt myself and your footman, Vi. Less trouble to bring this through the back. Good day, ladies. Is that port I smell?"

"No," said Althea as she shoved the bottle of port behind a pillow and sat on it.

"Not a bit," Mala said as she gulped the contents of her teacup and turned it upside down on its saucer.

"We were having a lovely coze and you're interrupting us. Go make certain those men don't make a mess." Violet made to shut the door, but Grantham had lost interest in his delivery and pushed past her.

"I'm certain I smelled port," he said, ambling across the workroom.

"Don't be silly," said Violet, taking one last look at the workmen before rejoining the group. "Respectable ladies would never be drinking in the middle of the afternoon."

"Hmmm." Grantham let her lie go unchallenged. Instead, he turned on one heel and surveyed the room. "Where can I find a sixty-gallon tub, Vi? I'd like the men to finish the setup tonight."

"Sixty-gallon . . . oh my goodness. What have you bought? Oh, Arthur will be livid."

Amusement lightened Grantham's face. His enjoyment had always been contagious, and even through her distress, Violet could not remain unaffected. The lines between her eyes smoothed, and Althea and Mala leaned toward him like flowerheads following the path of the sun.

Grantham didn't even glance at Margaret.

She traced a gilt ribbon on her teacup, scratching with her thumbnail at a spot where the gilt had flaked off. The teacups and saucers, jars and plates in Letty's workroom were comprised of castoffs. Pieces once unblemished and desirable eventually grew worn from careless handling and indifferent washings. The more familiar something became, the less precious it appeared. Eventually, anything shiny and new would be relegated to belowstairs.

Grantham might kiss women all the time. Hadn't the scandal sheets hinted at such? What happened last night at the ball after his confession may have held no great importance to him. Had she simply been another warm body on a cold night?

"You've interrupted Margaret telling us her marvelous news," Violet said, coming back to her seat and tossing a shawl over her teacup. "She has a commission."

Grantham beamed as though he'd been given a medal. "Of course she has," he exclaimed. "Whatever bridge she designs will be famous. I shall make it front page news in my broadsheet starting tomorrow," Grantham announced.

His what?

"Your what?" Violet asked.

Mala turned to peer at Grantham over the top of the sagging couch.

"You own a newspaper, my lord?"

"Yes, Mrs. Hill." Wrenching his gaze from Margaret's, Grantham beamed at Mala. "I own *The Capital's Chronicle*, this city's finest weekly broadsheet. A paper of record that has been enthralling London since 1836."

Althea tilted her head and Mala frowned. "I've never heard of it," she said.

"Me neither," Althea agreed.

"Oh?" Grantham scratched his head with a disappointed air. "Well, soon you will hear of nothing but *The Capital's Chronicle*."

He twirled his top hat between his fingers and beamed at Margaret. "Once I've delivered instructions to the workmen for my much-anticipated six-foot replica of Egeskov Castle, I am scheduled to visit *The Chronicle*'s offices and meet with the editor. I shall have him write a story about Madame Gault's tunnel."

"Egeskov Castle?" Violet squeaked.

"I don't think that is a good idea," Margaret said, the repercussions dawning on her. "In fact, I think—"

"The castle built in the center of a lake?" Mala asked.

"Oh, Grantham you go too far. Stop, please." Violet ran out of the room after the workmen without bidding them farewell.

"What kind of a newspaper is *The Chronicle*?" Althea asked.

Grantham, who'd been watching Violet's flight with pleasure, turned from the doorway and regarded Althea. "What kind? The regular kind, I suppose. Reports about the Railway Regulations Act. Articles about that business with the government reading the Italian bloke's mail."

Mala shook her head. "She means what are its political leanings. Tory? Whig?"

Grantham lifted one shoulder and held out his hand as though asking for the answer from them.

"Its leanings are anything the Guardians of Domesticity find offensive."

"What does that mean?" The sour taste from Margaret's bad conscience coated her tongue and slurred her words more than the port could. "What does your newspaper have to do with Victor Armitage's group?"

"I grow tired of leaving his insults unanswered," Grantham said. "If I must see ridiculous caricatures of myself in his magazine—"

"They were . . . revealing," Althea noted, blushing.

Unable to resist, Grantham flexed his arms. "Indeed. I begin my campaign against Victor Armitage and his Guardians this very day."

A weight settled on Margaret's chest. Grantham never did anything by halves.

Grantham's gaze settled on her. "Perhaps we might meet later to discuss the story, Madame Gault?"

The innuendo in his voice rattled her. Crossing her arms, she lifted her chin and scoffed. "*The Capital's Chronicle* will have to find something else with which to fill its pages."

He blinked twice at her scorn, such a small movement, all but unnoticeable, yet Margaret felt as though she'd kicked a puppy.

"I will take my leave, then." Grantham bowed to her, his eyes lingering for a scant second as he tried to read her face, then he smiled as though nothing had occurred.

"Good day, ladies," he said to Mala and Althea, then winked. "I must find a tank before we can begin construction."

Margaret scowled at the broad, muscular back of him, refusing to let her gaze linger on the way his trousers fit tight to his legs, rejecting the momentary sympathy infecting her when his smile had dimmed.

When Grantham left, the morning light left with him, but her friends did not notice. Their spirits remained high, and Althea pulled the port out from beneath the cushion with a flourish.

Mala held out her teacup despite what her mother-in-law might say and turned to Margaret.

"Now. Tell us every detail about the project from beginning to end."

"BEING AS YE dine with the queen and all, ye might no' be ready for the sight of men who dirty their hands for a livin', me lord."

A gnome-like man clad in rough woolen trousers and wrapped in an ink-stained apron stood beside a printer's press. Abel Runnymead was the head printer for *The Capital's Chronicle*. His squat stature and sloped shoulders belied the deftness of his stubby fingers when it came to pulling out the myriad shelves on the wall behind him, which held drawer after drawer of tiny type.

"I wasn't born an earl," Grantham retorted. "I've mucked plenty of stalls in my life and not until I left soldiering behind did I hide these baby-soft hands beneath a pair of gloves."

Abel made a derisory sound and continued his lecture. "Newssheets were taxed each page until a few years ago. Taxes have gone down, but thrift prevails, and we still use broadsheets for *The Chronicle*. We lays out two pages of print onto one side of the sheet, turn 'em, and print on the other side. After they come off the press, we folds 'em."

Abel pointed out the four separate layouts for one piece of paper. Each issue of *The Chronicle* used two broadsheets, which was the equivalent of eight pages of news.

For all his republican leanings and horror at the fact that an earl nosed about his beloved printing press, Abel was generous with his knowledge. He explained the presses at *The Chronicle* were Columbian hand presses designed by an American. This met with Abel's approval, as did their system of government. He lectured Grantham on both the process of printing and the benefits of a representational democracy with equal vigor.

As two assistants moved around them with the ease of men used to working in confined spaces, Grantham listened carefully to everything Abel had to say. He couldn't help but think Margaret would enjoy the process of laying type and watching the backward script become legible.

"Biggest change came a few years ago when *The Illustrated London News* started up," Abel said as they examined a wooden etching about to be molded so the image could be transferred to a metal plate before printing. "They are almost half pictures, half story but the process is expensive and takes a bit of time. We only print pictures when it's guaranteed the story will be a big one."

There was no newspaper in the village where Grantham grew up, and they were as rare and precious as gold when he was soldiering in Canada even when delivering news over a year old. He'd never once thought about the process of making a broadsheet and asked as many questions as he could think of in the moment.

Finally, Abel had enough of him and declared he'd work to do.

"There's some at other newspapers what use the steam press." Abel said, finishing his lessons as they left behind the press room and made their way upstairs to the ground floor. "We would certainly make more money if *The Chronicle* used the same, but we would lose half the men what works below."

At the top of the stairs, Grantham thanked the other man for his time and promised to visit the press room often. Abel stared a moment at the hand Grantham offered him but shook it gamely and trundled back to his kingdom of ink and paper.

"Abel convince you to renounce your title and join the radicals, yet?"

The editor of *The Capital's Chronicle*, Moses Wolfe, scratched his beard as he leaned back in a rickety chair behind his desk. At least, Grantham assumed a desk sat behind the piles of old broadsheets stacked nearly to the man's nose.

"He gave it his best effort, but I'm afraid I'm a monarchist through and through," Grantham confessed. He took a seat without waiting for an invitation and lifted his chin, dropping his shoulders and widening his legs slightly—posturing designed to show Wolfe he was not too high in the instep to hear what needed saying.

"Did you enjoy your tour of our offices?"

From the lack of inflection in his voice, the editor sounded disinterested, but Grantham wasn't fooled. No one at *The Capital's Chronicle* could believe it when he walked through the doors earlier today.

They'd assumed he'd forgotten them, or even if he hadn't, that he would send a man of business to root through their books and then be on his way. An enormous earl who wanted to explore the place from the cellars to the attic was beyond their ken.

Wolfe's office was on the second floor and well away from the main floor, where the majority of the newspaper's folks worked, but Grantham had no doubt every person there would know the contents of their conversation before he made it home later that night.

"I suppose you are here to tell me what I have to change?" the editor asked.

Skin color a dark olive that could point to mixed race or Southern European heritage, Wolfe had taken to the latest fashion and sported impressive raven-black muttonchops and he stared at Grantham with amber-colored eyes that took in everything.

Grantham liked that Wolfe was respectful but not deferential. The assumption that the earldom lent legitimacy to his pronouncements made Grantham uncomfortable. A title didn't confer upon him any wisdom or innate gifts. It made no sense if someone went and slapped a coronet on a costermonger, half of Parliament would be toasting him that night. This reluctance to embrace the benefits of the title was another reason his peers viewed him with suspicion.

"*The Chronicle* is losing money," Grantham said without preamble. "Why should I keep this place running if it cannot bring me profit?"

One of Wolfe's bushy black eyebrows perked at the statement in a gesture of surprise.

Grantham might not have shown much interest in *The Chronicle* before now, but he kept track of his assets and the paper had been in the losing column for almost a year.

Wolfe straightened in his chair. "There's been more broadsheets opening as the newspaper taxes have decreased. It's taken us some time to adjust to the competition, but I can assure you that—"

Grantham pointed to last week's issue sitting on the center of the desktop. "The other broadsheets are talking about the visit of Louis Philippe or the opening of the Royal Exchange."

Wolfe nodded.

"*The Chronicle*, on the other hand, has a profoundly pedantic article about the Parliamentary Boundaries Act and how it relates to the Counties Act, a column about cravats, and the worst serial mystery I have ever read."

"That means there's something for everyone." Wolfe's reply did not sound convincing.

"But not enough of that something to keep everyone interested," Grantham countered.

"I do not care to pander to everyone," Wolfe retorted. The first hint of irritation crept into the man's voice. "Yes, we print what is popular to keep readers, but it is also important to inform the public. That is the point of a broadsheet." He leaned back in his chair and folded his arms. "Profoundly pedantic it may be, but the Boundaries Act has a direct bearing on whether a landholder is fairly represented in Parliament."

Grantham said nothing and the two of them took each other's measure. Rather than talking around a subject, Wolfe was more like Arthur—without the three thousand knives and black stare of death.

"What do you want to print if not columns on cravats?" Grantham asked.

"I want to print the news without having to take a side," Wolfe said without hesitating. "I want to print stories to inform the public about what the people in charge are up to and how it will impact them. I want to change lives."

In light of those lofty goals, Grantham's mission to make Victor Armitage look a fool seemed small and petty. Damn his damnable conscience.

"That is a noble aim indeed," he said. "I might consider extending the life of the paper for another year and even investing more money if . . ."

Leaning back even more, Wolfe's eyes narrowed. "Why do I have the feeling I won't like what's coming next?"

"You will have a year of grace to print the news as you see fit, once we complete one small mission."

"What mission is that?" Wolfe asked.

"To bring down Victor Armitage."

Grantham exited the building two hours later after an enervating talk with Wolfe about what *The Chronicle* might accomplish. As was his wont, he glanced over at the offices of *Gentlemen's Monthly*, hoping to catch a glimpse of Armitage himself. While Victor was an unattractive man and Grantham could probably squeeze him out of existence just by sitting on him, it would be amusing to challenge him.

Instead of Armitage's pasty face and ridiculous hair, Grantham found himself face-to-face with a conundrum of another stripe.

"Good day, my lord."

Cool as a stream in winter, Margaret exited the building next door, glancing suspiciously at the sky then over at him as if he'd conjured the light mist.

"Good day, Margaret."

Delighted by her unexpected presence, he fell into step at her side, staring at the building. She still hadn't explained her connection to the place.

"You have to stop following me," he informed her. "As flattered as I am, I cannot return your fevered affections."

Margaret huffed so hard, her bonnet slipped.

"Me follow *you*?" she asked. "I cannot turn around in this city of hundreds of thousands without seeing your face. *If* I had any affections for you, they would indeed be the product of a fever."

When she reached to pull back the brim of her bonnet, she scowled at him. It pushed her lips together into a pinkish-plumlike whorl that made him dizzy.

"I've had women lie in wait for me before," Grantham said. "Usually, it's at a house party or a ball. They spring out from dark corners to trap me. Much more considerate of you to do it in the daylight."

"Women throw themselves at you?" Margaret stopped walking, studying him with those all-knowing eyes of hers. Her scrutiny made him shrink an inch or two. Ghastly woman.

Gorgeous woman.

"Yes," he said. "It gets so I have to walk slowly in case one of them throws herself at my feet when I'm not looking, and I trip and break my nose."

Margaret leaned in, squinting as she stared. The delicious scent of mother-of-pearl mixed with sawdust wafted beneath his nose and had a strange effect on his knees.

"I call a corker," she said. Setting her bonnet aright on her head, she walked away as though she hadn't accused him of lying right here in a public street.

Happiness frothed within him. Grantham followed two steps behind her, a giddy lightness lifting his feet and setting his heart to thumping. That *chappy* woman. They could be at the Abbey again, teasing one another until they resorted to the ultimate test.

"If you call a corker, you must be prepared to perform the 'Test of Truth,'" he reminded her. She stopped at the corner and pulled out a coin for the street sweeper. A scrawny lad with a crook-back tipped his hat and with a listing gait swept the street crossing, removing the leavings of the horse traffic from the day.

Something twisted in Grantham's chest at the sight of the tiny body hunched over the broom handle.

A steady stream of families from the countryside moved here every day in hopes of bettering their circumstances, abandoning the land which could no longer sustain them. Everyone needed to work if they wanted to eat, and some children worked harder than adults.

The work itself didn't cause Grantham's blue devils. To be certain, he'd put in his share of hours working the fields of his stepfather's farm. However, Grantham had the luxury of a belly full of nourishing food and the wonder of the Lincolnshire countryside to explore as a boy. This urchin most likely had the dubious pleasure of one room for his entire family, filthy air to coat his throat, and a dirty, dangerous street in which to work.

Children were not meant to live like this; crammed cheek by jowl in structures imprisoning them from the call of the earth and the balm of nature, working night and day, only to return to an over-crowded hovel with barely enough food to survive.

Margaret said something to the boy too low for Grantham to hear, but her expression caught him up short. The wickedness in her glance had fled and they shared a look in the middle of the noise and dirt. Was she remembering how verdant and pure their summers had been on the banks of the stream, surrounded by the bluest of skies and the richest of earth? The leaves had held hidden messages when the wind sailed through them and they spent hours hunting toads and singing back to the wagtails and thrushes. Only during childhood could one learn the secrets of the countryside in a way that turned the world magical.

Here in London, there was no magic.

Grantham could change some of that with this Reform Bill. Boys like the street sweeper could be in school instead of out on the street. The thought buoyed him. Margaret, unable to read his thoughts, turned away and broke the connection. The stench of the city streets smacked Grantham in the face, and he hurried after her, longing to catch her scent.

"Are you turning your back on the 'Test of Truth'?" he called out to her after tossing the boy a coin of his own.

"I have no time for such nonsense," she said sharply when he'd reached her side. "I am due across town in an hour."

He'd lost her, but he tried to keep her with him out of stubbornness. "I've run fair short of shame. Let's stop right here and you can twist my arm as hard as you'd like to see if I did tell a corker."

Margaret didn't even bother to glance over her shoulder when she answered, "I cannot. I have to meet a supplier for my project."

"I have not seen you since you made your announcement," Grantham said, unwilling to admit defeat. "Come with me to Gunter's Tea Shop and tell me about your project. I have a free afternoon and no one so pretty as you with whom to spend it."

Margaret made a gesture of dismissal with her shoulder so Gallic, it almost made Grantham smile.

"You are not my confidant, my lord," she informed a streetlight, walking two feet ahead of him, boots clipping on the wooden walkway. "I am not a source of information for your broadsheet. I do not give you permission to write a story about me."

Why was she so short with him?

"Of course, I won't write about you without your permission," he assured her.

They came to another corner, and Grantham caught her by the elbow under the guise of helping her negotiate a hole in the wooden walkway.

"Have I done something since the ball to offend you?" he asked. "I thought . . ."

"I forgave you the other night, but it meant nothing except we have closed our circle," she said, pulling at her arm. "There is no offense. I must work for a living and do not have the luxury to sit about all day like an aristocrat. Good day."

The strange turns their lives had taken struck him as the afternoon sun wrapped its fingers around the clouds and glowered sullenly on the street, putting her face in a half light. She spoke nothing but the truth.

"I must apologize, madame," he said gently. "I have kept you from your responsibilities. How inconsiderate of me. You are correct. We are no longer children, and I should not play with you as though we were."

Margaret clenched the handle of her reticule tightly and shook her head once as though to clear her ears of the sound of rushing water or a linnet's call.

As she walked away, Grantham shielded his eyes from the last of the autumn sun's rays.

She hadn't been annoyed with him, not truly. She'd looked lonely and bereft.

And she had been lying about one thing.

The circle was not closed.

7

"THE FUTURO CONSORTIUM is pleased to announce the world will be blessed with yet another British wonder. The future is upon us, gentlemen. The future is now."

The words carried on a breeze to where Margaret stood beneath the shade of a horse chestnut tree, moving her jaw to prevent it from freezing in an unattractive clench.

On the banks of the Thames a mile or so outside of London proper stood a crowd of seemingly identical men. They were varied in their height and width but otherwise were all clad in checked trousers; tight, high-collared cutaway coats; and grey or black toppers. Their well-fed faces were all white except where flushed red with self-satisfaction, like fleshy British flags. Some of the men were passersby, drawn by the promise of spectacle, but most of them either worked for or were associated with members of the Futuro Consortium, the name Geflitt had given to his group.

Margaret hated the name but that wasn't why she seethed. The reason for her fury—and her fright—stood to the left of Geflitt upon a raised platform next to a half-finished warehouse at the official groundbreaking of the Futuro Consortium's railway tunnel.

Margaret was not on the platform.

She had been told the announcement that her firm was to design the tunnel would take place later that month.

Discreetly.

"I am so pleased to share our celebration with supporters such as Mr. Victor Armitage. Mr. Armitage, would you care to say a few words?"

As the crowd applauded, Victor Armitage stepped forward and instead of lifting hearts with a stunning oration, he presented his audience with a list of grievances.

"The hardworking men of this country are under attack. Women are leaving their babies behind and taking men's jobs at lower wages. In an ascendant England, a glorious England, men must be the sole wage earners once again."

Ugh.

For a man who held such power, he presented an uninspiring figure. Shorter than Geflitt, Armitage had the florid coloring of one who indulged in the finer foods and wine that were beyond the reach of the kinds of men who followed him. His greying hair was longer on one side, and he'd pasted it over his head to hide a balding pate.

As if to make up for the thinning hair atop his head, he'd grown his side whiskers to cover his cheeks almost to the middle of his chin. Beady brown eyes surveyed the crowd as he spoke, one hand over his breast, full lips pursed, and jowls shivering with intensity.

"This tunnel will once again remind the world of the ingenuity of England's men, who have . . ."

England's *men*, indeed. Margaret wished he'd choke on his ignorant words and fall face first off the platform.

That was yet another irritant. The platform itself listed to the left, which made her ears itch. Constructed so it could easily be taken down, it served its purpose whether or not it sloped too much to one side, but Margaret could not bear the indifference of it.

The perfection of a squared corner bestowed its own pleasure along with the constancy of a right angle and the thrill of watching theory become reality. Even if it were a simple box, why accept mediocrity when perfection was achievable in this field as in no other?

This was what her teachers never understood about her decision not to continue with physics. Engineers married the beauty of theory with the gratification of practical execution. They were able to produce perfection beneath their fingertips. In her field, no problem existed that could not be solved with the aid of a slide rule.

In fact, she'd a slide rule in her reticule. If she were a braver woman, she would take it out and shove it up Armitage's . . .

"This tunnel will be a masterwork of English ingenuity. No foreigners are involved in its design or construction." Armitage went on to list a litany of folks he despised (foreigners, women, and men who didn't hate foreigners and women) as the Thames made its lugubrious way past the site. There were no residences in this patch of land outside the city proper, and unlike Richmond on the same side of the bank but the other side of London, no pleasure boats launched from here, no pretty parks or tidy little greens beckoned to the upper classes.

As far as Margaret could tell, there were more than enough railroads already being built in and around London. How would the consortium's trains compete with those who'd already laid lines of track? Were they hoping the notoriety of a tunnel would draw folks to their line instead? Why did they pick this somewhat isolated site instead of closer to the city?

The crowd grew slightly restless. Although the Guardians might be intimidating to common folk, this group today consisted of the consortium members and their associates. All of them were moneyed and some were even gentry—not the usual crowd for a rally. Most were wise enough to know Armitage didn't believe what he was saying. The Guardians appealed to men who feared for their livelihood and felt as though no one else would listen to them. Margaret knew a moment's pity for their plight but even greater was her anger that Armitage would turn those men and their stupid alliterative placards against innocent women.

Almost as if her thoughts had conjured them, the shouted cadence of a chant filled the air.

Rather than the raucous slogans of the Guardians, however, this group of folks presented a stark and welcome contrast to the men in the crowd as they marched over a knoll. Men and women of different ages and sizes, some wearing colorful bonnets topped with stuffed replicas of various birds, were shouting indistinct slogans.

A fellow member of Athena's Retreat, Flavia Smythe-Harrows, had created the hats and sold them anonymously at Fenley's Fantastic Fripperies, the largest emporium in London. The bonnets, and occasional matching top hats, were decorated with the feathers of common species of birds Flavia had either collected in her wanderings or other scientists had found and brought to her.

Flavia's bonnets were sold together with cards that told the owner something about that particular species.

For example, Violet had a truly horrific bonnet with a stuffed parrot atop it, the corpse of someone's lifelong pet. From Flavia's card, Margaret had learned parrots are long-lived, and that bird was fifty-four years old before it perished.

They had become immensely popular with ladies who were protesting the killing of songbirds for decorative bonnets. Margaret could not see the appeal of wearing a dead bird on one's head no matter how it had expired, but she thought highly of Flavia, who channeled her share of the profits to a fund which provided child carers for some of the club members who needed the help.

Margaret could read the signs now—some were festooned with ribbons; most were decorated with feathers and bore different messages.

TERMINATE THE TUNNEL

REJECT THE RAILWAY

MORE NESTS LESS MESS

FUTURO CONSORTIUM YOUR GOOSE IS COOKED

Stepping out from behind the tree to get a better look, she had to stifle a magnificent curse. An enormous blond man tagged behind the group.

Grantham.

Who was following whom?

At his side were two shorter men armed with small notebooks. They must be reporters from his blasted broadsheet. Whatever did this mean?

Armitage had been equating the Consortium with the crusaders—not a comparison Margaret found in any way compelling—but left off his speaking to goggle at the bird people. Geflitt leaned over and whispered something in Armitage's ear that turned him redder than usual.

Grantham spied her easily since she stood a head taller than anyone else and his face turned grim. He lifted a hand with a half-hearted wave.

Could she blame him for the lackluster greeting? Yesterday, Margaret had been on her way to meeting another of the consortium's preferred merchants, which had left her blue deviled and had sharpened her tongue when he'd made an appearance.

He hadn't deserved it.

What was she to do? Share with him what weighed down her heart? They could not pick up where they left off. Too much had changed. Although she'd assured him she bore him no ill will, the hurt she'd nursed for thirteen years could not disappear overnight.

Too much was at stake for Margaret to turn her attention to anything other than her Plan.

As ever, she had resigned herself to being alone on her journey.

"Your tunnel is simply another scar on an already wounded landscape!" The colorful crowd had quieted so a protestor holding his hands cupped around his mouth could be heard. "Adding to the noise and rubbish you leave in your wake, this tunnel will disrupt the only known nesting site in all of Britain for the greylag goose."

What was this?

Before Armitage could ascertain if the greylag goose was male or female and thus decide if it was worthy of existence, Geflitt patted him on the shoulder and gestured for him to step aside. Taking his place at the center of the platform, Geflitt bowed to the crowd as though the mass of protesting bird folks were guests who'd been unavoidably detained.

"No one loves the wildlife of the British Isles more than I, my friends. Why, my estate is a refuge for a population of black grouse I have prohibited folks from hunting."

The bird people murmured among themselves, a few of them lowering their signs. Armitage huffed but remained silent for the nonce as Geflitt's words made an impact.

Geflitt continued, "Yes, the fowl of Britain have a friend in the Futuro Consortium."

The bird man would not be dissuaded. "Why would you choose this site above all others? The greylag goose—"

Geflitt held up a hand. "The greylag goose"—he spoke over the other man—"has its breeding grounds in Iceland. Now, your organization has sent communications explaining a small group of them—"

"Gaggle!" someone shouted helpfully from the crowd.

"—have become confused and now nest here." A frown marred Geflitt's blandly handsome face. "This is against the natural order. We will simply move them to where they belong."

"That isn't how birds do things," shouted one woman. "You can't explain to them they're in the wrong country."

Impatient with the shift in attention, Armitage had had enough. Shoving Geflitt to the side, he strode to the edge of the platform with clenched fists.

"If you think a handful of placards and some silly slogans will change the path of progress, you are bound to be disappointed," he hollered. "You won't get anywhere by shouting at us."

The irony of Armitage's words was lost when he took another step and toppled off the edge of the slanted platform. Geflitt leaped forward but was too late to stop Armitage from flattening two or three men closest to him.

"It would be morally wrong to hope he retains permanent injury from his fall," Grantham said by way of greeting.

Margaret had been so caught up in the drama, his approach startled her.

"Better to wish for the rapid recovery of the poor men he's used to soften his landing," she answered.

The bird folk continued to chant their slogans and hold their signs, but their fervor was much diminished now their antagonists were distracted.

"Grantham, can you please explain to me what is happening?" Margaret asked, a terrible buzzing running down her spine.

What had he done?

The two men who had accompanied him stood amid the bird crowd, nodding their heads and scribbling in their notebooks. Armitage had been helped to his feet and limped alongside Geflitt and a handful of their audience toward waiting carriages bunched in front of the warehouse.

"What are you doing here and what does any of this have to do with geese?" she asked.

Grantham pulled at his cravat. "I was at the offices of *The Chronicle,* speaking with the editor, and a group of those people in Flavia's hats knocked on the door. They were trying to drum up interest in their cause."

Margaret let loose a string of silent curses. Each day this project became more of a nightmare. First Armitage, now Grantham and a group of bird-hatted agitators.

"And their complaint is the tunnel work will disturb geese's nests?" she asked, turning away from the crowd and walking toward the riverbank. A breeze carried the scent of lemon verbena from Grantham's handkerchief when he unfolded it to reveal pieces of stale pastry.

"Exactly. There is a breakaway group of geese," he said.

"Gaggle."

"Gaggle of geese who've turned their backs on Iceland and decided to live here year-round. There's a pair of them right now."

Indeed, two menacing birds sat staring at them from amid the reeds by the bank a few feet away. Grantham's grim countenance lightened, and he crumbled a piece of the scone.

"Don't feed them. You'll draw their attention," she said.

"You're not afraid of them, are you?"

Grantham tossed a few crumbs into the river and the birds zipped across the water with surprising speed. The larger of the two gobbled the crumbs down its long neck before the other one could do more than dip its beak in the rippling waters.

"You used to love visiting the farm to play with the geese and ducks."

Margaret shook her head in the negative when Grantham tried to persuade her to take a piece. Undaunted by her cowardice, he threw it to the birds as they drew closer to the shore.

"When I was eight," she said. "When a fence stood between me and them. Now I'm a grown woman, I've no desire to get any closer than this unless the goose is dressed and on my supper table."

The larger of the two geese made its way out of the water. On dry land, its webbed feet made it ungainly and it lost its grace. Grantham faced her even as he continued to toss crumbs to the birds.

"A small community out of the thousands of greylag geese live here year-round," Grantham explained. "All the rest of them fly off to Iceland and whatnot. Those two reporters were out the door like a shot to write about the rally and I came with them. I wasn't sure you'd be here, but if you were, I thought to warn you."

The big goose—Margaret decided to name him Victor—now stretched its neck and twisted its head to scrutinize Grantham with what seemed like annoyance.

Make that two of them.

"Warn me?"

"There will be articles printed about this. The editor, Wolfe, thinks it will sell papers."

At least Grantham had the decency to appear embarrassed. And well he should. Margaret thought the whole situation ridiculous.

"You cannot mean the British public will take seriously the plea to stop the construction of a major railway simply because there are *geese* nesting nearby?" Margaret asked.

Grantham stared at her as though she'd spoken in another language. "Victor Armitage just spoke in favor of this tunnel. His magazine is planning a series of articles in support of it. I would have thought the sight of Armitage would have you picking up one of the bird people's signs and doing bodily damage to him with it. What is his connection to the tunnel? Why is he even here?"

Margaret glanced between Grantham and Victor the Goose, who paced in an agitated manner, mimicking the frantic nature of her thoughts.

She wasn't ready to reveal Armitage's roll as her financial benefactor, but what other explanation could she offer?

"There were many well-known men on that platform." She leveled her voice, hoping Grantham would not hear her nervousness. "Geflitt is cultivating their support by inviting them here today. Armitage probably invited himself to speak. He craves attention."

The smaller goose, Fanny—named for Armitage's wife—reared her head, ignoring the crumbs scattered at her feet, and unfurled her wings as if to fly away. Victor the Goose joined his nasty missus now and the two birds circled Grantham, their heads snaking on long, narrow necks, wings askew, and blackened eyes narrowed in rage.

"Yes, but . . ." Grantham kicked at the goose nearest to him, never looking away from Margaret's face. "This tunnel project. If it draws the likes of Victor Armitage . . ."

Frustration welled until it constricted Margaret's throat. She'd love to be rid of the likes of Armitage. Did Grantham suppose she had some power over these men? With whom they consorted?

"In the end, what does it matter if Armitage is involved?" she snapped. "A tunnel is to be built; a huge, grandiose monument to these men's hubris. The question is whether you are pleased I will be the one to build it or if you will stand in my way."

Grantham's head swiveled between the carriages where Armitage made his exit, the cluster of bird hats, then to Margaret. Three lines appeared between his brows.

"What about the geese?" he asked. As he spoke, he threw away the rest of the scone, hitting Victor Goose in the head.

A low hiss emerged from the goose's beak, which made the hairs on her neck stand up.

Margaret took a step away from Grantham and the geese, who had him pinned between them. "Why don't we continue this discussion closer to the road?" Margaret said. "Whatever you fed them has upset their digestion."

"Digestion be damned, Margaret. If you would throw your lot in with those men, you should at least have been on the platform with them. Why are you defending them if they won't let you stand at the front?"

He would have sounded much angrier if he hadn't spoken while jogging backward. Victor and Fanny had advanced upon him in tandem, their wings jutting forward as though they might pummel him with their elbows.

"If you would . . ." Grantham darted to the side. "What in the . . . ?" Belatedly realizing the position he was in, Grantham issued an order to the geese to desist in his most authoritative tone.

"Stop right where you are."

Dismissive of aristocratic privilege, Victor and his wife neatly trapped Grantham, one in front, the other behind. Fanny Goose wasted no time in getting to the center of the matter and launched her attack straight between Grantham's thighs.

"Mother of God!" he bellowed, jumping straight in the air, utter panic forcing his eyes wide and mouth open.

Margaret couldn't move, frozen by the tableau unfolding before her.

"What are you doing standing there?" he called to her, stumbling toward the park as the geese advanced on him in earnest. "Are you going to watch me be bitten to death by these monsters and do nothing? Get help. Call the watch. Call the—feck!"

She should have, but the urge to get in the last word overcame her common sense.

"Did you perhaps want to try rescuing one of their goslings?" she asked. "Lift some great boulder in one hand and hold a baby bird in the other?"

Thus, did all great heroines fall. Moments later Margaret's skirt billowed in the river breeze and caught Fanny Goose's attention.

"Not so funny now, is it?" Grantham huffed as Margaret hopped over tufts of hawkweed and a rotting log to avoid the goose's terrible nips.

"Shut up and run," she cried, heedless of the spectacle a six-foot-tall woman and her giant companion might make as they fled in fear from a group of geese.

Gaggle.

"WILL IT BE forever?" Grantham asked some five minutes later from their hiding place in a small copse of twisted oaks.

Margaret paused in her monitoring of the geese and turned her attention to him. "I believe they must find more food at some point. Not more than a few hours at the most."

They stood in a tiny clearing at the center of the copse. The chanting of the bird folk carried on a slight breeze, but they were hidden from the view of the crowd. A few clouds overhead intermittently cast them in shadow as they passed over the sun, and the scent of wet leaves and crushed speedwell tickled his nose.

Grantham considered letting the misunderstanding remain, but Margaret's news had thrown him off-kilter.

"I meant, will it be forever, the way you hold me at arm's length?

All this time you have been working in the offices next door to the broadsheet and never said a word to me. Victor Armitage is making speeches in support of this project, yet you've made no mention of this and shown no concern for yourself or your safety. You were there last year when the Guardians of Domesticity set fire to Athena's Retreat."

Margaret cocked her head as though he'd said something in another language.

"At the ball, you said you forgave me, but . . . there is a distance between us you will not let me cross."

The breeze pulled at the bronze ribbons on her burgundy velvet paletot, and she fingered her bonnet strings. In their retreat, her bonnet had slipped backward and now she took it off and inspected the embroidery on its brim.

"The distance is time," she said, her attention fixed on the scarlet berries stitched into her bonnet's trim. "It is a span too wide to cross. We are adults now. Whatever ease we had with one another was years ago."

What of their kiss the night of the ball? The constant hum of attraction between them? Years may have separated them, but their bodies had recognized each other.

"There are days when you are a stranger," Grantham said. "Days you are so grounded into this new body of yours, when you forget anyone is watching and allow yourself to be still. You are different, then, from the girl you once were."

She inhaled sharply as though tasting the air between them and Grantham hastened to explain.

"You are so magnificent now. Determined. Thoughtful." He paused. "Quiet. Sad? I cannot read your face anymore and I *wish* to know."

Truly, he wished to know Margaret, the woman grown independent of the Maggie he remembered.

"Part of the distance is the gap between then and now," she said.

"Part of it is unfamiliarity. The man you were on your way to becoming, I have no idea what happened to him. I am not the only one who has changed."

Grantham walked to a fallen log and sat, staring at his knees rather than her.

"I could have come and found you in Paris when I returned to claim the title," he said. "Violet knew where you were. I could have asked her," he said.

Dried leaves lay crossways over each other in myriad layers. Ants and beetles made their way across the debris, to go do something industrious, no doubt, unlike the giant lazy humans who spent their time wandering aimlessly in search of useless goals like contentment and happiness.

Margaret took a seat on the same log, a fair distance between them. A distance as palpable as the wood beneath his backside.

"Why didn't you?" she asked.

"Because the man I was on my way to becoming was not anyone you'd care to know, I don't think."

Grantham had put his father's family out of his mind when his mother remarried the kind and prosperous farmer, James Alwyn. Mam never let him forget, however, he was of the aristocracy. The constant reminders by his mother of his noble blood had partly spurred his rash decision to become a soldier. No chance of becoming like his father if he left England behind.

"Soldiering was not the adventure I'd thought it to be," he confessed. "I told myself it would be exciting, and the pay was better than anything I could find near home. I'd grown resentful of Alwyn's attempts to civilize me, and certain Mam would never miss me for she had just had Lizzie. I was selfish and young and so very, very stupid."

Margaret did not disagree. Instead, she plucked at the ribbon on the bonnet in her lap. The line of her nose was perfection, and he could stare at it for hours, the way it sat stern and straight until the end, where it sloped upward in a surprise.

"I hated it."

Fingers stilled, Margaret set her elbows on her knees and leaned in to listen.

"I hated being a soldier and the disappointment—in myself for being so stupid and in the officers around me—it seeped into my body like a poison."

Grantham had found solace in a bottle most nights, and in a fight the others.

"Did you think of me?" she whispered, her voice thin and bleak. "Did you wonder what had become of me?"

"Ah, Maggie." He leaned forward, picking up a stick and using the point of it to disturb the leaves by his feet and no doubt causing grief for the dutiful ants and beetles. Keeping his gaze on the leaves made it easier to speak.

"I thought of you always and wished for you by my side every other minute of the day." The truth fell from his mouth like pieces of gravel, hard and uncomfortable—most likely unwelcomed, but she had asked and now it would out, like a contagion from his pores.

"The rest of the time I would thank God you were in England. I knew Violet's father would protect you from your mother's wish to see you married. I would imagine you sitting at a drafting table, talking to yourself that way you do when you are working. In my mind's eye, I stood behind you, watching you fill those huge pieces of parchment with your numbers and symbols I don't understand."

Margaret turned away from him and they both stared straight ahead.

"I didn't come to find you because I had little to offer, even after I took the title. My estate was in shambles. Farmer Alwyn died the year after I came back, and Mam was quieter, more fragile than she'd ever been. Lizzie was a stranger to me, and I had to learn to be responsible for dozens—" He broke off, visualizing the tenant houses, the laborers and servants at the estate, and their children. "No, hundreds of other souls who rely on the earldom. At first, I resented the title because anything that came from my father I thought of as poisoned. I think the soldiering was the breaking of me and the title has been the remaking of me. I have taken up my work in Parliament as a way of, well, cleansing the title, I suppose, of all it used to represent to me. To Mam as well."

They sat together in silence for a while, the low rush of the river a steady melody while the occasional birdsong made a sweet counterpart. Wind blew through the remaining leaves on the trees overhead and the carpet of leaves crackled and rustled. A powerful urge to leave the city and return to the estate gripped him. Harvest was over and there were decisions to be made. Which repairs would be undertaken this year, and which put off? What would they do with his sister already two years past the age to debut? Was his mother well enough to withstand a London season?

When Margaret rose, he stood as well. She brushed off her paletot and he settled his hat on his head.

She'd not said a word the entire time Grantham had unburdened himself to her. While her body might have stilled, her mind never would, and he bowed his head an inch, waiting for her judgment.

"You are not the boy who left me behind thirteen years ago," she said.

All but the smallest traces of the wild spirit that had been Maggie were muted now. The woman who stood before him was a study in elegance and had a presence extending two feet out from her in every direction.

"Neither are you the fierce lass who knocked me to the ground the first day we met," he countered.

"No, no, I am not her," Margaret agreed. Grantham longed for that girl. He'd caught a glimpse of her in the corridor of Beacon House the other night when she'd left him gasping for air on the cold floor.

"There is no blame in having grown up," she said, straightening her spine, as though speaking to an invisible audience as well as him. "I . . . I am glad I am no longer her. Being angry and confused all the time was difficult."

Grantham's heart clenched at the memory of Margaret's tears at the litany of complaints her mother would level at her on the rare occasions she would visit.

"It wouldn't be fair to wish you were her," he acknowledged. "You had your own lessons to learn. You were married. You realized a life-long dream. The person you are right now, Margaret . . ." He trailed off.

The sun went behind a bank of clouds, but she kept the light around her, the essence of who she was shining through her pale skin and auburn hair, which appeared warm to the touch.

"The woman you've become since we've been apart," he continued. "Can she be friends with the man I am become? Even if Georgie and Maggie would never consider it—can Margaret and George—"

He sounded foolish, but he kept on, needing to make himself understood even if in the most rudimentary way.

"It seems to me the world will never be right again if some iteration of us cannot be friends."

He didn't mean to whisper, but his throat had closed on the words as the force of his hope climbed in his chest.

Margaret studied him as she might a set of equations then set her bonnet on the log and held a hand to her breast as though making a pledge.

"I never stopped being your friend, George. I may have hated you at times, but I never stopped being your friend."

"Some nights—" He swallowed and tried again. "In Canada, the nights were long."

Hours took years to pass when home was thousands of miles away and the litany of a man's regrets could not be drowned by the voices of men singing songs around the campfires.

"Those nights, I would imagine what you might say to me if you caught me weeping into my bedroll."

The apple red slice of a smile appeared as her bottom lip turned up. It distracted from the pity in her eyes. He didn't want her pity. He wanted her to understand.

"*Button up yer gob, Georgie*, you might say," he continued.

A tendril of laughter curled from between Margaret's teeth. "I would never have said 'gob.'"

Holding his arms out slightly from his side, Grantham stepped toward her, not wanting to broach their new detente but needing to be close to her just the same.

Margaret's chin lowered in agreement and his heart thudded like a blacksmith's hammer against an anvil as he ever so gently gathered her in his arms. Her hair smelled like the straw of her bonnet and slightly of her sweat—a combination of salt and lemon that went straight to his chest. And to his groin, but he ignored that for the most part.

"You would have told me to stop sniveling and get on with the job I'd been sent to do," he said, delighting in the softness of her locks against his lips. "I made it through the worst nights by imagining you scolding me."

He thrilled to how Margaret fit against him. Most women were so small, but she could lower her head comfortably on his shoulder as if he were made to be her resting place.

"My first project was in Slavonia," she said, her breath tickling his ear. "There was an old Roman aqueduct, and instead of tearing it down, they wanted to incorporate it into the new bridge. Two firms told them it was structurally impossible."

She pulled away from him and fetched her bonnet, placing it deftly on her head and tucking her curls beneath the scuttle-shaped brim.

"I had to be lowered by rope to survey the base before I could complete my assessment."

His eyes went wide then narrowed and a real laugh escaped her. "Yes, the whole way down I kept remembering the time I made us a rope swing and you insisted on being the first to try it."

"My backside was sore for a week," he accused her. "You swore I'd be safe."

"The entire time I dangled over that river I pictured your face when you fell." She trailed off, the smile fading. "When you were crying into your bedroll, I cried into my pillow every time I lost a project because I was a woman. I would hear your voice in my head telling me not to stop. That those men who rejected me were daft *jobber-noules*."

Grantham tilted his head. "A fine Lincolnshire insult, to be sure."

Margaret grinned and the world righted itself with a click that reverberated in his bones.

"Perhaps time isn't so great a distance as we thought," he said.

"Or perhaps our definition of friendship has grown, just like we have," she replied.

Before Grantham could parse her words, she moved away, offering to check on the geese. Sure enough, the savage beasts had moved on, and he and Margaret made their way out of the clearing. Most of the bird people had gone home, but Evans and Dodson stood near Grantham's carriage, scribbling away in their small hand-sewn books filled with scraped-off and reused parchment cut into small squares.

Still not speaking, Margaret took hold of the elbow he offered as they stepped around tiny piles of goose droppings and feathers. Too unsettled to even peek at her ankles as Margaret pulled up her skirts, Grantham struggled to put a name to the warmth filling his chest as the clouds thickened and the wind turned from brisk to downright cutting.

8

"W HAT A LOVELY night rail, Margaret." Grantham's voice was low and scratchy. Only a single candle flame lit his face in the predawn darkness. "How quickly can you take it off?"

At four o'clock in the morning, Margaret had been awoken by an insistent knocking. Even before she'd tightened the sash over said night rail, she'd known whose face she would see in the hallway outside.

"Tell me this is a nightmare, and you are not at my door in the dead of night," she said.

"Remember yesterday, when the geese tried to eat us?" Grantham asked.

Staring at him without having wiped the sleep from her eyes, all Margaret could think was a goose *had* bitten him, and he suffered some rare bird fever.

"It's four o'clock in the morning," she pointed out.

"When we were hiding from the geese," Grantham continued as though it were normal to wake a woman at this hour, "you said we were friends."

Margaret did wipe her eyes then and smoothed the hair that had come loose from her braid while she slept. They stood toe to toe, the hallway outside her rooms at Athena's Retreat dim and cold. She was the sole guest on this wing and the only light came from the candle Grantham held over their heads, the shadows pouring across his stubbled chin. Was this some strange Grantham-like way of getting into her bed?

More important, would she deny him?

"I cannot fathom why you are here," she said finally. "Four o'clock is too early for coherent conversation. Come at eight. Bring tea."

But Grantham reached over and tugged at her braid, his face lightening with mischief.

"You agreed we could be friends, and friends help each other, isn't that right?" he asked.

Oh, no.

No, no, no.

She remembered this expression; thick blond eyebrows raised to a devilish point, a glimpse of his chipped incisor peeking through his smiling lips, the absolute commitment to trouble lighting his eyes. That *look* had preceded far too many an escapade in their youth, leading to her and Violet being subjected to hours-long lectures on how proper gentlewomen were to behave.

"Friends we may be, but I have work to do, even if your newspaper is about to make my job ten times—" Margaret broke off when Grantham set his palm on her shoulder. The heat from his skin burned through the thin cloth; where his thumb rested her collarbone tingled.

"I have a problem and I need your help."

When Margaret shook her head no, her chin brushed his knuckles and a blush raced unbidden across her cheeks.

"I am not—" she began.

"Maggie." Grantham leaned forward and brought the candle down so she could see the thick fringe of his eyelashes and the tiny white-gold hairs on his chin. "When was the last time you had *fun*?"

Seduction she might have resisted, but it truly had been ages since she'd had fun.

At least, that is what Margaret told herself when, after having hastily dressed, she followed Grantham to a cramped workroom on the Retreat's third floor which faced the back of Beacon House. He must have been here earlier setting the worktable with sticks of graphite, rolls of parchments, India rubber, and a handful of rulers.

"But why do we have to do this so early?" she complained.

"We must needs be as stealthy as possible. That man has preternatural powers to sniff out any plot before it's even hatched."

"That man" being Arthur Kneland. He and Grantham had a strange rivalry where they camouflaged their affection by insulting one another.

Men. They certainly were a mystery.

"He only sleeps between three and six," Grantham continued. "Even then he sniffs while he sleeps."

Margaret let her disbelief show in her stare, but Grantham was unmoved.

"He isn't natural, Maggie. I suspect it's something to do with his lack of height." Grantham scratched his chin in thought, then shook his head.

"That's a mystery we leave for another day. I need you to build a bridge between this workroom window and the window to the sitting room on the third floor of Beacon House. The room is next to Baby Georgie's nursery."

"A bridge?" she echoed, staring at the parchment and a platter of pastries to one side of the table.

Clearly, Grantham had anticipated her acceptance and prepared accordingly. She should have been annoyed at his confidence that she would say yes to his offer. Instead, a treacherous wave of comfort warmed her from her toes to her ears that he'd known what she would need.

"Not just any bridge," he assured her, far too cheerfully considering the obscenely early hour. "A *retractable* bridge."

While he plied her with tea and pastries, Margaret sat and sketched a series of schematics for a retractable bridge. Grantham perched himself nearby, after having offered her a crumpled piece of paper on which he'd written the distance between the window of this workroom and the third-floor sitting room, the heights of each of the windows, and the width of each windowsill.

Despite her assumption the prank would fail, Margaret's brain woke at the prospect of a challenge.

A bridge was always a study in contrasts. An engineer's task was to balance strength with lightness. The bridge had to carry a great weight but not be so heavy it collapsed on itself. This bridge would be temporary, however, and if something wasn't made to last, one could take certain risks.

That last thought stuck in Margaret's head as she considered then discarded various materials one might use to build a retractable bridge.

"First, is it you who will be using the bridge? That will impact the design as well as the materials I would use," Margaret explained. "It must be strong enough to hold you, but not so solid we cannot set it up and break it down without attracting a great deal of notice."

"Ye gads, woman, I didn't think of any of that," Grantham said round a mouthful of pastry. "How your brain works is a miracle. I'm amazed I can't hear the cams and linkages clicking around in there."

"Cams and linkages." Margaret peered at him. "You remembered."

His expression told her he remembered everything about their encounter in the nursery that day, including setting his hand to her back. More than the kisses they'd shared at the public ball, his casual touch lingered in her memory. Fevered kisses Margaret could explain away as only natural for a woman who'd been widowed for so long to enjoy.

What gave her pause was the way in which he'd embraced her yesterday at the rally, the way he'd set his palm upon her shoulder earlier. Tender, but not hesitant.

Familiar.

Intimate.

Her musings were interrupted when Grantham choked on his pastry, abruptly moving away from the table to pour a cup of tea from the flask he'd brought with him.

"If anyone could come up with a solution, it would be you," he said. "Kneland has some notion a baby should only have so many gifts. That's the Scot in him. I want Baby Georgie to grow up surrounded by everything she's ever wanted and more."

He set down his cup then picked up her slide ruler and played with it. Next, he repositioned her sticks of graphite and stacked the rolls of parchment.

"I'll sneak over there and drop off the gifts." He wandered over to the window, fiddling with the latch. "Then I'll come here and collect the bridge. Baby Georgie will have mountains of presents to play with and she'll never want for anything."

Margaret bent her head to a series of equations while her thoughts about what Grantham had said ordered themselves in her brain. After a moment, she put down her pencil and spoke.

"I think with Violet and Arthur as her parents and the whole world of Athena's Retreat steps from her nursery, Mirren Georgiana has everything she needs." Margaret softened her voice as she picked her words with care. "She will be surrounded by people who love her and will keep her safe. I suppose Arthur believes that is enough for a happy childhood."

She then erased a crooked line and held her breath.

The floorboards shifted beneath Grantham's weight as he left the window. From the corner of her eye, Margaret admired how his muscled thighs strained against the fine wool of his trousers when he sat on the stool next to hers. He refilled her tea, and she took it with a nod of thanks. The air between them thickened but Margaret did not peek at Grantham again, giving him privacy of a sort.

They had never talked about what his father did to him and his mother.

As children, they'd acted as though his bruises didn't exist. The summer they turned twelve, Violet's father had given Margaret permission to design a tree house in the willow where she and Grantham first met. Once she'd finished, Margaret would sometimes find him sleeping there, having found a place where he'd been safe from his father's fists. He never stayed more than one night at a time, however, unwilling to leave his mother alone with his father too long.

Margaret knew he had hated his father and his father claimed Grantham was a bastard, no matter how his mother insisted he was not. What she didn't understand was how a man could commit violence against his son and wife. As a gently bred young woman, Margaret had no vocabulary at the time for her worries over the boy and his mother. No guidance from her own mother as to what she might say or do to make things better for him.

Instead, Margaret had built him a haven.

"Is it so bad to want to give something to Baby Georgie I never had?" Grantham asked quietly.

His hesitant but genuine query woke a longing within her. Desire, Margaret could deflect.

Tenderness? Infinitely more compelling.

She grabbed hold of her slide ruler, pressing the sharp edge across the palm of her hand. She could not let Grantham reside in her head or her heart. They were friends again. That was all she could allow.

Shifting on her stool so she faced him at an angle, Margaret kept her voice steady and even.

"No, I don't think that's bad at all. But more important than any doll or frock you can give her would be to spend time with her yourself. Show her where the dormice live in the old stone fence between the Grange estate and Alwyn's fields. Teach her how to skip rocks in the stream and listen for the linnets."

Grantham's brows lifted in surprise. "Do you think she'd like that?"

"I think any girl who had your attention would count herself lucky."

Someone needed to cut his hair. His pomade could not keep a buttery forelock from falling over one eye, an invitation to touch, to push it aside and trail a finger down his cheek, coming to rest at the corner of his mouth.

That someone would not, could not be her.

Margaret twisted away from temptation and stared at the diagram before her.

The work came first. She mustn't ever forget when everyone abandoned her, the work was always there.

AS THE SUN battled to punch through the haze of coal smut hanging in the damp London air, Grantham sat in shadows, jealous of the lone shaft of light that fell through the window and landed on Margaret's left cheek. Her skin, which appeared almost blue in the dim room, now turned a delicate cream color where the sun kissed her.

"Balance."

Margaret spoke aloud as she worked, explaining to Grantham the factors she considered when designing a bridge.

"I've told you before, we must always consider the two opposing forces. There is compression, which pushes inward, and there is tension, which is pulling outward."

Grantham nodded, wryly acknowledging those same forces acting within him. The longing to touch any part of this woman was tension indeed, and he compressed the desire by sitting on his hands.

Friends. The name he'd agreed to when defining the newly reached accord between them.

It shouldn't be difficult. He'd spent the last six years in society acting as friend to every woman he met. Listening to what they said, rather than what he wanted to hear, encouraging their opinions rather than forcing them to parrot his own views—oh, he might be known as the Untamed Earl, but his interactions with ladies had been respectful.

One did not fondle one's *friends*.

Holding tight to this thought, Grantham leaned ever so slightly toward Margaret, drawn by the scent of oranges and competence.

Her hands were capable, her fingernails short and clean, knuckles slightly chafed. A small scar ran down the smallest finger of her left hand and a bruise-colored patch of graphite spread over the bottom of her palm as she rubbed out a series of calculations having to do with how she might channel the load—that would be him, plus the gifts, plus the weight of the bridge—without abutments or piers.

"A bridge is like a person in many ways—at least this is how I think of it," she said, her concentration centered on her work, no glances to spare his way. "A person can only carry a load for so long before they need to either share the weight or collapse beneath it."

Grantham considered her words. Did she want him to help bear her loads? Did she feel the same tension as he?

"The function of an abutment," she said, raising her eyes from the parchment, "is to help disperse the weight. Without it, we are forced to widen the bridge. Too wide, however, and we cannot string it between here and Beacon House."

His gaze followed her finger as it traced a mesh of dotted lines between her expertly sketched buildings.

"I have dragged you out of bed and forced you to eat cold pastries for a fruitless exercise," he said. "From what you say, I cannot see how we will make a bridge work."

Restless, the sunbeam gracing Margaret's cheek now slipped to rest in the curve where her neck met her shoulder.

"You promised me fun," she said. "This is fun."

"Hmph." He made a noise of disbelief. "When I said 'fun,' I had a vision of myself swinging between the buildings with a package beneath my arm or Arthur giving chase and falling out of a window, not you doing maths and drawing pictures."

A tiny curl made an auburn C at Margaret's temple, a secret message against her skin Grantham longed to taste and decipher. When she'd been a girl, her hair had been red and gold, the color of flames. The color of her temper. Everything about her had matured and mellowed: her hair, her temper, her expectations.

"This part where we begin, there is a tiny thrill," she explained. Pushing her stool from the table, she walked to the window and bent at the knees, nose to the windowsill, gauging the distance by eye.

"You can make plans, but nature has a way of throwing you off. That is the bigger thrill. When the columns go up and the span takes shape—will it be winds we never considered? Will the ground shift or will the road be widened and allow more traffic than expected?"

She stood and gazed at the parchment on the table, its surface half-covered in numbers and lines Grantham would never be able to make sense of.

"Aha, I've guessed your secret," he said.

"I doubt you have any idea of my secrets, Lord Grantham."

One eyebrow raised, she crossed her arms, leaning against the window frame. Excitement tickled the base of his spine and Grantham adjusted his seat. By God, was Margaret *flirting* with him?

Well, friends could certainly flirt, even if they couldn't fondle.

"Your secret," he said, waggling one eyebrow, "is you have not changed much on the inside. To the world, you present yourself as a serious businesswoman and engineer, but inside . . ."

A tiny flush rose on the tops of her cheeks and she bit her lip as he spoke. Grantham shifted again and cursed his overactive anatomy reacting to every sign of interest on her part. He wished to savor this easy air between the two of them.

". . . inside, you have the same spirit of adventure as the Maggie who figured out a way to swing between the trees with a rope tied to a brick—"

"But I measured wrong, and we crashed after the third tree," she said.

Didn't matter.

"—built a dam to keep the biggest fish from going upstream—"

"We flooded two fields that spring."

Grantham didn't care.

"—and designed a trebuchet in case of attack from marauders," he finished.

"We put a hole in the roof of Grange Abbey," she pointed out.

Violet's mother had been livid.

"This bridge will be the perfect project for that girl inside you," Grantham promised. "And the best part is, we're grown and there's no one to stop us."

"Is that so?"

The two of them turned in tandem toward the open door, which Grantham could have sworn he'd locked.

Arthur Kneland stood there, one hand at the breast pocket of his jacket, the other flexed. His black eyes promised a slow, painful death but his mouth quirked in a smug grin.

Damn.

"What gave us away?" Grantham asked.

Kneland set a finger to his nose and let the grin widen to an evil smile, casting a glance at the table. "I trust you'll have cleared this away by end of day, Grantham. Right around the time the maids will be . . . decluttering . . . Mirren's nursery."

He nodded to Margaret. "Good day, Madame Gault."

Margaret shook her head when Kneland left as silently as he'd arrived. "You were right after all," she said.

Kneland might have bested him this time, but Grantham would not give up. It might not be a retractable bridge, but he'd figure out a way to get Maggie to enjoy herself with him.

Grantham would let nothing come between them ever again.

9

A WOMAN SCIENTIST, ONE of our own, is poised to create history. Standing in her way is tantamount to blocking us all."

Murmurs of approval rose and fell through the room, a genteel wave of support buoying Margaret where she sat, hands clenched together in her lap, trying to appear unaffected.

Mildred Thornton, better known as Milly, a chemist, and one of the oldest members of Athena's Retreat, stood before an assembled group of Retreat members, her snow-white curls riotous as ever despite her valiant attempt to contain them beneath a garish orange linen day cap festooned with ribbons. Milly did not follow the fashion for puffed sleeves as they were ill-suited to laboratory work; however, a plethora of ruffles covered her blue and gold striped day dress, including an odd, bib-like tier of ruffles down her ample chest. Her round cheeks were flushed with emotion as she continued her impassioned plea.

"We formed this club to support one another, to ensure our work will not just continue, but will flourish. Madame Gault's decision to open an engineering firm in her own name is a momentous step forward. It will be a woman's name attached to a second Thames Tunnel. Can you not see how important this is?"

That last plea Milly had directed not at the crowd of scientists so much as at the woman standing opposite her, Wilhelmina Smythe, better known as Willy. They faced one another in the center of the common room on the second floor of the secret part of Athena's Retreat.

In the public areas, the walls were papered with a lovely crimson flocking made of powdered wool on fabric, the design hand-painted with varnish. Such decorative touches were far too flammable for what went on here. Instead, the walls of the common room on this side of the locked doors were a cheery yellow with a series of framed etchings of Mary Anning's fossil finds and small paintings depicting a variety of still lifes including a study of the insides of a sheep brain and an eerie arrangement of dead birds and tarantulas. Margaret averted her gaze from that particular picture as she listened to Willy speak.

"We do not stand in the way of Madame Gault by pointing out the consequences of her latest project," Willy said, her jaw set, one hand on a hip. "All scientists must reckon with the impact of their discoveries."

The physical opposite of Milly, tall and thin with steel grey hair decorously hidden beneath a lavender cap, Willy wore a simple but costly day dress made of grey silk as she was in half mourning for her father.

Willy once said her father didn't believe a girl needed an education for anything other than the basic skills one needed to run a household. He hadn't even been convinced she needed to learn to read.

"You know better than anyone, Mildred, we must reap the consequences of our scientific actions." Willy's tone shifted from irritated to somewhat wistful. "Why else has Ascanio Sobrero discontinued our correspondence on the development of pyroglicerine? Any further study or experimentation is too dangerous." Although her mouth softened, Willy shook her head. "The tunnel Madame Gault is to design will have terrible results for the greylag goose. And what of the project's association with men like Victor Armitage? We cannot let so-called progress go unchecked simply because it is progress."

The club members approved of this argument as well. They were scattered throughout the room, perched together on lumpy yet comfortable low-backed sofas and clusters of padded chairs. A mottled patchwork of scorch marks and stains wound its way across the carpet, ending in a blackened kidney-shaped spot directly in front of Flavia Smythe-Harrows.

She'd walked into the common room an hour before with a stack of newspapers in her hand. Margaret, Violet, and Althea had been chatting by the fire when Flavia handed them around.

By the time Margaret had finished the first paragraph of the story in *The Chronicle* detailing Armitage's speech—with a snide allusion to his "stumbles"—the common room was abuzz. Flavia then announced the Society for the Preservation of the Greylag Goose in Great Britain would be holding a rally against the tunnel next week where she would be giving a speech.

Margaret stared at the print, seeing only a mass of black smudges. Only a few hours earlier she and Grantham had . . .

Had what? Come to an accord? Begun to test the boundaries of what friendship between them might entail?

Damn it. They had been *flirting*. How could he not have told her this would happen today?

"Margaret, did you know about this?" Violet asked.

Margaret stared mutely at her friend, her pain at Grantham's omission leaving her speechless. Violet's mouth pursed as she read the article again and the bottom dropped out of Margaret's stomach.

Althea meanwhile had crossed the room and caught Flavia's sleeve, speaking quickly to her in a low voice. Margaret only realized her friend had been explaining Margaret's involvement in the tunnel project when an argument broke out between Milly and Willy, who had been standing nearby.

This was not part of Margaret's Plan. She had envisioned giving a presentation to club members replete with preliminary sketches finished to illustrate her designs. She'd even hoped to solicit the advice of some of the physicists about the calculations she'd used to estimate the shifting sediment of the riverbed.

"Without progress, we stagnate," Milly said now.

"Without cautious examination of our actions, we can cause harm," Willy countered.

Mortified her work had become the subject of contention between Milly and Willy, Margaret shrank into her chair. Flavia also appeared deeply uncomfortable, her wide mouth tight with embarrassment, large brown eyes cast to the floor.

Violet turned to Margaret and whispered, "If they keep this up, I am afraid the members will feel compelled to choose a side."

"I should have spoken with Flavia myself," Margaret replied. "I should have told you first. This isn't how I wanted anyone to hear of my Plan. I'm so sorry, Violet."

A thin, strained smile stretched across Violet's face.

"Do you think if I stare at Milly hard and you stare at Willy hard, they will hear our thoughts and announce tea?" Althea asked.

When Willy raised a pointed finger and opened her mouth, Violet rose and took a step forward, so she stood between the arguing chemists.

"Mrs. Sweet went to stay with Lady Greycliff for the duration of her pregnancy, which means Cook has baked shortbread biscuits for today's tea."

A surprised moment of silence followed Violet's announcement, then a frantic shushing and rustling of linen and silk as the room emptied out in seconds, leaving only a missing button and a few sheets of newspapers fluttering in the breeze.

Mrs. Sweet often oversaw the Retreat's afternoon teas and her steadfast belief in the evils of sugar meant few women partook of the meal. Cook's shortbread biscuits, on the other hand, contained a shocking amount of sugar—and tasted like sunlight and heaven.

As the room emptied, Violet turned and nodded at Margaret. Relief swept through her at Violet's tacit acceptance of her apology.

Flavia, clearly flustered, also headed toward the exit.

Margaret hurried after her. "Flavia. Can we speak?"

"Congratulations, my dear." Milly blocked Margaret's progress and Flavia left the room. "I should like to hear about your plans. How daring that you will go out into the world and practice your science."

Daring? The entire endeavor had Margaret doubting her sanity at every step. Staring into Milly's sweet face, Margaret had the urge to unburden herself.

Being the first was terrifying. Imagining the worst, praying for the best, and living with the uncertainty of the in-between had taken a toll on Margaret's appetite, her sleep, her better judgment.

"Madame Gault will make us proud," Althea enthused, coming to stand at their side. While Willy engaged in a hushed conversation with Mala, Margaret swallowed the confession sitting at the tip of her tongue.

How could she tell them she wasn't bold—she was terrified? She wasn't a pioneer; she simply had nothing else in her life that came close to the satisfaction of her work. The future was a void without anyone in front of her holding a light.

Taking the coward's way out, Margaret made her excuses. She hailed a hack and escaped to the safety of her office. Once there, she paid a boy some coin to fill her coal bin and stoked the small fireplace as high as it would go.

Work.

That was what Margaret fixed her attention on as her stomach cramped and the skin at her elbows and palms itched.

Do the work.

Draw the lines. Solve the equations. Double-check the measurements.

Everything would be fine if you *do the work*. Do not aim too high, do not set yourself out to be noticed. If you were a woman in a man's world, moving forward meant bending to their desires or just doing the work.

She pushed Grantham to the darkest regions of her mind and spread her hands over the papers in front of her.

For years, Margaret's greatest dream had been to design and carry out the construction of a major suspension bridge.

A suspension bridge was different than the bridges she'd been building for the past ten years. Those bridges were either truss or arch bridges. As she'd told Grantham this morning, the greatest danger for a bridge was if it collapsed under its own weight.

Rather than having any point on the bridge support weight on its own, an arch bridge, for example, pushed the weight evenly out to the supports. By design, no point of an arch is weaker than any other, with the arch working to hold itself up.

Elegant and simple.

Simply boring.

Suspension bridges had been in existence for as long as arch bridges. A rope bridge was a good example. The bridge deck was supported from above, through suspension cables, rather than from below.

Building materials had progressed and now there were cast iron chains rather than rope and—even more intriguing—wire cables.

Only a few years before, William Tierney Clark had unveiled his design for the first major suspension bridge in Europe, to be built in

England and transported piece by piece to Hungary, where it would cross the Danube between Buda and Pest.

The Hungarian political reformer, Count István Széchenyi, had proposed the idea and convinced a Greek businessman to finance the project. Of course, Henri had put forth a bid for the project. Margaret had wanted the commission so badly, she made herself sick with longing. Working sixteen, sometimes eighteen hours a day on the designs, Margaret pushed the limits of what physics allowed and created a masterpiece.

They favored Tierney Clark because he'd already built his first suspension bridge in Berkshire, but Margaret believed her own design to be vastly superior if a tad riskier. It could have made her a legend.

Unfortunately for her, the Greek businessman financing the project had definite ideas about where a woman should be found. Not behind a drafting table nor at a construction site. Certainly not as the engineer of a bridge with which his name would be forever associated.

The loss had influenced Henri's decision to close his firm and Margaret learned never to dream so big again. She went back to her simple, boring bridges and stone by stone, day by day, she did her job.

Now, Margaret forced all awareness of the world outside her office from her brain and focused on the soil reports and shore measurements Geflitt had sent over.

Never mind the women of Athena's Retreat might turn against her, never mind Grantham had betrayed her trust, never mind right now Tierney Clark reaped the accolades and payments that could have been hers. Today, all she could do, all she had ever wanted to do, was work.

GRANTHAM'S SCHOOLING HAD been erratic until his mother remarried and had money for tutors and books. Reading never came easy to him although his mam tried her best. As a result, when he needed a word to sum up a feeling or the aftermath of an event, he often came up empty, being too ashamed to ask if such a word existed.

Today as he sat in Lords, he racked his brain over whether he'd ever heard a term which might describe being simultaneously proud and deeply apprehensive.

"You certainly put Armitage in his place. I cannot wait to read what you will print about him next."

"Well-done, old boy. Looking forward to your speech."

"*Armitage, your goose is cooked.* I showed it to Bradley and Chatham at the club. We all had a good laugh."

Congratulations had poured over Grantham from left and right as he made his way to chambers this morning. Not until he stopped and spoke with a page did he see a copy of *The Chronicle* sitting on a bench and all became clear.

Wolfe had done his job. The front page of the broadsheet had an illustration—Grantham wondered if Abel had complained about the cost—that portrayed Victor Armitage's fall from the stage last week, except beneath his body sat a mother goose looking up in terror, six darling goslings gathered to her breast.

The story itself was far less dramatic. It described the Futuro Consortium's plans for a tunnel, going on to explain the Society for the Preservation of the Greylag Goose in Great Britain's objections to the site. The article repeated each side's argument without any obvious bias, but the caricature made clear whose side *The Chronicle* supported.

"Rather clever move on your part to fight fire with a more polished fire." Lord Fenwood, a horse-faced man who prefaced anything of import with a deep huffing sound, had barely spoken to Grantham since he'd attained the title and taken his seat in Lords. A baron whose family went back to the Domesday Book, Fenwood had made it clear Grantham's claim was suspect and how he'd been brought up was tantamount to being raised by wolves.

Grantham hadn't much cared so long as Fenwood invited him to work on the Education Reform Bill—or at least he'd told himself that.

It turned out he did care. Grantham enjoyed not having to fight for every scrap of respect he was owed for once.

Life was easier when your words carried real weight.

Later that afternoon, he headed toward *The Chronicle*'s offices, intent on delivering his congratulations for the first in their salvo against Armitage. He hadn't written the article, but the praise for it had filled his chest with a sort of pride, and the sepia-colored haze around him—a combination of coal smut and mist—didn't depress him as much as usual.

In fact, as he tossed the street sweeper an extra coin and made an obscene gesture toward the window of *Gentlemen's Monthly,* Grantham was in an excellent mood.

Until the door from the building he passed by swung open.

Margaret stood there in the entrance, staring at the sky before she left the safety of the vestibule. A cowardly urge to keep walking and hope she wouldn't notice him took the place of Grantham's high spirits until her eyes found his.

Tired.

No, exhausted. Margaret appeared exhausted and defeated.

After a moment, she grimaced and stepped back into the building, letting the large door slam shut between them.

No.

Not today.

With the length of her skirts and the slippery stairs, Margaret only made it to the second floor before Grantham was a few steps behind her.

"Maggie. I had no idea Wolfe planned to print a story so soon. Maggie. Maggie, stop and talk to me, will you?"

Margaret's shoulders hunched closer to her ears every time he called her by that name, and she hastened her steps. Grantham pursued her even faster, more afraid she would slip and fall than wanting to catch up with her for when she turned around, there would be hell to pay.

"Maggie, you don't need to—"

As he'd feared, Margaret's lovely kidskin boots, which made her ankles look so comely, were also too delicately shod to gain traction on the slick granite stairs. Without a pause, he caught her neatly as she went sliding backward and scooped her up.

"Come, show me to your office," he said. "You can give me a proper scold there."

"Put me down, Grantham," she hissed. Uneven crimson clouds dotted her face, and he kept his head away from her in case she decided to slam her forehead into his.

After kneeing him in the ballocks, he wouldn't put anything past her.

"All right, all right." Conscious this was her place of business and to be seen in a man's arms, no matter how innocent, could be catastrophic to her reputation, he took the stairs two at a time. Acutely aware of the soft round of her arse pushing against his cock, of the rightness of her in his arms, of the way she smelled and the mystery of how she tasted, he could neither slow down nor speed up, his body rigid and wanting.

And did Margaret help?

No, she remained supple, beguiling, and so fecking beautiful. Instead of turning stiff and holding herself away from him, when she realized he wouldn't put her down, her body went pliant; her chin pressed onto his shoulder and her breasts rubbed against his chest. When he lifted her slightly, so he had a better grip, she let out a surprised gasp that caused a tingle at the base of his spine.

At the top step, the torture ended. All the way up here, silence reigned except for the low cooing of the pigeons seated on the skylight above. He set her on the wooden floor in front of a door with a small brass plaque affixed to the right.

GAULT ENGINEERING
MME GAULT, PRESIDENT

"Get out."

Any pleasure she might have experienced in his arms was nowhere evident in her manner. Arms crossed, mouth twisted in a scowl, Margaret took two steps away from him until she backed against the wall.

"You have a plaque," he said stupidly.

She glared at him. "I do. I'd like you to—"

"I did not know the story would be printed today," he said.

Unmoved, Margaret lifted one shoulder in the French version of an English snort.

"Did you not? What *did* you know, Grantham? Did you know it would be the cause of a public debate at Athena's Retreat? Did you know I could not leave this building for a meal because a flock of bird-hatted people were marching outside for two hours? You know very little."

The plaque sat at eye level, glinting even in the low light of the dirty windows.

In fact, he knew a great deal. Grantham knew that even after she said she'd forgiven him, Margaret had taken this huge, brave, amazing step of opening a firm without telling him. If she'd shared this from the beginning instead of keeping him at arm's length, he would have brought her flowers and champagne and told everyone how damnably proud he was of her. Instead, he'd found out by chance while she shared secrets and port with her friends.

Just this morning they'd been happy in each other's company.

Grantham had nursed a secret hope their accord might strengthen into something more.

Now, whatever he did next would be the wrong thing. If he told *The Chronicle* to stop writing stories that touched on the tunnel, he would be losing a chance to damage Armitage's influence. If it kept printing those stories, they would make Margaret's life more difficult and drive them further apart.

"Victor Armitage is standing in the way of an Education Reform Bill that will allow girls to go to school." Frustration and the ever-present thwarted lust he felt in her presence roughened his voice. "I thought you would understand why this matters."

Margaret wore a piece of headwear which, while it did not stick out so far as those ridiculous poke bonnets, conspired to keep her face in shadow, hiding her eyes. Her firm mouth he could see, the plump lips pulled into a tight plum line, an upside-down question mark at either side.

"There are myriad other ways to get to Armitage without pulling me down along with him," she replied tersely. "You said you were my *friend*."

"Your *friend*," he repeated, voice so low it came out as a growl. He set his palms on either side of her, pushing into the flaking plaster wall.

Margaret tilted her head and her bonnet fell to expose her eyes to his sight, the hazel irises nearly eclipsed by the widening of her pupils. A soft pant escaped her lips and every ounce of control Grantham had mustered to remain a gentleman now frayed to the point of nonexistence while his cock grew so hard it pained him.

He was furious—at her, at himself, at Victor Armitage and geese and everything else conspiring to come between them. Most of all, he was furious he could not stop wanting her.

Dust rained to the floor as he dug his fingers into the wall, but Grantham did not care.

This woman. He could not think right around her, but he could not leave her be.

Leaning down to meet her eyes, Grantham spoke as gently as he could manage.

"I will do whatever I can to pass that bill and take down Armitage. At the same time, I will try my best to keep you out of the fray."

"If you were a good friend—" she began.

Grantham leaned a fraction of an inch closer and moved his mouth to her ear, desire and frustration pounding in his veins, unable to keep from shifting his hips so the evidence of his discomfort made itself known.

"It is because I am your *friend,* I will not move any closer to you. That I will not take your mouth and kiss you until you tremble. I will not press my cock against your belly, and I will not drop to my knees, lift your dress, and set my mouth to where you are needing."

A puff of warm air against his neck was the extent of Margaret's reply. Her knees bent a fraction of an inch and her breathing increased in pace.

Grantham kept his word, however, and did not set his lips to hers. Instead, he remained frozen, listening to the pounding of blood in his veins and watching a flush spread across her cheeks.

"I will not touch you, because I am your *friend,* but know this . . ." His lips were so close to the soft skin of her cheek, he could taste the salt of her skin just by breathing.

"Know that friendship goes both ways. If you but ask, I will give you everything you want and in return . . ."

Grantham stepped away. As he brushed the plaster from his knuckles, he drank in the sight of Margaret's pulse fluttering wildly at the base of her throat, her unfocused eyes and parted lips.

"In return," he said, "all I ask is that you let me in."

Only the low chortle of pigeons in love accompanied him as he walked away.

10

FECK.

Grantham's favorite curse reverberated in Margaret's head as she left the offices of Adams and Sons Foundry.

The place had been a disaster.

Neither Adams nor his sons had been in evidence. They were rarely to be seen, according to the foreman, a gloomy man who walked without ever completely lifting his feet from the ground. If Adams had bothered to show up, he might have had something to say about the ramshackle way he ran his foundry.

More than once, Margaret witnessed near mishaps in the loading of the unfinished iron into sorting bins. A foundry was always a sooty, smelly place filled with hazards, but the men here did not seem to be wary of them, and the foreman was more interested in sighing and glancing at his tiny office, where she'd found him asleep at his desk, than he was at the slow pace of the work.

Now when she stepped outside, the sky had darkened and the first few drops of a vile London rain had already fallen.

Feck again.

It would take her forever to find a hack and she'd have to ride home in damp clothes atop filthy cushions.

"Madame?"

A youth in tan and gold livery approached her on the street.

"Madame Gault?" he asked.

"Yes," she said hesitantly.

He touched his topper. "I've the carriage right around the corner, madame."

The carriage?

The youth gestured to the side of the building. "Couldn't stop out front because there were too many wagons. This way, madame. M'lord sent along hot tea or whiskey, whichever you prefer."

M'lord.

Grantham.

Sure enough, the same carriage that had taken her and Maisey home the other day waited for her.

All I ask is that you let me in.

No matter how long and imaginatively she'd cursed his name, Margaret had been unable to erase his words from her mind and the impact of his touch from her body. After two days spent restlessly pacing her office and getting nothing done, she'd gone to visit the foundry, hoping to clear her head.

"How did you know I would be here?" she asked the youth as he lowered the stairs for her.

"There's a boy what sweeps the street by your office. M'lord asked him where you said when you took a hack this afternoon."

He gestured toward the cab, surprised when she hesitated. "Oh, madame. The inside is proper flash, er, right pretty. Just look."

Margaret could not refuse when he offered her his hand with a small flourish.

Inside, clean blankets had been piled on the seat, and the boy clambered in to show her how to work a cunning compartment, which folded out into a tray and revealed a carafe of hot tea. It fit neatly into a circular depression so it would not fall over when the carriage moved, and the boy was as proud of it as though he'd thought of it himself.

Margaret relented and nodded her acceptance of the ride home. With a grin, the boy shut the door behind her and hopped up to join the driver. Sinking into the plush cushions, she pulled one of the blankets over her to ward against the autumn chill.

She should be annoyed by Grantham's presumptuousness. Angry at his interference.

Instead, she was exhausted.

The edges of Margaret's Plan were starting to fray, and it set fear roiling in her belly, her chest tight as if she were about to fall at any time. Sitting on her desk at the Retreat was the first cheque Geflitt had written her, unissued. The initial funds used to outfit her office were her own personal savings. One of the reasons she hadn't hired an assistant yet was she would have to use Armitage's money.

With Milly and Willy determined to insert themselves in the fight over the greylag goose, Margaret's hopes that Armitage's involvement would be forgotten were dashed. And if anyone looked closer at his relationship to Geflitt as someone other than just a supporter? Violet might champion Margaret's friendship despite the disparity in their stations, but what would happen when her friend discovered Margaret took his money?

Nothing was going as planned. As hard as Margaret tried to make the edges align, life was forever altering her designs.

The sound of rain on the roof of the carriage combined with the warmth of the blanket conspired to make her drowsy. After a few moments, she dozed until somehow Grantham appeared at her side.

She tried to apologize to him, but he wouldn't listen to her. Instead, he kept insisting she wake up. Why would he want her to leave this cozy nest? His big strong body pushed against her side and she relished how his muscles flexed beneath his skin, an enduring structure, solid and safe beneath its cladding.

"Wake up, Margaret. You cannot spend the night in my carriage, comfortable as it is."

With reluctance, Margaret opened her eyes to Grantham sitting next to her, gently shaking her shoulder. Not only had the carriage come to a stop, but it sat in an unfamiliar mews.

"You had the driver take me to your house," she mumbled the accusation, not completely awake.

"Not on purpose," he objected. "I'd told Chester to take you home but when he leaned down to ask where you needed to be set, you were asleep. So, he brought you here."

Should she believe Grantham or not?

"Take me to the office, please," she said. "I have another few hours of work I must do before supper."

"Hours of work?" he said. "It is eight o'clock."

"Eight?" Margaret had left the foundry at six o'clock. "Have I been sitting out here the whole time?"

"Well, you slept so deeply, I hadn't the heart to wake you."

When Margaret leaned forward, the muscles of her lower back complained. Expertly fitted by the most exclusive of seamstresses in Paris, her corsets never pinched. Even so, sleeping slouched in one for hours was extremely uncomfortable upon waking and . . .

"Have you been sitting here the whole time I slept?" she asked.

She'd been buttoned up in her pelisse with a blanket over her, but he sat in the unheated carriage in only his shirt and waistcoat. In the dim light, his buttery gold hair turned brown, the shadow along the line of his jaw even darker.

Grantham blushed. "I didn't want you to wake and be scared."

Something long frayed finally broke in her chest, and her throat closed around a lump formed of guilt and longing.

"I'm sorry," she whispered. "I'm sorry I was unkind the other day."

His brows came together into a line of distress, and she sat against the cushions and leaned her head against his shoulder, rain tapping on the carriage house roof while she waited for his reply.

The smell of Darjeeling tea filled the interior of his carriage and married with the humid air, the half-closed curtains lending an ochre cast to the interior. From his carriage house came the faint sounds of a few men trading words and the whinny of horses as they were uncoupled from the carriage and led into their stalls.

"I'm the one should be sorry," he said finally. "I truly had no idea *The Capital's Chronicle* crusade against Armitage would brush up against you."

"It isn't the paper." Margaret waved away the idea. "It's more that everything I've ever wanted is so close and at the same time so unachievable."

He shifted so she rested almost fully across his chest. Beneath her cheek rumbled his heartbeat, touching off a shiver of awareness.

Margaret continued, "Once I conceived of starting my own firm, I couldn't think of anything else. Violet's idea of a club is a stroke of genius, but it isn't enough. Women should be able to make their discoveries and be recognized—and be paid for them."

"Won't that set the Guardians' hair alight." He chuckled.

Margaret pushed the thought of the Guardians, and Armitage, away. This was about her and Grantham.

"I just—now you are here, and I am here, I don't know what I want from you. The old Georgie who would slay dragons for me to take up my cause no matter the consequences? Or is it easier to blame the Earl Grantham for throwing a gaggle of geese in my way?"

Comfortable with his silence, Margaret waited as Grantham sifted through her words. She relished the soft warmth of the linen of his shirt and ran a finger along the slick satin of his waistcoat. His body was a wrapped sweet, waiting for her to find a quiet place to open the treat.

"The other day, we reflected on how much we've changed," Grantham said, sliding his shoulder so her head would rest more comfortably. "This is one of the things that has changed. You admitting to uncertainty. The old Maggie would have picked one direction and charged toward it no matter the cost, fists at the ready."

In the embrace of the grey, damp folds of a London autumn, Margaret longed for the bright, clean days of summer in Lincolnshire. Life was so much easier beneath the willow branches.

"I suppose ambivalence is another sign of my advanced age," she said.

"Well, you cannot make a good decision on an empty stomach," he said to her. "Come inside and you can tell me if you'd rather dine with George Willis or Earl Grantham."

"Dine alone with an unmarried man without chaperone?" Margaret asked. "Bad enough I took a ride in your carriage. If I were an aristocratic widow, heads might turn the other way. Being a woman in a profession? How do you think other men would treat me if they found out?"

"My staff would never breathe a word," he said quickly but the two lines between his brows returned, and he shrugged in defeat. "You are right. It's not worth the risk."

Grantham would let her go. He would pull the crest from the side of the carriage and have her whisked to Beacon House, where Violet's staff would ensure discretion.

She should leave. Go to the Retreat and do her work. Stay safe. Risk nothing.

"I will not take your mouth and kiss you until you tremble. I will not press my cock against your belly, and I will not drop to my knees, lift your dress, and set my mouth to where you are needing."

Margaret had not forgotten his words. They lingered beneath her skin and made her lips tingle.

To remain with him would be a terrible idea.

Terrible ideas seemed to be her new specialty.

"YOU'VE TAKEN ON the church, the Tories, the mill owners—it is a wonder there are not more caricatures skewering you in the conservative broadsheets. Do you fear no one, my lord?"

Grantham shoved a piece of fish in his mouth to fend off the stupid grin he would otherwise be wearing at Margaret's compliments.

"Not all Tories," he pointed out once he'd finished swallowing. "Lord Ashley is the author of most of the bills I have supported. Now, there is a man to be admired."

"Hmmm." Margaret made a sound of agreement as she cut a piece of meat into a perfect triangle. "I read his speech in support of the Mines and Collieries Act."

The Mines Act outlawed the employment of women and girls underground in the mines and raised the legal age for boys to be employed to ten. Before then, children as young as five were sent in the mines, and since women and children were smaller than men, they were paid lower wages for their twelve-hour days. The conditions were horribly unsafe as evidenced by the tragedy at the Husker Collier, where twenty-five children under the age of sixteen were drowned in the tunnels. While the mine owners were intent on watering down the bill, the immediate effect on the children's health had been pronounced.

Pushing aside his plate, Grantham leaned forward. "To possess such skill as to write a speech that will move men to change lifetime views—that is something which I can never achieve."

The admission cost him nothing. Margaret would remember well his frustration with reading and writing from when they were children and he would escape his tutor and spend the day beneath the willow, hiding from his books and the disappointment on his mam's face.

Margaret set down her fork and considered him, her hazel eyes illuminated in the dancing candlelight, a small frown bending one side of her mouth.

"You are not a speech writer, but you have other gifts you can use to effect the same change," she said.

At his sound of disagreement, she held up her hand, palm facing outward as though to deflect his negation.

"Grantham. I have seen you charm the ladies of Athena's Retreat more times than I can count. You convinced Lady Potts to move her tarantulas to the cellar, away from Flavia's ornithology laboratory, when no one else could."

Poor Lady Potts. Her beloved arachnids were unpopular through no fault of their own. All she needed was for him to listen to her complaints with respect and pet her tarantulas a few times.

"Mala Hill no longer brings her hedgehogs to afternoon tea," she continued.

"Egads, Margaret. Don't bring them up at the table." Grantham shuddered. "They bathe themselves in a froth of their own spittle. Terrifying creatures. No wonder no one ever went for tea."

Her laugh was a ribbon of velvet that stroked his spine. Of a sudden, Grantham's enjoyment of their dinner conversation changed to something darker.

"No one goes for tea because no one can stomach Mrs. Sweet's biscuits. Except you."

True. They tasted like a scold.

"They're healthy," he said.

"You are kind, Grantham." Margaret pushed aside her plate as well. "You are afraid your upbringing has set you apart from those men in Lords. I believe your upbringing, your patience with others, your willingness to listen to their stories—these may be your key to cultivating votes."

Grantham wasn't convinced but neither was he about to argue with Margaret when she gave him compliments and gazed at him with admiration.

"In fact, I think this reputation of the Untamed Earl is misplaced," she said in a teasing voice. When a knowing smile stretched her lips, Grantham's virtuous intentions vanished in an instant.

The sight of Margaret's lips touching his silver and eating his food had a powerful effect on the dark and primal urge that had awoken in Grantham ever since he'd sat in the carriage watching her sleep.

Desire, thick and hot, replaced his blood and fogged his brain; a sensation unlike any he'd felt in years. He wanted to peel away every layer between them and lay Margaret out like the meal they'd just enjoyed and bury his face into every secret hollow she possessed, worshipping her mysteries.

Grantham was done with playing *friends*.

The moment she sensed the direction of his thoughts, she let the rim of her wineglass rest against her mouth. Grantham held his breath when she took a sip, licked a stray drop of wine from her bottom lip, and watched him watching her. A gorgeous tension pulled at his spine, and his cock twitched awake.

"I haven't shown you the rest of the house," he said, his voice low and nearly unrecognizable. There were words he should use, pleasant phrases, slick compliments, or charming distractions, but his brain wasn't working right.

"Perhaps you might like to stay for a while after dinner?" he asked. "I have some prints upstairs that are considered valuable."

When the candlelight flickered, the shadows beneath her cheekbones jumped wildly and he leaned forward, unable to read her face in the shifting light.

Was she intrigued? Disgusted? Amused?

Pearly white teeth peeped out when she sank them into her bottom lip as though she were biting into a slice of apple.

"I do believe I would enjoy seeing the rest of your house," she told him. "It has been a long time since I've . . ."

Her head bent and a blush appeared; two crimson spots of acquiescence that made his heart beat double time.

"I miss a man's company," she confessed to the snow-white linen of the table top.

The reminder she'd been used to a man's company dampened Grantham's anticipation somewhat.

Margaret had been married. She missed her husband. She'd even said so the night of the ball.

Her husband's ghost slipped behind Grantham as he rose from the table and walked to where she sat. What if she preferred her husband's touch? What if it were Marcel's name she whispered when she went to bed each night?

Despite his fears, he could not stop, not now. He stood at her side and took her hand in his. For the first time in so many years, her bare skin rested against his.

The sensation softened the edge of his misgivings.

"Come with me?" he asked.

Grantham parsed shadows until she nodded, and his heart resumed its rapid pace. He employed a bare minimum of household staff, uncomfortable with being waited on. The hallway, therefore, was empty as she preceded him up the stairs to the second floor.

When they entered his bedroom, a low fire crackled in the fireplace. A small candelabra sat on the credenza beneath the window, reflecting the tiny flames in the glass. Above them, he could make out the barest outline of Margaret and no sign of himself. As was right. His world narrowed to only this woman before him.

She peered at him coquettishly from beneath her lashes.

"Where were these prints you wanted to show me?"

Prints? He tried to recall what they had to do with anything. Instead, he reached over and cradled her cheek in his hand.

"By God, you are so soft," he said in wonder. How could this be? Her skin was a marvel, smooth as silk but, oh, so warm. He ran the side of his thumb along her cheek, reveling in the texture.

"Do you know where else I am soft?" she asked.

At that, his knees nearly went out from under him. He held her chin in his hand and leaned in for a kiss. The briefest of touches. Once, twice, three times, he let his partly closed mouth sweep against hers.

No urgency drove them. Unlike the kiss they'd shared the night of the ball, they'd no dire message to communicate. They had time to learn the shape of each other's mouths. Grantham set the tip of his tongue to her and tasted fleetingly the wine she'd had with supper. Lighter than the touch of butterflies' wings, their mouths met and danced away again.

Learning her anew layered atop of remembering from before colored the moment, increased the heady scent of oranges and parchment, raised his temperature, and heightened his hearing so the rustle of her skirts was louder than the pounding of his heart.

Each time they touched, a pulse of need built up within him, his cock stiffening, his grip on her tightening, pulling her closer and closer to him.

When she opened her lips and curled her tongue against his, the hesitancy burned away as the flickers of desire deepened to flames. In an instant, the mood shifted from exploring to demanding, and he forgot finesse, forgot everything except he wanted to be inside her in any way he could.

Grantham slid his fingers into her hair and held the back of her head in his palm, heedless of the hairpins falling to the floor as he kissed her harder, forcing her mouth wider again and again.

Margaret fumbled with his cravat, never leaving off her kisses, and finally yanked the length of linen from around his neck as she suckled his tongue. The sensation made him wild, and he pulled her hips against his, relishing and at the same time resenting the rough friction of cloth against his palms as his hands followed the path of her spine and smoothed over her hips until he couldn't stand it anymore.

The warm, supple body of this beautiful woman was mere inches away beneath the evil contraption of her dress. She'd apologized for having to dine in the same dress she'd worn to the foundry, but he hadn't cared while they ate.

Now Grantham broke off their kisses, panting, and studied the garment with agitation.

"How do you . . . where is the opening?" he complained while tugging at the buttons in the back and investigating the front to see if there were some easier means of access.

Laughing, Margaret tilted her head, baring her throat before him. Grantham left off his fumbling and paid homage to this miracle of nature instead.

The claret they'd had with dinner tasted like vinegar compared to the bouquet he inhaled at the perfectly formed curve where her neck met her shoulder. She was all salt and silk and smelled of lavender and parchment and something utterly unique to women. Unable to stop himself, he rested his teeth ever so gently in her soft flesh.

"I pulled you away from dinner too early if you are still so hungry," she said as he took small bites of her. If he let go of his control, he would leave a mark. At the thought, he stole her mouth again and pulled at her skirts, sweeping them in his arms as he sought more skin, more sensation.

God, how had he gone so long without touching her before now? He should have taken her in the gardens at the public ball, in the hallways of the club, anywhere they could be alone together.

Frustrated by the veritable waterfall of petticoats beneath his hand, Grantham picked her up and made his way toward the bed without breaking the kiss. A knife lay in his bedside drawer to cut the buttons from her dress.

Was that going too far?

When he set her on top of his bed, Margaret broke the kiss, staring at him with blatant hunger. As he leaned over to pull at her skirts, however, she set a hand on his arm.

"Before we go too far and cannot think straight . . . ," she said.

Too late, he thought.

"I must ask. Do you have any preventatives at hand?"

Grantham blinked and shook his head. Difficult to decipher her words when all he wanted to do was get rid of her damned dress.

"Preventatives?" he repeated.

"Yes." Her brows came together in consternation. "Do you keep a tin of condoms? I will confess I did not anticipate . . . this."

She sat onto her knees and unbuttoned his waistcoat. "And did not prepare for it."

Grantham's brain refused to work. How could it? Now she'd slipped the waistcoat from his shoulders, and when she'd gone onto her knees, her skirts had pulled to the side and he could see the arc of her calf, clad in sensible black stockings he wanted to pull off with his teeth.

"Did not prepare?" he repeated.

What was she saying?

Chill air came between them when Margaret paused in the act of pulling his shirt from his trousers. Her eyebrows raised to a point, a worrying sign. Grantham gathered the reins back from his penis and thought about what she had said.

Preventatives.

Prophylactics.

"I can't say I was prepared, either." Grantham looked wildly around the room as if a tin of condoms might fall from the sky. "It's not what one expects when you ask a lady to dinner."

The hectic flush drained from Margaret's face and he knew he'd put his foot in it.

"And if one is not a lady?" she asked.

Oh, dear God, there must be something he could do to save the situation.

"That is to say, I do not make a habit of inviting women *other* than ladies to dinner. Or having any expectations. Or not having them, either."

Her hands dropped to her sides.

Not an improvement.

Grantham thought fast.

"But you are not a woman other than a lady, of course. You are different."

"Different?" she asked, her voice icier than the Thames in December

No. *No!* Why was his mouth still opening and closing and spewing rubbish into the space between them?

Margaret swung around and climbed off the bed, rebuttoning all those evil little buttons that had made him so insane.

"I suppose I am not considered a lady. Not like your last paramour, Lady Phoebe Hunt."

How did Margaret know about Phoebe? She was the daughter of a marquess he'd halfway courted a few years ago, more out of concern for her safety at the hands of her father than out of anything close to love. She'd cut him off abruptly, however. Not long afterwards, she'd secretly developed a chemical weapon and put Violet in great danger. Luckily, Violet and Arthur had managed to stop Phoebe from doing terrible harm when she'd become a murderous maniac and betrayed Violet.

"What does Phoebe have to do with any of this?" Grantham asked, still trying to ascertain how he'd had Margaret nearly naked one moment and furious enough to gut him the next. "I never did anything like this with Phoebe."

"Never did anything like *this* with Lady Phoebe? What exactly do you mean by *this*? Have sex with her without preventatives or bring her to your bed in the first place?"

Storming across the room to pick up her hairpins, Margaret made a derisory noise. "Because I am not a lady, you have no qualms about seducing me, I suppose."

"No, no, I do have qualms."

Even as his big stupid mouth shaped the words, Grantham knew he'd said exactly the wrong thing and he slapped a hand over his face. When he opened his eyes, Margaret had collected her hairpins and had a hand on the doorknob.

"This was a terrible idea, George. If you'll excuse me," she said. "I have a busy day tomorrow. I shall see myself out."

Grantham said nothing because, by that point, she'd closed the door behind her and left him half-dressed, half-hard, and confused as to how he'd managed to muck this up.

11

R AIN.

Again.

All it had done since Margaret returned to London was rain.

The street gutters were black and brown rivers of manure and even worse. Last night on her way home from Grantham's, she'd seen a large rat riding a raft made of a piece of rotted wood floating beside the carriage.

The city and its weather perfectly mirrored her mood.

Margaret had slept poorly the night before, thinking of how she'd barely forgiven Grantham for breaking her heart and there she'd been wanting him all over again.

Sitting across from him at dinner had been like a dream. He'd spoken so passionately about his reform work, and she'd been fully introduced to a new side of Grantham. The next moment, her old friend had returned when he'd told silly stories to make her laugh. Every time she did, his pupils had widened and the power she had quickly went to her head.

The attraction between them lent color to the evening, made the food taste better, and sent the wine straight to her head.

Margaret had been tearing at his clothes, her blood fizzing and heart beating so loud, she could barely hear when she'd come to her senses to ask about preventatives.

That Grantham had been unprepared surprised her. Margaret had assumed any man known as the "Untamed Earl" would have had pro-phylactics at hand, if not for fear of disease, at least out of concerns for pregnancy. He might be obtuse on occasion, but Grantham was at heart a decent man and would never consciously put a woman in the position of having to carry an unwanted pregnancy.

"Not that I make a habit of inviting ladies for dinner."

Rather than giving him the benefit of the doubt—perhaps he actu-ally didn't invite women to his home—Margaret had let her insecuri-ties take control.

"You are different."

Seventeen had been very young to make the decision that changed her social status forever, but she could not change her past. Whether Grantham was a bean-headed clod, or she had jumped to conclusions, the fact remained that they were better off not becoming involved.

What if sex changed everything between them? What happened if she let Grantham get hold of her heart once more?

Margaret brooded in the damp seat of an ancient hack until it slowed, turning a corner then coming to a stop in front of Fenley's Fripperies. Leaping from the conveyance, she tossed the driver a coin and gulped the fresh air, shaking her fist at the banks of grey clouds pushing the sky down on the city like the heel of God's hand.

Before the hand could dump a bucket of water on her, she scuttled inside.

Last year when Margaret had stayed at Athena's Retreat, she'd struck up a friendship with Leticia Fenley—now Lady Greycliff. Many a night, Letty brought Margaret home to her warm and boisterous family in Clerkenwell for delicious meals and eventful evenings of chess with her father, Mr. Fenley; listening to the Fenley siblings bicker; and enjoying the adulation of Letty's younger sisters and the innocent flirtation of her younger brother, Sam.

It reminded Margaret of her summers with the Grange sisters, except no one in Letty's family shared her passion for science. Instead, they lived together and worked together to create the experience of Fenley's Fantastic Fripperies. Three stories of the most useless assortment of trinkets imaginable. In any other setting, half the wares of Fenley's would be passed over by the women of quality who flocked here. However, Mr. Fenley, his wife, their three other daughters, and Sam most of all, used their talents and imagination to create the illusion of spectacle and awe in their displays.

Ladies apparel and accoutrements took up the third floor, where Mrs. Fenley and her daughters reigned. The walls were hung with hundreds of tiny mirrors and from the ceiling were suspended modern paraffin lamps. Various tables of different sizes were covered in brightly colored silks and upon them rested boxes full of gloves, hatpins, and purses.

Beautiful gifts for women also crowded the second floor of the building. There were no mirrors there and the attendants were all male.

This was Sam Fenley's brainchild. A refuge for husbands who were searching for gifts for their wives. Some of the same wares as were sold above were laid out, but they came attached with various cards.

Have you done something terrible but she won't tell you what it is? asked a placard. Beneath the sign were boxes of bejeweled hatpins and brightly colored scarves, pretty bonnets and cleverly embroidered pincushions. *Want to make her happy before giving bad news?* asked another. A gentleman attendant would ask how dire the situation and guide a male customer to the perfect gift depending on what he heard. The more upset the gentleman, the more expensive the gift.

Pleased to see how men were as gullible if not more so than women—witness a display advertising beard oil made by blind virgins—Margaret always worried Fenley's encouraged men to buy presents rather than simply grovel.

Every man should be encouraged to grovel.

Margaret headed straight for the center of the first floor, where stood an attractive stand of umbrellas, similar to those designed by Jonas Hanway. They weighed more than the oiled silk Chinese parasols women held in Paris to protect their skin, but this way, Margaret could walk on the street without ruining her bonnets and not have to take as many hacks.

"Yes, yes, the toy is clever. My question is, can you make it bigger?"

Perhaps because she had been thinking of groveling, it called to mind the one person she would love to see on his knees.

That thought made her blush then grow angry with herself for blushing. Would she never learn?

Grantham stood deep in conversation with Sam Fenley. A delightful young man, Margaret thought he had an overabundance of intelligence and too few places to apply it. Perhaps six or seven years younger than her, the handsome youth with the distinctive Fenley wheat blond hair and cornflower blue eyes was well shaped and had an irresistible smile.

"Bigger is not always better, my lord," Sam said.

Had Sam matured since last they saw one another?

"More expensive, now that is always better."

No.

Same Sam.

"If you switch out the plain hat for the gilded one, it will shine like . . ."

Sam caught sight of Margaret and paused, mouth agape. A dreamy look drifted across his face, and she rolled her lips inward to keep from laughing at him.

"Madame Gault's eyes," he said in an awed tone.

Margaret picked the umbrella she'd selected and made her way toward his counter.

Grantham hadn't seen her; instead, he stared at Sam with consternation.

"How do you know Margaret's eyes shine like gilt?" he demanded.

"I'm certain Mr. Fenley meant something else altogether," Margaret said from behind him. She laid the umbrella on the counter, ignoring Grantham's surprise, and favored Sam with a smile.

Sam set one elbow on the counter and leaned toward her.

"I did mean you, madame. Why, my mother always says you epitomize the ideal woman with your grace and beauty, and of course your wit, and . . ."

"Hello?" said Grantham, scowling at Sam. He tapped the counter. Hard. "That is all well and good, but we were discussing something ungraceful, inelegant, and irritating."

Sam ignored him.

"But you cannot mean to purchase this umbrella," he said to Margaret. "It isn't magnificent enough for you. You should have something in russet or gold to highlight the color of your eyes."

Sam leaned even farther forward, the picture of adoration, and went to set his other elbow on the countertop. Unfortunately, because he stared at her and not the counter, he misjudged the distance and instead of leaning forward, he fell and smacked his head onto the counter's edge.

"Sh—" He swallowed a curse and stood quickly, his hands flying to his forehead, wobbled backward, and before Margaret could reach out to keep him upright, tripped on a box at his feet and fell over with a loud thud.

Margaret gasped.

Grantham, beholding the sight of a prone Sam Fenley, simply scowled with disgust.

"Christ Jesu, Fenley." He leaned over the counter and scolded the boy. "Have a little dignity."

"Grantham, stop." Margaret admonished him, hurrying round the counter to help Sam to his feet.

"Are you all right, Mr. Fenley?"

Sam, beet red from the part of his hair to where his neck disappeared beneath his collar, sat up. A large lump formed between his eyes and his stare was now glassy with pain rather than interest.

"Madame, when I am in your presence . . ." He leaned on her more than necessary as he made to stand. "There is no pain can touch me."

"Oh, I'm positive I can inflict enough pain even Madame Gault's presence won't protect you from," Grantham said, staring straight at Margaret.

"Lord Grantham." She spoke sharply, holding Sam's arm. "Do you not own a newspaper with which to occupy your time rather than purchasing frivolous gifts and tormenting poor Mr. Fenley?"

"A newspaper?" Sam exclaimed; injury forgotten. "Which one?"

"*The Capital's Chronicle*," said Grantham proudly.

"Oh. That one?" Sam's excitement faded and he turned his attention to Margaret. "But Madame Gault, Letty wrote us you are returned to London for good now. You must come and have dinner with the family."

Grantham frowned, head bouncing between her and Sam. "What do you mean, *oh, that one*? Yes. The one currently running a series of enthralling stories about geese."

Grantham's ears pinkened under Sam's stare of disbelief.

"*Enthralling* stories?" Sam's voice was thick with sarcasm. "I saw the article the other day and saved it for when I had trouble falling asleep."

"The article was informative and balanced," Grantham said tersely.

Sam tilted his head. "What kind of paper is *The Capital's Chronicle*?"

Grantham looked at Margaret as though for inspiration, but she just shrugged.

"By which I mean, what is the reason for the paper? Are you a political broadsheet? Literary? Gossip and fashion?" Sam asked.

"At the moment we are against anything Victor Armitage is for and for anything Victor Armitage is against."

"That isn't going to sell papers." Sam scrunched his brows. "To sell something, you need to be telling one grand story."

"It's a broadsheet," Grantham explained. "There are dozens of stories."

"No, it's more like—" Sam scratched his head, then pulled forward the tin soldier Grantham had been admiring. "See, I'm not selling you a toy."

"Oh, you aren't?" Grantham stared at the soldier and frowned. "I liked that toy."

Shaking his head and wincing, Sam gingerly touched the lump forming there. "That's not the point."

Margaret had spent enough time in the Fenley household to guess where Sam was heading and intervened before Grantham grew frustrated.

"You can have the toy, my lord. Along with the toy, Mr. Fenley is selling you the *idea* of the toy."

"Exactly." Sam favored her with a blinding smile full of surprisingly white teeth. "This toy is nothing but a few bits of tin screwed together by a bloke in Limehouse. You could buy it off him for a tuppence."

"A tuppence." Grantham pounded the counter with his fist. "You're selling it for three times as much!"

"I'm selling you the *idea* of it." Sam held the toy so it caught the light. "The exclusivity of finding it here. The story of land far away where men who more resemble elves than humans work their magic with tiny silver hammers."

Grantham grabbed the toy and moved its arms up and down. "I didn't believe you about the little men."

Unconvinced, Sam pulled out a small velvet box and packed the soldier away. "You say you're going to write about geese. These are the greylag geese Flavia is upset about?"

Grantham nodded.

"Maybe instead of an article about birds, you write about the way trains have changed our natural world forever," said Sam.

Margaret scowled. "The discovery of the steam engine has allowed us—"

"To sully the pristine British countryside with noise and dirt and smells," Sam said.

Gone were the adoring looks and pretty compliments he'd been throwing her way before. The true Sam Fenley had emerged. What energized him far more than a pretty woman was a prettier story to tell.

"And Armitage—the hypocrite. Presenting himself as the guardian of England while at the same time he wants to decimate all our geese." Sam tied the box with a huge ribbon.

Grantham, who had been eyeing another toy in a glass case, peered up in consternation. "What? I didn't say he wants to decimate all the geese in England."

"I shall tell Lucy to take my counter tomorrow." Sam spoke over him. "What time does the newspaper office open?"

"What do you . . . ?" Grantham's brows pulled together as Sam pushed the box toward him. "I don't think they—"

"Doesn't matter." Sam waved off Grantham's question. "I'll be there at eight. Tell them to expect me. Oh, and Madame Gault?" Sam handed her the umbrella. "Please, take this as a gift and use it in good health."

Margaret considered. She wasn't well pleased with Sam's interference, but the umbrella cost six shillings after all.

"Do not forget," Sam told her with a suggestive waggle in his brow. "Today is Wednesday. You remember what Mam makes on Wednesdays?"

Oh, did she ever. "Roast?"

"Da and Mam will be so pleased to see you again. Please say you'll come for dinner?"

Margaret said yes because of the roast and not because it made a vein stand out on Grantham's neck.

Served him right.

GRANTHAM BOUGHT THE damn toy anyway, despite his disillusionment, and followed Margaret out of the store.

"That stripling should stick with what he knows," Grantham grumbled. "And what was that doggerybaw about your eyes and such? The boy is far too forward."

Margaret unfurled the umbrella and Grantham jumped back a foot so as not to get poked in the eye.

"He did his job," she said. "He could make you buy a piece of stone and have you convinced it was a diamond from the Queen's coronet. You are lucky to have him come help you ruin my livelihood."

With that, she spun on her heel and walked away. Grantham kept behind her, trying to duck under the umbrella and having to fall off the walkway instead.

"I am not—ow," his foot slipped off the edge of a rotting board and he stepped in a pile of manure.

"Damn—Margaret, I am not trying to—oof." Having moved off the walkway while trying to scrape the manure off the bottom of his boot, he hadn't looked where he was going and ran into a gentleman walking the other way. "Excuse me," Grantham apologized, lifting his topper.

Margaret meanwhile was half a street away already with her firm stride. Grantham took a moment to admire the sway of her backside as folks made way for her.

"I am trying to apologize," he said to himself as she turned a corner and he lost sight of her. Apologize for what exactly, he wasn't sure. Everything, he supposed. Not having preventatives. Not foreseeing a need for preventatives. Not finding the words to explain while he'd imagined her naked in his bed hundreds of times since the kiss they'd shared at the ball, he'd never believed she would be there in the flesh, so to speak.

That she was so long a dream, he didn't know what to do with the real woman.

Too late.

Once again, he'd made everything worse between them.

Thick, greasy drops of rain fell on the brim of his hat and Grantham glanced at the beautifully wrapped box in his hands.

Ah well, at least the day wasn't a total waste.

"THE FECK THIS is made by elves on a mountainside. You can buy this in Limehouse for a tuppence." Arthur Kneland crowed with delight as he pulled the toy from its elaborate wrapping. Grantham had made his way to Beacon House after his unsatisfactory encounter with Margaret.

"The box you brought it in is worth more than this toy," Kneland said.

"Fine," said Grantham glumly. "Give Baby Georgie—"

"Her name is Mirren."

"—the box. She can use it to hide in when she learns she's half-Scottish."

Grantham selected a biscuit from the tray in front of him then set it down, his appetite having fled. He'd climbed through a window this time to avoid the footmen Kneland had set to watch him and nearly scared the wits from a parlor maid. In retaliation, Arthur had asked a footman to bring him the last of Mrs. Sweet's biscuits rather than Cook's shortbread.

Grantham rubbed his face and covered a yawn with his hand. After Margaret had left last night, he'd spent the hours until dawn castigating himself for having ruined the chance of a lifetime. Missing a night's sleep was a far sight easier in his boyhood than in his advancing years.

"What ails you?"

Grantham stared at the other man in surprise. "What?"

"What ails you, man?" Kneland asked again. "You look like you haven't slept in days, your jokes aren't even up to your worst standards, and you have this . . ."

He waved his hand around and frowned.

Annoyed, Grantham mirrored the gesture. "This what? Godlike physique? Abnormal beauty for a mortal?"

"No," Kneland spat. "You have this air about you as though you've lost your best friend."

Twenty years a protection officer for figures as varied as a corrupt

Italian prince and the head of the Greek Army had left Kneland with a rudimentary ability to read another man's face.

Which disconcerted him more? That his problems with Margaret had left such a mark on him or he had the sudden urge to confide in the other man? Both thoughts made him queasy.

"Simply a stomach upset," Grantham said.

They were in the Beacon House library, where Kneland had been in the act of letter writing when Grantham arrived.

Grantham enjoyed the library. A large room, all four walls fitted with dark oak bookshelves. Unlike the decorative libraries found in most of society's town houses, the books in here had been read and reread. Some of the spines were so creased, the titles were illegible. Thick blue brocade curtains kept the light from bleaching the cloth covers, and a huge mahogany desk sat next to a cozy arrangement of wide-seated Georgian chairs and settees. The fireplace wasn't lit yet and the lovely landscape by Joshua Reynolds of Richmond brightened the room. Bowls of dried lavender and rose petals scented the air and someone had left a shawl hanging over the back of a chair.

It reminded him of the library at Grange Abbey, where he and Violet had come up with their more outrageous schemes. Since Margaret was present only during the summers, she wasn't always able to temper his and Vi's ridiculous inventions, and the worst of their transgressions always occurred around Christmastime.

Kneland stared at him while he walked in a circle around Grantham's chair.

"'Tisn't a stomach upset. You've the intestinal constitution of a goat. No." Kneland stopped, leaned in close, and sniffed. He leaned back and scrutinized Grantham's shoes. Then he reached over and plucked a hair from Grantham's head.

"The devil!" Grantham roared.

Kneland didn't even blink as he squinted at the hair then held it to his ear, nodding mysteriously.

"As I suspected," he said, his near-black eyes narrowing as if in deep thought.

Grantham snorted. What rubbish was this?

"Woman trouble," the Scot pronounced.

"The only trouble I have is I haven't punched anyone in days," Grantham said, leaping to his feet. "You cannot tell me you've diagnosed women trouble from one hair."

Kneland dropped Grantham's hair in a small rubbish bin and took out a handkerchief with which to wipe his hands.

Bounder.

"No, but your face when I pulled it amused me. I don't need your hair to tell you what ails you. Although one of the members claims she can tell a person's sex from their hair."

"Ridiculous," said Grantham.

"Stuff and nonsense," he agreed, holding up a finger with obnoxious certainty. "The question is . . . who? I haven't heard your name linked with anyone lately. The gossip columns say the Untamed Earl is like a fox run to ground by the persistent pack of matrimonial mamas. Unless this obsession with the greylag goose . . . you're not sniffing 'round Flavia Smythe-Harrows, are you?"

Of all the . . .

"I am not sniffing after her. I don't sniff. I am man. I draw a powerful breath, or I inhale mightily. Either road, I am not courting Flavia."

Grantham threw himself onto the settee, taking great pleasure in the horrific creak of the wooden frame. "I don't *sniff.*"

"Obviously, whomever your sights are set on is not returning your attention or you'd be in a better mood." Kneland paused. "You might consider a grand gesture."

"I need a what?"

"A grand gesture," Kneland explained. "It's what will get you the girl every time."

"Get me the girl? Grand gesture?" Grantham moaned. "Have you been reading Mrs. Foster's books?"

"*The Perils of Miss Cordelia Braveheart and the Castle of Doom* is a brilliant piece of literature," Arthur said. "You see, there is always a grand gesture on the part of the hero at the end. That's what you need for the heroine to admit to her love."

"This is ridiculous. I cannot listen to this."

"I could shoot you," Kneland offered. "Violet proposed to me after I was shot."

What did it say about Grantham's mental state that he considered the offer for a second or two?

"I'm not getting shot. And I'm not dressing up and having a sword fight like Greycliff did. I'm not doing anything ridiculous or undignified or painful because I don't need to."

Kneland leaned back in his chair and crossed his arms over his chest with a self-satisfied air. "Then do not come here and mope because she wants nothing to do with you."

"She does want something to do with me, for your information," Grantham shot back. "Kissed me like there was no tomorrow just the other night."

"Flavia?" Kneland nearly rose from his chair in shock.

"No, not *Flavia*, you great gowke. Someone else," Grantham said. "Someone more mature, for one thing. Flavia is a child."

"Mature, eh? Well, there is no accounting for taste."

"I could shoot *you*," Grantham muttered under his breath.

"What is the problem?" Kneland asked. "She wants something to do with you. You most definitely want to do something with her."

Grantham hesitated. Could he discuss a matter as delicate as negotiating preventatives with another man?

"There is a misunderstanding between us," he began.

Kneland nodded and steepled his fingers. "Misunderstandings are common in Mrs. Foster's novels."

Oh, for the love of . . .

Greycliff had somehow gotten Kneland to read the romantic novels of Mrs. Foster, including the ridiculous *Perils of Miss Cordelia Braveheart*. The two of them were forever rattling on about abandoned mines and forced marriages. Personally, Grantham found her writing to be rather sesquipedalian and awfully reliant on bent spoons and the fortuitous wanderings by of sheep herders.

"This misunderstanding," Grantham said. "It is of a delicate nature."

The question of condoms aside, so much history lay between himself and Margaret. Would sex make their future interactions more fraught?

An even deeper fear niggled at the back of Grantham's head.

What if Margaret considered a night together as "closing the circle"? What if she slept with him simply to consummate a thirteen-year-old unfulfilled desire and finished with him after that? Worries tumbled through his brain.

"I don't know how to talk with her."

"Talk?" Kneland asked. "Talk about what?"

Realizing he'd said the last part out loud, Grantham pulled a pillow out from beneath his head and put it over his mouth, hoping perhaps he'd pass out. When he remained stubbornly conscious, he pulled the pillow away.

"Talk about my . . ." His voice dropped to a pained whisper. "My concerns. My fears."

"Christ Jesu," Kneland said. "Have you a fever? Or has your tiny excuse for a brain finally given up and dribbled out of your ear?" He shook his head. "Talk about *your* fears? Grantham, *men* do not talk about their fears. *Women* talk about their fears."

Grantham sat hugging the pillow to his midriff. "What do men do?"

"Men *act* to take the fear away," Kneland said. "They jump in front of bullets and kiss their wives until they're cross-eyed. They listen to whatever it is women want to tell them and they go and do it. They get up with the baby so she can sleep and gift her boxes of sulfite and carbonic acid when she's sad. They tell them they are beautiful when they cry about their figures and leave them tulips on their pillow on Tuesdays simply because it is a Tuesday. They never, ever admit they are afraid of anything bad happening. Ever. Because if they said it out loud..."

Kneland's mouth closed so tight, his jaw made a popping sound. For a charged second, the men scrutinized each other and saw uncertainty and a distressing vulnerability.

Somehow, they'd gone from joking to coming perilously close to revealing their *feelings* to each other.

Then what? What happened after you revealed the messy insides to someone else? How did you shove them back in once they'd been exposed? What if Grantham's fears were ugly or laughable or unsolvable? What if he lost Kneland's respect?

The realization brought Grantham to his feet. He had to do something to save this friendship or nothing would ever be the same between them again.

"When I'm standing, I can see the top of your head—one of the benefits of you being pathetically small for a grown man—and I do believe you are losing your hair. The lamplight is shining off your pate like sunlight off the North Sea."

Kneland nodded, relief washing across his face. "Your mouth is prettier than a lady's. You need a scar there to match the one on your enormous nose."

A stupid sort of happiness filled Grantham as he lowered his head and slammed into Kneland's gut. It persisted despite the Scot's uncanny ability to flip Grantham over onto his arse and bubbled up even more when Grantham managed to toss Kneland halfway across the room.

Violet came in soon after to break up their fun, scolding them for knocking over the statue of some archeologist or another but neither of them cared. Later that night Grantham surveyed the bruise on his chest and had to ice his knee, but it was well worth it.

No feelings had escaped in the course of the afternoon, and all was right with the world once again.

12

GRANTHAM'S "TALK" WITH Kneland had refreshed him and he woke up in a spirited mood. Before most of London arose, he'd drunk a pot of strong tea, boxed a few rounds at a down-on-its-heels gentlemen's club on the edge of Houndsditch, and gone for a long ramble.

Much as he'd loved his time during his childhood summers with Violet and Margaret, Grantham had also treasured his time alone. He could watch for hours as grumpy badgers dug their setts and knew the song of every species of bird nesting in the trees that created wind barriers between the fields. He followed generations of dormice who lived in the stone walls marking the farmer's property and insisted on helping repair them so the nests would continue undisturbed.

As a soldier, he'd been the only one who enjoyed the long marches, volunteering for scouting missions where he'd be alone in the woods for days on end, learning another landscape and coming to admire its stark beauty and fierce moods before he'd been pulled into the world of men once again.

Although Grantham hadn't the same knowledge of his estate as he'd had of his childhood home, he would learn in time. Six years he'd held the title, but his attention split between the work in Parliament and the needs of his tenants. Once he'd finished shepherding through the Reform Bill, he would retire to the countryside for good. His days left in London were few. If a fine pair of hazel eyes and a sharp tongue were not uppermost in his mind, the thought would bring him far more joy.

This morning he cut his ramble short. The skies were clear for once and he walked to Parliament, where he caught up with Lord Fenwood. Fenwood was close with Lord Ashley, the original author of the Reform Bill, and Grantham had a great deal of respect for him.

What had Margaret told him before he'd made a dog's dinner of the evening?

Listen to their stories.

"Good day, Grantham. You are just the man we wanted to see."

At Fenwood's side stood Mr. Benedict Locksley, a large man who smelled like camphor and held a seat in the Lower House of Parliament. He sent Fenwood a speaking look Grantham couldn't interpret.

"I bought a copy of *The Capital's Chronicle* this morning," Locksley said.

Grantham listened, all right. What he heard in Locksley's tone of voice did not bode well.

"They've a finger on the capital's pulse," Grantham said.

That was *The Chronicle*'s motto.

"Hmmm." Locksley cleared his throat with a derisory sound. "I had heard your paper was taking on the fight for the Reform Bill."

Grantham's gaze went to Fenwood, who lifted one shoulder in a quick shrug.

"Yes, that's the idea," Grantham said.

"One article about a group of geese is not going to solve the conflict between the Church and the Dissenters," Locksley said. "There were no articles in today's issue about the speeches Lord Ashley made to the Society for the Protection of Indigent Children about the planned improvements to the ragged schools. If you'd printed them, it would invite letters on the subject of education reform and a debate would spring up."

The ragged schools were a group of charitable organizations that took donations and relied on volunteers to educate those children too poor to attend the more common Sunday schools. Some folks spoke of forming a union of these schools, which were scattered about London.

While Wolfe had taken his mission to mock Armitage to heart, Grantham understood from Locksley's remarks this wasn't enough. His personal animosity toward the Guardians of Domesticity shouldn't overshadow an opportunity to advance a cause he cared about.

"Your insights are welcomed, Locksley," he said. "I will keep them in mind when I go to the newspaper today and speak with the editor."

Rather than appearing pleased that Grantham agreed with his critique, Locksley's mouth pinched into a kidney shape.

Hadn't Margaret said listening could effect change? If this was true, why did Locksley stare at him as though he'd grown a third eye?

"You weren't at the Demmings' ball last night," Fenwood remarked, drawing Grantham's attention. "You have not been seen at any evening events lately. The ladies miss the Untamed Earl. Can it be one special woman has finally caught your interest and you are spending your evenings pining beneath her window?"

Grantham forced himself to laugh and make a stupid comment about becoming boring in his old age.

Locksley frowned; his lips almost inverted with disapproval. "If you want to make your mark, stop courting notoriety." After an emphatic nod, he shambled off to find a large chair in which to nap.

The Untamed Earl. How Grantham hated that name. Not only did it imply he was uncivilized, but it also implied a woman's job was to tame him. What an unappealing thought.

He'd brought it on himself, to be sure. Did he allow himself to become a caricature because of his annoyance with the way society saw him and his disdain for the title? Yes. His greatest regret was not foreseeing it might hamper the one good thing he'd done with his life.

"I don't see myself scaring up a bride before the bill comes to a vote," Grantham said. "Other than attend dinners and print more articles on the Reform Bill, what else can I do?"

"You've come a long way toward restoring the title and making a name for yourself," Fenwood said kindly. "The last earl never bothered to take his seat in Lords and your father . . ."

The older man paused and cleared his throat diplomatically. Grantham lifted one shoulder to signal nothing more needed to be said.

"If you are patient and surround yourself with the right sort of folk, bide your time, and learn from others, someday you will have the power to lead in Lords," Fenwood explained.

Bide your time.

Be patient.

Someday.

Grantham thought of the boy who cowered in a corner as his father terrorized his mam and drank their last coins away. He thought of the children who might be saved from such a fate if this bill passed, how they could get an education and leave behind generation upon generation of poverty and violence. Everything inside him called for *action*, not patience.

If he'd been raised in the bosom of his father's family, none of this would be so difficult for him. Grantham would have understood these men without pause, would have known how to wait them out while they spewed platitudes and fattened themselves at the expense of the poor.

Then again, if he'd been raised by his father's family, he would never have met Vi and Margaret, never understood the ways society ground them down to silent acquiescence. If girls were allowed to be educated the same as boys, there would be no need for a secret group of women scientists. Women like Margaret would not have to work twice as hard as a man with less intelligence.

Locksley's admonitions ringing in his head, Grantham soon took his leave. Upon entering the offices of *The Capital's Chronicle*, Grantham's sour mood grew even worse as Sam Fenley's voice reverberating off the plaster walls served as his greeting.

The first floor of *The Chronicle* was shaped like an H with a long narrow desk sitting right in the middle. This was where a timid clerk received the mail and listened to the complaints, most of which were directed toward Mr. Poppers, the columnist who wrote about haberdashery. Mr. Poppers was actually Evans, a reporter who'd never set foot in half the establishments whose wares he extolled.

Another clerk accepted payments and wrote out the descriptions of the various advertisements that were placed at the back of the newspaper and paid for the bulk of *The Chronicle*'s expenses.

Upstairs, Wolfe kept his office alongside a storage room for older issues of *The Chronicle* and a meeting room that doubled as a bedroom when one of the employees worked late and could not go home. Downstairs, the main work of the paper happened in the area between Evan's and Dodson's desks and a smaller meeting room where Wolfe ate his meals. In this room, Grantham found Sam Fenley, springing about like a grasshopper. Evans, Dodson, and Wolfe were sitting at a table in the center of the room, watching the young man with a mixture of suspicion and amusement.

"Sales have dropped how much?" Sam asked. "Sixty percent? Which folks are no longer reading the paper?"

"All of them," answered Wolfe dryly. When he caught sight of

Grantham, Wolfe pointed at Sam with a half-eaten pasty. "Young Fenley here claims you sent him. He's got 'ideas' for us."

Sam popped up from his seat, enthusiasm written on his face. "Lord Grantham. I have toured the entire building."

"Never stopped talking the entire time," said Wolfe from around the lump of pasty in his mouth.

"The ideas are coming to me faster than I can write them," Sam exclaimed.

Wolfe brushed the last of the pasty crumbs from his shirt front and considered the young man. "What do you want, Fenley? To give us your opinions? Your da might not appreciate you giving them away for free."

Sam scoffed. "Everything has its price." He held his topper in his hands and rocked on his heels for a moment. "What I propose is Fenley's receives a half sheet of paper for its advertisements each week."

He held up his hand at Wolfe's stuttered protest. "In return, I will recruit enough advertisers to more than make up for the lack of revenue from the half page. In addition, I will devote two days a week to the newspaper, without a salary."

"Two days a week for a wet-behind-the-ears emporium clerk to run around and tell us how to do what we already know?" asked Wolfe.

Sam didn't take offense. Working with the public must have given him thick skin, for his mood remained buoyant.

"Two days a week for the brain that increased the sales of Fenley's Fripperies by thirty percent over the past two years," boasted the young man. "Who do you think came up with the ideas that have landed our emporium in the press time and again? Why, if you'll remember, gentlemen, the watch had to be called this summer to stop a stampede when Fenley's launched its line of Cora's Comfort Corsets."

Grantham scratched his chin. "I don't remember that."

"It's true. We wrote a story about it. Evans wasn't the same for weeks after witnessing it," Wolfe said.

"Yes, and no other emporium in London sells hand cream made by the Queen's beehives. Royal Bee Balm. I arranged that." Sam ran a hand through his hair, which fell in a stylish wave over his forehead, nearly covering one eye. "I'm young, but I've done more to convince people to part with their coin than anyone here."

Now Wolfe frowned, crumpling the greasy newsprint in which his pasty had been wrapped. Idly, Grantham wondered if it was a copy of *The Chronicle*.

"Parting with coin is secondary," said Wolfe. "The men here write stories that aim to inform the public."

"Inform the public of something you want them to believe," Sam countered. "Perhaps I want to do more than sell beard oil. Perhaps I want to turn my talents to selling ideas."

"Seems to me Mr. Fenley is exactly the kind of man we need at *The Chronicle* if it's going to be profitable enough to pay for your vision, Mr. Wolfe," Grantham said.

"Must it be a man?"

Grantham turned in surprise. Standing in the doorway were Miss Althea Dertlinger and Mrs. Mala Hill.

Mala's hand gripped a covered basket.

Within the space of a heartbeat, Grantham leaped onto a chair, hat held out in front of him and ready to use it if necessary. To do what, he wasn't certain.

"Good day, Lord Grantham." Mala said. She held up her basket. "Hedgehogs are nocturnal, I've told you before."

When he did not move, she sighed. "I don't have any with me."

This did not assuage Grantham in the slightest.

"One might have crawled in your basket when you weren't looking," he said, pointing at the cloth.

"Really?" asked Sam, delighted.

"No." Mala peeled back the cover of her basket and showed them tidy rows of scones. "No hedgehogs."

Sam deflated, but Wolfe perked up enough to rise from his seat.

"Might I be introduced?" he asked.

Introductions were made and scones dispensed while Grantham hesitantly stepped onto the floor. Evans went and fetched another chair to set at the round weathered oak table that sat in the center of the room, while Dodson cleared a low shelf of piles of paper and furtively dusted the surface with a dirty handkerchief. The room had three windows on one side of the wall and the rare London sunshine shone through the hazy glass, exposing the shoddy housekeeping of Wolfe's staff.

Grantham supposed they were there to write stories, not to dust the furniture. Still, he was grateful the women seemed not to notice. Sam and Mala chatted merrily about his pet hedgehog, Fermat, and Althea inspected the office, asking Evans and Dodson fifty thousand questions. Wolfe stared at them all the while he chewed his scone. When he'd finished, he crossed his arms over his chest.

"An earl, an unmarried society miss, the wife of a barrister, and the scion of Fenley's Fripperies. Hedgehogs. Hmmmm. What is the connection?"

Sam spoke quickly. "My sister, Letty, was a member of Athena's Retreat, as are Mrs. Hill and Miss Dertlinger."

"Ah. The ladies club," Wolfe said. "Of which Victor Armitage strongly disapproves." His grey-green eyes alit on Grantham. "And your involvement, my lord?"

"Is easily sussed for anyone who reads the society pages," Grantham said curtly. He did not want Wolfe delving too deeply into the club. "To what do we owe the pleasure of your visit, ladies?"

Mala and Althea took their seats at the table next to one another.

"We want to help with the newspaper," Mala announced.

Wolfe choked on his second scone. "You what?"

"The ladies of Athena's Retreat wish to contribute to your newspaper," Althea said. "Considering the terrible things the Guardians of Domesticity have said about us, we would like the chance to rebut their arguments. Especially their assertion that ladies should not gather outside the home to learn about the natural world."

"What would you write about?" Grantham inquired.

"Science," said Mala.

Althea leaned forward, her spectacles glittering in the wan sunlight. "More specifically, the role science plays in our lives. For example, we could have a column for women on how to use science in cleaning and housekeeping."

"Why would we run a column for women in the newspaper?" asked Wolfe. "Women don't read newspapers."

Silence fell as Mala and Althea turned as one and pierced Wolfe with their stares. At least the man had the wherewithal to appear concerned. Little did he know Mala had access to an endless source of hedgehogs. Things could go badly at that moment.

An icy voice sounded from the door. "On what do you base your supposition?"

Wolfe's mouth dropped open and Grantham whipped around. Behind him, Margaret had entered the office. Despite the way in which they had parted yesterday, he could not help but smile. Her presence made the day brighter, her unique scent of competence and lavender settling around him like an embrace.

"It's considered unfeminine. I've never seen a woman reading a newspaper. I suppose . . ." Wolfe stopped speaking, his head lowering and shoulders dropping as if waiting for a blow.

"Considering the state of your beard, the stains on your shirt, and the excruciating color of your waistcoat, I assume you do not live with a woman and thus do not know what you are talking about. This is quite common among most men," Margaret said as she came all the way into the room and stood behind Mala and Althea.

"Studies bear this out," Mala added.

"Even casual observation confirms this statement," said Althea.

Sam raised a finger as if to object and Grantham shook his head. Silly boy. Nothing good could come of arguing with a trio of scientists. They start talking about variables and datum and y axes and made the man look like an even bigger idiot.

"I can assure you women indeed read newspapers," said Margaret. "They read the discarded papers left by their husbands."

"Or sneak them from their papas before they're used as kindling," said Althea.

"Or they read days-old ones left in the reading rooms," offered Mala.

"You don't think women read your paper because you've never gone out and sold it to them," Margaret concluded.

Wolfe shook his head, like a dog come in from a rain. "It's not a ladies' magazine; why would I sell it to ladies? And who are you?"

"Allow me to introduce you," said Grantham. "This is Madame Gault. Our neighbor and the proprietor of Gault Engineering, soon to be the preeminent engineering firm in all of Britain."

For the first time since she'd entered the office, Margaret glanced at him, and her grateful smile warmed him from his toes. He fought a blush and executed a bow to cover his sudden awkwardness.

"'Tis a pleasure to have you visit. To what do we owe the honor?" he asked.

"Mala sent round a note she and Althea were here and might need my assistance."

Sam, meanwhile, had pulled the brim of his topper nearly shapeless in his excitement. "But this is brilliant. Your problem is you don't have anything that makes you stand out from the other broadsheets."

"We have a column on haberdashery," Evans pointed out.

"So does every other magazine and newspaper out there," Sam said.

"We've fine reporting on the bills before Parliament." Wolfe tipped the basket of scones toward himself and frowned at the crumbs. "We give the public information it needs to make sound choices."

"But it's *boring* information reported in a *boring* manner," Sam shot back. "The ladies have a brilliant idea. You write your stories, but you write them in such a way they relate to science."

"Science?" Wolfe asked, one hand paused in the act of reaching over to take Dodson's last scone.

"Science," Grantham echoed thoughtfully.

"I think it's a marvelous idea," Margaret said.

Sam preened while Wolfe stared at the scone thoughtfully, set it down, then studied Grantham.

"What about Armitage?" Wolfe asked.

Already thinking about this, Grantham leaned back in his chair and surveyed the motley collection of people gathered around him.

"We will not let up on him. The Guardians of Domesticity are against women gaining a scientific education. We make the case in favor of it."

From the corner of his eye, Grantham gauged Margaret's reaction and continued, "I was reminded today my argument with Armitage stemmed originally from his opposition to education reform. I want to see Lord Ashley's speeches on reforms reprinted on our front pages from now on. Education goes hand in hand with science."

The others spoke over one another in excitement, but Grantham ignored them, watching Margaret instead. She stood back from the table, the weak sunlight glancing off the shiny aubergine-colored ribbon trimming her dark blue bonnet. Like most of her clothing, the trimming was simple and elegant.

She must think a great deal about how she appeared to others. A woman who worked in a man's profession found herself constantly in men's company. Men being what they were, there must have been some who thought because she was a woman, she was there for their pleasure.

Her clothing communicated nothing to Grantham about the woman within. There were no extraneous details, no whimsical touches, or bright colors.

Having to go through your day wearing an armor that shouted "unexceptional" must be a chore for a woman with Margaret's beauty. And Grantham, was he any different from those men?

For here he sat, staring at her respectable dress and nondescript bonnet, wondering if he would ever have another chance to see her naked.

"You are the owner, my lord." Wolfe did not seem especially put out, but neither did he bubble over with excitement like the others. "If you want to try this, it is up to you."

Decisions were presented to Grantham nearly every day. Unlike Margaret, he had the luxury of making a terrible choice without having an employer take him to task over it. In fact, there were few people in England who had the power to condemn his actions, and none of them ever would.

The consequences of his decisions rolled downhill.

The power sometimes left him with a hollow ache in his gut. It would be nice to have someone with whom he could consult, someone to whom he would be accountable.

Right now? His decisions all centered around Margaret's approval.

LATER THAT EVENING, Margaret pulled a copy of *The Capital's Chronicle* closer to her eyes. Could she blame the small print, her exhaustion, or finally starting to feel her age as she squinted at the listings of rooms for rent? A single candle sputtered on the desk and Margaret interlocked her fingers, stretching her arms over her head. The chair squeaked in protest, and she got to her feet, shuffling in a worn pair of Turkish slippers over to the window.

Since accepting the commission to design the tunnel, Margaret had concluded she must separate herself from the Retreat. Eventually a piece of information would slip out and the members would realize she hadn't just Armitage's tangential support of the project she'd accepted—she'd taken his money as well.

She'd spoken with Milly earlier when she, Lady Potts, and a handful of other scientists were getting ready to leave for the day.

"I do not think you should make my work the subject of a subcommittee," Margaret had told her.

"Why not? You are a woman who is progressing science and you will be given public credit," Milly insisted. "More important, you did this on your own without family connections or an aristocratic title to protect you. Imagine what young women will think when they learn of what you've done."

Yes, and imagine what they would think if Margaret failed? If they learned she spent every day unsure of her talents and worried about exposure? Shouldn't she feel like a role model if she was going to be one?

"What of Flavia?" Margaret asked. "She is a scientist as well. Shouldn't we be considering her arguments? Finding a compromise?"

Lady Potts sniffed. "Compromise. That is what women are forced to do, day in and day out. Never allowed to take credit. Never allowed to stand at the front. Is a group of reactionaries going to water down your success?"

Violet had been right. This was not only about the tunnel. Lady Potts and Milly were motivated by their own history of having been deterred from pursuing their passions.

"Why do we have to set ourselves against one another?" Margaret asked.

"Someone has to win." Milly's gaze sharpened. "If we slow down, we are going to be trampled over. One compromise forces another. Who might the next group be to object? Or the next? How will you lead us into the future if you allow others to hold you back?"

Was Milly correct? Could progress come only with a determination that set aside other concerns?

"Wilhelmina is simply indulging in a misguided nostalgia in the wake of her father's passing," Milly explained. "He did not approve of the railways, nor canals. The English countryside should remain unsullied by commerce, never mind how the common folk are supposed to make a living."

"You would do well to stop inviting Victor Armitage to speak at those events," Lady Potts added. "It draws sympathy away from your cause. That man is poison, and anything associated with him will surely pay a price."

Thanks to Grantham, the damage had been done. Margaret's tunnel had become a subject of controversy and she would once again lose a refuge.

Pity. She loved the guest rooms here. The walls were painted in soothing shades of peach and plum with bright rag rugs and pretty curtains. In the main room was a comfortable bed, a desk, a dresser, and a large armoire. In the smaller room at the front two large armchairs stood next to a settee and she'd room enough for friends to gather for a pot of tea and a coze. At night if she couldn't sleep, there were two separate libraries full of books and periodicals on the second and third floors of the club.

The delightful lethargy after her bath had cooled with her thoughts.

Leaning against the windowpane, she peered at the kitchen garden. In the moonlight, she could make out the rows of herbs Mrs. Sweet grew for her cures and the flattened dog roses that had suffered Grantham's attentions on the day of her arrival.

Turning away from the view, Margaret pulled a nightgown from her drawer and inspected it before pulling it over her head. The seams at the shoulder were starting to fray. Margaret had no skill with the needle—had never contemplated learning such a useless task when studying physics as a girl.

Her father had been convinced she would follow him into cryptology, but Margaret had no patience and no aptitude for that branch of mathematics. Disappointed, he'd taken solace in her studies of physics. A kind man who lived always in his head, he'd naively assumed women would be accepted into university during her lifetime and she would carry on the Strong name by publishing fantastic new theories.

He'd died before she found her love for the science of engineering. Margaret had only one parent left to horrify with her choices.

A tapping at her door prevented her from becoming too maudlin. Margaret threw a blanket over her shoulders and opened the door, half expecting to see Violet come to pry her secrets loose as she had in the old days.

The other half already knew who it would be at this time of night, considering what lay unfinished between them.

"Here." Grantham thrust an enormous arrangement of hothouse flowers at her. Margaret fell back at the sheer weight of them, and he took the opportunity to follow her into the room.

"What are these for?" she asked.

He forbore from answering as he stood in the center of the ante-chamber and surveyed the room.

"This is rather small," he observed, walking over to fireplace to peer at a framed print.

"It's a perfectly reasonable-sized set of rooms," she said. Setting the arrangement on an end table, Margaret marveled at the size and variety of the blooms. "Bought out a greenhouse, did you?"

"Huh. This one has blue hind legs. I thought tarantulas were brown."

She jumped away from the arrangement. Had Lady Potts's tarantulas gotten loose again? The entomologist has sworn she had perfected her feeding system so the spiders would never again escape.

Grantham pointed at a print hanging above her mantle. "This is one of those pictures of Lady Potts's collection of tarantulas she had made for the baby's nursery. Kneland has been taking them down and putting them in different rooms over the house but somehow they keep reappearing on Baby Georgie's walls."

Oh, thank goodness.

Nodding with satisfaction, Grantham crossed his arms and smirked. "Devious woman. I enjoy her company, spiders and all."

Without another word, he walked past her into the bedroom. Margaret considered whether she should follow him or take herself downstairs away from temptation.

For he was here to tempt her.

Tempt her away from her determination not to let herself be distracted from her Plan, tempt her to remember the boy he'd been and how much he'd meant to her. Tempt her to let down her guard—and take off her clothes.

Margaret wasn't fooled by his apparent nonchalance.

"You have a copy of *The Capital's Chronicle*?" he called from the bedchamber. "Did you read the review of Lender's Chophouse? That reporter, Evans, he's too free with the adverbs if you ask me."

Margaret sighed.

Temptation wouldn't leave without a swift kick in the arse.

Inside her bedroom, Grantham had made himself at home, having removed his bulky overcoat and hung it from a hook on the wall and taken a seat at her desk, booted feet on the chest at the foot of her bed. He wore a claret-colored dinner jacket with a brocaded salmon waistcoat beneath and a black silk cravat. One of the candles on the two-pronged candelabra on her desk sputtered and tiny orange and gold sparks illuminated the robin's-egg blue marbling in his indigo irises. A thick forelock of his hair fell across his forehead in a way designed to make her fingertips tingle with the desire to smooth it back.

He might as well have come dressed in the silver and burgundy cloth that wrapped the most desirable gifts from Fenley's Fripperies the way he made her heart leap in her chest and her body take notice. In his presence her skin buzzed with awareness like the low hum of a tuning fork. If he left now, the resonance of their attraction would linger for hours.

The only relief was friction, the slow slide of skin against skin.

"Why did you bring me flowers?" she asked, mouth dry at the direction of her thoughts.

Grantham studied her for a moment, nodding as if having a conversation only he could hear. "I am making a grand gesture," he said.

"Oh, no." Margaret lost some of her abstraction. "You haven't been reading Mrs. Foster's novels, have you? No one is going to burst in here and shoot you, are they?"

He shrugged but a blush appeared high on his cheeks. "No. Nothing like that. A grand gesture is the prerequisite for an apology, I am told. I wanted to apologize for what happened the other night."

Pushing his boots off the chest to make room, Margaret walked past him to stand by the fire. Not until she turned around to say some-thing about romance novels and reality did she realize the fire made her nightgown transparent.

Judging by Grantham's face, he'd seen it as well and her stomach flipped over.

"What happened the other night was to be expected," she said.

Grantham hung his head. "That I wouldn't have thought of pre-ventatives before trying to make love with you?"

"No," she said. His hair fell forward like a sheet of gold and Mar-garet gave in to the urge plaguing her for weeks. She walked over to where he sat and ran her hands through his hair. The sound he made—half gasp, half groan—reverberated on the floorboards. Be-tween her legs, a low humming vibration answered back.

Pulling her into his lap, he held her hips as she straddled him, thrill-ing at the sensation of his thick, hard cock pressed against her core.

"We act as though we still know each other," she explained.

Margaret was constantly being reminded of her great height and size, but when Grantham wrapped his palms around her calves and smoothed his hands upward, lifting her nightgown and leaving in his wake a prickly heat, she felt fragile in a way she never had before.

Undoing the knot of his cravat with steady fingers, she shivered low in her belly. The linen was thick and of excellent quality, and the buttons on his waistcoat she slipped from their fastenings were real brass.

"You are not my old playmate. You are an earl. It behooves me to remember that and not scold you for whatever behavior you have or have not been indulging in since we have been parted," she said. "I must apologize as well. I could have asked you questions instead of making assumptions."

Grantham stilled her actions and held her hands in his, holding her gaze.

"Instead of acting as though you were making assumptions, I could have given you answers. The subject is not one I have a great deal of experience speaking about with a lady, which accounts for how I reacted but does not excuse it."

He pulled her hands to his mouth and gently kissed the tips of her fingers.

"I am sorry, Margaret, I did not think to use preventatives before going to bed with you."

A prickling behind her eyes had Margaret blinking rapidly. His apology moved her—the words were unembellished and simple but what touched Margaret most deeply was his sincerity.

How many men would have said the same?

"I am sorry for thinking ill of you in the moment. I know you would never put a woman in jeopardy," Margaret said. "You are too kind."

Grantham frowned. "You will ruin my reputation as a rake."

She set her forehead against his, her heart swelling with tenderness. "Would you like to try again?" she whispered.

Robin's-egg blue turned to indigo at her words, and his smile sharpened with avarice.

"Oh, yes," he said, voice low and dark.

Pulling her hands from his grasp, Margaret slipped the waistcoat from his torso, and ran her fingers over the fine lawn of his shirt.

Grantham lifted her off his lap and carried her over to her bed as if she weighed nothing. Setting her there, he stood back, undid his boots, and placed them against the wall. In his stockinged feet, he walked to where his greatcoat hung.

Reaching into one large pocket, he pulled out a bundle wrapped in brown paper and tied with a string.

"Behold," he said with utmost dignity. "Four tins of Mrs. Philips's finest condoms." He tossed the packet to her, and she caught it.

"You must think highly of your stamina you've brought that many," Margaret said, laughing. "I hope you have the knack of them. They can be tricky to keep on sometimes."

Grantham's forehead wrinkled, but he turned again to the coat and pulled out a flask. "Vinegar," he said, setting the bottle on her desk. From another pocket, he pulled a pink and white striped silk pouch. "A sponge."

"Are you presenting me with choices?" she asked. How incredibly thoughtful.

Grantham reached into yet another pocket and removed a small lemon. "Lemon," he said. "It's a preventative. Apparently, you put it . . . er . . . I read a pamphlet but . . ."

"I'm certain you don't need the advice of a pamphlet," she teased him. "A man such as yourself most likely invented ten of the twelve different ways to make such an undertaking extremely pleasurable."

A lovely blush colored his skin and Margaret reclined, making certain her nightgown pulled up as she did, displaying the sight of her naked legs to her thighs.

"Come here," she whispered when he glanced at the lemon then to her again.

Grantham set the lemon on the desk and pushed his hair out of his eyes. "Didn't you want to . . ."

He studied the vinegar and the lemon, biting his lip.

"How do you . . . what should I—" He broke off, rubbed his mouth, then backed up.

Why had he moved away rather than toward her?

"If you don't want to use it, we have other options, thanks to your foresight," she assured him. "Which is your preference?"

The blush had faded from Grantham's face, and he'd turned slightly grey. "My preference?" he repeated.

Margaret sat up, her delightful fog of desire quickly dissipating.

"Do not tell me you don't want to use them," she said.

"No, no. I want to, I simply . . . er . . ."

What ailed the man?

Without warning, Grantham spun round and grabbed his boots.

"I forgot I have to go do something important."

He had to *what*?

"You have to *what*?" she asked.

Without bothering to sit, he pushed his feet into the boots and could only fit them in halfway so he wobbled like a colt as he grabbed his cravat. "Very important thing to do that requires me to leave right now," he babbled.

Leave?

"You," said Margaret as she slid off the bed, ". . . are going nowhere."

"You can keep the lemon," he offered, trying to unhook his coat while shoving his feet even farther into his boots. "Use it for lemonade or somesuch. Lemon tart. Pie. Good with tea."

A strange but important thought occurred to her.

"Really must, ow! Margaret! What are you doing?"

He was going nowhere. To be certain of this, Margaret had launched herself at him, and grabbed him around the neck, clinging to his back.

"You take your clothes off and finish what you have started," she said.

Grantham spun in a circle, trying to unlock her hands, which she'd clasped tightly around his neck.

"Can' bree. Maggie," he wheezed. "Leggo. Leggo."

"No." She wrapped her legs around his waist and held on as he bucked and arched. "Tell me what the devil is going on, George Willis. Is this some sort of revenge?"

Grantham made an inarticulate noise. Margaret relaxed her pressure on his windpipe and slipped off. Gasping for air, Grantham stumbled over the edge of the rug and fell onto the floor, his head barely missing the side of the bed.

"Are you trying to kill me?" he gasped.

Margaret lowered herself and sat on his chest, her legs trapping his arms to his side. She leaned forward, hands on either side of his head, and her braid fell over her shoulder, hitting him in the face.

"You tell me what is happening here," she demanded.

"Maggie."

"Don't Maggie me. You . . ." Margaret stopped speaking and studied his face.

She thought about his lack of preventatives, about the fact he was over thirty and not yet married, and the way he'd struggled with her dress the other night.

"George," she said softly. "Can it be you've not a great deal of experience with preventatives?"

Grantham pulled an arm out from beneath her leg with a grunt and covered his eyes with it.

"Could be," he said grudgingly.

Margaret waited a moment, then pulled his arm away. "Can it be you have little experience with preventatives because you don't have much experience with . . . intercourse?"

"Could be," he repeated, a blush creeping from his neck to his cheeks.

Well, this was unexpected.

"How little experience, exactly?" she asked.

George blew a breath out from between his lips and stared up at the ceiling.

"All things considered," he said, "and not telling tales or breaking confidences, if one tallied it up, which one could, if one were so in-clined to do such a thing, one could reasonably . . ."

"George." Margaret shook him by the shoulders.

"None," he said, squeezing his eyes shut as he made the revelation. "No experience with intercourse. I have never made love with a woman."

How could this be?

George Willis, Earl Grantham, one of the most eligible bachelors in the peerage, known throughout London as having the ability to charm almost any lady, was a virgin.

13

MARGARET SAT ON her haunches and studied Grantham like a damned specimen beneath one of those thinga mascopers. The women at Athena's Retreat did it all the time. The sensation of being scrutinized wasn't unfamiliar, but he wished he knew more about what went on in Margaret's brain.

"Don't be embarrassed," she said gently.

"Too late for that," he replied.

Rolling off him, she rested on her side next to him on the colorful rug, her head propped on her hand. Beneath her nightgown, her breasts moved freely, unrestrained by any corset or chemise.

The thought would have excited him beyond belief only moments before, but . . . could embarrassment be permanent?

"Was it the Army?" she asked.

It took him a moment to understand the non sequitur, the fear of impotence born from shame occupying the largest part of his thoughts.

"Was what the—oh." Grantham shook his head and rolled over on to his side, mirroring her position. The rug was soft so far as rugs went, but the floor beneath was hard.

"No. It isn't due to any physical condition. I just haven't done it—made love—with anyone."

There would be a lump on the back of his head later. Grantham groaned as he got to his feet and held out a hand to Margaret. She took it and rose, her soft, unbound breasts brushing against his torso as she stood.

"Come," she said, and pulled him onto the bed.

Grantham admired her rounded arse beneath the nearly sheer muslin as Margaret clambered onto the bed before him.

He settled himself beside her and they mimicked their pose from the floor, face-to-face.

"How many times have you tried? Was the woman—"

Grantham cut her off.

"I haven't ever tried," he said. "Let's be clear about that from the outset, shall we? My pieces are in working order were I to . . . go ahead."

Those eyes of hers, they were not soft, nor did they shine like stars. They were the passageway for information to reach her brain, and Margaret had an active brain. Grantham let himself be scrutinized while he tried to gather his thoughts. Thoughts kept getting scrambled by the scent of her, the way her body dipped and curved in such a way he wanted to run his hands along her side and over her belly.

"Then why, Grantham?"

Margaret reached over and pushed his hair out of his face, but he rolled away from her. He couldn't look at her if he was going to tell her the truth.

"There never was a right time." He pondered that sentence and tried again. "There never was the right person."

Margaret hovered over him, blocking his excellent view of the plaster molding on her ceiling. "I don't understand. You and I could barely keep ourselves from consummation that summer. I remember it as an exercise in torture. I would have thought you would be like a stag in rut when you were a young man."

Grantham took hold of her arms and rolled them both, so he was now atop her. He kept his body a few inches over hers, propping himself on his arms. He'd known somewhere in the back of his head he would have to tell her. He couldn't pretend a great deal of experience despite the naughty books he'd read in anticipation of the act.

Knowing he would have to speak and saying the words aloud were very different experiences.

"When we were young, I wanted to be with you so badly, I thought about it every second of every day."

Her lips parted slightly and the pink arc of the tip of her tongue peeked out in invitation. He wanted to meld his mouth to hers and taste her, lapping up the secret parts of her with relish.

Instead, he told Margaret his most tightly held secrets.

For they were friends, were they not?

"I walked around in too-tight skin. Every brush of my smallclothes against my cock made me harder, every time I caught the scent of something floral or feminine, I would want to seek you out and touch you. I imagined what you would look like, what we would do, so many times I feared the village priest was correct, and I would go blind from lusting after you."

The smallest of touches between them, the brush of the back of his hand against hers when they sat with Violet beneath the willow, the fortuitous times when they were alone and would hesitantly clasp hands before desire bolstered courage and they would set their lips to each other conspired to keep Grantham from eating or sleeping. He would replay the sensation of her fingers on his skin for hours in his bed at night.

"Remember Tommy Peyton?"

"The boy from your village who could spit ten feet?" she asked.

"The spitter," he confirmed. "He had two older brothers that worked for a printer in Alford. The boys would pass pictures around—tame enough stuff but it fed the fire that burned inside me every single moment. All I wanted, all I dreamed of, all I could think about was making love to you, Margaret."

When he paused, she raised her hands up from where they lay across her stomach and set them on either side of his face, tracing his lips with her thumb.

What began as a tender gesture turned deeply erotic when she pressed her thumb into his bottom lip, then sucked her own bottom lip into her mouth. Grantham dipped his head to kiss her but she dragged her thumb down his chin to his chest and undid the last of his buttons, pulled the shirt from his trousers, and tugged it over his head. Rising onto his knees, he took the shirt from her and tossed it to the floor.

She scooted out from beneath him and rose to her knees, so they were once again facing each other.

"Tell me the rest," she said, brows drawn together as if she were working one of her equations.

The rest? "Then I left."

Her nose scrunched in question. "What do you mean?"

He shrugged. "Then I left for Canada."

She cocked her head, trying to hear something he hadn't yet confessed. "But surely you must have wanted to try it with another woman."

Giving in to curiosity, Grantham ran one finger along her collarbone, close to where her pulse fluttered in her throat. Softer than down, softer than the finest silk, her skin released the scent of lilacs and salt and something uniquely Margaret.

"I did, but it wasn't the *same*." Running his finger over her breast-bone, he stopped at her heartbeat and placed his palm there, relishing the warmth of her.

"There were women who followed the drum." He pushed lightly against her, marking the bones beneath her skin, amazed at how someone so strong could be at the same time so fragile. "They were obliging—or so I hoped—but I never wanted to be obliged."

Grantham said nothing about the other women. Officers' wives. Women in the small outposts they sometimes visited. Women whose lives had been so bleak, he'd felt only a frustrated sympathy.

"I kept waiting for it to be the same with someone else," he explained. "Wanted so much to know that reverence, that fever we both came down with that summer."

Dear God, she was beautiful, his Maggie, staring at him in the waning light of a candle stub. Some might find her too tall, her shoulders too broad, or her hair not a pleasing shade. They were blind, ignorant fools. This woman was perfection, and he would gladly spend forever worshipping the body that housed her. He simply had to tell her one last thing.

"I could not find another woman that did all those things at once. No other woman made me wild with longing, no other woman had me wanting to peel my own skin from my bones so I could be free of the constant desire."

She placed her hand over his and bowed her head slightly. "Those are the feelings of first awakening. They fade over time."

Ah. She thought he didn't understand.

"As I grew older, I realized I chased the dream of a seventeen-year-old boy. Still, it didn't take away my longing."

Her face turned slightly to the side as if searching out an invisible answer.

"Longing for . . . ?"

Now Grantham moved his hand, so he cupped her chin and met her gaze with his own. The world drew into a tight circle and consisted only of the thrum of their heartbeats, the shush of their breath, the lightning sitting dormant at the tips of their fingers.

"If it could not be perfection, I could at least ask for grace," he whispered. "And so, I waited. I waited until I met someone I respected. Someone who would be kind and generous. Someone I could trust."

"Grace," she repeated.

Margaret reached both hands out and set them to his cheeks, pulling him slightly closer, palms warm against his hot skin. The tension in his belly tightened and a distant rumble of thunder echoed in his pulse.

"Is that me, George?" she whispered. "Have I earned your trust?"

What he wanted to say was this.

Who else could it be in all the world?

He wanted to say this as well.

I have been waiting for this moment for so long.

Instead, he said this.

"I trust you to be patient. To tell me if I am too clumsy or too—"

She cut him off with a kiss. Not a hungry kiss or a kiss of longing, but with a closemouthed sweetness that brought him back to their first tender fumbling.

They weren't young anymore. Margaret had been married, had known another man intimately, and Grantham had closed a part of himself off since they parted.

It didn't matter.

When they kissed, a sense of comfort settled into him, deep in his bones, and the world, which had been shaking and heaving beneath his feet since this woman walked back into his life, it stopped and breathed a sigh of contentment as if to say, *Here.*

Here is where you always should be.

MARGARET BROKE THE kiss and stared at Grantham, trying hard to reconcile the pieces of him into one. The enormity of the gift he offered staggered her and she hoped she would be worthy. Something of her concern must have shown on her face.

"Of course, the issue is moot," he said lightly. "Confessions of virginity have a deleterious effect on a man's libido. I might as well leave now."

Oh, this silly, glorious, wonderful man.

"Is that so?" she asked. "There is no way I can arouse your interest?"

Grantham sighed a long, put-upon sigh. "I doubt even you could . . . Oh, I say . . . well, would you look at that?"

Having reached over and stroked the back of her hand along the outline of his already hard cock, she bit the bottom of her lip to keep from giggling.

"George," she said, grateful his humor had dispelled her misgivings, cognizant of the importance of the act to him. To her. "May I undress you?"

If he hadn't left her years ago, they would have done this by the light of the moon, hidden beneath the curtain of willow leaves. They would have been bound forever, neither of them having enough willpower to see beyond the act itself and worry about the consequences.

A few moments of physical release and Margaret would have committed herself to traveling thousands of miles away and given up any hope of becoming an engineer.

The last of her resentment or grief for what could have been detached itself and floated away forever.

"Stand up."

When he climbed off the bed and stood, she knelt before him, letting her nightgown slip from her shoulder and reveal the top half of her breast as she unbuttoned his trousers and pulled them over his muscled thighs. Pretending she did not hear the rasp of an indrawn breath, she nudged his legs, so he stepped out of his trousers. She pulled at his stockings and sat on her heels, taking the time to admire the long arc of his thighs, the bunched muscles of his calves. His penis was hard and curved in toward his belly, its outline clear beneath the fine lawn of his drawers. Reaching up, she untied the tapes, pulling him free of the soft material and baring him before her.

Remaining on her knees, she let her hands learn the landscape of him. The soft curls ran down the center of his stomach and grew thicker and dark at the root of his cock. The way his quadriceps twitched when she cupped his heavy sac in her hand.

"Are you . . ." He cleared his throat. "Are you going to let me do the same?"

"In a moment," she told him. "Right now, I am listening to you."

Indeed, she listened to an exhale that ended in a hiss when she set the tip of her tongue along the skin bisecting his ballocks, then the length of his cock. She listened as well to the low groan when she took the whole of him in her hand and pulled the silken sheath to expose the plum-colored head of his penis, and the quick pant of delight when she licked the head of him like a spoonful of flavored ice.

"Sweet Jesu, Maggie. What are you doing to me?" he asked.

Splaying her hands on either side of his narrow waist, she pulled herself upright, dragging her breasts against him the whole time until they stood, nearly eye to eye.

"I'm tasting you," she whispered. "You are like the most delicious platter of Robeson's pastries. Every part of you is beautiful and must be savored."

Grantham set his hand against her face and pushed her mouth open with his thumb while at the same time he grabbed her waist and pulled her hips against his, his cock pressed against the center of her, their hipbones rubbing together.

Sparks skittered to life beneath her skin. Margaret opened her mouth wider in invitation, suckling his thumb when he pushed it in over her bottom lip.

"Is it feasting, what we will be doing tonight?" he rasped.

She nodded, keeping his thumb between her lips, canting her hips against his and relishing the friction of his skin against the muslin gown at the juncture of her thighs.

He pulled his thumb out and kissed her, thrusting his tongue into her mouth, rough but not unpleasant. Lapping at her mouth, he cupped her bottom then dragged her nightgown over her head.

When she made to lie back, he held her still.

"I am listening," he chided.

This time, he was the one who sank to his knees, running a finger over the arc of her toes, circling the bone of her ankle, massaging her calf. When he sent his palms skimming her thighs, she rested her hands on his head in a benediction, in an invitation.

Grantham brought his mouth to the center of her and whispered, "I may not have done this before. Doesn't mean I do not know what I am supposed to do here."

His thick hair fell back when he looked at her and she ran it through her fingers.

"I might need a bit of direction," he said. "Remember, I am listening."

Her silent laugh shook itself loose and rippled down to her stomach, where he kissed the tail end of it.

Pausing every so often to tell Margaret how beautifully she was made, how she tasted of lavender and stars, how soft and wet and pretty and pink her parts were, Grantham *listened*.

Warm, large hands ran over the length of her, pulling her closer when he found a place he wanted to savor. When his thumbs brushed the curls between her legs, she let out a gasp of pleasure, then another of discomfort when his explorations grew too rough.

Without hesitation, Grantham pulled back.

"Tell me what to do," he said.

They moved to the bed and curled around one another like furled petals as Margaret whispered her secrets. When to be gentle and when to be rough. Where to put lips and tongue and sometimes teeth. How slick she became when he whispered against her clit, how to touch her just so and how to hold her close, so close, when she came against his mouth.

Still clinging and writhing, Margaret learned him in return. She let him twist her hair into a wild mass as she swallowed the head of him then the whole of him, swirling her tongue around the length of him as his breathing stuttered and caught and the hot splash of seed hit the back of her throat.

Time unspooled itself as they needed, slowing when they drowsed and speeding up again when they woke to the sensation of skin-to-skin pebbling in the cold night air. Grantham stoked the fire and Margaret squeezed her thighs together at the sight of his body outlined against the flames, the indent of his flank, the thick length of him as he hardened. She showed him how to soak the tiny sponge in vinegar and how to insert it.

They teased one another, adopting French accents—hers far superior—as they praised their favorite parts of one another and named them for pastries. Grantham bent his head to the *cerises parfaites* as he insisted on calling her nipples. Their laughter mellowed and disappeared as Margaret's attention shifted from silly names to the flush beneath her skin and the beautiful tension pulling like a string from her breasts to the center of her.

He slipped a finger inside her and, at her urging, kept his thumb moving in a steady circle on the outside.

"I want to watch you come again," he whispered. Pushing himself on his knees, he stared into her eyes as his fingers worked and she trembled in anticipation. "I want to keep you naked beneath me for days until I know every way there is to make you come."

Margaret wrapped her arms around his hips and pulled him close. He slipped his fingers from her sheath and rested his hand beside her head, hovering over her. Part of her reveled in his possessive words and the way his large body surrounded her, blocking out the rest of the world.

A tiny voice in her brain cautioned her to stay wary. Not to believe his rough words of praise for her scent, for the shape of her hips, for the slickness of her sheath.

"God. Oh God, Margaret. Is this . . . ?"

His head tipped as he pushed into her. It had been so long since she'd made love, the sensation of his penis stretching her tight passage startled her with its mix of pleasure and pain. He was too big, too overwhelming, with no place to hide from him. Once deep inside her, Grantham paused. His gaze locked with hers, and although Margaret wished to break the stare, she was trapped beneath his hips, by what they shared in this moment, by the weight of all that had come before and all that would come afterward.

"I can feel you." He breathed the words, more a prayer than a whisper. "I can feel you all around me."

She wanted that to be a stupid piece of poetry he might say to any woman in the midst of lovemaking but every part of her body knew his words were truth for she could feel him as well; his labored breath, her sheath around his cock, her every nerve singing his name. When she raised her hips, he sank even deeper, and his gasp of pleasure was half a sob and Margaret grabbed his head and pulled him in for a kiss so he could not see her own eyes tear.

Hesitantly, he pulled out halfway, then sank into her.

"This," he said against her lips, kissing her so hard, their teeth clicked and her lips felt bruised.

His movements were more assured now and the friction was too much, was not enough. When Margaret matched his thrusts, he tore his mouth from hers to laugh, a beautiful golden note that made her heart race even more and had her clutching his taught backside.

"It only needed you," he said, no longer whispering as he angled his hips so the base of his penis rubbed over her clit in shallow, shattering strokes. "All this time, and it was always only you."

Grantham pushed her legs wider as he moved even faster, and sensation took over. Everything narrowed to the white-hot need and the force of his thrusts and she'd no time to protest he'd made her more naked than she'd ever been, he was at the heart of her and beyond, that nothing would ever be the same now.

All this time. All this time. The words echoed in Margaret's head until they lost meaning, and the shaking of the bedstead broke them into tiny stars until Grantham's hips jerked once, twice, and as he let out a bellow of joy, the world around them exploded and the stars burned too bright for her to bear.

14

H OW DO I woo her?"

"You must first understand the reason for courting behaviors. If we compare her to a red squirrel, for example, would you say she exhibited the signs of estrus?"

Sweet Jesu.

Grantham pushed open the door to *The Chronicle*'s meeting room and took in the sight of Jacob Wolfe sitting at the head of the table, head in hands, flanked by the reporters, Evans and Dodson. At the other end of the table sat Althea Dertlinger and Mala Hill. Everyone had teacup and saucer and a plate of Mala's scones. Grantham shot a suspicious glare at the basket on the center of the table, but it was empty.

He was in a foul mood and had been for a week. After finally making love to Margaret after all these years, he'd thought . . . well, he wasn't sure what he thought might happen. Certainly not that she'd refuse to see him the next day.

The chappy woman had the gall to send *him* flowers, along with a note thanking him for his company and apologies that she could not present them in person, but she had her courses and was unwell.

Grantham had laughed at the gesture, but when she'd declined a dinner invitation two days later, he couldn't help but wonder if he'd done something wrong that night. Had he been too eager? Too rough?

He'd thrown himself into lobbying for the reform act, attending dull dinners and stultifying evening entertainments in the hopes of finding one or two sympathetic ears before the final vote. Barney had been there as well, remaining on the fence while making comments about which lords might be amenable and whether they had unmarried daughters.

In the meantime, ever more activity happened at the offices of *The Chronicle*.

Today, Sam Fenley stood in front of a slate board, where Wolfe often wrote out story ideas for the coming week. Across the top stood the words: The Science of Romance. How a Gentleman can use the Knowledge of the Natural World to find a Wife and Helpmeet.

"How, exactly, are any of us to know if a red squirrel is showing signs of estrus?" Wolfe inquired of the table, head in his palms.

"Might their tails be wagging?" asked Evans.

"Do they have an excited gleam in their eye?" asked Dodson.

"Please don't," said Grantham when Mala opened her mouth to explain. "Please. Give me the gift of not knowing when the squirrels in Hyde Park are ready to mate."

Mala shrugged.

"I thought you were going to write a column on the domestic uses of science. For the ladies," Grantham said.

"We have decided not to be limited." Althea brandished last week's *Chronicle*. "You print advice columns on haberdashery and questions of etiquette. Why would you be averse to a column for the lovelorn? Other broadsheets do it all the time."

Wolfe grimaced at these words and jabbed a finger toward the slate board. "We're talking about *romance* here. Romance cannot be explained by science." He glared at Althea and Mala, rubbing a hand against his muttonchop whiskers. "Romance is about magic. Kismet. Fate, in other words."

Dodson nodded. "Ephemeral stuff, romance."

Evans leaned back in his chair with an air of finality. "True love is destiny and all. Ever read one of Mrs. Foster's novels? I highly recommend *The Perils of Miss Cordelia Braveheart and the Castle of Doom*."

Althea fell into her seat, eyes wide with amazement, while Mala scrutinized the three men with a faint air of pity.

"Gentlemen," said Althea with an exaggerated show of patience. "Romance is a human construct, made up to describe a series of behaviors that are otherwise, to the nonscientist, inexplicable. We cannot measure it in a laboratory, cannot predict its occurrence, and cannot find a reason for why it strikes some and not others."

Wolfe frowned, head swiveling between Sam and Grantham as if for support. "It's not a disease."

"It is a word used to describe the wide and varying effects of chemical and physical changes in the human body on emotions and behaviors," said Mala.

Althea nodded at her friend. "The more people understand, the more they can make rational choices when it comes to matrimonial adventures."

What an idea. Was romance simply a word they gave to the effects of some invisible goings-on inside the body? The thought depressed Grantham, and by the look on the other men's faces, it depressed them as well.

"This doesn't sound right to my ears," Grantham said. He held up a hand, palm facing out, when Wolfe tried to speak.

"I don't know much about science—excepting a bit about tarantulas because they are fuzzy, delightful creatures," he said—ignoring Mala's gasp of outrage—"but I *do* know simply because a scientific theory makes you uncomfortable or doesn't fit into your set beliefs, doesn't make it wrong. I am certain *The Chronicle* can find space for a column about science and romance."

At Wolfe's dark glare, Grantham threw up his hands.

"One issue. If no one buys it, we don't do it again. At this rate, we have nothing much to lose."

He could be home in his own office with a warm fire and chair large enough to hold him comfortably. Instead, Grantham made his way to the back of the building, where he'd shoved a desk against the window.

The window faced the courtyard shared by his building and the one next door. If he leaned to the left and looked up, he could see the third-floor window in that building and its tiny balcony. He'd come to this office every day for the past week to see if he could glimpse Margaret.

The more he reflected on what happened between them, the more his brain had been churning toward a fuzzy conclusion he'd yet to fully define.

Lovemaking had been a revelation.

Objectively, Grantham had known it would be pleasurable.

What happened had been beyond pleasure. In fact, he doubted a word existed to describe it.

Even now, a week later, his skin had grown tighter around his muscles and bones, sensitive to every surface it encountered. He had trouble with his memory, finding himself on unfamiliar streets when he meant to go a different way. Smells and colors were stronger—more intense.

Mostly, he thought about Margaret. She could have taken his admission of virginity in so many ways—as a burden or curiosity or something to laugh about.

Instead, she'd seen right to the heart of him and treated him with a tender respect that had him closing his eyes and remembering the feel of her lips against his.

The aftermath of making love with Margaret had left him so exposed, he could barely look at himself, let alone figure out how to act around her. This didn't stop him from wanting to see her.

Perhaps she had the same reaction as him and was trying to figure out who they would be together from now on.

Lovers? Friends?

More?

The thought stuttered through his brain like a candlewick refusing to light.

What could Grantham offer that would compete with the realization of a lifelong dream? Margaret certainly couldn't marry him and run her own business.

He was an earl, like it or not. If she married him, she would be a countess and responsible for the attending duties that came with the title. Poor Violet nearly killed herself trying to fulfill the role of Viscountess Greycliff. Her work lay barely touched for all seven years of her marriage. Any wife of Grantham's could never have a *career*. The idea a woman might prefer work over marriage was too radical for most folks to accept.

If Grantham wished to see the Factory Education Reform Bill passed, he couldn't marry a woman who built railway tunnels. His reputation would tip over from notorious to radical, his judgment would be questioned, and any influence he'd gained would disappear. Victor Armitage would waste no time targeting him and demonizing Margaret. Even owning a newspaper of his own would not shield him—or her—from the attention. Marriage would do them both more harm than good.

Margaret Gault didn't need him now. She had once, years ago, and he'd failed her. Today, nothing threatened her autonomy and thus she'd no reason to marry again.

As for what they'd shared? That slight shock whenever he touched her, that buzzing in his veins when her glance settled on him, the way her scent evoked images of naked flesh on soft sheets—certainly, this would fade over time.

What had Mala said about romance?

Romance is a human construct, made up to describe a series of behaviors that are otherwise, to the nonscientist, inexplicable.

Margaret was a scientist. Did she believe in romance? Did she tie what they had done in any way to the finer emotions?

Had it simply been sex to her?

Grantham stared out into the sliver of grey sky and left his speech unwritten and rubbed his chest where it ached.

Right above his heart.

"THERE IS NO right time when you have no time left."

The words rang out from the common area of Athena's Retreat stopping Margaret in her tracks. She walked to the entryway and peered in.

Milly stood in conversation with a group of ten or so members. Violet sat among them on an armless chair, listing to one side, her mouth slack, and hands limp at her sides.

"Flavia means well, I am sure. Of course, she is worried for the well-being of the greylag geese. They are delightful creatures," Milly continued.

Margaret's mouth fell open in shock. No. No, they were not.

Geese were *terrifying* creatures as she and Grantham could attest.

"She cannot allow her emotions to stand in the way of progress," opined another woman. The indomitable Lady Potts sat close to the fire, which gilded her enormous wig. The hennaed pile of hair resembled a bee's hive if it had been sprayed with a lacquer smelling of cheese. Her gout had been plaguing her all autumn, and she held a gold-tipped ebony cane in one hand, which she thumped against the carpet to punctuate her sentences.

"Madame Gault is literally paving the way for women engineers who come after her," Lady Potts said. "Subjecting her person to scrutiny as well as her science. These bird people must stand aside for the greater good."

Oh no.

Margaret had been hiding for the past week. From Grantham, from the club members, from herself. Her excuse was her monthly courses, which had come the day after they'd made love. As usual, they were debilitatingly painful. Some months she was unable to rise from her bed, the cramps were so terrible.

Her courses were not the only reason she avoided Grantham.

Somehow, a man with no sexual experience had stripped her down to the woman she'd been on the brink of becoming all those years ago. He'd reawakened her sense of wonder, her ultimate trust in him, her tender concern for the most wounded parts of him.

The temptation to go and do it again, to fall into his arms and sweat out her worries beneath him, was strong. Margaret could let go of everything she held on to so tightly. Her fears. Her insecurities. Her frustrations and loneliness.

If she asked, Grantham would give her enough pleasure to bring oblivion, but only for a short time. The world would be there waiting for her no matter how many times she gave in and made love to him.

The world which included the stupid tunnel, the stupid birds, stupid Victor Armitage and his stupid Guardians and . . . Margaret had a long list of what she found stupid, made longer by the pain and discomfort of menstruation.

"Why, there she is now. Our very own pioneer of women's advancement. Come and join us, Madame Gault," Milly called. "Welcome to the first meeting of the Subcommittee for the Advancement of Women Scientists in the World Beyond."

Margaret stared over at Violet and tugged at her ear, while she took a hesitant step forward. Hopefully, Violet would remember their secret signal.

Violet, however, was napping with her eyes open.

"Do you have an itch, my dear?" Lady Potts inquired.

"Urm, just a . . ." Margaret tugged and opened her eyes wider at Violet, who stared off into the distance. "Just a little . . ." She tugged again.

"We are banding together to support your venture into the world and force those who live in the past to let go of their fears. We cannot wait for the world to accept us," Milly said.

"Oh, you mustn't do anything drastic on my account," Margaret said, hastening to Milly's side. "We can come to some sort of compromise about the birds, I am sure. Move their nests or change the angle of—"

"No. This is about more than the geese." Milly turned to the rest of the committee; her hands clasped tightly at her breast. "This is about change. We cannot wait for the world to adjust to our ideas. We must take a stand and force them to wake up."

The women cheered and Lady Potts thumped her cane. A snort

came from Violet as her head snapped up, awoken by the noise. Margaret turned toward her friend and yanked on her ear one last time out of desperation.

"I do believe the baby must be awake from her nap by now," Violet said abruptly.

Finally.

She came to stand near Margaret and laid a palm on Milly's shoulder.

"While I applaud your incentive in forming this subcommittee, I cannot approve it until I bring it before the entire club for a vote."

"A vote? Another delay in the march toward progress." Milly huffed. "I do not have much time left on this earth, Mrs. Kneland. I will make use of it as best as I can."

What might it be like to draw close to the end of one's life not having seen progress toward one's greatest wish? Violet, not without sympathy, told Milly she might petition the rest of the members to hold an early vote as she bustled Margaret out of the room.

"Violet, why is Milly so adamant about my project?" Margaret asked as they went through the hallways over to Beacon House. Settling themselves in the cozy blue parlor, Violet called for a tray.

"I don't think it is just about your tunnel," she assured Margaret. "Their work on pyroglicerin has been halted, John Waterstone rebuffed a proposal by Milly for a joint project in unkind terms, and Willy's father died."

The maid brought in a platter of sweets and lit the fire for them. With Mrs. Sweet away, Cook had free reign in the kitchen and the two friends indulged in her famous shortbread biscuits.

"I do believe Willy always hoped to reconcile her family with her love for science," Violet said.

Margaret stared at the fire glumly. Worries over the project soon replaced sympathy for Willy. Away for three weeks before the annual meeting of the consortium, Geflitt had left her a letter that had sent her under the covers with a plate of scones for a good cry.

Her series of initial sketches and reports had been shared with his consortium members. A sharp-eyed gentleman had seen her name at the bottom and had kicked up a fuss, doubting her abilities to see the job through. Geflitt had thus instructed her to create a convincing presentation defending her budget and methods.

". . . the University of Pisa has contacted me. I have been in correspondence with Raffaele Piria and I have hopes he will copublish a paper with me on Avogadro's law."

Margaret pulled her thoughts to the present. It took a moment for Violet's words to sink in.

"But this is wonderful, Violet," she said. "This will be the first time your work is published under your own name."

"I just . . ." Violet yawned loudly before she could cover her mouth. "I don't think I'll be able to finish in time."

"When is the deadline?"

"Six months."

Six months? Margaret goggled at the thought. So much time.

Meanwhile, Margaret had a deadline of three weeks to come up with a presentation, was not publicly acknowledged by her employer, had no money to hire an assistant unless she used Armitage's cheque, and certainly had no one waiting upstairs to provide comfort and support in the evenings.

"My goodness, what is the problem? Just do the work. What is stopping you from—" Margaret closed her mouth.

Tears were gathering at the corners of Violet's eyes.

"Violet?" she whispered. Rising from her seat by the fireplace, Margaret settled herself on the settee next to Vi who'd slumped against a cushion.

"Tell me what is wrong."

"Nothing is wrong," Violet said, sitting up straight and busying herself stacking the biscuits into tiny shortbread towers. "You are right. I need to finish it. I'm just . . ."

When the towers fell, so did Violet's tears. "I'm just so stupid. Nothing makes sense anymore. I am tired all the time. When I spend time with Mirren and Arthur, I feel guilty I am neglecting the ladies and the club. When I am at the club, I am missing Mirren and Arthur. I do not know what to do about this rift between Milly and Willy, and with Mrs. Sweet gone to be with Letty, Cook has been making potatoes and crumpets and rashers again and all I do is eat."

Violet collapsed backward onto the cushions and stared at the ceiling. "Whatever I set out to do, it's as though I am doing it halfway and through a fog."

"Oh, Violet." Margaret reached over and hugged her fiercely, breathing deep of her best friend's scent, a unique blend of lemon drops and sulfur.

"You are trying too hard to be everything for everyone. No one needs you to be *everything*. They only need you to be *you*."

Violet was not convinced. "Yes, well, me is tired and plump and forgetful and—"

"—and kind and loving and the best wife and mother and friend in the whole world," Margaret said. "Not because you are perfect. Because you listen to others and have a big heart and laugh at yourself and the world."

She leaned over and restacked the shortbread, setting two more pieces on a plate and handing them to Violet.

"As for Mirren and Arthur, there is nothing you can do that will make them love you any more or any less. Simply being yourself is all they want and need."

"I know," Violet said, wiping her tears. "You are right, but the doubts nip at my heels regardless."

Margaret offered her own handkerchief when Violet's grew damp.

"Doubt doesn't nip at my heels," Margaret said in commiseration. "It grabs me by the knees and throws me to the ground. I am waiting for someone to come and tell me the game is up and I am to turn in my slide rule and go home."

"This is not what I thought life would be like when we were little," Violet confessed. "I thought we would be friends forever, you and me and George. I thought life would be a series of sweet vignettes where we would play with each other's babies and create a liquid explosive—"

"Oh, yes. We were going to buy a mine and blow the tunnels out instead of digging them."

"That's right." Violet stopped snuffling. "I must apologize. I have a tendency toward tears ever since I had the baby."

Margaret frowned. Violet shouldn't be apologizing. "No, dear. It is I who must ask forgiveness. I have been selfish. I should have been here more to remind you to nap and help with the baby and do whatever else it is a new mother needs."

Violet went to her bookshelves and pulled out a large leatherbound tome. When she carried it to the settee, Margaret looked at her askance.

"What does Friedrich Accum have to do with . . . ahhhhh."

Opening the book, Violet revealed the pages had been cut away to create the perfect hiding place for a small bottle of amber liquid.

"You were not selfish." Violet poured them each a measure of wellaged Scotch whisky in delicately etched glasses meant for sherry. Ha.

Sherry be damned.

"You are trying to make your way in a man's world. It isn't like the rest of us at the Retreat. You must do your work out in the world because you have chosen it as your profession. To compete with men, we have to think like men, act like men, and comforting cozes with your friends or tears into your teacups are not what men do."

Margaret sighed. "If only men did cry into their teacups more often, the world might be an easier place."

"Indeed. To male tears," Violet said.

The two of them solemnly clinked their glasses and drank at the same time, then coughed violently.

Goodness, that was strong.

"But you truly are the best of friends, Violet. You have been patient with me while I have been impatient." Margaret finished her drink.

"No, you are the best of friends, Margaret. You always encouraged me, no matter how outlandish or wild my ideas when we were younger. You left your work and your home to come and help manage the club last year when Arthur and I went north."

Violet finished her drink as well, and Margaret poured them both another.

"No, you are the best of friends, Violet. You are forgiving, even when I don't deserve it."

Violet took another sip and leaned into Margaret, setting her head on her shoulder.

"No, you are the best of friends. Remember when I was madly in love with Gerald Wentworth and he would come to visit? You told my mother I was bringing food to Widow Elmsgrove. Instead, I spent the week spying on him from the platform you built in the oak tree outside the guest room window."

Margaret had lost count of how many times they'd refilled each other's glasses. She should confess to Violet right now. Her friend would forgive her, and they would figure out a way for Margaret to take Armitage's money without somehow being of service to him.

"No. You are the best of friends," Margaret said. "Because when I disappoint you horribly, you will try your best to forgive me, even though I will not deserve it."

Violet lifted her head, eyes bleary from her earlier tears. Or at least,

Margaret assumed so. It could be Margaret's own eyes were having trouble focusing.

"You couldn't disappoint me, Margaret. You are so strong and determined. You would never make a mistake. You can do anything you set your mind to without any help. You are incredible."

Incredible was more a burden than a compliment. Margaret didn't want to have to be strong and determined. She wanted to ask for help.

"I have been so worried about what the Guardians might do next," Violet continued. "Arthur and I are both so grateful you were here when the persecution first began. What would we do without you?"

The planned confession curdled on Margaret's tongue. She didn't want Violet to look at her with scorn or disdain. She wanted her friend to always look at her with a mixture of trust and love. She wanted a home here with these wonderful women.

She didn't want to have to feel so alone.

Margaret poured them both another drink and they nibbled the last of Cook's biscuits until Violet fell asleep, snoring so hard a footman came running to see if one of the members was sawing through the floorboards.

Margaret waved him away. She would watch over her friend for as long as she could, until the truth came out and she was no longer welcome.

15

SOMETIMES ONE HAD to swallow a glass of something worse than one's pride. Sometimes one had to drink a cup of Mrs. Sweet's special tea.

Margaret stared balefully at what looked like bilgewater and swore to Athena herself she was never going to drink whiskey again.

Never.

Ever.

It tasted five times worse than it looked and Margaret shuddered for ten minutes afterward as she finished dressing. However, like most of the women in the club, Mrs. Sweet was a genius. By the time Margaret arrived at the office, her stomach had calmed and her head had cleared.

As she alit from the hack, Margaret spied the two reporters for *The Chronicle* hurrying out the entrance, laughing with one another. Grantham had spent some money on the upkeep of the building and the windows had been reglazed and cleaned. A new sign hung above the door and the cobbled street out front had been swept.

In front of the building on the other side, two men stood in the bow window of *Gentlemen's Monthly*, watching the activity over at *The Chronicle*.

She hadn't seen Victor Armitage himself since the speech at the tunnel site. The Armitages were in high demand as the social season wound down before the nobility retired to their estates for the winter. *Gentlemen's Monthly* had printed a picture of Armitage and his wife, Fanny, an unhappy woman who made certain everyone around her was equally unhappy, at a charitable event for widows of soldiers just the other week. The story insinuated without the support of Armitage, these women would be forced into the streets, or—worse—must take employment outside the home.

While the piece lauded the society women who'd raised the funds, it failed to specify how much they'd raised or how many widows it would help.

"Feckless man," Margaret muttered to herself as she marched past the newspaper offices.

She entered her own building and walked up the stairs past Geflitt's empty offices. That he'd left for his estate in the weeks leading to the Consortium annual meeting was the worst possible timing. Not only did she have questions about the presentation, but Margaret also needed his intervention with a strange invoice she'd received.

Somehow, one of the merchants on his list had mistaken her inquiries as actual orders and billed them for two wagon loads of lumber Margaret hadn't wanted. Worse, when she went to the warehouse to arrange its return, she found they'd never delivered it.

If Geflitt and his fellow investors trusted firms like this to do their business, whom else had they trusted? Unease rested in the pit of her belly.

Lighting a few oil lamps against the gloom, Margaret sat at her worktable. The headache of the morning returned as she reviewed her plans for the twentieth time.

"When was the last time you had fun?"

Margaret swept the beginnings of her report to one side and tapped a pencil to her bottom lip. She certainly did not have time to . . .

An hour later, she'd hammered together three boards to make a U shape with a flat bottom. The width between the boards was 1/100th the distance between Beacon House and Athena's Retreat if one were standing in a small, cramped workroom at the back.

All of her projects began as small-scale models. Some of her bridges took years to build and Margaret often began a new design while the last project broke ground. She couldn't wait years to see if her projects would work, so she created them in miniature first.

The other night, she'd relieved Violet of a few skeins of grey wool while she slept and now Margaret sat on the floor next to a rough sketch and tied the yarn into a complex series of knots.

A retractable bridge wouldn't work if it were made of wood unless she designed a system of cranks and gears to push it out from the workroom to the parlor. While this would be a delightful invention that might one day see the light of day, it would not work for Grantham's plans.

If only because now she believed him about Arthur's omniscience.

No, she had to figure out how to distribute Grantham's weight using nothing but ropes and pulleys.

A suspension bridge made of hemp rather than steel cables.

Margaret chuckled to herself as she envisioned Grantham trying to cross the bridge with a package in one hand, the rope swaying beneath him. Of course, she would have to tell Violet. It would be like old times.

Except Violet would be kept in the dark until the last minute because she couldn't keep a secret.

Besides, rope was flammable.

Geese and tunnels and the last vestiges of a hangover disappeared, as questions of how to attach a pulley to Beacon House without notice filled her head. When the sun dipped low enough to shine in her eyes, she'd spent too much time having "fun" and regretfully heaved herself from the floor.

Back aching from sitting for too long, she paced the chamber. Like an itch where she couldn't reach, the double doors of the balcony of her office beckoned to her. She knew what she would find when she walked out there and leaned over the balcony railing. A sliver of glass faced the back office of *The Chronicle*. A back office that had recently been cleared of shelves and outfitted with a large desk.

Grantham.

He stood at the window in his office, looking at her.

Startled, he jumped out of sight and the resulting crash reverberated through the shared courtyard. After a moment, he reappeared sheepishly holding a hand to his head.

"Oh, George," she whispered.

Every time she turned around, he was there. Waiting. As reliable and kindhearted as he'd been through her childhood.

He wasn't the same boy, however.

Not just his outside had changed. Grantham had grown more reflective of his own actions and more observant of others'. As much as he tried to mask this with his foolish stories and air of unconcerned bonhomie, he'd become discerning in his old age.

Thank goodness. He'd always been too quick to believe the best in others. Certainly, he'd always believed the best about Margaret. Even when she hadn't deserved it.

Like right now.

"What do you think you're doing?" she called out, half-amused, half-worried.

He'd climbed out of his window, and now stood in the courtyard surveying her building. Nodding once, he took hold of the windowsill on the first floor.

"You're going to fall, you great gnaw-post."

Appearing unconcerned, Grantham hoisted himself to the lintel jutting out over the first-floor window and grabbed hold of the decorative frieze above it.

"Did I ever tell you the story of how I rescued a baby possum in Canada? A bear had chased it up a tree," he called out to her. With a grunt, he pulled himself up and swung his leg to a brick jutting out of the wall, heaving himself to the next windowsill.

"I climbed the tree, tucked the possum in my shirt, and swung from branch to branch until we were well away from that bear." He performed the same maneuver again until he'd reached her balcony, grabbed the railings, and pulled himself over with an ease belying his strength.

"Did the mother possum try to trap you into marriage afterward?" she asked.

Grantham threw his head back and laughed.

At the sound of sunlight flung from his throat, the earth shifted beneath her. Not literally, of course.

Metaphorically, the world moved like an earthquake and the lovely construction she'd erected around her heart cracked.

How could it not?

When they were young and had discovered each other in that way young loves do, he'd brought her gifts. Not books or ribbons, but the kind of gifts he knew were precious to her. Pieces of marble found when plowing a farmer's field, squared and mysterious, grey veins running through the ancient white, sometimes with the chisel marks on them. Oddly shaped branches and scavenged nails he'd pounded straight and polished.

If he wanted her heart again, these were the gifts she would treasure. Laughter. Respite. Attention. Joy. Rarities in her world, so shiny and appealing from where she stood so far away from everyone around her.

A natural phenomenon, like a windstorm or a waterfall, Grantham was fashioned from desire and humor and unabashed delight, and he battered against her defenses. Not even her trusted slide ruler would make a difference. When he laughed at her, when he pushed her into her office, when he took her by the waist and pulled her close and kissed her as though he might simply die if his mouth weren't against hers—there were no straight lines. Everything was soft and blurred and so damned delightful. He made her head spin with memories of what they'd done and images of what more they might do together. The tiny pulse that woke in between her thighs reminded her of how perfectly they'd fit together despite the awkward start the other night.

"Where have you been this week?" he asked, lips against her neck.

"I'm sorry," she said.

She was always apologizing to him. The thought hurt her heart and she bent her head and rested it on her shoulder.

"Maggie," he whispered, lips grazing the lobe of her ear in a way that had her shivering. "If I did anything wrong or made you feel—"

"Oh, George."

Margaret held him close, blinking against tears. How could a heart as great and tender as his be allowed in the world? It should be kept like a treasure, cased in glass with guards set to keep it from ever being hurt.

"Is that a no? If it is, could you let go, I'm starting to get dizzy," he rasped.

Releasing her hold, Margaret laughed at his puffed cheeks and crossed eyes. She set her hand to his cheek and shook her head.

"You were wonderful," she said.

A proud smile lit his face.

"I was, wasn't I? Made your eyes roll back in your head."

She giggled. "You did."

"Then . . . ?"

The memory of his face above hers, the sound of his voice when he cried out her name, the way her whole body glowed beneath his touch—it made her tremble even now. What could she say that would not unravel her?

"I don't think I was prepared for how wonderful you actually are," she said.

He swallowed and set his forehead against hers, the sooty mist curling round the open balcony door and echoes of shopkeepers calling out to each other wrapping them in the grey cloak of London; a city of millions who went on about their lives as though a woman was not at this moment about to take a great fall.

One ill-tempered shopkeeper called out a word that broke the spell and Margaret took hold of herself, pushing him away like a plate of tarts she'd much rather be eating.

"I have work to do."

He made a show of holding up his hands and stepped away. A dimple appeared to the right of his lips, the single parenthesis bracketing one side of his beautiful mouth, an open invitation to put her mouth there and finish the sentence.

"Of course, you have to build a . . . Holy mother of pearl, Maggie. You did it!"

It took ten minutes to explain her idea and two seconds for Grantham to somehow unravel the bridge then retie it into knots, but it didn't matter. His laughter was the low, long peal of a French horn in a Beethoven sonata and it rippled up her fingers and down her spine.

The magic could only last for so long. When she cast a glance in the direction of her drafting table, her worries descended, dampening the excitement of his appearance.

"May I?" He gestured to the table, and she joined him, studying her messy plans.

"I don't understand anything I'm looking at," he said genially. "But this doesn't resemble a giant hole to me."

"Do you know," she said, momentarily distracted, "you are perhaps the only man of my acquaintance who would admit to not understanding something a woman has created?"

One muscular shoulder rose, then dropped. "Well, I don't think Kneland pretends to understand when Vi starts talking about avocados and such."

Winking when Margaret rolled her eyes at him, Grantham continued, "I've never seen the point of pretending I will ever understand any of you scientists. What does it gain me?"

Margaret fought not to sigh like a ninny nonny. "At the risk of inflating your already enormous ego, you must know how attractive I find such an admission."

He might have swallowed the sun, so bright was his smile.

"I'm an idiot," he declared with outsized cheer. "Explain to me what you're doing here, and I'll just assume that will act as an aphrodisiac."

Pulling one of the sheets closer, Margaret shook her head in mock despair. "You don't have to be an idiot to be confused by this mess. It's not really a design yet. This is just me beginning to put together my ideas. I've been thinking about both the slope of the riverbank and the composition of the soil and rock beneath it."

Grantham nodded. "This part I understand. I've dug a few holes in my lifetime and it doesn't go well if there's a boulder in the way."

A smatter of raindrops tapped at the skylights above and the shadows reached out from the corners of the room. The wick of the heavy oil lamp Margaret used to illuminate her work needed trimming and the circle of light around them shrank.

"One of the reasons they want a tunnel rather than a bridge at this site is the differing height of the opposite bank. If they were the same height, I would design long approach viaducts on either side," she explained, tracing the viaducts with her finger so he could see what she meant. "This raises the entrance and exit of a bridge from the low ground on either side of the shores to allow for vessels to sail beneath your arches."

Margaret pushed aside one plan and pulled over another.

"In the case of a tunnel, we do this almost in reverse. We create a ramp going down, rather than up."

Grantham took his time peering at the two designs, running a gloved forefinger over a column of equations.

"Are you enjoying the work?" he asked.

Margaret's own hands were ungloved. As much as she tried to care for her skin, her hands would never be fine and soft like a gentlewoman's. Perhaps if she wore gloves while she drafted and slathered lanolin on them like some.

The urge to see her equations translated into reality was too strong, however. Much like the cupboard for her parchments she'd constructed, Margaret enjoyed making small models of her projects, testing theories against reality. One of her thumbnails was uneven, a casualty of distraction while hammering a bookshelf together. Her skin was rough, and ink stained the first three fingers of her right hand.

"I am challenged by the design," she said. "Won't they miss you at *The Chronicle*?" Margaret asked in an attempt to shift the conversation away from her work.

Grantham chuckled. "I have as much influence there as I have in Lords."

"What do you mean?" she asked.

Instead of answering, Grantham paced the room, asking questions. Margaret followed in his wake, biting her lip to keep from telling him not to touch anything. Touch was an easier way for him to learn than reading or listening. He removed his tan gloves and caressed the satin wood of her cupboard, traced the vines carved into a frame holding a sketch of her first bridge design, and pulled open drawers full of maps and surveys of the worksite and surrounding areas.

Unable to bear his fidgeting any longer, she left him to his exploring and went out into the street, beckoning to Jeb, the street sweeper she'd met the other day. She'd taken to searching him out and sending him on small errands and had convinced Geflitt's clerk to do the same. Handing him a shilling, she sent him to fetch them some luncheon.

"Mind, don't you buy the pasties from Mrs. Lovett's pie shop," she told the boy, having been warned sometimes they tasted off.

By the time she returned upstairs, Grantham had settled somewhat, leafing through the maps that showed the riverbank on the opposite side of the Thames from where Geflitt had held his event.

She'd one chair for her drafting table, and the settee in the corner had only three legs. While she could balance on it, she doubted it would survive an encounter with Grantham. Instead, Margaret took the quilt from the settee and spread it on the floor. They set their impromptu picnic in the center and sat opposite one another, both facing the balcony, legs stretched out before them.

A dusty floor, greasy pies, and the drumming of the constant London rain—this was the most perfect meal Margaret had shared in years.

"Is your sister graduated from the academy yet?" Margaret asked idly as she set aside her bottle of ginger beer the boy had brought along with the pasties.

Grantham's half sister Lizzie was a student at the same school Violet and Margaret had attended as girls, the Yorkshire Academy for the Education of Exceptional Young Women.

"Ugh. That place. Better call it the asylum than the academy," Grantham complained. "The last time I went to visit, there were trebuchets in the kitchen garden, tobacco plants in the solarium, and multiple scorch marks on the carpet. And the chairs. And the men's retiring room, for goodness' sakes."

"Ahhh, the trebuchets," Margaret said, overcome with nostalgia.

"Lizzie has put off leaving for two years. She almost made her debut last year," Grantham said. "Violet was ill, however, and Mam doesn't have the connections to bring her out by herself. Besides, Mam hasn't been well."

"What do you mean?"

Grantham stared at the tiny squares of grey that could be glimpsed through the thick glass doors.

"Farmer Alwyn's death certainly shook her but moving to Morningside did something to Mam's spirit. She met my father there. Mam was a poor relation come to work as a companion to some great-aunt, and next thing you know, my scapegrace father went and put a baby in her belly."

Margaret studied his profile. What had he done to break such a strong nose? "I'm surprised they married," she said. "The family could have denied your mother's claims and kept your father free for a more advantageous marriage."

Tilting his head, he stared at the skylights and the silvery sheet of clouds above them. The sounds of traffic from the front of the buildings were filtered through the stuccoed walls and only the occasional shout from an irate wagon driver or pack of boys could be picked out from the general rumbling of commerce in the great capital around them.

"'Twas the great-aunt who insisted," Grantham told the sky. "On the one hand, Mam didn't have to bear a bastard alone. On the other hand . . ."

He didn't need to complete the sentence. Margaret knew well enough the suffering both Grantham and his mother had had at his father's hands.

He peered into the bottle, closing one eye, then the other. "I believe she is lonely." Setting the bottle on its side, Grantham kept his attention there, rolling it back and forth. "She's buried two husbands, and her daughter will leave her soon enough. She's too shy to spend time with the tenants and there's not much else to do on the estate, but she has no liking for London."

"You are a good son." At his frown, Margaret reached over and touched his hand, speaking gently. "You always were. Please do not think her sadness has aught to do with you."

Leaving off playing with the bottle, Grantham turned his torso toward Margaret.

"I need someone to keep Mam company, see to the tenants, and manage the house. If I am called to London, I cannot ask Lizzie to be my hostess. Instead, I need . . ."

Ah.

"You need a countess," Margaret said.

The words were solid and bitter, but truthful. Grantham had to marry.

"Dunno 'bout that," he mumbled.

An earl needed a wife to continue his title, help run his estate, bring out his sister, and be company for his mother. The care and keeping of Grantham and his possessions would be his wife's sole occupation. And in time, the care and keeping of his children as well.

Margaret had a profession—an occupation having nothing to do with estates or mothers or anything domestic. Following through with her Plan meant spontaneous picnics and handsome earls must be kept at bay. The logical thing to do would be to send him on his way now.

Sitting here like a fool and drinking in the sight of him? That was illogical. A waste of time. An unnecessary indulgence and the prelude to a heartbreak. He needed to leave.

Grantham could not be her partner.

With a grace that belied his great size, Grantham got to his feet in a single movement. Margaret caught her breath as his body clenched then unfurled to standing. A small miracle of muscle and sinew occurred when his thighs bunched beneath the lawn of his trousers and the linen of his shirt clung to the slope of his biceps.

Lust as thick and sweet as treacle rippled through her. The ghost of horehound sweets and willow leaves filled her nose and Margaret marveled at the way her body, which she'd been so convinced had succumbed to age, now sprung to life the same way it had fifteen years earlier.

"Do you need help?" he asked, extending a hand.

Here was another revelation. Something as mundane as a man's hand could be erotic; the tripod of bones moving beneath the skin on his hands, the pulsing blue veins, the knobs of his knuckles and the dips between them. Margaret set her hands in his and bit her lip at the bliss of contact.

Grantham's pupils widened and he hissed as he pulled her up, not being subtle when he wrapped her arms around his waist, pushing his hips against hers, giving her the evidence he'd noticed and approved of her attraction.

His kisses were hot and hungry. Although Grantham had told her he no longer felt the urgent lust of his seventeen-year-old self, the terrible yearning from that summer settled beneath Margaret's skin. She fumbled for his buttons, for the knots and folds keeping his body hidden from hers, searching his mouth for the remembered taste of licorice and bliss, teeth against teeth, tongue against tongue. Margaret couldn't pull her mouth from his even when he groaned in frustration at the buttons of her dress.

"Pick me up," she told him between biting kisses, making an approving sound when he wrapped his arms around her waist and lifted her so she could wrap her legs around his narrow hips.

"Desk."

Grantham hesitated until she bit his lower lip and sucked away the sting. Within seconds he had her bottom on the edge of her drafting desk and had laid her on the slanted surface.

"Brilliant." He spoke with his lips against her neck, hands reaching beneath her skirts even as his hips ground against hers.

For a moment they writhed, stymied by the layers of linen and canvas, rows of buttons and knots, then Grantham reared back and yanked Margaret's skirts to her waist in one move, pulling the tapes of her drawers apart with shocking speed. Pushing her higher on the desk, he set his shoulder beneath her leg, exposing her to him. With one hand palming her breast, he put his mouth to her core and with the flat of his tongue licked the seam of her.

"Oh, wh . . . oh . . . yes, please," she managed to stutter as he proved to her he'd remembered well the lessons from the other night. Gentle at first, he pressed his forefinger into her slick passage, pressing against her delicate flesh as he pushed down with his mouth. She squeezed her eyes shut while red and gold sparks flew as her toes curled under in her boots and she breathed in and out in tiny pants.

Clever, clever man, he twirled his tongue around her clit and she arched off the desk, the sensation so strong, she almost told him to stop, but it reached a point where there was no need for words, no need for any communication, because he'd driven her so high into the atmosphere, she'd crashed into the stars, and as she exploded, the tiny sparks from the collision burned away the last of her defenses.

16

◈

"SHE HAS MY eyes," Grantham told Kneland as they sat in the library of Beacon House. He held Baby Georgie in his lap and tried to make her laugh. "Probably got my brains as well."

"Out of respect for your family, I believe I shall leave them a body part after I kill you, so they have something to bury," said Kneland conversationally without looking up from his newspaper.

"Be sure to leave them my cock," Grantham said as he breathed deeply the smell of baby, delighted when she opened her eyes wide and laughed at him. "The women of England will need a relic for their shrine."

"Do not say the word 'cock' in front of my daughter," said Kneland, setting down a copy of *The Chronicle* in outrage.

Baby Georgie giggled again.

"It makes her laugh," Grantham protested. "Watch." He made a face at the baby and enunciated, "Cock."

A stream of hysterical laughter followed, and Grantham grinned at the baby, giddy with joy.

Kneland left his desk and stood behind Grantham, hands on hips. "She is laughing at your face."

Grantham knew better and said it again. "Cock."

This time there was no mistaking the baby's amusement. Her laughter was like tiny golden bubbles going straight to Grantham's head.

Kneland's as well, for he nudged Grantham aside and leaned over his daughter.

"Cock," he said.

Baby Georgie screwed up her face and for a moment both men reared back, ready for one of her famous vomit spouts. Instead, she screamed with laughter, the kind that left her red-faced and breathless.

"Cock," said Grantham merrily.

"Cock," echoed Kneland. "Cockity cockity cocks."

"It's one o'cock. Time for tea," Grantham informed the baby.

Peals of laughter bounced off the spines of the musty old books and brought sunshine in through the crimson velvet curtains.

"And at two o'cock, we take our nap," Kneland added.

They made it to eleven o'cock before Baby Georgie laughed so hard, she forced a surprise out from her other end and Kneland hastily rang for the maid.

Grantham made rhymes with cock under his breath when the baby was taken upstairs to be changed and Kneland returned to his seat, resuming his perusal of *The Chronicle*.

"*Dear Sir Science,*" he read aloud. "*I have lately been visiting with a lady of my acquaintance. While I would like to ask her to go walking, I cannot ascertain whether her interest in my company is of an amorous nature or not. How can you tell if a lady has an interest? Sincerely, Wondering in Woolsley.*"

Against all odds, the Sir Science column had become a sensation. They sold out of every issue of the newspaper this week and the offices were flooded with heaps of letters from young men desperate to learn the science behind romance.

Wolfe had accepted the teasing of the staff with good-natured grace and he, Sam, Mala, and Althea were in talks about expanding the women's role at the paper.

Kneland continued reading.

"Dear Wondering in Woolsley, have you considered instead whether you are showing the lady signs of your interest?"

"Hence we return to the importance of cocks," said Grantham.

Kneland frowned over the top of the paper. "A cock is not the answer to every woman's dilemma."

"I beg to differ."

Margaret had come undone in his arms yesterday. She'd melted into a puddle of woman that he drank like the finest of wines. His mind was full of nothing but her skin and her smile—her *smile*.

For the first time in so long, her smiles had come without pause, without hesitation or fear. He tried to imagine sex with anyone other than her and could not. How could his release be anywhere near as poignant, as all-encompassing if it weren't with her?

She must feel the same, must she not?

"Women need more than sex to be happy," Kneland said.

Grantham resented Kneland's knowing tone. Simply because the man had more experience did not render him some sort of expert on what women needed.

"You were the one who said actions were better than words," Grantham reminded him. "My actions leave Marg—er, women, lots and lots of women—very, *very* happy."

Kneland studied him so long and hard, Grantham's glow cooled.

"First," Arthur said, "I consider Madame Gault to be under my roof for all she resides at Athena's Retreat. If your intentions . . ."

"Oh ho. I've known Margaret since she was eight years old," Grantham said, pointing a finger at Kneland. "Your intentions are irrelevant when it comes to her. *Her* intentions are what matters. No one does anything to Maggie without her permission."

The Scot swallowed this and nodded. "Violet has no idea, does she?"

"No," Grantham said quickly. "To protect Margaret from any embarrassment, you shall not breathe a word of this to Vi."

There was no argument from Kneland. Everyone knew Violet could not keep a secret if her life depended on it.

Kneland wasn't finished lecturing. "Second, you might consider Madame Gault's situation."

"Her situation is she is being adroitly taken care of by a man with a large—"

"Her situation is she is an untitled woman in a man's profession, not an aristocratic debutante. There is a difference in your stations that in polite society is unbreachable."

Grantham scoffed. "I am aware—"

Kneland's voice carried a rough edge to it. "I know what it is to marry someone with a title and drag them down. Madame Gault is in an untenable position."

That shut Grantham's mouth. *Drag them down?*

Did Kneland see himself as a burden to Violet? How could that be?

"You do not drag Violet down, Kneland," Grantham said. "You lift her up. Violet is the happiest I have ever known her. You've made her *whole*."

Kneland's gaze burned despite the blackness of his eyes. "That may be, but I cannot change I am the son of a tenant farmer and work for a living. She is the daughter of a viscount and the widow of the same. We are not accepted any longer in certain homes where Violet was once welcomed. It affects the club, and though she might deny it, it affects her. And from what Violet tells me, Madame Gault has a plan for herself."

"Yes, she is starting an engineering firm," said Grantham.

"And you are an earl. With properties and a title you must maintain—even if they came to you unexpectedly. Isn't that why you wanted to marry Violet in the first place?"

Grantham knew this. He'd said it to himself a hundred times.

"Madame Gault cannot do both," Kneland said. "She cannot be a woman who earns a wage and a countess at the same time."

True.

"Greycliff whisked Letty away to Herefordshire so she wouldn't be subject to so much attention. She can continue with her mathematics because it's theoretical and done behind closed doors," Kneland continued. "Even so, once she has her child, the work will be put aside. Madame Gault does not have either of those luxuries."

Picking the paper up, Kneland raised it in front of his face.

"If and when she realizes she cannot have both you and her profession . . ." Kneland cleared his throat and gentled his voice. "She's not the only one who might be hurt."

It was the nicest thing Kneland had ever said to Grantham.

Feelings.

They were bound and determined to escape, weren't they?

MARGARET SAT SLUMPED over her drafting desk and thumped her head against its surface.

Damn. Damn. Damn.

After a moment, she stood and stretched, setting her hands to the small of her back. Her stomach rumbled but she was too far gone to worry about food.

She needed a breakthrough.

Geflitt had procured her the drawings by the Thames Tunnel's chief draughtsman, Joseph Pinchbeck, and she pored over them with a deep appreciation for their detail.

In 1818, Marc Brunel had invented a tunnel shield that made it possible to dig the first tunnel ever constructed below a navigable river like the Thames. At first, the biggest hurdle was the construction of the initial shaft, which sank in under its own weight. Margaret would not have that problem as engineers now understood the shaft should be wider at the bottom than at the top.

Once they reached the optimal depth, they would install the shield. The iron structure was made up of twelve frames lying side by side over three stories, which equated to thirty-six spaces for workmen. The back end of those spaces was open, and the front had removable boards. As the workmen removed the earth from the front and dumped it out the back of each cell, bricklayers would follow behind, shoring up the tunnel.

Closing her eyes, Margaret visualized the riverbank. In her head she placed her workmen and prepared the site. Lower and lower, she sank below the earth and her imaginary workers constructed the tunnel borer.

Sitting at her drafting desk, Margaret rubbed her forehead and scrabbled through the pile of reports on her desk.

No matter how hard she tried, the images would not stick. For the hundredth time, Margaret pulled out the report on the soil composition of the riverbank and reexamined the path of the railway.

Geflitt and his preliminary surveyors insisted the placement of the tracks called for a tunnel rather than a bridge. That part of the Thames bent sharply. To reach the preferred location on the opposite bank, they couldn't use a viaduct bridge because of the uneven elevations of both sides.

Something about the soil composition report had Margaret reading it a third and fourth time.

If it were up to her, Margaret would simply alter the proposed locations and design a suspension bridge. Such an undertaking would be as difficult and controversial as a tunnel. However, what if . . . ?

Margaret stopped and placed a finger on the reports.

She wished her father were here.

A quiet man who lived in his head most of the time, he'd been the first to prompt Margaret to ask, "What if?"

"Science is much like art," he would tell her as they sat together on a rotting wood bench in the tiny garden of their London home. "Both the scientist and the artist ask themselves, what if? The artist has no restrictions on his answer. He might paint or sculpt any solution that strikes his fancy."

This struck Margaret as unfair, and she told her father so.

"Yes. A scientist must answer the question 'what if' using scientific principles," her father said. "He must work within the confines of what has been proven—unless he figures out what has been accepted before was incorrect."

"I would much rather be a scientist than an artist," she'd told him solemnly. "I like to follow the rules."

Those had been wonderful times before her father became too sick to work and when her mother believed Margaret would stop growing.

Now, Margaret stared at the reports and the frustrating equations that added up to a disaster. On a whim, she went downstairs and spoke with Geflitt's clerk. Half an hour later, she'd gotten the name of the geologist who had completed the soil surveys and wrote to him, asking for more details than she'd been given.

Unable to sit still any longer, Margaret returned to Athena's Retreat and walked through the halls in search of company.

"The greylag geese are majestic creatures deserving of our respect."

That stopped Margaret in her tracks. Majestic *flesh-eating terrors* is what they were, but Margaret kept that opinion to herself.

As she peeked around the doorway to the small lecture hall, Flavia stood at the other end of the room at the lectern in front of a row of mismatched chairs. There sat a handful of scientists, Violet and Althea among them.

"Railways cause great devastation to the animals and fauna around them when they are built. The amount of . . ." Flavia halted and stared over at her audience. "Is 'poisonous residues' too scientific? Should I say 'nasty rubbish' instead?"

Violet set a finger beneath her chin in thought. "'Nasty rubbish' has a nice ring to it."

"Do not be afraid to use scientific language," said Willy. "You must use all the gravitas you can muster. The more scientific the better, in fact, for most folks will have dismissed half your arguments before you open your mouth since you are a pretty young woman."

Damn. There must be another rally scheduled for the Society for the Preservation of the Greylag Goose in Great Britain, and Flavia was practicing her speech.

"If she is to use scientific arguments, why not simply declare herself a scientist like Madame Gault has declared herself an engineer and be done with it?"

Milly was there as well.

Margaret hadn't seen her at first since she sat on the far side of the room, her arms crossed over her chest, a truly magnificent cap of burnt gold silk with bright puce ribbons folded into roses at either side.

She looked furious. Willy appeared similarly angry, and tension saturated the air.

An immediate and overwhelming urge to go find Grantham swept through Margaret as she pulled away from the doorway and stood against the opposite wall. Certainly, he could distract from her worries, but for how long? Grantham could hold the world at bay for only a few hours at most. The women of Athena's Retreat and the conflict between them would not disappear anytime soon. Not unless Geflitt could be made to change the site.

Margaret peered back into the room. Flavia seemed flustered by

Willy's directions and Milly's remarks. Margaret considered intervening, despite her conflicting interests. Poor Flavia had worked so hard over the past two years to overcome her self-doubt.

"Well," Flavia soldiered on. "I thought I would tell people about the history of the greylag goose throughout Europe. The Romans credit the greylag geese with warning the city of the Gauls' approach in 390 BC."

"Hmmm." Willy frowned and crossed her arms over her chest. "Why don't you describe the goslings and how they will suffer if the railway trains run over their nests?"

Margaret hovered in the doorway, heart heavy. Here were her friends, doing what they were supposed to do—helping one of their members protect her field of study.

Did there always have to be a winner and a loser when two fields of study conflicted?

"Pictures of dead goslings?" Flavia shook her head, the worry lines of her forehead deepening. "That would make folks scared and upset. That isn't my aim."

"Scared and upset is how we feel every time those Guardians march around with their signs and their shouting," Milly said, rising to standing. "If you impede Madame Gault's progress, you—"

"You maintain the integrity of the British landscape. You force industry to question the consequences of constant industrialization," Willy said, her voice rising to cover Milly's protest.

"Your father is dead, Wilhelmina." Milly's words were like tiny missiles, puncturing Willy's anger. "He's dead and he will never accept you. You cannot go back and change his mind. You might save a hundred geese, breed a thousand grouse, do whatever it is he would have approved of, but it won't matter."

Willy gasped, clenching her fist between her breasts. The women in the room stared at one another in consternation and Flavia's face paled.

Milly's round cheeks were streaked with crimson, and tears stood in her eyes. "You can't take back anything you've done, and why should you? Your work is brilliant and so are you."

Even in distress, Willy remained poised. She lowered her hands and smoothed her skirts, posture perfect, chin slightly raised.

"You ascribe to him more power than he truly had, Mildred." Willy lifted her chin a fraction higher. "While I do not agree with his *reasons* for disliking the railways, I agree we have adopted scientific advancements without thinking through the consequences. Look what results from these new machines we have introduced in garment mills. More waste. Child labor. Hardship for those craftspeople losing their jobs."

Violet spoke now. "I don't believe Edmund Cartwright thought he would change the British economy for the worse when he invented the mechanical loom. I believe he hoped to make work easier for people."

"Be that as it may, in this instance we *do* know the result of this progress," Willy replied.

Milly threw her hands in the air and shook her head. "I cannot agree."

"I don't need you to agree," said Willy. "I need you to respect my opinion." Her perfectly squared shoulders bowed as if burdened by an invisible weight and her mouth softened. "But if it means I am in danger of losing you, I will stop speaking out."

"Oh." Milly's hands went to her cheeks, her rosebud mouth open in surprise. "Oh, my dearest," she said. "You will never lose me."

She closed the distance and came to stand before Willy, studying the other woman's face, relaxing at whatever she saw there.

"You may not agree with me now, but I am confident I will wear you down eventually."

Willy shook her head, but a smile slipped across her face. "It is I who will change your stubborn mind."

A blush rose on Margaret's cheeks at the way the two women regarded each other. She had a fairly good idea how this argument would be settled. So did the other women in the room, given how quickly it cleared out so Milly and Willy could reconcile in private.

Violet greeted Margaret with a hug and accompanied her to a small parlor for a chat.

"It's Grantham's stupid newspaper," Margaret muttered as she built a fire. "It's convinced people the greylag goose is in danger. It is not. The populations are healthy and thriving. It is simply one group of geese too lazy to fly to Iceland that will be displaced."

Margaret had been to Iceland once. Despite their ferocity, and the role they played now in her troubles, she understood the geese's reluctance to travel so far to a place where one couldn't find a decent cup of tea for love or money.

She wasn't a monster, for goodness' sake.

"Flavia believes differently," Violet said. "She has been documenting the migration patterns of various species over the whole of England. The introduction of railways into rural landscapes has displaced many nesting sites."

"And allowed for a stronger economy," Margaret replied. "We can move goods and people at twenty times the rate as we did ten years ago."

"At what cost?" Violet asked. She held her hand up when Margaret opened her mouth to answer. "I don't mean pounds. I mean what cost to the land and animals?"

Rising from her knees, Margaret made her way to the red velvet curtains, a lump of hurt sitting in her throat. Shouldn't Violet be arguing against Flavia? Isn't that what friends did? She closed the curtains to shut out the draft, yanking tight on a fraying rope tie.

"I don't believe *The Chronicle* is solely to blame for the controversy," Violet remarked. "This is the doing of Victor Armitage and his

Guardians." She yawned, small wrinkles drawing attention to the dark circles beneath her eyes.

Poor dear.

Sympathy warred with hurt that Violet had taken Flavia's side over Margaret's.

"If it weren't for Armitage, everything would be so much easier," Violet continued.

"Victor Armitage did not invent the controversy surrounding Athena's Retreat," Margaret pointed out. "That existed well before the Guardians came on the rise. Even if he is gone tomorrow, we will have to hide what we do here."

As usual, Violet had sensed Margaret's mood. "You mustn't worry, dear." Her friend gazed at her with warmth. "Flavia came to the members and asked for help. Of course they would rally around her. If you do the same, they will support you as well."

Yes. Flavia had asked for help.

Margaret, on the other hand, had assumed she would have to face the consequences alone. Her perfectly fitting corset became too tight, and the walls loomed inward at her. The sensation of taking up too much space, of being too big, of not getting it *right* threatened to suffocate her.

Ask for help? How did one do that exactly without admitting to flaws or seeming weak and stupid?

Instead, Margaret distracted Violet with talk of babies and physics and anything but how the walls were closing in.

17

I T'S TIME TO talk geese."

Grantham set down his pen and stared at Wolfe with trepidation.

"Are there any here?" he asked.

Wolfe squinted in confusion. "No." He ambled over to a spare chair Grantham had shoved against the wall, pulled it across the room, and set it next to Grantham's chair, then took a seat.

"Did you know they mate for life?" he asked. Leaning back, he peered through Grantham's window. "Interesting view."

Both men watched Margaret pace in front of her balcony doors, backlit by her oil lamps and the light from her skylights.

"It appears she is having an argument," Wolfe remarked.

"Talking to herself about angles. Those angles, they're always causing havoc," Grantham explained. "They have to be in the right place in order for everything else to happen."

"'Sat so?" Wolfe pursed his lips and rubbed his whiskers, perhaps contemplating what life might be like if all the angles fell into the right place. They sat in a comfortable silence for a while, and Grantham returned his attention to the speech.

Words were difficult for him. When he tried to write out his ideas, they banged around the inside of his head like rabbits, going this way and that. Trying to turn those ideas into full sentences took a great deal of time and concentration. Much easier to have a conversation with another person, to watch their face as they spoke, listen to their voice and how they held themselves. If left with merely words to either understand a concept or convey one, Grantham felt as if he were walking through quicksand.

"Did you choose to work in this room so you could watch Madame Gault without her knowing?" Wolfe asked.

Grantham dropped his pen, mouth agape. "Absolutely not," he admonished the other man. "First, I work here so I can oversee the excellent reporting you are doing on the Reform Bill as well as exact revenge on Victor Armitage. Second, I don't watch her without her knowing."

As he spoke the words, Margaret paused in her perambulations. She walked to the balcony doors, scowled at them, and pulled shut a pair of curtains.

"See?" Grantham said. "She knows."

"Interesting you mention Armitage." Wolfe leaned back even more until the front legs of the chair were in the air. Neat trick, that. If Grantham tried it, the chair would collapse.

"I've had Evans out doing some digging."

Grantham rolled his eyes. "Was he digging his way through another plate of steaks? I've noticed the restaurant reviews column is now weekly. The man eats like an elephant. No wonder the paper is losing money."

Truly, he did not care how often Evans escaped his wife's cooking.

Other than to remark to Evans perhaps *he* ought to learn how to make a meal, Grantham left the managing of such decisions to Wolfe.

This morning the first bite of winter woke him. Having left his town house without a greatcoat for his morning ramble, he'd had to increase the pace to keep from shivering. The uneven rows of brick and stucco houses stood along the street like poorly placed pickets in a gate, hedging the city's residents closer and closer to one another. Seeking the horizon, he walked to the river, where the scent of rubbish fires made him sneeze. He'd stood there for a while watching cargo ships pass by on their way out to sea.

Time to go home.

November meant the harvest had been taken in and winter preparations would have begun. Even when he was a boy who could not stay still, winter chores indoors were pleasant enough: fixing frayed harnesses and polishing tack, feeding the animals, and repairing any holes in the barns and outbuildings, all the time surrounded by the warm smell of manure and hay and the sounds of men laughing softly as they livened the monotonous work with songs and jest.

Another life called to Grantham.

The bill came for a vote in three weeks. Three weeks of him watching Margaret though a window and perhaps stealing a few more nights together.

What happened then? Did he migrate to London every spring and fall and try to see her? What if she met someone? Another engineer perhaps? And what of his mother and the estate?

"The key is Victor Armitage."

Grantham stared at Wolfe as though he'd two heads. "The key to what? Purgatory?"

Wind tapped a message at the windows and Grantham reminded himself to call the plasterers when a draft curled around his ankles.

"The key to the Futuro Consortium."

Something about Wolfe's manner made Grantham shift in his seat to face the editor. A canny light glowed in the man's eyes, giving him a predatory air.

"You have something to tell me and I'm not going to like it," said Grantham.

The other man's smile was a hairsbreadth away from a smirk and Grantham's stomach lurched.

"When Sir Royce Geflitt put together his consortium, he had trouble finding anyone to sign on. This seemed odd, seeing as folks are throwing money at railroads hand over fist."

Grantham rubbed his chin, the slight stubble persisting no matter how clean a shave he'd begun the day with. "True, it's all they talk about at parties these days, who has invested in which railway. Do you think this will be like the canals thirty years ago, where people invest so manically, the entire scheme collapses?"

Wolfe pulled a bag of boiled sweets from a coat pocket and offered it to Grantham first before selecting one himself and rolling it around his mouth. "If it is, we're nowhere near the crash, but there are warning signs. There are an awful lot of tracks being laid and not many places left to go. Last year the Gremende Consortium had to stop construction of their railway line only a fourth of the way into laying rails. Luckily, they bought insurance for the project and got their money back."

The scent of burnt sugar filled the office and Grantham's nose itched. "But Geflitt had trouble raising capital? Odd. Geflitt has a good reputation as a businessman. He's gentry as well."

Nodding, Wolfe popped another candy in his mouth. "Gentry, yes, but with a manse and lands that need to be paid for and not enough folk left to care for it. You see, the problem wasn't Geflitt. The problem was, like you, other folks are wondering how long this bubble will last. They're a wee bit more careful about investing. Geflitt found his money in the end."

The relish with which Wolfe said those words gave Grantham a bad feeling.

"I won't like where that money came from, will I?" he asked glumly.

Wolfe glanced out the window at where Margaret's curtains remained closed. Grantham had contemplated climbing the building earlier this morning, but she'd sent a note telling him she was preparing for a meeting and could not be disturbed.

"Victor Armitage is nowhere listed on the paperwork that issued the consortium," said Wolfe. "He did, however, take out a bank loan for a goodly sum of money two months ago. The same amount enabled Geflitt to qualify for insurance, and once he did, suddenly there were men lining up to invest."

The leaden sky punched down around the building and Grantham struggled to draw breath. A faint wash of soot stained the windows and colored his view of the world a dingy shade of brown.

Victor Armitage had paid for Margaret's grand project.

"The engineering firm tapped to design the tunnel has not been announced," said Wolfe.

"No." Grantham's voice sounded tinny to his ears, as if it came from far away.

"It is Madame Gault's firm, is it not?"

If Grantham squinted, he could see the curtains ripple every so often. He pictured Margaret pacing her rooms, pencil in her hair, frown pulling at the corners of her mouth.

"Mrs. Hill and Miss Dertlinger have spoken of her with great admiration and affection. I believe Miss Dertlinger sees her as something of a sisterly figure."

Althea and Mala would be devastated. Violet would be devastated. All of Athena's Retreat would be aghast.

They would never forgive her.

Grantham didn't know if *he* could forgive her.

Why? Why had she taken that man's money after he'd tried to shut down Athena's Retreat?

"Here's what I'm thinking," said Wolfe. "We put out an issue revisiting the terrible things Armitage has said about women then point out he has employed a woman engineer to design the tunnel. Evans is a master of metaphors. We could even come up with a few slogans of our own. *Engineer a way for women to work,* for example."

"It is not illegal, is it?" Grantham asked.

It took a moment for Wolfe to understand what Grantham was asking.

"That Armitage lent Geflitt the money but is not listed as a member of the consortium? It is not."

Grantham nodded. He pushed himself out of the chair and wandered over to a bookshelf. There were forty-three volumes on the shelves; he'd counted them one day when trying to find the right words to convince a group of privileged men who'd never wanted for anything they should care about the plight of anonymous children whom they would never encounter.

Now Grantham touched the spine of each of the books as he wrestled with what to do. It did nothing to clear his head.

Wolfe was going to print news. Not hyperbole. Not innuendo. These were facts that would sway popular opinion against Armitage forever. Grantham had worked toward that man's demise for months now, and the entire time, Margaret was in his employ.

What would the women of Athena's Retreat do to her when they found out? What would Violet say?

"Put together an alternate issue without the story about Armitage," Grantham said. "In case we need to do more research."

Wolfe's lips thinned. "And what would that alternate issue contain, my lord? Alternate facts? The truth is Armitage is a hypocrite, and he deserves to be exposed. He is a silent investor in a project that will make Madame Gault one of the most famous women in this country."

"Just do as I say." Grantham cringed inwardly at the imperious tone he'd adopted.

Might Margaret be ignorant of Armitage's funding?

God, he hoped so.

He needed to hear the truth from her before they printed anything.

"The papers go out the door at six sharp tomorrow morning, my lord." Wolfe stared at him, disappointment clear in his gaze.

"Yes, yes." Grantham waved a hand. "Give me until then to look into something. If you don't hear from me, print the issue with the story about Victor Armitage."

MARGARET DID NOT cry at her father's funeral.

When Marcel died, she did not leave her apartment for two weeks, but she did not cry.

When her father-in-law, Henri, blamed her barrenness on her insistence on working, she was furious, but she did not cry.

She did not even cry when George told her he wouldn't marry her after all.

As Margaret left the first annual meeting of the Futuro Consortium, she was not crying but every ounce of her willpower went into keeping her eyes dry.

Those shriveled gnomes with their white muttonchops and stupid medals they probably earned by sending men to die needlessly. How she loathed the condescension of such men, born of their self-satisfaction and having nothing to do with their decidedly lacking personal attributes. Margaret doubted they even understood the theory behind combustion engines.

These were the types of men who ruled her country.

When she'd proposed an alternative to the tunnel which would cost less, be ready in half the time, and avoid the issue of the greylag geese's nesting site, they'd stared at her as though she'd sung an opera in Greek.

"A suspension bridge?" asked one gentleman. "We asked for a tunnel. How difficult could it be to dig a hole in the ground?"

"This sort of nonsense at the last minute is why we cannot justify paying your exorbitant salary without having a man in charge along with you," intoned another.

Exorbitant salary? Her rate was half of what any other engineer in England would charge. She'd spent almost nothing because of her worries about Armitage.

"This project was bound to be expensive, but the initial outlay is more than I'd bargained for," another man grumbled. "This is what comes of having women involved in men's matters."

He peered at her, his eyes traveling from her face to her breasts and lingering for a moment, making Margaret feel as though she'd been doused with a bucket of spiders.

Finally, he turned to Geflitt. "You haven't failed us before, but I want an accounting of every penny she's spent since you agreed to this farce."

Geflitt agreed without a word of protest, as if it mattered not to him that this was her life in his hands.

"Madame Gault will go back to the original designs without delay and deliver on time," he'd assured them. "A more pressing concern is the bird people. It appears there is an encampment at the worksite, and we cannot proceed with the groundbreaking as planned."

"Get rid of them," one man shouted. "That piece of land is ours. Shoot them if you must."

"Between these stupid geese people and this ridiculous notion of hiring a woman, we are bound to be a laughingstock. Our shares will be worth nothing," the man said.

The discussion continued. Over her. Around her. Through her.

Margaret waited for breath to return to her. Once it did, she calculated her options while the men moved on to discuss cast iron versus wrought iron and the new influx of upstart Americans into the railway industry.

She could stand and condemn them for being overfed, overbred, and downright ignorant. As satisfying as that might be, Margaret harbored little hope they would change their behavior based on a string of insults. Another option would be to try and explain the science behind her idea to change their plans. Perhaps she hadn't used the right diagrams? If, for example, she drew a man shooting a person with a bird hat at the end of it, might they pay more attention?

None of these options would make any difference. Instead, Margaret adjusted her bonnet strings, collected her reticule, and left the room.

"Madame Gault?"

Geflitt hurried out of the room and caught up to her as she approached the cloakroom, where she'd left her paletot and umbrella.

"You mustn't take their criticisms to heart."

"Must I not?"

"They pay a good deal of money to have opinions," Geflitt said. "They air them, then we open a window and let them float away."

He nodded at her as if to say, *We understand, we two.*

But he didn't understand. He would never understand.

"I worked for a long time under trying conditions to become an engineer," she said, refurling her umbrella and making sure to secure it before she left the building. "I spent twelve years proving myself every day to men who had half my brains and a quarter of my vision."

Geflitt opened his mouth then shut it again, appearing mildly amused by her revelation.

"I am tired of it," she said. "The geologists I contacted say I am correct. If we change the location an insignificant amount, a bridge will work as easily if not better than a tunnel. They sent me a copy of the surveys they did last year, which are far more optimistic than the ones you received. You see . . ."

The words slid off him like the greasy rain outside. "Yes, yes. I understand but a tunnel will bring us the attention we need to stand out from competing railways."

Another question occurred to her. "Why did they say the project is already mounting exorbitant costs?"

Geflitt hesitated. So slight she might not have noticed if she weren't staring straight at him, his eyes shifted to the side, then to her. "They wouldn't know how much it costs to hire laborers or the price of iron or timber struts. Anything paid for instead of written out as an IOU is foolish to them."

Unease crept along Margaret's spine and her palms grew wet.

Something was wrong here.

"I won't do it."

Geflitt chuckled. "Come now. I've told you there's nothing to worry about. You continue with your plans, and I will handle the consortium members."

"I don't think you understand," she said. "I am finished. I won't be dismissed by a group of men who can't even count past twenty."

His laughter ceased abruptly, and goose bumps broke out on Margaret's skin.

"You will not stop, Madame Gault." Something about Geflitt's voice carved a thin line of fear down her spine. "You will abandon your plans for a suspension bridge, and you will turn in your designs for that tunnel."

Without turning her head, Margaret ensured there were other people walking in and out of the hotel's corridors. The tips of her fingers felt numb. Gone was the handsome, enthusiastic gentleman who'd encouraged her designs a few weeks ago.

In his place was a man who had heard a threat.

"You have a contract," he said, each word dropped into the space between them with the aim of a marksman. "You will fulfill it, or you will never again work anywhere in the English-speaking world."

Trying to swallow, Margaret righted her shoulders, hoping her fear didn't show on her face. "That contract includes language giving me the right to cease services if I have concerns—"

"One word from me to Armitage and you will be lucky to find work as a washerwoman, let alone as an engineer." He stared at her as though she were one of Althea's specimens beneath a microscope. "Did you not understand this from the beginning? Your reputation, the reputation of anyone who is close to you, it could all come crashing down with a single article in *Gentlemen's Monthly*. Such is the power of the pen, my dear."

All feeling left her limbs as Geflitt's genial smile returned as though he'd never threatened her and he patted her shoulder, like a master petting a dog.

"There, now. I shall be away next week. Write that accounting of your spending Walters asked for and see if you can't lower the cost for the tunnel borer. We will meet when I return. By then, I am certain, you will be as enthusiastic and optimistic about the project as I am. As are we all."

Margaret said nothing, but her surrender must have shown in her expression, for he nodded happily and walked away.

Your reputation, the reputation of anyone who is close to you, it could all come crashing down.

Who else would Geflitt hurt if she did not comply with his demands?

What had she done?

With no moisture in her mouth, Margaret could barely pry her lips open to refuse the footman who stood outside the hotel when she left a few seconds later. Like a heaving beast, Grantham's carriage waited a few feet away, horses pawing at the muddied streets.

Of course he was here today of all days.

With an awkward jerk of her head, she signaled her acquiescence, and the footman opened the door and pulled down the stairs. It took most of her energy to concentrate on not tripping or falling as she climbed in, so little blood circulated to her extremities. All of it froze in residual fear.

The interior of the carriage had changed since the last time she'd found respite within. There were no piles of blankets or clever cups of tea. Neither was there any hint of sympathy in Grantham's gaze where he sat opposite her, his arms crossed over his body, blue eyes narrowed, mouth bent downward.

He knew.

"The Stafford Arms Hotel," said Grantham as Margaret settled into the seat opposite him. "Quite a spectacular setting. Did Armitage pay for that as well?"

"Bring me to my office, please." She managed to force the words past what felt like cotton in her mouth.

Grantham said nothing as the carriage pulled away from the hotel. He might be furious with her, but Margaret was not immune to his presence near hers in the dark. His thighs were slightly splayed, and she could picture them as she'd seen them last. Perfectly sculpted to display the intricate layers of muscle, skin, and sinew; she wanted to press herself against one, feel the golden curls against the uncovered core of herself.

Pointless fantasy in a world about to crash around her.

"Why don't I bring you to Athena's Retreat? You can tell the ladies there about the outcome of your meeting," he said. Not a hint of emotion colored his voice.

"You know why I couldn't tell you," she said.

With a derisory huff, he shook his head. "Because you were ashamed?"

Margaret lifted her chin and looked away from him, catching glimpses of the city through a crack in the curtains.

"Why, Margaret?" he asked.

She wouldn't meet his gaze, staring instead at the flashes of color outside the carriage, the bright crimson of a town house door, the deep indigo of a gentleman's greatcoat.

"In all the world, there has always been one person who I could trust. Even you failed me once," she whispered.

Grantham's head jerked back against the cushions as if she'd slapped him.

"I told you why, Maggie," he said. "I couldn't take you away from a future as an engineer."

"I don't blame you," she told him. "When you came back into my life, I thought it might be a sign." The pressure in her chest building since Geflitt had threatened her grew more intense by the second. She had to relieve the pressure. There were words she needed to say.

"A sign I'd paid whatever dues I've owed for not following in my father's footsteps, for disappointing my mother for being so big and unnatural, for not wanting to be just a wife or mother like every other girl, for working so hard for so little reward. I thought having you back meant the world would hold me gently in its hands for one. *Damn. Minute.*"

"Maggie?" Grantham reached across the carriage for her, but Margaret forestalled him.

"It wasn't a sign, Georgie. There was no forgiveness. I am still that same stupid gangly girl who wants to build towers instead of pour tea and no one will ever . . ." Something was wrong. Her face heated and her nose burned, and the air left the carriage.

"I . . . stay away, don't—" Something was wrong. Something was very wrong. "My eyes, I'm . . ."

For the first time since she was a child, Margaret Gault began to cry.

18

❧

THEY WERE TEARS. Water and something else, probably some disgusting chemical stuffs Violet would tell him about in detail. Not the plague. Not anything fatal.

Grantham's heart beat triple time, a cold sweat beading his brow. "How can I . . . what can I . . ."

Margaret peered at him through her tears and the world shifted again. *Again.* Every time this woman was in his presence, the damned universe kept tossing him to his knees.

She never cried. Not when she fell from the tree house and broke her ankle, not when her father died, and not when he told her he couldn't marry her.

"Those stupid, stupid men," she said in between sobs.

The world made sense again at those words. Someone had hurt her feelings, most likely doubted her. Easy to fix.

"Tell me who is stupid, and I shall find them and beat them bloody," he said, shifting himself over to sit next to her despite her protests. Her handkerchief was damp from her weeping, and he offered his own, gathering her in his arms as they rode through the city.

When she bent her head and rested on his shoulder, Grantham knew she was where she needed to be.

"All of them. All of them are stupid and shortsighted and I hate them." She spoke into his greatcoat, her bonnet poking him in the eye, but he didn't mind.

"Come, we will go home to my house for tea. We are practically there," he said when she tried to object. "Unlike the kitchens of Beacon House, mine is never in short supply of delicious sugary biscuits."

Grantham's cook did not make a liar of him. He called for the cozy upstairs parlor to be readied, and by the time he got Margaret out of the carriage and hung her paletot and bonnet, a merry fire burned in the fireplace. Soon enough, a pot of tea and a heaping platter of biscuits and tea cakes appeared.

One of the few rooms Grantham's mother had refurbished before she lost interest in coming to London, the parlor had walls papered with a crimson damask and pretty polished end tables covered in bright gold silk cloth. On the mantel a chinoiserie porcelain clock took pride of place and the old portraits of some forgotten ancestors had been replaced with a landscape by the late Richard Bonington.

"How did you find out about Armitage's funding?" Margaret asked.

Grantham oversaw the selection of a goodly portion of cakes to her plate then his own before he took a seat on the soft moss-colored sofa.

The fire battled the worst of the cold, but the room was still chilled. With only himself in residence during the fall season, most of the rooms were shut up and took ages to heat. It nettled him, that he could not warm her properly. Margaret didn't complain. Her eyes remained on the plate in front of her, the strong line of her nose slanted downward, lashes lowered—his indomitable Amazon drooped.

"Wolfe figured it out. He smelled a story and sent Evans and Dodson digging." Grantham thought about the details of Wolfe's reporting. "Geflitt was desperate for money and Armitage stepped in to save him. I thought Geflitt had a better head for business."

"Yes, well, Geflitt is not all he seems," she said.

Something in her voice worried him.

"Margaret?" he asked. "Has Geflitt—"

"It doesn't matter," she said quickly. "I suppose if someone like Evans, who uses 'smashing' to describe everything from steak to spring flooding, can find out Armitage funded the consortium, he didn't do a good job at covering his tracks."

Grantham thought about it. "Unless he didn't expect Geflitt to ever hire a woman."

"Perhaps," said Margaret glumly. "Although he is one of those men who says one thing and does the opposite, and because he does it so brazenly, others let him get away with it."

"Why are you taking his money?" Grantham asked.

The question had been sitting like a stone in his throat since Wolfe gave him the news. How could this woman who championed other women accept Armitage's funds?

Margaret set down the plate, the lovely biscuits untouched, and picked up her gloves. She'd set them aside to eat, and now she smoothed out each finger against her knee.

"You have been a long time among the aristocracy. Have you forgotten what your mother had to endure to make a living while your father took himself off for months at a time?"

He had not.

All the hours and hours Mam hunched over her cushion and bobbins making her lace. It took weeks to make a piece large and fine enough to sell and she was never paid what she thought it was worth. If she complained, the shopkeeper would tell her to leave; he could always find another lace maker.

When people came to her to write letters for them, sometimes they would pay her less than they'd promised. She had no man to defend her, and half a shilling was better than none.

"If I am to run a firm full of women engineers, I cannot be discerning," Margaret insisted. "It is easy for the scientists inside the laboratories of the club to remain protected and unsullied by commerce. Once you step out of the lab, there are myriad sacrifices and compromises you must make if you would also *eat*."

"There will be other projects . . . ," he said half-heartedly, and stopped talking when she cast him a cutting glance.

The second ever tunnel beneath the Thames. What other projects would come along and give her such fame?

"Why must *I* give way?" she said, fists balled, launching herself from the settee to pace the room. "Why do I have to wait for what I want? Why can't I be first? I can't be beautiful like my mother. I can't be a genius like my father—I can do *one* thing well. Why must I give it up?"

She clasped her hands together in a gesture of supplication. "You understand. Of all people, I know you do."

"Yes, but will happen afterward?" he asked her. "You do not see it, but Althea lights up when you walk in a room. Violet is so happy you are together again. Those connections will be lost, and you will be alone."

"I hoped if I could achieve the Plan, perhaps it would be a first step to opening Athena's Retreat."

"Do you mean revealing the secret of you scientists?" Grantham asked. "Won't that be dangerous?"

Margaret's reddened eyes widened. "It is already dangerous. We are trapped in hidden rooms while the Guardians shout slogans and Armitage demeans us in his magazine. We are at the mercy of unscrupulous men who can ruin our lives with just one word."

Those men included himself. If he let Wolfe print the article, it would expose her not only to her friends, but to the world.

"Margaret..."

She held her hands out to the fire, her back so straight, head held high. Grantham rose from his seat and came to stand at her side, running a comforting hand down her spine. Beneath the cotton of her dress was the outline of her corset and the laces that kept it wrapped tight around her, like a caress.

Should he tell her about the story?

"What will you do when the members of Athena's Retreat find out about Armitage?" he asked. "I mean . . . eventually this information will come out. Evans and Wolfe will not keep it to themselves forever."

The winds outside pressed their boneless fingers against the glass in his windowpanes, the fire sputtering as some of the rain outside made its way down the chimney.

"I will continue my work for the Futuro Consortium until the terms of my contract come to an end," she said. "I cannot walk away."

A terrible foreboding sat on his chest, an invisible weight he could not define. Was this the end of them? Would Margaret retreat to her office alone like a princess deliberately locking herself away from the rest of the world? Was it his role to bring her down?

Would it be fair to try and rescue her if she didn't want to be rescued?

"It is cold in here," she said.

Grantham reached over and took her hands between his own, tugging at her until she turned to face him. Such beautiful hands she had. They were not petite and chubby, like Violet's, nor pale and soft like other ladies'. They were the hands of a capable woman who might leave him in the next breath. A woman who did not need him, but who might be convinced to want him, one last time.

"Let me warm you."

Never letting go of her hands, he brought her upstairs to his bed-chamber, where the fire between them kept away the cold.

In the morning, Grantham would send word to hold the presses for one day. He couldn't tell her about the story right now. It would be cruel. He would keep her here by his side tonight. Tomorrow, he would be there with her as she told the women of Athena's Retreat about what she had done.

As for what might happen the day after tomorrow, Grantham hoped for the best.

And feared for the worst.

GRANTHAM SLEPT IN the same way he made love—exposed, no attempt to hide himself. He snored lightly now, sheet around his ankles, baring himself to the world.

If Margaret ever told him how magnificent he was, she'd never hear the end of it.

He was, though.

When she lit a candle to help her find her clothes, the rust-colored flame revealed the outlines of Grantham's sleeping body.

His chest was broad as a blacksmith's, a great arch of muscles and bone. The smooth indentations delineated symmetrical bands of muscles carving a path along his torso, bisected by a line of fine blond hair that spread around the base of his thick penis, which lay curled between his thighs.

His arms were splayed out across the bed, and one hand came off the side of the mattress, pointer finger extended. She could see a vein at his wrist marking the seconds, bouncing beneath his skin, as if part of him must be moving, even when asleep.

Now she noticed there were other signs of Grantham's ever-present energy. A muscle twitched above his knee, and his eyelids flickered.

"A bit like Michelangelo's *David*, aren't I?"

Startled, Margaret laughed too loud, then caught herself, although Grantham's staff must have been aware she'd spent the night in his bed. Too late to be worried about discretion, she supposed.

"You are insufferable," she told him.

Grantham opened his eyes and reached his arms above his head, bowing his back and flexing his buttocks.

Preening.

"Where are you going?" he asked. "It isn't yet dawn. We've plenty of time ahead of us."

Margaret studied the clothes she'd collected, then set them at the foot of the bed. She didn't tell him behind the thick curtains the sun was already climbing the iron grey November skies. Instead, she pretended it was still night and there were hours and hours to go before morning. Clad in only her chemise, she returned to the mattress and settled herself beside him.

Madness.

"I must go to the club to change my clothes. I have to be out to the warehouse today before nine o'clock. There have been two deliveries there that don't make any sense and I must clear them up."

Grantham said nothing but took her hand in his and ran a thumb along the side of her palm. The action soothed her, and Margaret let her brain rest and, for a few stolen minutes, imagined spending every morning waking in this bed.

"Do you ever wonder," Grantham said idly, ". . . now we know our present selves, if I'd have taken you to Canada . . ."

Rolling onto his side, he stared at her face, running a finger over the bridge of her nose.

". . . do you think we would have been happy?"

What kind of question was this?

"I don't know. I can't . . ."

What to say? She stared deliberately at the ceiling, not wanted to see his reaction to her words.

"I do not see the world the same way as you," Margaret explained. "The story you told me the night of the ball, of walking over my bridge and coming to an understanding of who I am and how I needed to live—" She stopped and breathed in the scent of his warm skin, salt and sweat and something that made her feel as though they were beneath the willow.

"I would have walked that bridge a thousand times and not have made the same connection as you did," she said. "I want the world to work in straight lines and right angles. If I try to imagine the future or reimagine the past, it becomes a blur."

He laughed, low and rich like treacle. Unexpected, the sound vibrated in her belly and she grew wet between her legs at the way his breath caressed her skin, at the languorous possession in his touch as he gently palmed her breast.

"Can it be my tiny man brain is better at something than yours?"

Foolish to tease her so.

As an answer, Margaret sat and pulled her chemise over her head, reveling in the way his eyes grew dark, and his breath hitched.

She'd spoken the truth. To imagine a life other than the one she'd made left her dizzy and confused. Why revisit the past? Would it have any bearing on the fact they'd found each other again?

"I imagine all sorts of scenarios," he said, turning the back of his hand and skating it over the slope of her breast, flipping it and gently rolling her nipple between his thumb and forefinger.

How easily he touched her now, as if they were long-standing lovers. Margaret, on the other hand, felt like a child who'd opened a toy box. The dip in his clavicle, the smooth circles of his nipples in the centers of his massive pectorals were endlessly fascinating.

She marveled at the symmetry of his body, the way the muscles of his abdomen rippled in waves when she ran her fingers along them, delighted with the sensation of strength beneath the softness.

"You are lost to me," he whispered. "Where have you gone to in that head of yours?"

Margaret raised her head and bit her lip, sheepish. "I wondered if one might use thin cables, like the fibers of a muscle, and wrap them around iron beams, almost like bones."

Rather than be annoyed, Grantham laughed without restraint. "By God, Margaret. Does your brain ever rest itself? I suppose I should be flattered you are inspired by the magnificence of the body before you."

Pulling her atop him, her breasts pushed against his chest, he kissed her firmly, then slipped his hand down her spine to rest on her bottom.

"You should be," she agreed.

"Hmmm." He kissed her again, more slowly this time, his fingers kneading the crease where her bottom met her thighs. Between their stomachs, he grew hard again. Margaret slipped from his embrace and retrieved a condom, relishing the hard length of him as she fitted him with the sheath.

Grantham studied her face while she did, eyes unreadable.

"If you ever do build that bridge, I hope you name it for the part of me you admire the most."

A flippant answer sat on the tip of her tongue, but she swallowed it. The truth sat in her chest, squeezing some of the breath from her. The parts of him she admired most were the parts she couldn't find in herself these days. Honesty. Hope. A willingness to trust and believe in the goodness of the world.

Soon she would leave him. It could not be this way—Grantham touching her with unabashed affection and joy while she hid the deepest parts of herself from him. Everything about this man was an affront to her love of straight lines and orderly processes and a separation of herself from the messiness of the real world.

She could not resist when he set his mouth to her skin and wrote naughty words on her breast with his tongue. She could not say no when he asked if he could touch her there, if it felt good, would she like it harder, softer, longer. She could not hold back a cry of wonder when he moved within her while touching her in such a way that sparks went off behind her eyelids.

Her release lay close and everything in this room, in all of London, in all the world, held her tethered to this moment and this man, and she rode him harder, wanting to be closer, closer than having him inside her. She bit on her bottom lip to keep from spilling her secret.

Margaret loved him.

Oh, she'd always loved him in the way of fast friends and first loves, but this emotion coursing through her veins was different. He was the dawn, the first light, the way home, and she had to strangle the powerful urge to tell him.

What good would that do if they couldn't be together? What if she told him and he left her again?

Leaning down, she pressed her torso against his, moving her hips in a rhythm faster and faster until her mind quieted in the pursuit of climax, the sensation leaving her fingers and toes as pleasure pulled her away from the world.

A groan issued from somewhere deep in her belly as her vision went dark then exploded in light. The terrible tension pulling at the bundle of nerves between her legs now snapped and she contracted around Grantham's penis deep within her.

Again and again, she shuddered, torrents of pleasure tossing her about like a leaf caught in a windstorm. She flew unfettered, unable to stop the sensation.

Grantham's hips thrust upward throughout her climax, prolonging her pleasure. Her swollen clit pulsed over and over, sending bliss along her spine every time he pushed his hips up until the pleasure threaded with pain.

"Let go," he urged her. "You can trust me. You can let go."

A second orgasm took her by surprise, and she lost her breath as a huge rush of warmth swept through her body from her head to her toes.

"Maggie," he whispered.

Her arms shook as she raised herself over him, head down and nodding with every lazy thrust of his hips.

"I need to turn you over."

Allowing Grantham to move her like a rag doll, his thick cock hard within her, Margaret looked at him through a haze of bliss. Her legs fell open and he pulled one close against his torso, hooking it over his shoulder as he pushed deep within her.

"Can you still feel pleasure?" he asked, the strain of holding back his thrusts apparent in his voice. A vein stood out on his neck, and she wanted to put her mouth to it, but was too spent to move. "I can stop if you wish."

Speech was lost to her, as if her brain had finally managed to detach from her body and she was only left with a sense for pleasure. Only when he paused did she manage to form words.

"No." The word came out like a grunt, his hips locked with hers, pressing her into the mattress as he continued to bear down on her in a slow, maddening rhythm. "Don't stop, I think . . ."

From somewhere deep inside, another culmination approached.

"Once more," she confessed, grabbing hold of his arse and pulling him against her, grinding herself against his pubic bone and arching. "I'm going to come once more."

Jaw clenched so tightly the muscles in his face grew impossibly taut, a bead of sweat rolling from Grantham's temple to his cheek. Her focus narrowed to the place where they joined, his entire body giving her as much pleasure as the friction of his cock within her. Their skin slid and slapped while an ache of pleasure deeper than anything she'd ever felt spiraled low in her belly.

Her fingers slipped as they ran up his spine and tried for purchase on his shoulders, wet and slick. He swiveled his hips until she had no place to go.

Her climax came slowly, like a wave. It began at the core of her and rolled outward, a surge of pleasure flooding every part from the roots of her hair to the tips of her toes. So all-encompassing, the pleasure felt detached from their frantic lovemaking. It overwhelmed the confines of her skin and flowed outward, her mouth opening in a low moan, tears streaming down her cheeks.

With a muted roar, Grantham arched his back, his arms holding her close as he pulsed within her. For long hazy moments after his release Margaret listened to the sound of their heartbeats echoing in the space around them.

"Maggie," he whispered, nuzzling her temple, kissing away the tears that wet the sides of her face.

Why was she crying? What strange and terrible reaction was this?

"I didn't hurt you?" he asked.

There were words for what had happened between them. There were declarations to be made and vows to be delivered, but Margaret couldn't speak. Instead, she took his head between her hands and stared at the miracle of his face, the way he glowed like newly minted sovereigns when he was happy.

"That was . . ." Margaret searched her brain for words to describe how she felt without exposing the core of her. "That was good."

"Good?" He laughed with genuine mirth, sounding like a church bell, solid and clear. Pulling himself from the clasp of her body, he slipped an arm beneath her, then rolled her over, laying her body fully atop his, toes nearly touching.

"You must stop with the flattery, Margaret." Once more he laughed, then kissed her forehead and her lips.

She slipped sideways so she could rest her head on his chest.

"That was . . . very good?" she ventured.

"I am embarrassed by your praises," he said dryly.

Chuckling, she breathed in the scent of him, committing it to memory.

"Margaret." Grantham traced the line of her spine with his thumb, and she shivered. "Considering how wild you are for my skills in bed . . ."

"Are they skills?" she asked. "Or is it beginner's luck?"

He nipped her ear, then continued, "Considering as well how we get on, and furthermore considering what a remarkable specimen of virility and intelligence I am . . ."

"'Remarkable' is one word," she said.

"Don't you think it would be advantageous for you if we married?"

All Margaret's relaxed muscles stiffened in an instant, pain flaring in her jaw, she clenched it so tight.

Grantham reacted by enfolding her in his arms, but she pushed away, wanting to see his face.

"Do not jest, please," she scolded him.

Even as she spoke, the flush on his cheeks and the tilt of his mouth told her he hadn't jested.

"We rub on well enough," he said. "We could do worse than look forward to this every morning."

Not the most romantic proposal Margaret had ever imagined, but then she'd not imagined any proposal—other than the one Grantham had made when he asked her the first time. The ache of loss for what might have been sat like a brick in her belly as she tried to figure out why Grantham would propose at all.

"We can do this every morning without having to be married," she pointed out.

He reached out to touch her face, but his hand stopped halfway, and he pulled it to his side. The sweet sky blue in his eyes darkened despite the sliver of candlelight lying across his face and the rest of his pillow, pulling out strands of brown and silver from the mass of buttery gold hair falling over his forehead.

"I . . ."

He took her hand in his and scrutinized it as if he'd never seen it before, then raised his gaze to hers.

Margaret held her breath, staying perfectly still. Perhaps something deeper than lust, deeper than companionship, spurred him. If he loved her in return, loved her with the same intensity as she loved him, surely now he should say so.

"Wouldn't it be more practical if we married?" he asked.

Margaret yanked her hand from his.

Practical.

What an oaf.

Oblivious, Grantham continued, "Awfully convenient when we're in the same house anyway. Then there's your office. You could take my carriage instead of taking a hack every morning. Makes sense when you think about it . . ."

Slipping off the mattress, she made her way to the washstand and cleaned herself with cold water and a flannel.

"Don't be silly, George," she said to the spotted looking glass hanging above the milky white pitcher and bowl. "What countenance would you have left if you married a businesswoman? I work in a man's occupation—I'm not even considered a gentlewoman anymore."

She undid her hair from a loose braid, combing it out with her fingers. From the corner of her eye, she watched him, lying flat, staring at the salmon and gold brocaded canopy of his enormous bed.

"Don't have much countenance to speak of as it is," he mumbled. "Whatever I have, thought it might do you some good."

"Borrowed countenance?" she asked. Pulling her hair back, she set her pins in place, taming a few rogue whisps trying to escape.

"When the club members find out about Armitage, I can . . ."

There might have been a chance to ask for help but Geflitt had made it impossible. He would tear her down and bring Violet and maybe even Grantham along with her.

No. Margaret had no choice but to go through with the project.

"You can what?" she asked. "Rescue me? Hold me in one hand while you carry me away from my worries? You tried that before, remember?"

A trick of the light made it appear as though he shrank at her words.

"I cannot marry you, George. You must know that." Margaret adopted a brusque tone, devoid of any hurt from his lack of sentiment. "An engineer cannot be a countess, and a countess cannot be an engineer. Now. Where are my clothes?"

19

As Grantham's carriage pulled out of the mews, Margaret distracted herself from his confusing proposal by thinking of everything she needed to do today. First, she had to sort out the strange orders by this week or they would show on the explanation of expenses she was supposed to do for the consortium.

Otherwise, Geflitt would have even more ammunition to use against her should she muster the courage to part ways with him.

After she went out to the warehouse to send back the goods that were mistakenly delivered, Margaret planned on paying a call to Flavia. Even if Geflitt would not let her refuse the commission, she would find a way to keep the geese safe.

She and Flavia would work together to find a compromise that allowed for progress alongside conservation. It might not be ideal, but nothing ever was.

By the time the carriage pulled around to Athena's Retreat, the morning had advanced enough that a footman stood at the side entrance. Margaret had no wish to advertise she'd spent a night elsewhere. Yesterday, her encounter with Geflitt had disturbed her enough that she'd forgotten about discretion. However, if anyone saw her getting into Grantham's carriage without a maid and recognized her clothes today as the same . . . well, that would be one way of escaping Geflitt's threats. A scandal bigger than either she or Grantham could contain would certainly change Geflitt's mind.

Thoughts on potential scandal and how she would carry on working with Geflitt's true nature distracted her and she turned down the wrong hallway. Instead of heading toward the stairs leading directly to the Retreat's guest rooms, she walked toward the front hallway and straight into Althea.

"Oh, Althea." Margaret switched her reticule from one arm to the other and reached to check her bonnet ties.

Damn. Most mornings she worked in her laboratory before dawn, so Margaret wasn't surprised she walked the halls this early.

"Good morning, Margaret. I mean—not that I'm—that is . . ." Her mouth opened in shock, Althea took a step back, then forward again. "Are you . . ." Her skin was pale, her lips lacking color.

Poor thing needed a nap.

"Have you come to confess?" Althea asked.

Confess?

The sensation of Grantham's hands on her breasts lingered; the marks he'd made with his mouth and teeth no doubt still stood out red and pink against her pale skin. Margaret opened her mouth to lie but the scent of his skin had imprinted over her own. Did this show in her face or had Althea seen the carriage?

"How did you . . . ?" Margaret groped for words. Althea was a gently bred young woman for all she understood about human physiology. What could Margaret say to her?

"Is it only you who knows of us?" she asked.

Althea's head reared back in surprise. "Only me? By this time, all of London knows."

All of London?

"All of London?" Margaret cried. "How? How could that be? I . . ."

Wait.

Althea wasn't scandalized or embarrassed.

She was *bereft*.

This was not about last night. This was about something much worse.

Pressing her glasses up the bridge of her nose, Althea appraised Margaret with a searching intensity, her delicate mouth bowing beneath the weight of a frown.

My God. Somehow Althea knew about Armitage.

"I must . . ." Margaret gathered her thoughts.

Violet. Violet would understand.

"I have to find Violet and . . ."

Althea pointed at the small parlor. "She is in there with Mr. Kneland. Milly and Willy are with them and we . . ."

Somehow Margaret managed to walk without stumbling into the small parlor where Violet sat by the fire, a newspaper clutched loosely in her hands. Milly and Willy stood next to her, Willy's arm around Milly's shoulder.

The Capital's Chronicle.

What had Grantham said?

"*. . . eventually this information will come out. Dodson and Wolfe will not keep it to themselves forever.*"

Violet held it for Margaret to see. The print was so large, she could read it from three feet away.

VICTOR ARMITAGE SINKS HIS POUNDS
UNDER THE THAMES

Margaret could not form words. She held out a trembling hand for the paper. Rather than letting Violet get up, Arthur handed it to Margaret.

Beneath the bold letters, the entire first page of the broadsheet carried a single story about how the Futuro Consortium had partnered with Victor Armitage. The details of Armitage's deal were laid out for all of London to read. How Geflitt had tried two years before to get funding for a railway and failed. How Armitage had stepped in to save the project.

At the bottom of the page, Margaret found what she feared most. Grey spots appeared before her, and she forced herself to breathe.

While Armitage's desire to keep quiet a relatively risky financial investment might be seen as mere prudence, *The Capital's Chronicle* has found a deeper, more insidious reason for his silence.

The Futuro Consortium has hired England's first and only female engineer, Madame Margaret Gault, to design their innovative tunnel. Madame Gault, the renowned designer of railway bridges across the continent, has recently left Henri Gault and Son to set up a firm on our shores.

Mme. Gault is highly respected for her engineering acumen as well as her savvy business practices. However, Mr. Armitage has been vociferous in his distaste for women working outside of their role as keepers of the hearth. Could his secrecy around his payments to the consortium be to hide his hypocrisy? In public, he whips his Guardians into mobs to harass poor women who are trying to feed their children. In private, he makes financial deals with firms employing women to line his own pockets.

The paper slipped from her numb fingers, cutting through the still air to land in a pile at her feet. All she could think of was Grantham's body laid out before her in the flickering candlelight. His words of praise and comfort as they lay facing one another amid his tousled sheets. The way he'd made love to her as if he searched for a way inside her skin while he knew this article would come out today. Had his proposal been a clumsy way to rescue her after the fact?

"Why didn't you tell me?" Violet's voice held not a hint of anger. Instead, she radiated sympathy and concern.

Sympathy.

What was Margaret supposed to do with sympathy? She could not push back against sympathy and hope to remain standing.

Rage. Sorrow. Those, Margaret could acknowledge and endure. Sympathy meant she could have told her friend everything.

Sympathy meant Margaret had done this all wrong.

"Armitage's men have terrorized the women of this club for two years," Arthur said. No inflection in his voice denoted his opinion of Margaret's actions but his eyes were hard and black as coal. "Now, you are in his employ. Are you certain it is safe for the club members to have you here? Does he know what we do here?"

Grantham called it the black stare of impending death and Margaret met the stare with her own.

Grantham.

Margaret wished he were here with her now. He would say something idiotic and maybe he and Arthur would knock over a plant stand or two, but it would have been lovely to feel his strength at her back.

Ironic, considering he was the reason she was in this mess.

Or was he?

Margaret had done this to herself, by taking the job and by keeping this a secret for as long as she had. Keeping everyone at arm's length so they would never know how inadequate she truly felt, no matter how deep she buried it beneath a facade of competence and industry.

Violet turned to Arthur with a frown. "Margaret would never put the club in danger."

"How are we to trust her?" Willy asked. "She has taken his thirty pieces."

Perhaps a bit overwrought, but Margaret bowed her head to accept the condemnation and waited for more.

"Enough!" Althea snapped. Willy frowned and Violet exchanged surprised glances with Margaret at Althea's unusual display of temper.

"We all make similar compromises." Althea rubbed her forehead, staring at nothing in the center of the room, the heat gone from her voice. "Why, the entire reason for women to marry is financial stability. Margaret had to take a man's money because so few of us have money of our own. How many of our members stay silent when their husband's employer says something prejudiced about science or women because they can't afford for them to lose their jobs?"

She rounded on Willy, setting her hands on her hips. "She took his money, but it is Margaret's name that will be forever attached to that tunnel. A woman engineer. That is *important*."

"What does it matter how amazing this tunnel is if its construction enriches men like Armitage?" Willy retorted. "You climb in bed with men like him and you lose your integrity along with your virtue."

Margaret bent and picked up the folded sheets of paper then looked around for somewhere to set them.

"She intends to create the first all-woman engineering firm in the country," Althea argued. "Are there not concessions we should be willing to make for a woman to be the first in something? How long do we have to wait?"

Althea, Milly, and Willy were standing in front of the low table near the settee. Violet and Arthur blocked the rosewood secretary. Margaret was left standing before them like an unruly student called before the headmistress, her gloves becoming grey with the ink from the papers.

"It doesn't matter, Althea," Margaret said, numbness receding and acceptance taking its place. "A hundred years from now, we will still be at their mercy."

This was not hyperbole. While men like Arthur and Grantham existed, they were exceptions.

"It's true," said Milly. "Mary Astell wrote pamphlets in support of equal education for women in 1696. Mary Leapor was condemning the injustice of unequal education and the oppression of the lower classes in 1730."

She stepped away from Willy's embrace and spoke to her. "Fifty years ago, Olympe de Gouges was denounced as unnatural and beheaded for advocating for communal property in a marriage. Nothing will change, Wilhelmina, unless we force it. In this case, the *results* of Margaret's actions are more important than who funds them."

Violet spoke from the chair where she sat. "I've learned over the years there are no hard-and-fast lines between what is wrong and what is right. There are gradients. There are compromises and those are not necessarily bad."

Willy opened her mouth, then closed it tight.

"There are very few true villains or heroes," Violet continued. "Only people who see the world in different ways."

At his wife's words, Arthur set a palm on her shoulder. The two exchanged an unreadable glance and Margaret again mourned the lack of Grantham's company.

How stupid of her.

"I have to leave," Margaret said.

Althea crossed the room and clasped her hands. "The members will understand. No one is forcing you from the club. If they so much as—"

"I meant I must clear out my office." Margaret squeezed her friend's palms, stepping away from them all. "There is no chance I will have a contract for employment after this."

She blessed whatever force kept her upright and regarded Willy with resignation. "Your point we must consider the far-reaching consequence of scientific progress is not wrong. I wanted so much to be the first, it drowned out most other considerations."

"I understand," said Willy softly. "As much as I want to stop the march of progress from trampling the most vulnerable, I, too, want to see a world where women can leave a permanent mark."

"What will you do afterward?" Violet asked.

Afterward, Margaret would take down her plaque from the wall and pack it away. She would apologize to the women of Athena's Retreat and accept their condemnation.

And then?

Then, she would find Grantham.

GRANTHAM WATCHED FROM the bedroom as his carriage left the mews, shading his eyes against the morning light so he could catch a last glimpse of Margaret's head in the carriage's rear window and cursed himself ten times over a fool for his terrible attempt at a proposal.

Greycliff and Kneland had been right after all. If he'd just reread a passage or two from *The Perils of Miss Cordelia* . . .

His hand dropped and he turned toward the bed when the meaning of what he'd done sank into his bones like the chill from a fever.

The sun was high enough to reach over the carriage house roof.

In the aftermath of their lovemaking and his pathetic proposal, he'd lost all sense of time.

Hollering for his horse, he'd known already it was too late. By now *The Chronicle* had left the press rooms and was out on the street. Still, he rode faster than was safe and nigh flew over the horse's head when he reached the doors of *The Chronicle*'s office.

"Those papers will be out on the streets or I—" Wolfe stood in the center of the office, hair standing in tufts on his head, where he'd no doubt run his fingers through in frustration. Mala Hill stood opposite him, arms full of cloth-bound periodicals and a basket at her elbow.

Both leveled frustrated stares at Grantham when he burst into the room.

"Here is Lord Grantham," Mala said with a tone of satisfaction. "He will agree with my actions and then he will no doubt punch you. Very hard. Twice."

Grantham rested his hands on his thighs while he fought to catch his breath.

"No . . . papers . . . stop them . . ."

"You said by six o'clock, my lord," Wolfe protested. "Six o'clock came and went. I waited an extra ten minutes."

Mala dumped the periodicals on the desk in front of her and set her hands on her hips.

"I spent the night in my laboratory at Athena's Retreat since two of my hedgehogs are due to give birth."

"Aargh!" Grantham stared at the basket in horror, convinced this day was sent directly from hell.

"Christ Jesu, Grantham," Wolfe said. "Those are scones."

"I came to deposit these materials before I went home and saw the first of the barrow boys leaving," Mala continued. "When I read the headline, I had Mr. Wolfe stop them until you arrived."

Relief washed through Grantham, and he took Mala's hand in his. "Thank you, Mrs. Hill. How did you manage to do that?"

Wolfe's ears turned a shocking shade of pink and Mala's mouth turned down into a frown. "Let us say some secrets are meant to be kept."

Another time, Grantham would do everything in his power to find out what Mala held over Moses Wolfe, but he had to speak with Margaret immediately.

"About the article," he said to Mala. "While you will want to speak with Margaret about her choices, I hope you will do her the kindness of listening to her reasons."

Curious brown eyes studied him, then Mala pulled her hand from his clasp. "I arrived here at twenty minutes after six o'clock. Three barrow boys had already left. One of them to the environs of Knightsbridge."

Grantham was out the door before she'd finished her sentence.

By the time he caught sight of Athena's Retreat, it was well past eight. Throwing the reins at the groom, he dashed inside, nearly knocking down the footman, Johnson.

"Is she here?"

Johnson, pale around the mouth, knew exactly about whom Grantham spoke.

"No, milord. She just left." He gestured with his chin toward the main rooms of the Retreat. "They're talking about the article right now. Maybe you want come back later?"

Tempting, but his mam didn't raise a coward.

Just a fool.

When he entered the small parlor, Althea leaned on the tiny mantelpiece in one of her ill-fitting dresses with tight sleeves most women here wore to keep from dipping a cuff into their experiments. The olive green shade of the dress made her look sallow, and dark circles accentuated her hollowed cheeks.

Violet and Kneland were speaking quietly in front of a street-facing window, and Milly and Willy were sitting close together on a pair of cushioned chairs. Milly wore one of her painfully bright day caps and Grantham suppressed a shudder.

Were the two ladies color-blind? Could Willy not say something to Milly before they left the house?

"Grantham." Kneland greeted him with a slow shake of his head. "What have you done?"

Milly and Willy wore matching expressions of disapproval, and Violet stared at him balefully as he told them the whole story.

"It is all my fault, Violet," he said at the end, holding his hands in the air as though she had an imaginary rifle instead of an expression making him feel two feet high. "The distribution of all but three barrows of the paper have been stopped."

"How were we able to get ours?" Milly asked.

"This part of Knightsbridge and west of Brompton Road were two of the three barrows that left before Mrs. Hill arrived. I've got boys out seeing if they can buy back the ones that've been sold."

For the first time since Grantham arrived, Althea spoke.

"Mala was at *The Chronicle* this morning? When did she . . . ? Did she see . . . ?"

Interesting.

Grantham had no time for intrigue now, but once he'd sorted everything with Margaret, he planned on having a long talk with Moses Wolfe.

Because he *would* sort everything with Margaret. Grantham was not going to lose her a second time.

"I don't understand. You say you knew about this since yesterday?" Violet asked. "You let her go back to work for Geflitt knowing he took money from Victor Armitage? Why didn't you stop her?"

Did Violet not know a thing about her friend?

"Margaret has a plan. She will not give up the project for anything or anyone. Least of all me." He sighed, rubbing his face as the truth of the words sank into his bones.

Courageous, yes, and oh so admirably bold, Margaret would let nothing stand in her way.

"I tried to protect her," he said. Unable to bear Violet's scrutiny, he turned his hat in his hands. "I was afraid for what would happen when the news got out. I asked her to marry me."

"Oh, George." Violet clasped her hands and gazed up at him with joy. "Marry? You and Margaret? How wonderful."

"She said no."

Violet bit her lip; pity clear in her gaze. Grantham brushed a spot of dirt from the brim of his topper with far more force than necessary.

"I've been racking my brains all morning about what to do." He infused bravado into his voice. "I have a plan in mind."

"A plan?" Kneland echoed.

"What exactly are you thinking?" Violet asked in a cautionary tone.

Grantham looked over at Kneland for a dose of male solidarity amid this ocean of womanhood. "Grand gesture, of course."

"A grand gesture?" Willy asked, one brow raised in a disapproving arch.

"Yes. Like in the book. Thinking of patching things up with Prince Albert and borrowing some crowns and swords." Grantham stopped. All the women now stared at him as though he'd grown another head.

"Haven't you read the book with all the sighs and alligators?" he asked. "*Miss Cordelia Strongbow and the Castle of Whathaveyous*?"

"George," Violet asked, "do you love her?"

"Do I *love* her?" Grantham stared at Violet, unable to comprehend a world where this could be in question.

"I have always loved her," he said. "I breathe her and bleed her, and if you open me up, my heart is the shape of Margaret Gault. I have loved her from the moment she knocked me to the ground, a blow from which I have never tried to recover. *Of course* I love her."

Violet's mouth remained taut in a frown, filling Grantham with unease.

"When you proposed marriage to her," Violet asked, "did you tell her you loved her, or you wanted to protect her because you were worried for her?"

"No. I didn't say any of that." Grantham turned to Kneland for support. "Margaret doesn't need to be burdened with my worries for her. It's up to me to make grand gestures and the like. Right, Kneland?"

Violet's thick black brows pulled together to create a straight line. "You don't believe that, do you, Arthur?"

"Er . . ." Kneland frowned and glanced around at all the women's faces. "You can't be laying all your troubles on someone else's shoulders, especially if they are sad themselves."

"And so, you remain silent about what is in your heart?" Violet asked. "Did you not think that in itself would be a burden?" Violet shook her head as though chastising a child.

"Sharing your fears is an act of love greater than buying a store full of lemon drops or a hothouse full of tulips," she admonished him.

Milly and Willy nodded in tandem, as though it should have been obvious, while Althea peered at Grantham with an air of sympathy.

Wait.

What was this?

If this was true, Grantham had made a terrible mistake when he proposed to Margaret.

He had not spoken from his heart.

His fears had clotted in his throat, and instead of admitting to them, he'd spoken around them and in the end said nothing.

Fixing this might take more than a plate of pastries and an armful of flowers.

"Right." He bowed to the ladies and gave Kneland a black stare of impending death of his own. Later, he and Kneland were going to have a little talk about Mrs. Foster.

"I'm going to find Margaret and this time . . ." Grantham set his topper on his head with a flourish. "This time I'm going to get it right."

20

IN THE ANTEROOM of Geflitt's office, the kind young clerk whistled as he sorted the day's post.

"Has Sir Royce left for the countryside yet?" Margaret asked.

The clerk shook his head. "He has to make a stop at the warehouse first, madame. Says he must receive an order."

Why would Geflitt personally receive an order?

"From whom is he receiving the order?" Margaret asked.

"Dunno for sure. Think it might be the wrought iron."

That couldn't be. She had decided last week not to engage Adams and Sons Foundry. The place was so lax, she was certain such a large order would tax their small staff and an accident was inevitable.

Not one death was worth the culmination of her dreams.

There shouldn't be a single order for any iron placed yet—unless Geflitt had done it himself?

"I believe the receipts from the past week are on his desk, if you want to have a look there," said the young man.

Margaret thanked the clerk and let herself into Geflitt's office, which smelled invitingly of tea and sandalwood.

Sure enough, a stack of paperwork sat on his desk. To her surprise, not only was there a receipt for payment for wrought iron from Adams and Sons, but another two invoices for the same amount of iron from two other foundries lay beneath it. With trembling fingers Margaret shifted through a stack of similar invoices including the mysterious order of wood from a few days ago.

All of the orders had been placed under the name of Gault Engineering.

Across the room, a stack of *Gentlemen's Monthly* magazines squatted on the credenza but the plans for the consortium's tunnel were gone. Crossing to the table where Geflitt had originally laid out what she suspected now was bait, Margaret found nothing about the tunnel and only one or two preliminary sketches of the riverbank.

The acid taste of panic coated her tongue.

There must be some mistake. She had misread the receipts. She had misinterpreted Geflitt's manner toward her the other day.

She took the papers back to her office and compared them to the records she'd kept of every visit and every order she'd made. None of them matched up.

For the first time in her life, Margaret wanted to believe herself to be "hysterical" and the terrible scenarios floating in her head to be the products of feminine humors or something equally ridiculous.

That strange wish sustained her as she hailed a hack and stared at the greying brick and opaque windows of the buildings outside until they came to the site of the rally a few weeks ago, but reason returned when she alighted from the hack and made her way to the warehouse.

Nothing.

The place was empty.

Margaret stood in the center of the incomplete structure and surveyed the building. Only one story with a half-finished roof and no place to hide a single piece of iron or the lumber purchased and marked as delivered.

Purchased under the name of Gault Engineering and not the Futuro Consortium.

The strengthening wind outside reached in through the hole in the roof, sweeping handfuls of dust from the packed earth floor. Margaret jumped when a lone starling swooped low and nearly brushed her bonnet. Flying straight up again, it perched on one of the rafters overhead, its bright eyes surveying the vacant space. Perhaps it had come to the same conclusion as Margaret, although it had taken her much longer to comprehend.

The Futuro Consortium and Sir Royce Geflitt were committing fraud.

"I am not clear on the details," Margaret said to the figure that appeared in the doorway. For a moment, he stood still, backlit by the late afternoon sun. He doffed his top hat and stepped into the dark.

"I had hoped you would stay out of here for at least another month," Geflitt said. He sauntered in but stopped about three feet from her, the beating of the starling's wings catching his attention for a moment.

"Thousands of pounds' worth of material has been charged under my name and yet there is nothing here to show for it," Margaret said, watching him intently.

"We were hoodwinked, obviously," Geflitt said. He transferred his gaze from the disappearing bird to Margaret's face. Blandly handsome, but now she knew what to look for, Margaret fancied she could see the glitter of greed in his eyes, a curve of cruelty in his upper lip.

"By scurrilous merchants?" she said, a tiny bit of hope in her heart the least likely explanation was the truth.

"By a *woman,* my dear Madame Gault."

Chilled, Margaret took a step away from Geflitt. The hairs on her neck stood at attention as her mind raced.

"No one will believe I would destroy any hope at creating a successful firm by cheating my benefactor," she said, scrutinizing the warehouse. There were two large doors opening outward on one side of the rectangular building, meant for the unloading of wagons, but they were held shut by a heavy iron bolt. The only other means of exit were the doors through which Geflitt had entered.

And which he now blocked.

Not that he would hurt her. He was a baronet. A gentleman.

And a liar.

"You are once again committing the mistake of assuming men pay attention to anything you say," Geflitt said, his jovial tone at odds with the cruelty of his words. "All anyone will know is what we tell them in *Gentlemen's Monthly*. The Futuro Consortium made the grave mistake of giving a woman engineer the chance of a lifetime. The responsibility was too much. It sickened her brain and made her hysterical, just as Victor Armitage warned us. Suicide will be hinted at but not publicly claimed out of respect for your family."

Suicide.

He meant to kill her.

"The broadsheet," she blurted out. In her shock, she'd forgotten the article. "There is an article in The Chronicle about the tunnel. It exposes your difficulties finding funding and how Armitage's money saved you."

Geflitt uttered a crude and especially ugly oath. As he moved his jaw, most likely calculating the harm such an article would cause him, Margaret considered her hands. The mechanics of a punch were etched in her brain. Her legs were long, and her height gave her an advantage. She simply had to lunge for him, push him down, and run away.

A nasty leer split his face. "It will work," he declared. "In fact, Armitage will be vindicated. He listened carefully to the arguments you made and gave you a chance. Your betrayal will be all the greater and you will have proved his point."

"You cannot hope to get away with crimes as serious as fraud and murder. You will be found out," she said, her voice cracking.

Disgusting man. He sensed her fear—smelled it if the flaring of his nostrils was any indication.

"Found out by whom?" he spat. "The Untamed Earl? You don't think I know the two of you are lovers?"

Dizzy, Margaret clasped her hands to her stomach. How?

"Grantham is a fool. If he held Prince Albert's regard, I might have been worried, but he is too much of an oaf." Geflitt's voice held nothing but contempt. "Staring after you like a mooncalf. Loitering in the street outside our building. Paying a street sweeper to keep abreast of your whereabouts. If, out of some misguided sense of loyalty, he tries to defend you, it will be discounted as a desperate attempt to sell his newspapers. Not to mention he will lose whatever influence he has in Lords."

Grantham.

A wild strain of hope rose in her breast. Nearly every five minutes that giant irritation of a man had appeared at her side out of nowhere since she'd returned from Paris. She could not sneeze without him jumping out of a nearby hedgerow with a handkerchief.

What if he were about to walk in the door?

What if he were outside right now?

Right.

Now . . .

Tilting his head slightly, Geflitt glanced at the exit then at her.

No one stood in the doorway.

No one was coming.

No one would miss her.

Margaret had turned away the one person who might have rescued her.

Geflitt let his gaze roam her body, evincing no pleasure in the act other than satisfaction at her shudder of disgust.

"Let's go," he said.

Margaret curled her fingers once, twice, and inhaled a breath of cold air before readying herself to run.

Until Geflitt reached into the pocket of his greatcoat and removed a pistol.

The fear holding Margaret's knees locked now slithered up the backs of her thighs and her reticule fell from her numb fingers. The sound of the bag hitting the packed dirt floor came from far away.

"A pistol? How am I supposed to have committed suicide with a pistol?" she said, forcing bravado into her voice. "I don't know how to shoot."

A single shoulder rose in a half-hearted gesture of ambivalence at Margaret's words. "There won't be much left of your body once they pull it from the river," Geflitt said without any remorse. "It will be impossible to tell how you died."

Died by her own damn stupidity. How foolish of Margaret to believe she could have her dream. How naive to think a group of men might value her for her talent and skill and see beyond her gender.

Despite her terror staring at the black hole at the end of the pistol, anger propelled Margaret forward when Geflitt gestured to the exit. He stood behind and to the right of her, the pistol aimed at her back as he directed her toward the riverbank. The wind now whipped about them, yanking at her bonnet and flattening her skirts against her ankles. A few drops of rain spattered against her cheek, the chilled air forcing itself through the thick wool of her cloak.

A good-sized skiff bumped against a poorly constructed dock.

"It would be a lovely bit of irony if this boat were as full of holes as your story about me being a hysterical cheat," Margaret said between clenched teeth.

Geflitt glanced around but no one else was in sight. The weather was raw and unappealing and the river too choppy for any stray fishermen to be about.

"Get in the back," he ordered her.

Briefly, she contemplated jumping into the river and swimming away, but she could see the tips of the reeds above the waterline. It would be too shallow, and her skirts would weigh her down. Margaret had no desire to be shot while running away. She stepped from the dock into the rocking skiff while trying to think of a way to get hold of Geflitt's pistol.

Once more, Margaret thought of Grantham. As she pulled her skirts around her and sat gingerly on a rotting board at the back of the boat, she scanned the banks of both sides of the river.

Empty. Woolwich lay a quarter mile away on the opposite side of the riverbank—there were certain to be folks nearby if she could only get there.

Geflitt hopped into the boat with an annoying lightness of ease and directed her to take the oars.

"I left word I would visit you at the warehouse," Margaret said, rowing as slowly as she could. "People will be searching for me."

"Not until tonight. You enter your office at the crack of dawn and stay all day," he said. "Other than Lord Grantham, no one has been seen coming in or out of your offices."

True. She had made a point of working alone this whole time.

The irony that because Margaret was so determined to do everything by herself, she'd landed in this boat with a gun pointed at her did nothing to quell her anger. It only made it worse. Now she was angry at Geflitt *and* herself.

"If it is of any consolation, you are talented," Geflitt said. He must have been out hunting on his estates, for his skin had darkened since last she'd seen him, leaving fine white lines where his wrinkles were.

"If I were to do something as risky as building another tunnel under the Thames, you would have been the perfect engineer."

"We can salvage the project," Margaret said quickly. "My father-in-law was a genius with building excitement around his projects. You can make the money back . . ."

Geflitt dismissed her with a shake of his head. "Years. It would take years to make the money back. This way, we claim the insurance, and everyone gets paid."

"Except for me!" she reminded him.

"Oh, and the geese are to remain. A wonderful story all around for everyone. A nice touch, wasn't it?" he asked rhetorically. The hollow wail of the wind increased, and it rained even harder. Geflitt seemed not to notice, but he raised his voice, practically shouting at her.

"If anything happened with you, the geese were the backup plan. We were going to burn the warehouse and blame it on that bird girl from your club."

Margaret would feel more sympathy for Flavia being relegated to "bird girl" except Flavia got to live.

Geflitt peered at her with curiosity when she huffed and slapped the water with her oars. The water was more agitated now and her cheeks hurt from the cold and the wind. Rain dripped over the brim of her bonnet and ran down her chin.

"Did you truly think you could have a woman-owned engineering firm?" he asked. "No one would have hired you. Even if I never came along, you would have still failed."

"I might have failed," she agreed, "but I would have been the first to try and that means something."

As she spoke, a renewed sense of purpose filled her. "It is so much easier to make a choice if someone has done it before you."

Geflitt gestured with his chin. "Fascinating. Keep rowing, please."

Something in the arrogance with which he directed her to move closer to her own death dislodged the fog of fear that had descended on her since he appeared in the warehouse.

Why should Margaret do as he ordered?

She would not let her last action on earth be to obey this man.

Or any man for that matter.

"I will not."

Staring straight at Geflitt, she let go of the oars.

His brows rose nearly to his receding hairline as the oars sank into the Thames. "Pick them up!" he shouted.

The skiff passed beneath a low stone walking bridge, and Margaret gauged the distance from the boat to the shore.

"Reach down and get them," Geflitt ordered her.

If she were lucky, she would reach the cluster of reeds before the weight of her skirts and the river's currents pulled her under. She hadn't been swimming since that last summer at Violet's before everything went awry and Margaret hoped she would remember how.

"Listen to me, woman—"

The sound of a body hitting the water drowned out Geflitt's final words.

WHAT IN THE name of God was Margaret doing?

Grantham stood on a wet stone bridge a quarter mile away from Geflitt's warehouse and watched in amazement as Margaret and Geflitt rowed a damned fishing skiff on the Thames in the middle of a rainstorm.

And people thought Grantham was an idiot?

"Margaret!" Grantham called her name through cupped hands, but the wind tore it away from his lips and sent it over his shoulder.

Feck.

He'd left Athena's Retreat in search of Margaret two hours ago.

Waving off Violet's offer of a carriage, he'd pulled his coat tight and fought the wind as he rode his horse down Fleet Street.

He'd poked his head into Geflitt's office, where a young clerk told him Margaret had been there earlier.

"She wanted to speak with Sir Royce, but he's been out at the warehouse all morning." The young man craned his neck and nodded at the clock on the wall. "He's due to leave for his estate after so you should hurry if you don't want to miss him."

Grantham went to Margaret's office next, finding it open and empty. She hadn't locked the door and he studied the space. It felt strange, as though Margaret left something unfinished.

Perhaps he should leave her a message?

Making his way to her sketches, he leaned toward the paper, inhaling the scent of graphite and lavender. Tiny worms of unease wriggled in his gut. The sensation went beyond a fear Margaret would be furious with him over the newspaper article.

Straightening, he considered the skylights and the drops of rain tapping at the glass.

Where was she?

It had been many years since he'd undertaken to do a favor for Prince Albert. Mostly he had sat in various crowds and listened as the speakers called for reforms—reforms which Grantham came to agree with after a time.

Sometimes, he had found his way into empty rooms where private papers were kept. Grantham had always had a healthy sense of when danger approached. Not only would he get a thrashing if he were caught, but it would also look bad if it were revealed a peer of the realm spied on British citizens at the behest of a foreign prince. Albert had little popularity in those early years.

That awareness which had warned him of someone's approach in the past now picked at the hairs on his neck. Stepping away from the sketches, Grantham made his way to the battered secretary where Margaret kept her books. There, splayed across the surface, were a handful of half-crumpled invoices and receipts. A bell sounded in the back of Grantham's head. Hadn't Margaret said she had to visit the warehouse to sort out why a delivery had been made which she hadn't ordered?

He laid the papers out before him on the desk and studied them. There were duplicate orders from different suppliers and all the charges had been made in Margaret's name. The bell moved from the back of Grantham's head to the front.

Geflitt couldn't find enough money or support for this project until Armitage signed on. Despite Armitage's views, Geflitt went ahead and hired a woman engineer. Now, a pile of charges had been made in her name and she had gone to investigate them.

Grantham had told Margaret he never searched her out in Paris because he was not the man he wished her to know. This was true.

The other reason he stayed away was Margaret had not needed him. Somehow, Grantham had known across continents—across years—if she were ever truly in need, if she were in some sort of peril, he would be there.

Margaret needed him now.

Stopping only to deliver a message and a coin to the street sweeper, Jeb, he rode his horse as fast as the London traffic would allow.

The wind howled and the rain poured as if from buckets by the time he pulled his horse up to the empty warehouse. The half-built structure leaned crazily against the darkening skies, its exposed rafters staring at him like empty sockets in a leering face. He needed to get his poor horse to a stable and have him rubbed down, but the feeling in his gut wouldn't recede. If anything, it grew worse.

Tying the horse to a beam inside the warehouse, Grantham stood in the doorway and squinted through the rain. He could barely see the opposite shore, but nothing moved over there. No one was on the road in either direction on this side of the river. The Thames had come to life beneath the wind and rain, tiny white points capping its rough waves.

Only an idiot would be outside in weather like this.

Disgusted that he'd let himself be distracted by a stupid whim, he removed his top hat, poured off the water, swept back his hair, and settled the hat on his head while gazing at the river when a strange shape caught his eye.

A tiny skiff sat bobbing like a child's toy in a lake. Some fool had misread the weather, no doubt. The person in the front of the boat was definitely a man—one could see his hat in silhouette—but a smudge of pink and the bell-shaped curves of the second figure could only mean a woman was on board the tiny vessel.

Even as his brain recognized these details, his body moved. Not even stopping to untie his horse, Grantham raced toward the stone bridge in the distance.

"Margaret," he called now.

The wind fought him but surely she saw him? Grantham leaned over the side and bellowed to her.

Grabbing hold of the cold slick stone, he said a blasphemous prayer beneath his breath. It was one thing to climb a building on a dry windless day. Quite another to heave himself onto the railing of a stone bridge in the middle of a windstorm, but for Margaret, he would do anything.

Grantham laughed out loud when he realized what this meant.

He had gotten his grand gesture after all!

The sight of him teetering on the edge of a bridge would win Margaret over. All he had to do now was tell her he loved her.

"Margaret, I love you," he shouted into a gale that muted his voice to barely a whisper.

A nasty gust came from behind and smacked the top hat from his head. Bareheaded and shivering, he stared at the river below. Margaret and Geflitt were coming out from beneath the bridge. Grantham could see them better now. Margaret's snow-white skin stood in stark contrast against the darkened skies, her hands gripping the oars as she swung her head, examining the riverbanks on either side.

Geflitt looked nowhere but at her. He said something, but the words were lost in the storm. Why, the bounder made Margaret row against the current. Instead of helping her, Geflitt leaned forward, holding a—

Sometimes the world shifts beneath a person's feet.

Or, it could be, they lose their balance on a slippery surface and fall headlong into blackness.

Either way, life is forever changed.

As the freezing water swallowed him up, Grantham's final thought was perhaps the world had started moving beneath him on the same day a tearstained girl went and knocked him to the ground.

The world had always meant it to be this way, pushing him in the direction of Margaret Gault until the day he drew his last breath.

21

❧

EARING FOR ONE'S life does odd things to a woman's brain. Somehow, Margaret confused irritation with relief. Thus, her initial greeting to Grantham when he emerged from the waters of the Thames and threw one enormous arm into the skiff, trying to pull himself in: "Good God, you're going to drown us all. Where have you been?"

"What the devil?" Geflitt shouted. "Don't touch the boat, don't..." He beat at Grantham's head ineffectually with one hand, trying to hold the gun on Margaret with another.

The first time Margaret ever set eyes on Georgie Willis, she'd known he was hers. He'd offered to rescue her that day from whatever evil he'd imagined had caused her to cry. Later, when he understood her pain wasn't caused by a dragon he might slay or a bully he could punch, he'd still championed her.

Everything the world told Margaret was unappealing about her— her height, her intellect, her temper, and her ambition—George Willis would go out of his way to praise.

And now here he was, leaping off a bridge in the middle of a rainstorm into the Thames. Larger than life and grinning like mad despite Geflitt's flailing.

Oh, her heart.

Her heart had always lived in this man's palm.

If she had to give up her Plan to keep him close, she would.

Because plans could be changed.

They could even be improved upon.

But first, Grantham needed to get in the damn boat.

Geflitt jumped to his feet, setting the boat to swaying precariously when he realized Grantham was coming aboard.

"Sit, you fool!" Margaret shouted, grabbing the side of the skiff as it lurched to the left. Curtains of rain separated them from sight of the land, but she judged them to be drifting farther from the shore.

"You'll tip the boat," she scolded her captor. "Sit down!"

Did Geflitt listen to her?

Of course not.

Once again, he dismissed her counsel, bellowing nonsense no one could hear over the wind.

If he had just shut up and done as she said, when Grantham heaved his whole self into the boat, he wouldn't have lost his balance and fallen forward, gun gripped in his hand.

Margaret threw herself to the side as Geflitt's arms spun in the air, mouth gaping and hat falling forward to cover his eyes. At the same time, Grantham tucked himself into a ball and rolled over onto all fours, settling the rocking of the boat.

The shot, when it rang out, didn't surprise her. Geflitt would not be able to resist making a big noise.

What did surprise her was how much it hurt.

THE HOWL THAT left Grantham's lips did not sound human.

How could it when his entire being was consumed in a conflagration of rage? With one hand, he lifted Sir Royce Geflitt into the air and tossed him from the skiff. It mattered not to him in the moment whether the man drowned or not.

Maggie was bleeding.

That degenerate piece of offal had shot her.

"I was the one supposed to get shot," he told her as he gathered her into his chest.

She mumbled something into his coat, but he couldn't hear her over the wind and slapping of waves against the side of the skiff. Didn't matter. He had to get her to shore and to a doctor then in his bed.

Forever.

Looking around one last time to be sure nothing in the boat could help, Grantham shucked his greatcoat, pulled Margaret's bonnet from her head, then reached beneath her skirts.

"...not the time, George."

He couldn't help it. Grantham let loose a laugh that sounded more like a sob toward the end. There was his darling Maggie, scolding him no matter the time or place.

He ripped off the ties of her petticoats and shoved them down her legs.

"The less you are wearing if you enter the water, the easier it will be for you to swim to shore," he said into her ear. With that, he tore a petticoat in three pieces, ignoring another complaint from her thinned lips.

"I don't care how expensive your petticoats are," he told her, wrapping the rent muslin around the wound in her upper arm. Mrs. Sweet had gone and hied herself to Herefordshire, of all places, but the lectures she'd given them over the years had stuck in his head. Far better for Margaret to suffer loss of blood than to expose her wound to the filthy waters of the Thames.

Satisfied with his impromptu bandage, Grantham eyed the distance between the skiff and the riverbank. The water had soaked through his boots, which meant they would be impossible to remove, but he could swim in them. He nodded once, grabbed Margaret, kissed her on her frozen lips, then pushed her onto a seat and dove overboard.

Feck but the water was cold.

Grabbing hold of the skiff, he pushed it toward shore. Without his greatcoat, he swam faster but a strong current ran beneath the surface here, right before the bend, and he had to kick with all his might.

". . . more to the left."

Setting his shoulder to the stern, Grantham tried his best to steer them according to Margaret's directions. After a moment, he glanced at her but could see nothing except the pale smudge of her face, and he redoubled his efforts.

When his toe hit the muddy bottom, he called to her, but she didn't answer. Terror cleared away his exhaustion and he kicked the water as hard as he could until he could set both feet down. Pushing the boat aground, he heaved his feet from the mud sucking at him.

"Maggie!" he hollered, squinting through the fog now rolling in with the lessening of the rain. "Maggie, can you hear me?"

She slumped against the gunwale, one arm reaching over the side. The utter stillness of her stopped his heart even though his feet kept moving.

"Maggie?"

Lifting her into his arms, he pressed his open mouth against her closed lips, the only way he could think of warming her. He would have to carry her to the warehouse where his horse waited. He couldn't tell how far down the river they'd gone. Quarter mile? Half?

Didn't matter. Holding her close, he ran. The wet leather of his boots rubbed his ankles raw while the wind pummeled him like a kitten being batted about by a mastiff.

"I am terrified of the back garden at Morningside," he told Margaret between huffs as he clambered up the bank past tangles of roots and moss-covered rocks to reach the main road. There must be businesses or homes nearby where he could stop and send for help. Only a small distance.

"I thought I saw a hedgehog there once. Lizzie asked if she could have a birthday tea in the garden, for it's a lovely setting, but I said no and never told her why not."

Once his boots had hit the flat surface of the road, he set a frantic pace, his soles squelching in the mud and gravel, but at least the earth beneath him was level.

"I am terrified Lizzie will fail as a debutante because of something stupid or uncouth I have said."

Margaret's hair was flat against her scalp, the color of red marl and the contrast made her skin all the more ghostly white. He paused for a moment to set his lips against the hollow of her throat and ran once he felt her pulse beneath his lips, continuing his confessions.

"I am afraid if the education reform act does not pass, I will be no better than my father. A man who did nothing with the privilege the world gifted him for no reason other than his birth. I fear the future for girls like you and Violet will be even more confining than it is now and that will partly be my fault."

His throat ached and his legs wobbled like green twigs, but he kept on running, talking to Margaret, willing her to hear him.

"I used to wake every day expecting the world to show me something marvelous and every day I found it. I am afraid the longer I stay in London, the more blind I will become to marvels."

Soon he would come to the end of his strength without any sight of people or homes and with no boats on the heaving river.

"I am terrified I have lost you before I even tried to keep you. I am afraid you will find me an unsatisfactory lover; I will never measure up to your late husband, and nothing I can offer will come close to convincing you to stay with me."

When his legs gave out, he barely felt the stones tear the knees of his trousers. His attention was on keeping Margaret shielded from the jolt of his fall.

"I fear losing you more than all of my other fears combined, Maggie. I cannot lose you. I cannot. Please, please stay with me."

"Hallooo?" a familiar voice called from close by.

Grantham gasped and coughed when he drew breath to shout his reply.

"Here," he croaked.

It didn't matter, there were people coming toward him. Arthur was running, his compact body slicing through the drizzle like a knife. Behind him clattered Violet's carriage, Althea Dertlinger's entire torso hanging out of the window as she called to him.

Grantham wanted to scold her about the dangers of jostling out of a carriage like that, but he couldn't speak.

Even when they had been gathered into the carriage and Althea babbled about how Jeb had come with the message and Violet explaining how they arrived at the warehouse to find Margaret's abandoned reticule and Grantham's horse—Grantham could not speak. He kept his entire focus on pulling the wet cloak from Margaret's body and wrapping her in all the blankets they could scrounge from the carriage.

Despite the wind and fog, they arrived at Beacon House in good time, no doubt due to the lack of traffic on such a horrible day.

Violet issued orders and Althea rushed off to carry them out as he brought Margaret through the kitchen to the tiny chamber off Mrs. Sweet's set of rooms. Grantham almost balked when he caught sight of the sitting room. Shelves lined the walls laden with jars of all sizes full of murky liquid and unrecognizable objects; a skeleton hung from a metal arm and danced in the breeze conjured in their wake and the entire area smelled like one of those vile teas.

The organs reminded Grantham of what he wanted to do to Geflitt.

"Sir Royce," he said. "He went overboard and—"

"Arthur remained behind." Violet patted his arm. "Geflitt will be taken care of."

That worry assuaged, he helped Violet remove the last of Margaret's clothing and slipped her beneath the covers on a sturdy wooden cot. The chamber was comfortably furnished with a thick rug, two cushioned chairs, and a small end table. Lemon yellow curtains framed the single window above the foot of the cot and two pretty etchings of the River Severn hung on the opposite wall.

Maisey, the maid Grantham had met a few weeks ago, entered and set a tray full of hot tea, piles of clean linen bandages, and all manner of jars and tins on a bedside table.

"Maisey has been working with Mrs. Sweet for over a year now," Violet said softly as she moved him out of the way so the young woman could see to Margaret's wound. Grantham nodded but could not speak as Maisey examined the wound, frowning in concentration. Once it was ascertained the bullet had gone clean through, Grantham leaned against the wall and stared at the floor as Maisey applied a series of strong-smelling unguents and rebandaged the wound with clean cloths.

While Maisey and Violet tidied up, he pulled the larger of the chairs to the edge of Margaret's bed and sat as close as he could to her but did not reach for her hand as he did not want to jostle her arm. After a while, he could not tell how long, everyone left them. The rain fell but more softly now, an apologetic patter that did nothing to soothe him. Occasionally an errant drop would hit the pile of coals in the grate and hiss, reminding Grantham of the myriad jars and objects in the room next door.

Stupid, mundane thoughts with which he occupied himself so as not to go mad at the steady rise and fall of Margaret's chest. In that, he could take comfort.

Losing track of time, the rhythm of the rain and the gradual warming of the room conspired to make him drowsy, and he could barely keep his eyes open when he was confronted by this question.

"Where did you have Lizzie's birthday party if not the garden?"

Instead of answering this burning question, Grantham poured Margaret a glass of water, his hands shaking so badly, he spilled half of it on the floor. When she sat up, he propped a few pillows beneath her and took the glass away when she'd drunk it all.

"We held the festivities in the gazebo, and if you ask me, it was a smashing success. Far better venue than some overgrown jungle full of prickly beasts."

Her lovely auburn hair fell around her shoulders, contrasting with her pale, almost grey skin.

"Are you in much pain?" he asked. "I can call Maisey. She said Mrs. Sweet has teas that can make you more comfortable."

When Margaret rolled her eyes, some of the tension that had skewered his body like nails ebbed.

"If you think to feed me one of those disgusting teas, I will never speak to you again."

"Fair enough," he told her.

She settled against the pillows.

"I am so sorry about *The Chronicle*'s article," Grantham said. "I should have told you about it immediately and not put it off. You must believe me when we spent the night together, I had every intention of killing the story—"

He paused. "That is a newspaper term. It means not to go ahead with a planned—"

"I gathered as much," Margaret said. "Continue with your apology, please."

"Yes. I was supposed to get to the offices by six to keep it from being printed." Dropping his head, Grantham remembered his panic.

Her fingers plucked at the edge of the blanket then smoothed it back.

"I am to blame, I suppose, for distracting you with my female wiles?" she asked.

"I do not have the stomach for assigning blame to anyone in this debacle," Grantham said.

Pushing her head deeper into the pillow, Margaret peered at the ceiling. "There will be many members who think different."

Fie on them.

"It's easy to make choices based on experience," he said. "You were in a situation which none of them have encountered. Who is to say they would not make the same decision?"

If he could, Grantham would protect her from any repercussions, but Margaret would never let him fight her battles.

"Why did you tell me those things before?" she asked. "Your fears?"

With a great deal of care, Grantham set his hand over hers. When she didn't complain, he ran his thumb over her palm.

"I have been under the mistaken impression men ought to hold back their fears. When you were injured, I realized . . ."

He wasn't trying to be dramatic, but the breath left his lungs when he pictured her again, limp in his arms and bleeding.

Clearing his throat, Grantham tried again. "I realized this might be the last chance to tell you what weighed on my heart. I hoped if I shared my fears with you, you might be moved to share yours with me."

Margaret frowned. "What would you do with my fears if I shared them?"

Letting go of her hand for the moment, Grantham stood and set the chair where it had been, returned to her bedside, and knelt before her. Once again, he took her hand in his.

"If I had been honest with you that night years ago. If I had told you I was scared I could not make you happy, do you think our lives would have been different?"

She lifted her chin to better assess him. When understanding flickered in her eyes, he nodded.

"If you say your fears aloud, they become less powerful, I promise," he said.

A single line formed between her brows until she spoke.

"I am afraid I am not feminine enough for other women to want to be my friend."

Grantham blinked but remained silent.

"I am afraid I am not beautiful enough to keep your interest. I am afraid I am not strong enough or smart enough to build a firm on my own."

The tip of her nose turned red, but Margaret's eyes remained dry. Those fears must be so familiar, they no longer had the power to bring her to tears.

"I am afraid everyone will find out I am successful only because I work so hard. Not because I am brilliant or exceptional or any of those words they use. I am not a pioneer, I am not unique, I am just . . . me."

He wasn't certain what he'd expected to hear, but not this. How extraordinarily complex she was, how difficult to see into her heart if she never shared her secrets.

"Does it make the fear go away if I tell you I find you to be the most beautiful woman I have ever encountered?" he asked.

Grantham set the tip of his finger to the line on her forehead, wishing he had the power to dismiss her fears with one touch. "You do not have to be brilliant or exceptional to be a success. Hard work is as admirable as sheer talent—maybe more so."

When he lifted his finger, she peered around the room, then shook her head.

"The fear didn't go away," she complained.

Course not. That would be too easy. He and Maggie were destined to struggle. Didn't matter as long as they did it together.

"You were right, however," she continued. "It does make the fear smaller, somehow, when you say it aloud."

Grantham placed his lips carefully on the back of her hand, then brushed a lock of hair away from her face. He didn't like that she looked so frail—he wanted his fierce girl.

"It does, doesn't it? Would you like to hear my greatest fear?"

"They're nocturnal," Maggie said.

"No. Not the hedgehogs." Grantham scowled.

Abominable woman.

"My greatest fear is you will never ask for help, and the more you insist on going it alone, the further away you will push me. I do not want to live in the margins of your life, Margaret. I want to be front and center."

"YOU CANNOT FIT in the margins of anything," Margaret said, but without rancor.

Grantham cupped her cheek in his hand. "I want to share your burdens. I want to be the first person you ask for help, even if I have no clue what the solution might be to your problems. I love you, Margaret."

In all the world, there was only one person who could pick Margaret up and spin her around until nothing was where it started, and the world was both unfamiliar and exactly what she'd always dreamed it might be like.

I love you.

Margaret had never heard those words spoken aloud, let alone directed to her.

How incredibly powerful that handful of syllables. What courage it took to speak them, like presenting a set of keys that opened one's heart. Grantham was more naked in that moment than he'd ever been in bed.

Margaret took a deep breath, terrified and exhilarated at the same time.

"I love you, George. I have loved you since the moment I knocked you to the ground," Margaret said.

"I tripped," Grantham corrected her.

She pulled their entwined hands to her mouth and reciprocated with a kiss upon the back of his hand.

"The second after you fell, I regretted my actions. Here was a boy offering to help me and I pushed him away. Again and again, I have turned aside the kindest, bravest, most beautiful heart I've ever encountered."

His blue eyes shone with unshed tears and Margaret fell even deeper in love. Good thing she had decided never to leave this man's side.

"It won't be easy," she said, "but I will try not to push you away when next I need help."

A vow more difficult to honor than any oath of fidelity or everlasting love, but Margaret would endeavor to keep it.

"We shall both become the stronger for it," he promised.

A lightness spread within her. Despite her wound, she knew in this moment she was the safest and most treasured she'd ever been. It freed her to speak her most pressing fear, one she'd not dared say aloud until now.

"What if being with me costs your political reputation?"

He stole her fears with a kiss, soft and sweet.

"I can only hope that my reputation will be enhanced due to my wise choice of a brilliant, beautiful woman as my wife."

Wife.

Yes. Yes, she wanted that as well.

"You are very presumptuous, considering I haven't proposed yet," Margaret said.

Grantham maneuvered himself into the cot, taking care not to overturn it, and settled at Margaret's side. As the rain stopped and the night sky cleared, the stars shone their silvered light through the window overhead.

"I am resigned to waiting patiently until the moment you make me the happiest man in London," he whispered into her ear. "Only, I beg of you, please do not succumb to the current craze for grand gestures beforehand. I doubt my nerves can take such an event."

Margaret giggled, then winced at the pain in her arm. "I can promise you there will be no firearms involved."

"Excellent." Ever so carefully, Grantham lifted her in his arms so that she rested against his chest. "Then I am content to be here, by your side, forever."

Sometimes the world stops spinning, comes to a slow halt, and allows you to take a courageous step in the right direction.

Whether that step leads you to where you were always meant to be depends on how you define courage. Is it the tenacity to forge ahead no matter the obstacles, or the ability to ask for help when those obstacles seem insurmountable?

Or is it both?

Epilogue

❧

Morningside Estate, 1849

I AM GOING TO kill you."

Margaret glanced between her husband and his best friend and hid a smile.

Sated after a picnic lunch, Mirren Kneland had dragged her mama away from their repast and across the lawns of Morningside to go and visit with her "Uncle" George's latest gift. Arthur had remained behind to finish his tart and level a black stare of impending doom at Grantham.

"It is a single pony," Grantham protested. "It could easily have been a herd, Kneland. Keep that in mind."

Arthur, unappeased by Grantham's generosity, gritted his teeth and grunted before following in his family's wake.

"You are cruel," Margaret told Grantham, laughing when he used a long blade of grass to tickle under her chin.

"I give the man something to worry over other than his wife and child," Grantham retorted.

Arthur took Mirren's other hand and walked with her and Violet over to a low wooden gate. Beneath an ancient apple tree, a pretty brown pony stood grazing, looking at the small figure that giggled and waved.

No matter how delightful, the pony lost interest in the girl when Jeb exited the nearby barn with a pail of grain. The adoration of a six-year-old girl was nothing compared to the prospect of lunch.

"Jeb's grown so much in the few months since we've been gone," Margaret said. Indeed, not even his mam would recognize the little street sweeper after four years in the countryside. "We'll have to have the boys measured again before winter to make sure they have clothes that fit before the weather changes."

"Aye. It's amazing how fast young folks grow when you take them out of the city and put them in the country air."

No scientific evidence supported her husband's theory the fetid air of London had an impact on a child's height. However, the children who lived at the Morningside Academy for the Study of Agriculture Sciences on the far side of the estate did appear larger and healthier than those young women attending the Gault School for Engineering in London.

"Perhaps we should arrange for the girls to come out to the country for a few weeks between sessions," Margaret said, leaning on her elbows and watching the clouds drift across the sky. The warm spring breeze brought the scent of lilacs and the flavored ices the servants had packed in sawdust to keep cold in the afternoon sun.

Marrying an earl had its benefits.

Aside from lovely picnics on a well-run estate, Grantham had brought the wrath of the peerage on the heads of Sir Royce Geflitt and Victor Armitage when Geflitt had confessed to his scheme five years ago. Geflitt had narrowly avoided prison—although he lost his estate—and the insurance company had refused to pay the consortium members. Meanwhile, Armitage was forced to sell *Gentlemen's Monthly* and had faded into obscurity, although the Guardians of Domesticity had not completely disbanded.

Marrying an earl also had its drawbacks.

The Reform Bill had failed.

In the end, it hadn't been all Grantham's fault. The Church was against the bill and was too powerful for a handful of lords to counteract. Still, there were some who blamed their marriage. Although they managed to keep *The Chronicle*'s story quiet for a week or two while Margaret mended fences at the Retreat, the marriage of an earl to a woman engineer amid an insurance scandal kept the other broadsheets busy for months. Their notoriety cost Grantham the influence he'd so carefully built, and Margaret had to close her office.

Disinvited to the working group that reintroduced the bill the next year, Grantham found another way to keep his promise to make the title mean something.

"We could do a games day—or even a festival like Violet's aunt manages each year in Yorkshire," he said now. Margaret nodded along as he laid out his plans, distracted by the light in his eyes and the healthy glow of his sun-kissed cheeks.

Instead of fighting the structure of a society desperate to keep people neatly labeled and socially static, Grantham had decided to change what he could and educate as many children as his finances would allow for. His school was small but gained the attention of education reformers across the United Kingdom. Next year, he and his Board of Governors hoped to open two more schools on other large estates.

After the gossip had died down, Margaret reopened her firm, keeping it under the Gault name. She was not wildly successful, but had enough commissions each year to pay for an apprentice. Only, there hadn't been any applications. So, she and Grantham opened a school for women engineers in London. It wasn't easy, but not much of what they had in life that mattered came easily. There had been tears and frustrated silences alongside the laughter and the lovemaking.

Over time, they'd constructed a life allowing for her to own a business and for him to craft a legacy for the title he could be proud of at the end of day. Together, they formed a bridge, for what is marriage if not a balance between tension and compression? Their lives did not have to be one way or the other. They compromised and found a way forward. Not what they'd planned, and certainly not perfect, but it was the way things should be.

"Mirren will no doubt keep her parents entertained this afternoon until naptime," Grantham remarked. The blue of his eyes darkened, and his easy smile transformed into a flirtatious grin. "I don't think they'll miss us if we sneak to the house for a time."

Margaret winked and let him help her to standing.

"I've a mind to peruse some folios in the library," she told him as she took the elbow he offered.

"Is that so?"

"Yes," she said. "It's been too long since I gazed upon Michelangelo's David."

Grantham tapped his chin thoughtfully. "You know, I have an idea."

They laughed and made their way toward the house and the rest of their perfectly imperfect life.

Author's Note

ENGINEERING. IS IT a science? Most would argue it is a discipline that takes scientific discoveries and applies them to the real world. I believe Margaret Gault would agree with this definition, but also point out that engineers in her time were educated as scientists, thus her inclusion as a Secret Scientist. Some of Margaret's ideas and experiences are very loosely inspired by the fascinating life of Sarah Guppy, a woman engineer and the first woman to patent a bridge in 1811. She was, in fact, friendly with Isambard Kingdom Brunel, whose father, Marc, was the chief engineer of the Thames Tunnel.

Margaret was a woman of her time and that meant she had access to birth control. The scene in which Grantham presents her with contraceptive choices is not an historical anachronism and not limited to women in the United Kingdom. Women have used contraception and methods of inducing postcoital menstruation throughout history and it is a terrible irony that a woman in 1844 had more reproductive choice and autonomy than some women in the United States today. As maddening as it is to watch our government try to limit our liberties, I believe that women in this country will continue to advance until we can fully control our political, economic, and reproductive destinies.

> It was we, the people; not we, the white male citizens; nor yet we, the male citizens; but we, the whole people, who formed the Union. And we formed it, not to give the blessings of liberty, but to secure them; not to the half of ourselves and the half of our posterity, but to the whole people—women as well as men.
>
> —Susan B. Anthony

Acknowledgments

Writing a romance during a pandemic was hard and lots of people helped me along the way. I would like to thank my wonderful husband for being such a supportive partner during the writing of this book and for continually inspiring me to be a better person. Thanks as well go to my amazing children who went through a difficult time during Covid but kept cheering me on the whole time. Thank you to Mom and Doug for all the child care—and I'm including Miss Bear—and the unconditional love and support. Thank you to my agent, Ann Leslie Tuttle, who is such a warm and positive human being. I'm so grateful for her help. Thank you to everyone at Berkley Romance, especially to Sarah Blumenstock, my editor, for helping me to become a better writer and for believing in my scientists and all they represent. Thank you to Jessica Mangicaro, my marketing Yoda and an all-around goddamned delight. Thank you to Stephanie Felty for all her help with PR and putting up with my dumb emails. Thank you to Rita Frangie for the cover designs for the series and to everyone in the PRH design and graphics departments—you are all amazing talents and I so appreciate your work. Thank you to Laura Blumenstock, a real-life engineer who took the time to make sure there were no glaring errors. Thank you to my Berkletes for being the gorgeous, anxious, talented, and generous women that you are—here's to more in-person meet ups in 2023. Special thanks to my Big Brained Broads—Mazey Eddings, Ali Hazelwood, and Libby Hubscher. I love you guys. Thank you to the Park Ave Moms for your friendship and for modeling how to go into this next phase of life with a balance of grace and humor. Thanks to the Highland Hotties for emergency carpooling, wine nights, and long walks. Thank you to the amazing community of bookstagrammers on IG who have consistently supported my Secret Scientists and have been a source of sheer delight in the miasma of social media. Finally, thank you to my fellow romance authors who have been so generous and kind—it is lovely to be part of such a wonderful community and I am so grateful to all of you.

Don't miss Elizabeth Everett's new series starring more daring
women in science and their happily ever afters!

THE LOVE REMEDY

'**O**W MUCH FOR pulling a toof?"

Any other day, Lucinda Peterson's answer would have been however much the man standing before her could afford.

Since its founding, Peterson's Apothecary held a reputation for charging fair prices for real cures. If a customer had no money, Lucy and her siblings would often accept goods or services in trade.

Today, however, was not any other day.

Today was officially the worst day of Lucy's life.

Yes, there had been other worst days, but that was before today. Today was *absolutely* the worst.

"Half shilling," Lucy said, steel in her voice as she crossed her arms, exuding determination.

"'Alf shilling?" the man wailed. "Ow'm I supposed to buy food for me we'uns?"

With a dramatic sigh, he slumped against the large wooden counter that ran the length of the apothecary. The counter, a mammoth construction made of imported walnut, was the dividing line between Lucy's two worlds.

Until she was seven, Lucy existed with everyone else on the public side. Over there, the shop was crowded with customers who spoke in myriad accents and dialects as they waited in line for a consultation held in hushed voices at the end of the counter. Not all patients were concerned with privacy, however, and lively discussions went on between folks in line on the severity of their symptoms, the veracity of the diagnosis, and the general merits of cures suggested.

Laughter, tears, and the occasional spontaneous bout of poetry happened on the public side of the counter. Seven-year-old Lucy would sweep the floor and dust the shelves as the voices flowed over and around her, waiting for the day when she could cross the dividing line and begin her apprenticeship on the other side.

All four walls of the apothecary were lined with the tools of her trade. Some shelves held rows of glass jars containing medicinal roots such as ginger and turmeric. Other shelves held tin cannisters full of ground powders, tiny tin scoops tied to the handles with coarse black yarn. A series of drawers covered the back half of the shop, each of them labeled in a painstaking round running hand by Lucy's grandfather. There hadn't been any dried crocodile dung in stock for eighty years or so, but the label remained, a source of amusement and conjecture for those waiting in line.

The shop had stood in Rounders Lane since the beginning of the last century and even on this, her absolute worst day, Lucy gave in. She wasn't going to be the Peterson that broke tradition and turned a patient away.

Even though today was Lucy's worst day ever didn't mean it should be terrible for everyone.

"For anyone else a tooth is thruppence," Lucy said as she pulled on her brown linen treatment coat. "So I'm not accused of taking food from the mouth of your we'uns," she paused to pull a jar of eucalyptus oil out from a drawer and set it on the counter. "I suppose I can charge you two pence and throw in a boiled sweet for each of them."

Satisfied with the bargain, the man climbed into her treatment chair in the back room, holding on to the padded armrests and squeezing his eyes shut in anticipation. Lucy spilled a few drops of the oil on a handkerchief and tied it over her nose.

While the scent of eucalyptus was strong enough to bring tears to her eyes, the smell from the man's rotted tooth was even stronger.

She numbed his gums with oil of clove as she examined the tooth and explained to him what she was going to do. His discomfort was so great the man waved away her warnings and with a practiced grip, Lucy pulled out the offending tooth.

Both of them wept for a bit, him from the pain, her from the stench, as Lucy explained how to best keep the rest of his teeth from suffering the same fate.

"You're an angel, Miss," the man exclaimed. At least, Lucy hoped he said angel, his mouth was still numb, and his cheek was beginning to swell. She sent him off with the promised sweets as well as a tin of tooth powder.

Seeing there were no customers in the shop, she locked the front door and closed the green curtains over the street-facing windows to indicate the store was closed.

Lucy's younger sister, Juliet, was out seeing patients who were not well enough to visit the store, and her brother, David, could be any-where in the capital city. Some days he was up with the sun, dusting the shelves and charming the clientele into doubling or even tripling their purchases. Other days, he was nowhere to be found. Days like today.

Worst days.

Lucy sighed a long, drawn-out sigh that she was embarrassed to hear exuded a low note of self-pity along with despair. Exhaustion weighed down her legs and pulled at her elbows while she cleaned the treatment chair and wrote the details of the man's procedure in her record book. She'd not slept well last night. Nor the night before. In fact, Lucy hadn't had an uninterrupted night's sleep for nine years.

Standing with a quill in her hand, she gazed at the etching hanging on the far wall of the back room, sandwiched between a tall, thin chest of drawers and a coat rack covered in bonnets and caps left behind by forgetful patients. Drawn in exchange for a treatment long forgotten, the artist had captured her mother and father posed side by side in a rare moment of rest.

"Through sloth the roof sinks in, and through indolence the house leaks," her mother would quote. Constantly moving, and yet always time for a smile for whomever was in pain or in need of a sympathetic ear, she'd been a woman of great faith in God and even greater faith in her husband.

"We work all day so we can make merry afterwards," her father would tell Lucy when she complained about the long hours. Indeed, evenings in the Peterson household were redolent with the sound of music and comradery, her father loving nothing more than an impromptu concert with his children, no matter their mistakes on the instruments he'd chosen for them.

The etching was an amateurish work, yet it managed to convey the genuine delight on her father's face when he found himself in company of his wife.

It had been nine years since her parents died of cholera, a loathsome disease most likely brought home by British soldiers serving with the East India company. When the first few patients came to the apothecary with symptoms, the Petersons had sent their children to stay with a cousin in the countryside to wait out the disease. Lucy and Juliet had protested, both of them having trained for such scenarios, but their father held firm.

Her parents' death had come as less of a shock to Lucy than her father's will. Everything was left to her as the eldest; the apothecary and the building in which it stood as well as the proprietary formulas of her father and her grandfather's tonics and salves.

She had been eighteen years old.

"What were you thinking, da?" she asked the etching now, the smell of vinegar and eucalyptus stinging the back of her throat. "Why would you put this all on my shoulders?"

Her father had nothing to say. He stared out from the picture with his round cheeks and patchy whiskers, eyes crinkled in such a way that Lucy fancied he heard her laments and would give her words of advice if he could speak.

What would they be?

A yawn so large it cracked her jaw made Lucy break off her musings and remove her apron.

Exhaustion had played a huge role in her string of bad decisions over the past four months. Ultimately, however, the fault lay with her, and Lucy's guilt had been squeezing the breath from her lungs for weeks.

On the counter, slightly dented from having been crushed in her fist, then thrown to the ground and stepped on, then heaved against the wall, sat a grimy little tin. Affixed to the top was a label with the all too familiar initials *RSA*. Rider and Son Apothecary.

Rider and *Son*. The latter being the primary reason for this very worst of days.

The longer she stared at the tin, the less Lucy felt the strain of responsibility for running Peterson's Apothecary and keeping her siblings housed and fed. Beneath the initials were printed the words *Rider's Lozenges*. The ever-present exhaustion that had weighed her down moments ago began to dissipate at the sight of the smaller print beneath which read "exclusive." The more she stared, the more her guilt subsided beneath a wave of anger that coursed through her blood. "Exclusive patented formula for the relief of putrid throats."

Exclusive patented formula.

The anger simmered and simmered the longer she stared until it reached a boil and turned to rage.

Grabbing her paletote from the coat rack and a random bonnet that may or may not have matched, Lucy stormed out of the store, slamming the door behind her with a vengeance that was less impressive when she had to turn around the next second to lock it.

Exclusive patent.

The words burned in her brain, and she clenched her hands into fists.

One warm summer afternoon four months ago Lucy had been so tired, she'd stopped to sit on a park bench and closed her eyes. Only for a minute or two but long enough for a young gentleman passing by to notice and be concerned enough for her safety to enquire as to her well-being.

While the brief rest had been involuntary, remaining on the bench and striking up a conversation with the handsome stranger was her choice and a terrible one at that. Lucy had allowed Duncan Rider to walk her home, too weary to question the coincidence that the son of her father's rival had been the one to find her vulnerable and offer his protection.

Now, Lucy barreled down the rotting walkways of Calthorpe Street, barely registering the admiring glances from the gentlemen walking in the opposite direction or the sudden appearance of the wan November sun as it poked through the grey clouds of autumn.

Instead, her head was filled with memories so excruciating they poked at her chest like heated needles rousing feelings of shame alongside her resentment.

Such as the next time she'd seen Duncan when he appeared during a busy day at the apothecary with a pretty nosegay of violets. He'd smelled like barley water and soap, a combination so simple and appealing it had scrambled her brains and left her giddy as a goose.

Or the memory of how their kisses had unfolded in the back rooms of the apothecary, turning from delightfully sweet to something much more carnal. How kisses had proceeded to touches and from there even more and how much she'd enjoyed herself and believed it all a harbinger of what would come once they married.

A shout ripped Lucy's attention back to the present and she jerked back from the road, missing the broad side of a carriage by inches. The driver called out curses at her over his shoulder, but they bounced off her and scattered across the muddied street as Lucy turned the corner onto Gray's Inn Road.

Halfway through a row of dun-colored stone buildings, almost invisible unless one knew what to look for, a discreet brass plaque to the left of a blackened oak door read

Tierney & Co., Bookkeeping Services

Lucy took a deep breath, pulling the dirty brown beginnings of a London fog into her lungs and expelled it along with the remorse and shame that accompanied her last memory. The sight of Duncan holding her handwritten formula for a new kind of throat lozenge she'd worked two years to perfect.

"I'll just test it out for you, shall I?" he'd said, eyes roaming the page. His lips curled up on one side as he read and forever after Lucy would recalls the slight shadow of foreboding that moved across the candlelight in the back storeroom where they carried out their affair.

"I don't know," she'd hedged.

Too late. He'd folded the formula and distracted her with kisses.

"I've more space and materials at my disposal. I know you think this is ready to sell, but isn't it better that we take the time to make sure?"

Yes. It might have been exhaustion that weakened Lucy just enough that she took advantage of an offer to help shoulder some of her burdens, but the decision to let Duncan Rider walk out of Peterson's apothecary with a formula that was worth a fortune was due not to her sleepless nights, but to a weakness in her character that allowed her to believe a man when he told her he loved her.

"AND THAT IS why I would like you to kill him. Or, perhaps not so drastic. Maybe torture him first. At the very least, leave him in great discomfort. I have plenty of ideas how you might do this and am happy to present them in writing along with anatomically correct diagrams."

Jonathan Thorne blinked at the incongruity of the bloodthirsty demand and the composed nature of the woman who issued it.

He almost blinked again at the sight of her face when she leaned forward and into the light but stopped himself at the last second.

None of that, now.

Never again.

He'd been in the back room when he heard her come in off the street, asking for Winthram, the tenor of her husky voice sounding sadly familiar. The sound of a woman almost drained of hope.

"Miss Peterson, I appreciate your—erm, enthusiasm?" Winthram had said. He'd brought the woman into the small receiving room where prospective clients met with Tierney's agents. "However, Tierney and Company is in the business of helping clients solve burdensome problems."

"It would relieve me of a great burden would you torture that bastard, Duncan Rider."

"Generally we try not to torture folks willy-nilly." Winthram's head turned at the sound of squeaking floorboards and Thorne came all the way in into the room from the hall where he'd been lurking.

"Allow me to introduce you to one of the senior agents," the young man said without bothering to hide his relief. "Mr. Jonathan Thorne, I'm pleased to present to you to Miss Lucinda Peterson, the owner of Peterson's Apothecary."

For close to thirty years, the brass plaque affixed beside the front door of Tierney & Co. had advertised a bookkeeping service but in fact, the five agents working here, Thorne and Winthram among them, did little to no accounting.

The books they balanced were more metaphorical.

When the government had a domestic situation that could not be resolved through official channels and might lead to some embarrassment of the extended royal family or members of the government, Tierney's received a visit from a bland, middle-aged functionary who pushed an envelope across the desk then disappeared. Shortly thereafter a certain dignitary might find himself transferred back home after his superiors received information about said dignitary's unsavory predilections. A palace servant might suddenly leave their post the day after a cache of love letters was returned to one of the Queen's ladies-in-waiting.

On occasion, Tierney's would agree to take on *pro bono* discreet services for an ordinary citizen who had been wronged. A widow would suddenly receive her late husband's back wages or a poor family's home be spared a tax rise.

The request by an apothecary owner for the assassination of a rival apothecary might be a bit out of the ordinary but the fact that the apothecary owner was a woman—an almost preternaturally beautiful woman—would have been unique in Tierney's history except since Henry Winthram began working here, exceptional women had been showing up in droves.

Thorne nodded at Winthram and steeled himself to indifference before he walked to the ladder-back chair where Miss Peterson had just risen to her feet and presented her hand in greeting.

There were some ladies of the ton, the most elite circles of British Society, who used to come and watch Thorne when he was a famous prize fighter. They would scream for blood and shout for pain alongside the common rabble from behind the safety of long cloaks and heavy veils. Afterward they would remove their veils and ogle him as though regarding an animal let loose from a menagerie. Thorne hadn't cared. When he was drinking, he hadn't accounted himself much better than an animal.

Over time the tally of his fights wrote themselves on his face; ears that puffed to the side like lopsided mushrooms, a poorly sewn cut high on his left cheek that left him with a permanent sneer, and a bent nose all conspired to change his appearance so much that his own mother had difficulty recognizing him and the ladies no longer simpered at him. Instead, they would hold their gaze in such a way that took in the whole of him without having to look too closely at his face.

A technique Thorne employed now as he bowed slightly over Miss Peterson's hand, eyes taking in the cut of her plain day dress, a faded India cotton print with a shawl collar that went right to her neck and her sturdy but well-worn boots, serviceable gloves, and ten-years-out-of-date straw bonnet that could not have provided much warmth on such a windy day.

What he didn't do was stare directly at her face. Beauty like Miss Peterson's elicited a reaction.

Thorne preferred to remain impassive.

She would be accustomed to some response, what with her perfectly round eyes and irises so dark blue they resembled the Mediterranean on the morning of a storm, full lips the color of a bruised rose petal and cream-colored skin pulled taut over high cheekbones.

Fascinating how each person's face contained the exact same elements but in one person, Miss Peterson for example, they were arranged so as to make a man stammer and blush, shuffle his feet and work to wet his suddenly dry mouth.

Fascinating and dangerous.

Miss Peterson took her seat and Thorne rang the bell for a servant to build up the fire and fetch another pot of hot water while he made small talk about the weather and asked a bit about her apothecary and its clientele. When he judged Miss Peterson's blood lust to have calmed a bit, Thorne took a chair from against the wall and set it and himself in between Winthram and Miss Peterson.

"You must know Winthram from his days as the doorman at Athena's Retreat," Thorne said.

Miss Peterson sat straighter in her chair, clasping the strings of her reticule tight in her hands as she shot a worried glance at Winthram, who held up a hand to ward off her concern.

"The agents at Tierney's already knew about the club before I came to work here," Winthram assured her. "They've worked with Lord Greycliff and Mr. Kneland before."

That would be the Viscount Greycliff. His stepmother, Lady Greycliff, had used the money left to her by Greycliff's late father to convert a series of outbuildings behind her townhouse into a club. Most of London believed it to be a ladies social club where women with an interest in the natural sciences would gather for tea and listen to lectures on subjects as varied as the proper means of cultivating orchids or how to use botanicals for better housekeeping.

Behind closed doors, however, women scientists used the three floors of hidden laboratories to further their work in fields as varied as organic chemistry, ornithology, and experimental physics. When Lady Greycliff had come under threat, a former counterassassin, Arthur Kneland, had been hired to protect her.

Much to Thorne's amusement, the intimidating man had not only gone and gotten himself shot for the umpteenth time, but he'd also fallen in love with the lady and now tried desperately to keep the scientists from wreaking havoc on the club and one another. On occasion, Kneland would help Winthram with small missions both to keep himself sharp and pass on some of his skills to the younger man.

Having poached Winthram from the duties of doorman to serve as one of their employees, Tierney's agents had not entirely reckoned with the fact that the women scientists who had long relied on Winthram to help them when their experiments got out of hand now came to him for assistance with other quandaries.

"I use the laboratories of the Retreat since all our space at the apothecary is taken up by supplies and treatment rooms for our patients," Miss Peterson said now. "For *years* I worked to create the formula for a throat lozenge that reduces the swelling of a putrid throat as well as soothes the pain. I planned on patenting the formula, but—"

Despite his best effort, Thorne let his gaze rest on Miss Peterson's face, perhaps assuming the anguish contained in her voice would diminish the luminosity of her beauty. In fact, it only added to it and Thorne redirected his eyes to her clenched hands and listened to her tremulous story and any clues it might provide.

"Before I could bring the formula to market myself," Miss Peterson continued, "I showed it to Duncan Rider. The son in Rider and Son Apothecary."

Unexpectedly, she launched from her chair and began pacing the room. Accustomed to the demure responses of the occasional gentlewoman or the humility of the domestic servants who sought their services, Thorne was taken aback by the ferocity in her manner.

Winthram showed no sign of surprise and Thorne presumed this behavior was common among women scientists.

"Once I realized what this fungus-sucking tumor of a man had done to me—"

Thorne swallowed a laugh and nearly choked while Winthram nodded his head in appreciation of the insult.

"—patenting *my* formula, I went and pleaded with him to do the right thing and either put my name on the patent or fulfill his promise to marry me. He did neither. I was tempted then to do him bodily harm, but I refrained."

"Most likely for the best," Winthram offered.

Miss Peterson stopped mid-stride, pointed a finger at the poor boy's face and leveled a ferocious glare at him.

Still beautiful.

"Do you think so, Winthram?" Her voice rose now, and she advanced on Winthram, who sensibly leaned back in his chair, realizing it would have been better to keep his mouth shut until the end.

"Do you think so? Let me tell you, as bad as it is that thieving pustule now makes a fortune from my hard work, today I learned something even worse. That walking boil has somehow come into my home and once *again* stolen my work."

She paused and regarded them both. "Now, will you kill him, or do I have to do it?"

ELIZABETH EVERETT lives in upstate New York with her family. She likes going for long walks or (very) short runs to nearby sites that figure prominently in the history of civil rights and women's suffrage. The Secret Scientists of London series is inspired by her admiration for rule breakers and belief in the power of love to change the world.

CONNECT ONLINE

ElizabethEverettAuthor.com
ElizabethEverettAuthorBooks
ElizabethEverettAuthor